3-IN-1 HISTORICAL COLLECTION

CALIFORNIA

Romance

3-IN-1 HISTORICAL COLLECTION

CALIFORNIA
Romance

COLLEEN L. REECE

BARBOUR
PUBLISHING

Print ISBN 978-1-62416-220-6
eBook Editions:
Adobe Digital Edition (.epub) 978-1-62416-501-6
Kindle and MobiPocket Edition (.prc) 978-1-62416-500-9

All scripture quotations are taken from the King James Version of the Bible.

This book is a work of fiction. Names, characters, places, and incidents are either products of the author's imagination or used fictitiously. Any similarity to actual people, organizations, and/or events is purely coincidental.

Cover design: Kirk DouPonce

Published by Barbour Publishing, Inc., P.O. Box 719, Uhrichsville, Ohio 44683, www.barbourbooks.com

Our mission is to publish and distribute inspirational products offering exceptional value and biblical encouragement to the masses.

 Member of the
Evangelical Christian
Publishers Association

Printed in the United States of America.

9/14
gift

COLLEEN L. REECE was born and raised in a small western Washington logging town. She learned to read by kerosene lamplight and dreamed of someday writing a book. God has multiplied Colleen's "someday" book into more than 140 titles that have sold six million copies. Colleen was twice voted Heartsong Presents' Favorite Author and later inducted into Heartsong's Hall of Fame. Several of her books have appeared on the CBA bestseller list.

ROMANCE RIDES THE RANGE

Dedication

For Susan K. Marlow,
author of the Circle C Adventures series—who not only
insisted I write this book but took me to California to research it!

A Note from the Author

God uses many ways to lead His children, including through the written word. I learned to read by kerosene lamplight. One night I said, "I wish we had a magic lamp and a magic carpet like Aladdin." My parents pointed out that our new lamp was an "Aladdin" lamp and that books were our magic carpet. I vowed to someday write a book of my own.

In 1977 I wanted to write for God. He used a passage from Emilie Loring's *There is Always Love* to encourage me: "There is only one common-sense [sic] move when you don't like your life. Do something about it. Get out. Go somewhere. Follow a rainbow. Who knows? You may find the legendary pot of gold at the end of it." I walked off my government job a few days later.

My "someday" book has grown to more than 140 titles and six million copies sold. Many, such as *Frontiers* and *Frontier Brides* (Barbour books) were inspired by Dad's love of western lore. How my eleven-year-old heart pounded when I saw my first cowboy. If only I could live on a cattle ranch! (I still hope to visit one.)

I hope you get as much pleasure from reading this story as I did writing it.

Blessings,
Colleen

Chapter 1

Spring 1882
St. Louis, Missouri

I t's over, girl. Git up." Gus Stoddard's gruff voice crackled with impatience. Seventeen-year-old Sarah Joy Anderson ignored the command and continued to bend over the freshly dug grave. Her tears fell freely, mixing with the recent rain shower. The April morning's sudden cloudburst symbolized her grief. It was as if all heaven wept on her behalf. The shower had cleared the air of the usual humidity of the St. Louis, Missouri, day and left the morning refreshingly cool and clean. A rainbow spread its half circle over her mother's grave just as the minister read John 14:1–3—a fitting eulogy for a God-fearing woman like Virginia Anderson Stoddard.

"'Let not your heart be troubled: ye believe in God, believe also in me. In my Father's house are many mansions: if it were not so, I would have told you. I go to prepare a place for you. And if I go and prepare a place for you, I will come again, and receive you unto myself; that where I am, there ye may be also.'"

The familiar words brought a measure of comfort, but it fled like darkness from dawn at her stepfather's harsh voice.

"I said git up, girl." This time, the hard prod of a leather boot accompanied Gus's voice. "The young'uns are hungry. You take 'em back to the house and fix 'em some dinner. I've got business down at the docks."

A wave of rebellion swept through Sarah. "I want to stay here awhile."

"It doesn't matter what you want. Do as I say. Now." Gus yanked Sarah up from the mound of dirt. He spun her around so hard her worn bonnet slipped to her shoulders, revealing a thick braid of red-gold hair circling her head. "Look at you. There's no call to shame yourself in front of the preacher and mourners by crawling all over the grave. You've got mud on your Sunday-go-to-meeting dress. You're a disgrace! What would your mother think of you wallowing in the mud instead of minding your brothers and sister?"

They are no kin of mine, Sarah silently protested. Long experience with Gus Stoddard had taught her to hold her tongue even when she wanted to cry out against him.

Sarah glanced down through tears at her blue-sprigged calico dress. Several large, dark splotches covered the skirt and the undersides of the long sleeves. Her hands were caked with mud from falling onto the mound of dirt that held the last remains of the dearest person she'd ever known. *Oh Mama. What will become of me now?* She read the tombstone once more: VIRGINIA STODDARD. 1840–82. Nothing more. No words of endearment, no mention of the other little life that lay in the woman's arms—the tiny baby girl who had never even been named. Engraving cost money—more than the unfeeling man standing next to Sarah cared to pay. He certainly wouldn't see the need to write anything other than the bare-bones facts.

Sarah looked up and blinked back tears. Most of the twenty-five or so mourners had gone, leaving her alone with the man who now had control over her life. She gazed silently into Gus Stoddard's face. It seemed chiseled from stone. The hard black eyes staring at her from beneath heavy brows made Sarah wonder what her gentle mother had ever seen in this man. Perhaps Gus had been handsome at one time, with his thick, curling dark hair and solid muscular build. Sadly, whatever charms he'd used to win Virginia Anderson had quickly worn off after the marriage vows. It had been the longest three years of Sarah's life.

"What are you staring at, girl?" Gus demanded, giving her a hard shake.

She fought back fear and revulsion. "Nothing." Her voice was so devoid of emotion it earned her a sharp smack across the cheek. She ignored the slap as she had learned to ignore so many things from her stepfather.

"Mind your impertinence, missy," Gus snapped. "We can't stand around all day grieving over a dead woman. There's work t'be done, you hear? Take your brothers and sister home while I mosey down to the docks. I've got business with Tice Edwards."

The look on Gus's face convinced Sarah he was in no mood to be trifled with. She grabbed eight-year-old Ellianna by the hand. "Come on. Let's go home." With her other hand she reached for five-year-old Timmy and motioned for the two older boys to follow. Together they headed back to the three-room cottage on the edge of town, the Stoddards' most recent residence. It was a two-mile hike through the bustling city of St. Louis; the humidity that had for a short time relented would soon be back in full force.

You're not my pa. Sarah shouted silently. *These are not my brothers and sister.* She gave Ellie's hand an impatient tug. "You're always dragging your feet, Ellie. Can't you walk a little faster? Timmy doesn't have any trouble keeping up."

In response, the child bit Sarah's hand.

"Ouch!" Sarah yelped. "What did you do that for?"

"You were pulling too hard," Ellie answered spitefully, glancing at the older boys walking alongside. They grinned.

Ian, the oldest at thirteen, stopped and shoved his hands into his pockets. "I ain't goin' home," he announced, kicking at a rock with one bare foot. "I'm goin' t'catch me some rats down by the riverboats."

"I'm goin', too," declared eleven-year-old Peter. He pulled back on his suspenders and let them go, grinning at the loud crack they made.

"Fine," Sarah muttered. "The rest of us are going home for nice hot stew and my special biscuits. You two aren't getting any if you don't come now."

The older boys looked at each other. Ian shrugged his shoulders then turned and took off toward the docks. Peter glanced briefly at Sarah then hurried after his brother.

The two youngest children whined and kicked. "We wanna go, too!"

Sarah held firmly to their arms. "You'll fall into the river and drown; then where will I be?" she growled over their screams of rage. "Just settle down and come along."

When they finally reached home, the need to heat yesterday's stew and mix up a batch of biscuits pushed Sarah's grief to the back of her mind for a few minutes. But as she pulled the hot pan from the small, black beast of a cookstove, the familiar odor of her mother's baking powder biscuits wafted on the air and set Sarah to crying again. She dropped the pan on the top of the stove, hastily dished up the stew, and placed the food before the two hungry children. They instantly set to eating with fingers and spoons.

"You're welcome," Sarah muttered past the lump in her throat. She untied her apron, hung it on a nail, and headed for the ladder to the loft she shared with Ellie and the boys. A thin blanket hanging from a tightly stretched rope separated the attic into two rooms. Sarah pushed past the flimsy partition and flung herself down on her corn-husk mattress, sobbing. Why had God taken Mama and the newborn baby?

When no more tears came, Sarah rolled over and stared at the attic ceiling. The pine boards were old and warped. Here and there a chink of sunlight showed through the tar paper and rough shake roof. Was there any hope it would be repaired before fall? *Hardly.* Gus Stoddard was not long on work. He could usually be found doing the least strenuous job for the most money. Gambling figured highly in his income opportunities, but Sarah knew he lost far more money than he won. She only had to look around the cramped shack and count the number of times she mended britches and lowered hems to figure out Gus was just as poor at gambling as he was at any honest venture. When things got too lean, he'd find work on the docks just long enough to tide them over for a few weeks.

"Oh God!" Sarah cried out to the ceiling. "Why did You let Mama die? How will I get along without her?" A vision of what lay ahead sent a cold chill into the girl's aching heart. Virginia had named her only daughter Sarah Joy, but what little joy Sarah had known during the past few years was buried in a lonely grave.

Thinking about her mother's death plunged Sarah into the past—to the

13

tragic death of her father five years before: the lingering illness that transformed the tall, strong but gentle Scandinavian giant into a thin, pale shadow. The anguish of watching their once-productive farm slowly deteriorate into disrepair when John Anderson could no longer work it. The final, agonizing hours of a wonderful husband and father. Although he had no fear of death, he mourned for his family, who would soon be left alone in the world. Seeing him so had wrenched Sarah's heart but not like this most recent, terrible loss. Now she was alone. Alone with—

"Why did you have to marry that horrible Gus Stoddard?" she sobbed. "We were getting along all right. You, Seth, and me." Even as she spoke, Sarah knew it wasn't quite true. Although her brother, Seth, had worked hard, he couldn't make the farm pay. Forced to sell Pleasant Acres, the family relocated to St. Louis, but every day was a struggle to live.

A year later Virginia Anderson had informed her eighteen-year-old son and thirteen-year-old daughter that she was remarrying. "He's a widower," she said. "A kind, God-fearing Christian man I met at a church social. He has four motherless children. The youngest is only two years old. Mr. Stoddard is anxious to share his home with a woman who will treat his children as her own. In exchange he will make a good husband and provide a home for us."

Sarah snorted. "A good husband?" she said disgustedly. She pulled herself to a sitting position on her bed, clenched her fists, and savagely slammed them onto her thin, uncomfortable mattress. Gus Stoddard had been desperate for a woman. A woman who would do all the work without even a thank-you. A woman who would care for his unruly, disrespectful children and go for days wondering when her new husband would return from his many "business" deals.

"Translation," Sarah sneered, "gambling and drinking binges. We were better off starving to death by ourselves."

She closed her eyes and tried to shove the pain of the last three years from her mind. "It's over," she insisted. "No point in digging up old memories. They should stay buried. I've got enough trouble right now without borrowing from the past." *"Sufficient unto the day is the evil thereof."* The verse from Matthew's Gospel popped into her head, but it did little to quiet her anxiety. Sarah knew the verse referred to worrying about tomorrow, but was God also trying to tell her to let the past take care of itself?

It was no use. Memories flooded her troubled mind, and Sarah could do nothing to stop them. At last she gave in and relived the heart-wrenching weeks that had followed her mother's marriage to Gus.

❧

Sarah and her brother saw through their new stepfather immediately. Gus Stoddard proved himself a hypocrite from the honeymoon on. Not once did he step into a church after the marriage ceremony. He dragged Seth to the docks to work, beating him if he raised the slightest objection. He forced Sarah to accept work as a laundress. Her hands turned raw and bled. Did she or Seth see a penny of their wages? Of course not! Gus pocketed the money then gambled it away.

A year later Seth made a bold move. "I'm going west," he confided to his sister one spring evening near the back fence. "I can't take old man Stoddard one day longer." Seth squared his shoulders, and a parting ray of sunlight rested on the red-gold hair that matched his sister's. His once-laughing mouth tightened into a straight line. With a pang, Sarah realized the childhood companion she adored was now a man. A man like their father, who had set his course and would not deviate from it.

"What about. . .what about Mama. . .and me?" Sarah asked, frightened. Seth leave? Unthinkable! Who'd stand between her and Gus when the disreputable man had had too much to drink and started on a rampage?

Chapter 2

Seth looked troubled. His blue eyes, so like Sarah's, darkened in concern. "I talked to Mama," he assured her. "She agrees it's best for me to leave. Gus is bound and determined to apprentice me to some wheelwright or blacksmith. Even worse, he wants me to learn the gambling trade." Seth laughed bitterly. "What do you think our pa would say about that?"

Sarah shook her head. "Pa never gambled a day in his life. Nor drank a drop of whiskey. He loved God and Mother. And us." Her voice quavered. "Seth, what will become of Mama and me?"

He reached out and pulled his young sister close. "Never you mind. Just hang on for a year or two. I'll go west and become a cowboy. I've heard they don't make much money, but if you're good at your job, you can get steady work all year 'round." He paused and added softly, "I'll pray every day for God to watch over you until I can save enough to send for you and Mama."

Sarah shook her head. "You know Mama won't leave Gus and the kids. She made a promise, remember? 'In sickness and in health. Till death do us part.' Just like she promised Pa. Mama will honor her vows—even if it costs her everything." A sob rose in her throat, but she hastily swallowed it. Seth *had* to go. She must not make it harder for him than she knew it already was.

"All right then. I'll send for *you*, little sister."

Sarah felt her heart leap with sudden hope. To be free of her brutal stepfather would be the greatest gift her brother could give her. Just as quickly her joy vanished and a dull ache entered her heart. *How can I leave? Mama relies on me for more than just help in managing the house. The kids don't listen—they make more work for her. Who would she talk with in the long evenings when Gus is gone? I'm Mama's only confidante. God, I simply can't leave her.*

Sarah felt torn in two. She loved her mother, yet she adored her brother. Since their father's death, Seth had been her protector, her cherished companion, her safeguard against some of her stepfather's unpredictable moods. More than once Gus's upraised hand had been stayed because of Seth's presence. What would happen when her brother left? She shuddered. She dared not remind Seth of this, or he might stay on her account. That must not happen. Although Gus held back from brutalizing the women, he clearly had no qualms about laying into Seth for the smallest offense. One of these days the beast would beat Seth senseless—or kill him in a drunken rage.

Sarah sighed, her decision made. "I can't leave. I'll get by." She clasped one of Seth's hands. "But you're right. You've got to leave before our stepfather does something terrible to you. He's a mean one. Stubborn, too. He'll no doubt have the law after you, seeing you're not yet of age. If you can only stay out of his clutches for two years, you'll be safe."

Seth heaved a sigh. "I know. I don't want to leave you and Mama, but I've got her blessing. She gave me what money she could spare. It must mean the Lord's going to look after me."

"I hope so, Seth." Sarah gave her brother a hug. "Write to us, would you? Let us know where you are."

"I'll try. But it'll probably be some time before I settle down in one place long enough to write."

"When are you leaving?"

"Right away." His face gleamed in the growing dusk. "I already said good-bye to Mama. Gus is down at the docks, hanging around his favorite riverboat. He'll no doubt be gone all night. By the time he staggers home, I'll be long gone." Seth paused then quickly added, "Thank God that for once in their marriage Mama stood up to Gus when he wanted to sell Copper! I wouldn't get far on foot. Even so, I can only carry food and a few extras in the saddle-bags. Look after what little else I have, won't you, and bring it when you come."

He paused. "Don't worry if you don't hear from me for a while. When I do write, I'll send the letters to. . ." He named a trusted friend. "We can't take a chance on Gus intercepting them."

Sarah sadly nodded and watched her brother walk off into the night. The sound of creaking leather, followed by the soft thud of the sorrel's hooves diminished, leaving her alone in the darkness. Hot tears fell as she hurried to hide her brother's few pitiful childhood treasures. The Stoddard children mustn't get their greedy little hands on Seth's belongings, especially the toy pistol Seth's pa had painstakingly carved for him years before, so perfect in detail it closely resembled the real thing.

&

Days passed. Gus Stoddard's initial fury at Seth's departure waned. A muttered "good riddance" a few weeks later assured Sarah and her mother that he had no immediate plans to track the young man down and drag him home. Life settled into routine—an empty routine for Sarah, who missed Seth's hearty laugh and reassuring presence more than she had dreamed possible.

Months limped by with no news of Seth. Sarah feared some misfortune had befallen her brother in the wild West. Each night after the youngsters had been put to bed, Sarah and her mother fell to their knees, asking God to keep His strong hand upon Seth. They also prayed for a letter.

More than a year later the longed-for missive finally arrived, delivered by Seth's friend. Seth was safe! Sarah and her mother rejoiced but kept the news to themselves, hiding the letter long before Gus returned from spending most of the afternoon and evening gambling away the little money he had. It would do Seth no good for Gus to learn the young man was now in California.

Seth had written that he loved learning the cowboy trade on the Diamond S Ranch. "I'm the greenest greenhorn in the entire outfit," he lamented in his letter. "I don't know why my boss, Matt Sterling, has taken such a shine to me, but if it weren't for him, I'd probably be lying dead in some back alley in Madera." He closed his letter by writing, "Don't worry. I'm alive, I've got a good job, and I am saving all I can. Keep praying for me. I know it's those prayers that have seen me through some hard times."

Other letters arrived, secretly delivered by Seth's friend. Usually they were short, with just bits and pieces of news about Seth's new life. He loved the mild climate and the opportunity to make something of himself by working hard. He was happy, Sarah could tell. She only wished—

❧

A crash and a piercing scream jerked Sarah abruptly from her musing. She leaped from the mattress and scrambled down the ladder. Ellie and Timmy were at each other's throats—biting, pinching, and hitting. Timmy was crying; Ellie shrieked at the top of her lungs.

"Stop that at once!" Sarah ordered, grasping the back of Timmy's overalls. She gave a yank, which forced the little boy to let go of his sister. "What's going on?"

Ellie threw herself at Timmy. Sarah had all she could do to avoid the child's flailing fists. "He stole it!" Ellie screamed. "Give it back, you crybaby!"

Timmy howled. "She's killin' me, Sarah! Make her stop!"

Just then the door to the cottage burst open. Ian and Peter strolled through—dirty and rumpled. They whooped in delight at the scuffle but made no move to aid Sarah. Instead they watched from the doorway as their stepsister fought to control the two children.

"You two give me a hand here," she ordered the boys.

"We're hungry," Peter answered, ignoring her request. He and Ian grinned, stepped around the ruckus, and began opening and closing cupboards in search of something to eat.

Ellie and Timmy screamed louder. Sarah held them at arm's length and tried to make them hush. A swift kick from the little girl sent a chair tumbling over.

"Can't a man return to his home without finding it in an uproar?" A bellow from behind Sarah sliced through the commotion.

Silence fell. Sarah released the children. They turned to stare at Gus Stoddard and a dark-haired, dark-eyed stranger standing in the open doorway of their tiny cottage.

"Here I am bringing a guest home and what greets us?" Gus roared. "A barroom brawl! Shame on you all." He turned and focused most of his wrath on Sarah. "You, Sarah. You're a grown woman. I expect you to keep these kids under control." He waved an arm toward the cluttered room that served as both the kitchen and sitting room. "Look at this mess. You've let it fall apart the past couple of weeks. Rubbish everywhere." He kicked at an empty whiskey bottle. "You're to be keeping the place clean, girl. I've told you time and time again."

Sarah felt her cheeks flame in red-hot anger. *Keep this place clean? How dare you!* She wanted to shout into his face that it was he and his disheveled pack of rowdy youngsters who turned this tiny shack into a garbage heap most days. If Mama hadn't worked so hard that she collapsed a few days before the baby came, perhaps both of them wouldn't have died in childbirth. Sarah had been too overwhelmed with trying to care for her dying mother to keep the place straightened up.

Gus glowered at her and continued his rampage. He waggled a finger in her face. "You, m'girl, are not making a very good impression on Mr. Edwards. I told him you kept a tidy house."

Sarah shoved her anger to a corner of her mind and shifted her gaze from her stepfather to the stranger. So this was Tice Edwards, with whom her stepfather did business. An older man, but not as old as Gus, he stood tall and proud, with coal-black hair cut short and slicked back. No ragged beard or mustache marred his chiseled face. Above a straight nose, his dark eyes gleamed with interest and amusement. When he caught Sarah's appraising look, he nodded slightly. "Good evening." His words were refined, silky, polished, but his bold stare made Sarah squirm.

She dropped her gaze and stared at a crack in the floor, mind awhirl. Just who was this obviously wealthy and high-class Tice Edwards? Certainly not one of Gus's usual companions. Many a night Sarah and her mother had been forced to endure the company of rowdy and ill-mannered guests crowded into the house, but Mr. Edwards had never been part of those gatherings. Whatever did he see in her stepfather?

While she was still trying to piece together the significance of Mr. Edwards's unexpected visit, Gus strode across the room, draped a heavy, dirty arm across Sarah's shoulders and grinned at his guest. The matter of the filthy cabin suddenly seemed insignificant. "So, what do you think of her, Tice? We sort of caught my daughter unawares, and I know she ain't dressed for company, but you can see she's a real looker. Think she'll do?"

Sarah flinched at her stepfather's touch and twisted free. Her throat went dry. *Do?* What kind of employment was Gus arranging for her *this* time? Scullery maid? Cook? Upstairs maid? Probably not, she reasoned, if the cottage was intended to be a job reference. It really *was* a jumble tonight. Perhaps

Mr. Tice Edwards would turn up his nose and stalk out the door in a huff. Judging from appearances, the man could afford many servants. Why would he consider hiring anyone Gus Stoddard put forward? Sarah swallowed and chewed thoughtfully on her lower lip. Perhaps working in a fine home would be a step up from serving as a drudge to Gus.

The next instant she saw the intense, eager look on Tice's face. Sarah decided she did not want to work for him after all—no matter how much he might pay. As unpleasant as her life was with Gus Stoddard, now that her mother was gone, she didn't like the looks of this expensively clad stranger. He stared at her like she was a slab of prime beef hanging in the butcher's window. She couldn't abide the thought of those probing eyes watching her carry out her duties in his home. Sarah steeled herself to refuse his offer of employment.

Tice strolled leisurely across the floor and came to a stop a few inches from where she stood next to Gus. He caught her chin and forced her to meet his gaze. "She'll do nicely." He chuckled. "Needs a bit of cleaning up, but you're right. She's real pretty."

"Then it's a deal?" Gus asked eagerly.

Tice dropped his hand and smiled. Straight, white teeth flashed. A line from a fairy tale crossed Sarah's mind. *The better to eat you with, my dear.* "It's a deal."

Sarah rubbed her chin and turned on her stepfather. "What's a deal?" she demanded. "If you think I'm going to work for Mr. Edwards, you're mistaken."

Gus's slap sent Sarah reeling. He shot an apologetic look toward Tice. "She's a mite feisty sometimes, Tice. Didn't have real good bringing up, I'm afraid." He waggled a finger at Sarah. "You're not going to work for Mr. Edwards, m'girl. You're going to be his wife."

Chapter 3

S arah staggered to her feet. "His—his—*wife?*" she stuttered, unable to grasp what Gus was saying. The stinging pain of her stepfather's slap went unheeded. She stumbled to the crude table and leaned against it, breathing hard. *This can't be happening. Please, God, let it all be a bad dream.*

Tice Edwards quickly joined Sarah. "If I may?" he offered, pulling out a chair. His silken words flowed over Sarah like sweet, sticky honey.

She shivered and closed her eyes then crumpled into the chair. She buried her head in her arms and fought against the nausea that threatened to overwhelm her. Hot tears sprang to her eyes, but she forced them back. *This is not a crying matter,* Sarah told herself fiercely. *I must think. I must get control of myself.*

A whimper brought Sarah's head up. Timmy stood at the end of the table, biting his lip. His light brown hair curled around his ears and fell into his wide, dark eyes. His hands were thrust into the pockets of his overalls, and he sniffled. When Sarah caught his gaze, he blinked hard and whispered, "Sarah?"

Her heart softened at the uncertainty on the little boy's face. But before she could respond to him, Gus barked, "Get outside—all of you. Don't come in till I tell you."

"I want Sarah," Timmy pleaded. He'd swiftly changed from the screaming, fighting little tiger of a few minutes ago to a scared child in need of a hug. No matter how irritated Sarah found herself at the antics of Gus's children, it was clear Timmy knew where he could find shelter during his father's many angry storms. He reached for her in spite of his father's order.

"Git, I told you!" Gus took a swipe at Timmy, but the boy was too quick. He ducked under Gus's arm and scampered outdoors with a frightened yelp. The other children had already disappeared through the door, away from their father's rotten temper and heavy hand.

Sarah heard the harsh teasing of the older boys and Timmy's sobbing through the open door. She clenched her fists. She wanted to rush outside and gather Timmy into her arms. Of Gus's four children, Timmy was the sensitive one, the child who had known Sarah's mother as his only mother and Sarah as his real sister. When he wasn't being influenced for evil by his older siblings, he was a loving little boy.

21

The brush of Tice's hand across the braid on the top of Sarah's head brought her around. She shook herself free of his touch and stood. She looked up, gripped the edge of the table to steady herself, and took a deep breath. Ice tinkled in her voice as she said, "I will not marry you, Mr. Edwards."

Gus lurched forward, hand raised, but Tice motioned him away with a curt wave. "No more of that, Gus. I don't want my future wife marred for her wedding day." He gave Sarah a rueful smile. "I'm sorry the arrangements are not to your liking, Miss Stoddard—"

"*Anderson*," Sarah corrected between clenched teeth.

Tice bowed. "My mistake, Miss Anderson. I apologize. I regret I haven't made a good impression on you, but contrary to what your stepfather told you earlier, you *have* made a good first impression on me." He grinned. "Actually, a second impression."

Sarah's stomach lurched. "I've never seen you before. How could I have made any impression on you?"

"You'd better explain it to her, Gus," Tice suggested quietly. He waved toward the chair Sarah had recently vacated. "Please sit down."

Sarah sat. Her palms turned clammy. She rubbed them against her skirt and then clenched them in her lap. She kept her expression stony when she turned to face her stepfather, dreading and fearing what he would say.

Gus sauntered over to the cookstove and peered into the speckled enamel coffeepot. He grunted, poured himself a cup of the steaming brew, crossed the room, and plunked himself down into an overstuffed armchair that had seen better days. "Well now, Sarah, the truth of the matter is this: My friend Tice has had his eye on you for quite some time. He saw you one day down by the docks and decided you were the girl for him. O'course, that was a few years back, but I promised I'd make arrangements for your—*betrothal*—as soon as an opportunity presented itself." He paused and looked at her over the rim of his coffee cup.

Sarah saw in Gus's steely eyes the truth of the past three years. He had used her mother from the very beginning—used her as nothing more than a slave. He had run her ragged taking care of his four kids and trying to keep everyone fed. He took, took, took and never returned a shred of decency, never regarded Virginia Anderson Stoddard as the companion and confidante that God intended a wife should be to her husband. Now Gus planned to use her, too. But why would he be willing to have her marry Tice and leave his children without anyone to care for them?

An ugly thought sprang to life in Sarah's head, and she leaped to her feet. *Money. It's got to have something to do with money.*

Disgust permeated her. It blotted out fear. Slow, hot rage slowly worked its way from the pit of her belly to the roots of her strawberry blond, braided coronet. "You waited until my mother died," she lashed out in sudden realization.

"She never would have stood for this, you—you—*swine*; I despise you!"

Sarah's outburst brought a bark of laughter from Tice. "Yes sir, Gus. I like her. She's got spirit. I've had more than my share of clinging, simpering females over the years. Your girl will be a welcome diversion. I'll be proud to stroll with her along the deck of the *River Queen* and show her off to all those luckless gentlemen who missed such a catch."

The gumption inherited from her strong Scandinavian father now served her in good stead. She drew herself up to her full five-feet, four-inch height, raised her chin, and slowly paid out words like a miser pays out gold. "I already told you, Mr. Edwards: I will not marry you—*ever*." Sarah felt stronger now. Her angry response to Gus had helped her gather her wits and prepare for battle. It *was* a battle—one she dared not lose. She took a few steps toward the ladder that led to her attic sanctuary. "If you will excuse me, I'm tired." She nodded at Tice. "I could say it was a pleasure meeting you, Mr. Edwards, but it wasn't. Good evening."

Gus lurched from his chair and hurled his half-empty coffee cup across the room. It slammed into the ladder steps, inches from Sarah's face. Dark brown liquid splattered her skirt. She froze. "You stay put and hear us out, girl." Gus's eyes blazed. "Your playacting and putting on fancy airs won't get you anywhere." He caught Sarah by the wrist and gave it a painful twist.

"Gus," Tice protested, "that's enough."

Gus ignored the warning. With a practiced hand he maneuvered Sarah toward the overstuffed chair and forced her to sit. Then he shook a bony finger in her face. "The fact is, missy, you've belonged to Tice Edwards for some time," he gloated. "Your signature on the marriage papers is all that remains to make it legal."

Sarah opened her mouth to protest, but the sudden, desperate look on Gus's face made her close it again.

"Perhaps I should continue, Gus," Tice broke in. "Miss Anderson, you are overwrought." He crossed the room and knelt down beside the armchair. "You must forgive your stepfather, Sarah, my dear. He's been under quite a strain the past two years. Gus owes me money—a *lot* of money. He's accumulated quite a gambling debt aboard the *River Queen*. I should have tossed him overboard long ago, but. . ." He allowed his gaze to linger on Sarah's face. "He assured me his collateral was worth allowing him a chance to win his losses back." Tice sighed. "Unfortunately Gus is not an especially good gambler. His losses keep piling up. The good news is that when you become my wife, I will cancel all debts against him. In addition, as my father-in-law, he will have the privilege of gambling as often and for as much as he likes aboard the *Queen*. Your brothers and sister need never worry about going hungry again." He grinned. "They could stay on board ship if they liked."

"They're not my brothers and sister," Sarah choked out. It was a stupid thing to say. But she could think of nothing else—not while her heart was slamming against her chest like a mighty fist and her stomach threatened to empty itself. The look in Tice Edwards's eyes reminded her of a reptile's eyes, a reptile waiting to strike its prey.

Tice smiled and patted her hand. "You may leave the children here, if you wish. It is immaterial to me *where* they live, my dear."

Sarah snatched her hand away and sent a shriveling glance at her stepfather. "This can't be legal. You can't force me to marry this—this—*snake*! I'll go to the police. I'll tell them, tell them—"

"Tell them what, Sarah?" Tice stood and smiled down at her. "That your *legal guardian*—under whose authority you must remain until you are eighteen years of age—has made a perfectly good marriage contract for you? I am more than qualified for the position of a caring husband. I can provide not only for you but also for your entire family. I am one of the most prominent men of this city. The police would laugh at your foolish talk and send you home." Tice grinned. "Trust me. I know. The chief of police is one of my regulars aboard the *Queen*."

Sarah ignored his remarks and focused on what he'd said earlier. "What do you mean, my *legal guardian*? That's rubbish. My real father is dead, and Gus is nothing more than a poor excuse for a stand-in."

Tice raised a sardonic eyebrow. "An attorney friend of mine and I helped arrange the matter of guardianship papers a little over a year ago." He turned to Gus. "You never told her?"

"Must've slipped my mind." Gus ambled over to the cookstove and poured himself a second cup of coffee. Then he looked at Sarah and smirked. "Sorry."

Sarah tried to absorb this new and unwelcome news. It was no use. Instead she did what she had promised herself she would not do in front of these men—she curled into a small ball in the depths of the armchair and burst into uncontrollable sobs.

When no more tears fell, Sarah rubbed her eyes and looked around. The cabin lay empty and quiet. She heard nothing except an occasional cockroach skittering across the wooden floor on its nightly round of foraging. The three small lamps that provided light burned low, casting the room into deep shadows. Sarah shivered. Where was Gus? Where were the children?

"Who cares?" she said, rising from the chair. For the first time since her mother had taken sick, Sarah was alone in the cottage. She crossed to the stove and checked the fire. Several coals still burned a dull red. Sarah quickly tossed a few sticks of firewood onto the bed of coals, fanned them to life, and slammed the door shut. She settled the coffeepot over the hottest spot, opened the lid, and peeked inside. There was enough for another cup. Good! She needed a hot, strong cup of coffee to sharpen her wits.

Her stomach rumbled, and Sarah remembered she'd eaten nothing since breakfast. She glanced over at the crude table, but not one biscuit remained of the batch she'd made for Timmy and Ellie. Had it been only a few short hours ago that she'd tossed the food on the table and fled to her attic refuge? It seemed like a century since she'd bade her mother good bye that morning. Nothing seemed real. How could her life suddenly turn so much worse in just one day? She'd thought there could be no more terrible fate than drudging for Gus. Now she knew better. Being married to a man she did not love, a man like Tice Edwards, was even worse than being a servant in her stepfather's house. *Infinitely worse!*

Chapter 4

All Sarah's dreams of what she imagined the perfect marriage would be came from her own parents' life together. She couldn't have had a better example. Her father and mother had honored and respected as well as loved each other. Sarah, even in the earliest stages of budding womanhood, recognized how important that was in a godly marriage. She thrilled when she caught the look that sometimes passed between her mother and father as they shared a secret joke or wanted to communicate without letting Seth and Sarah know. It was like magic, Sarah realized. It had made such a deep impression that she vowed never to give her life into another's keeping until God sent someone of His own choosing—and she looked forward to the time when she and her future husband would share such special moments.

An overheard conversation had deepened Sarah's determination. One bright summer morning Sarah had started lightly down the stairs of the farmhouse where she had been born. Halfway down she heard voices from the parlor. Mama had a caller. Sarah sighed and cast a longing look out the open screen door into the lovely, beckoning day. If Mama heard her, she'd be summoned into the parlor and forced to be polite to some tiresome neighbor.

Sarah turned to tiptoe back upstairs but froze when she heard a recently married young woman, scarcely more than a girl, say, "Mrs. Anderson—Virginia—everyone knows what a wonderful marriage you have. I want to work hard to have the same. I know a lot of it is because you are both strong Christians, but there must be something more. Please. Tell me your secret to finding happiness."

The unseen eavesdropper held her breath, waiting for her mother's reply. After a low, amused laugh, Virginia Anderson's voice rang like a silver bell. "Letty, John and I have always been so busy making sure the other person is happy that we haven't needed to 'find happiness,' as you put it. It's just there. In abundance."

Sarah never forgot her mother's simple recipe for joy in marriage. The words sank into her pounding heart and glowed like a precious gem.

Now, years later, Sarah mourned while she rummaged through the cupboards for something to fill her stomach. "This can't be happening. I cannot, *will not* marry Tice Edwards. I don't even know him. Why would such a man want to marry me in the first place? He doesn't know me. How could he just up and decide he wants me based on one or two stingy little glimpses? It's absurd!"

Sarah slammed the cupboard door shut and stepped to the stove to pour a cup of warmed-over coffee. With a tired sigh she settled herself at the table and pondered her situation. She wanted a husband with whom she could laugh, enjoy life, and confide. One who would put God first and lead his family in Bible readings and evening prayers. "It wouldn't hurt if he was a hardworking man like Pa," she added, sipping the bitter brew. She made a face. "Maybe I'm expecting too much. Maybe they're all like Gus. At least the boys and men from around here are all cut from the same bolt of burlap— rough and ugly."

The image of two men instantly came to mind: her brother Seth, no longer troubled-looking but smiling at her from a faded photograph he'd sent in one of his rare letters, and the tall, dark-haired stranger posing beside him. A rough-clad stranger whose steady gaze and half smile reassured Sarah that her brother had found a true friend. Her heartbeat quickened. "I'll bet he isn't like Gus," she whispered. "Matthew Sterling looks kind and good. According to Seth, he's as solid and true as his name."

She closed her eyes and imagined the stranger riding up to rescue her from the unspeakable future Gus and Tice planned. The next instant Sarah shook her head. "Appearances are just that—appearances. Seth might be mistaken about his friend. Even though Matthew means *gift of the Lord*, he might be no better than Gus and Tice."

Sarah sighed. If all men were like those two, she would *never* marry. Better to live alone than live married to someone she didn't love—or worse, who would never really love her the way God meant a husband to love his wife.

"So, God, what am I supposed to do?" she pleaded. "Tice Edwards is obviously a man used to getting his own way. He's no doubt got a justice or a preacher or two under his thumb. How am I going to escape this trap they've laid for me?" She took another gulp of coffee and stared at the tabletop.

Like a gentle breeze a scripture verse whispered in her mind. *"There hath no temptation taken you but such as is common to man: but God is faithful, who will not suffer you to be tempted above that ye are able; but will with the temptation also make a way to escape, that ye may be able to bear it."*

Escape? Yes! Sarah's heartbeat quickened. She must flee from the fate Gus intended for her. But how? Gus was clearly trapped in Tice's web of debt as surely as they intended to trap Sarah. "Perhaps there's a different way," she murmured. "If I could offer Gus another way out of his debt, he might not be so keen on marrying me off." She managed a small smile of hope. Maybe Gus could ask Tice Edwards to extend the loan one more time. If he—

The door swung open and smashed against the wall in the middle of Sarah's musings. Timmy entered first. He ran to Sarah and threw his thin little arms around her neck. The other boys shuffled past and plopped themselves on the floor in the center of the room with a pack of playing cards. Ellie sat down at the table near Sarah and just looked at her. As usual nobody said a word. No one offered an explanation of their recent whereabouts.

Sarah sighed. Keeping track of the Stoddard children was worse than trying to corral a flock of frightened chickens. The only relief she got was the days they were in school and she had the house to herself. Some days the older boys played hooky and surprised her by crashing in through the door and upsetting all her carefully laid plans.

Gus burst in and kicked the door shut with the heel of his boot. He lifted a bottle filled with amber liquid to his lips and took a swallow. "Well, Sarah," he drawled, "I gave you a few minutes by yourself to work things through." He fell into the ragged armchair and waited.

If Gus thinks I'll thank him for this small consideration, he is greatly mistaken, Sarah decided. Just looking at him made the bile rise in her throat. She swallowed hard and determined to work on an escape plan right away. "I'm not going to marry Tice," she stated. Before Gus could strike out, Sarah continued. "Promise you won't force me to marry Mr. Edwards, and I'll pay off the debt you owe him. I'll find work—good-paying work—and I'll pay back every cent. I'll keep this place clean and care for the kids. Just don't make me marry him."

Gus grinned and took a swallow of whiskey. "Sarah, Sarah." He chuckled softly, shaking his head. "You are such an innocent. Have you any idea how much I owe Tice Edwards?"

She shook her head.

"I owe him more than six thousand dollars."

Sarah blanched. "Six thousand dollars?" If she worked day and night until she was an old woman, she could never hope to pay back such a sum. Her hopes crashed. In desperation she threw herself to the floor in front of Gus. "Please," she pleaded, "don't force me to marry Mr. Edwards. Who will take care of the children if I'm gone? Timmy's still little. Ellie's too young to look after him all day while you're out of the house."

"Who'd take care of 'em if you hired yourself out to work?" Gus growled. He sat up and leaned closer to his stepdaughter. "I can get me another woman anytime I want. Just like I got your ma. It ain't hard to do. Your ma is proof of that."

It took every ounce of self-control Sarah had to keep from grabbing a frying pan off the dilapidated stove and giving him a whack. How could he speak that way, with Mama barely cold in the grave?

Gus reached out and grasped Sarah's wrist. "I'll tell you another thing, missy. Tice Edwards sees something in you he likes. I don't know what, but you'll not do anything to make him change his mind, you hear? He's a gentleman. Told me he plans to court you right and proper for a week or two—starting tomorrow. You'd best get yourself cleaned up and ready when he comes calling in the afternoon. Or else." He thrust her aside and went back to his bottle. Soon he was snoring loudly, sprawled across the chair with his head thrown back.

Tiptoeing so as not to wake his father, Timmy crept to Sarah and whispered, "I'm hungry."

"It's too late to fix you anything," Sarah muttered, getting up. She turned to Ian and Peter. "Go up to bed, boys. The night's half over."

Ian glared at her while Peter remarked, "We don't have to."

"Fine. Stay up all night. See if I care." Wearily she took Timmy's hand and glanced around the room for Ellie. The little girl lay sound asleep in a corner, curled into a small, tattered ball. Wisps of dark brown hair fell across her face, pouting even in sleep. Sarah thought about rousing her, but what was the point? Ellie would certainly protest against being wakened and dragged up to the attic. Why care if the child spent the night on the cold, hard floor?

A sliver of guilt stabbed Sarah as she guided Timmy up the steep ladder to the room above. Her mother never would have allowed Ellie to huddle in the corner. Virginia always had a tender word for the fractious little girl, no matter how weary and heartsore she felt after a long day's work.

"I'm not like you, Mama," Sarah confessed in a whisper, giving Timmy one last boost onto the attic floor. "I can't be patient and kind to these rowdy youngsters when my own world is falling apart. I'm sorry."

"What did you say, Sarah?" Timmy asked quietly.

"Never you mind." She tumbled him onto his pallet and tucked the quilt around his peaked face. She rose. "You just go to sleep. It's late."

"Sarah?"

"What now?" Sarah snapped.

"You—you ain't leavin' us to marry that gambler fellow, are you?"

Sarah caught her breath at the fear she heard in Timmy's voice. Reaching down, she patted him on the leg. "I don't know, Timmy. I hope not. But it's nothing you have to worry about right now."

Before he could reply, Sarah crept around the partition and onto her own mattress. The corn husks rustled and crackled while she tried to find a comfortable position for her weary body. Soon she lay still. The rustling ceased. Only the soft laughter of the boys downstairs and the occasional snore of a drunken Gus Stoddard floated up through the hole in the ceiling.

Although Sarah's body was at last at rest, her mind was spinning. The verse from Corinthians about escaping temptation repeated itself in her mind. Her escape from Tice Edwards by offering to pay Gus's debt was obviously not a viable plan. There must be another way to escape.

A familiar verse from Genesis 12 popped into her head. *"Get thee out of thy country, and from thy kindred, and from thy father's house, unto a land that I will shew thee."*

Leave? Sarah held her breath and stared at the pale moonlight peeking through the cracks in the attic roof. *Run away?* She shivered in the dark. How could she just up and leave? She had no place to go, no money to get there. Worse, she would be alone—dreadfully alone.

"Lo, I am with you always, even unto the end of the world."

Sarah held her breath in wonder. All those Bible verses she'd learned as a child were coming back to her just when she needed them most. But again, the word *how* kept rearing its ugly head—mocking her, urging her to stay and accept her future. She wavered. In spite of her unspoken vows never to marry until she felt God approved, maybe marrying Tice Edwards wouldn't be as bad as she was making it out to be. He was rich. He seemed polite and was obviously interested in her. He had spoken gently to her and prevented Gus from striking her.

She chewed on her lip in deep thought and rolled onto her side. The corn husks rustled loudly. There would be no corn-husk mattress waiting for her if she married Tice. Only silks and satins. Soft, smooth bedcoverings. No leaking roof. Then, like a clap of thunder, the memory of her mother's marriage to Gus resounded in her memory. Sarah remembered how content her mother had appeared when she knew she was marrying a man who would care for her and for her children. Gus had also seemed the perfect gentleman—before the wedding.

"I can't marry Tice Edwards," Sarah resolved between clenched teeth. "I don't love him. I don't even know him. I must escape. I have no choice." That decided, she gave the situation over to the One who knew exactly what He was doing. "I don't know how I'm going to escape, God, or where I'm going to go," she whispered in the darkness of the attic, "but I do know You're the only One who can help me now. Show me the way." She sighed, turned over, and fell into an uneasy sleep.

Chapter 5

Eighteen months earlier
Central California

Matthew Sterling rode into Madera and dismounted in front of Moore's General Store—which housed the post office—thirsty enough to drain a well. It was over a hundred degrees in the shade, and there was no shade on the ten miles between town and Matt's Diamond S Ranch. Just flat land, dry grass, and a glimpse of the snowcapped Sierra Nevada in the distance, so far away and hazy in the shimmering late September air that the mountains looked like a mirage.

With a practiced flick of his wrist Matt led his favorite buckskin gelding, Chase, to the well-filled horse trough in the middle of town, being careful not to let him drink his fill. "Whoa there," he ordered. "You don't want to founder." He raised his canteen to his own parched lips and grimaced when the lukewarm water poured down his throat.

Matt forced the reluctant horse away from the trough and secured the reins around a nearby hitching rail before giving Chase an affectionate slap on the chest. "Won't be more than a minute, old boy. Gotta pick up the mail, swap a quick 'howdy' with the captain, then it's back to the ranch for a cool drink and some shade." He chuckled as he always did when he thought about stopping by the hotel to greet the captain. He'd known Captain Russell Perry Mace ever since he was a small child, but Matt had never heard the stocky adventurer called anything but *the captain. I guess once a captain, always a captain. Even if the Mexican War's been over for ages,* Matt thought. Between his title and his ever-present top hat, Captain Mace was an easily recognized figure anywhere in Madera.

Chase shook his dark mane and snorted as if to hurry his master along. He stamped a hoof, and a swirl of pale yellow dust rose up and billowed around the young man.

"Hey!" Matt admonished with a laugh. "None of that. I won't be long." He glanced down at his dust-caked shirt and chaps. What was a little extra dust at this point? He'd been out on the range all day and had built up a good supply of dirt long before Chase showered him.

"Howdy, Matt. Haven't seen you around town for a spell. How're things

31

on the Diamond S?"

Matt turned. Evan Moore, Madera's portly postmaster stood in the doorway of his store grinning. His bald head glistened in the hot afternoon sun. Matt smiled back. "Busy, Evan. Fall roundup's just around the corner."

"Got a full crew?"

"Pretty much. Wish I didn't have to hire on drifters." Matt shook his head and joined the postmaster on the wooden sidewalk. "They're nothing but trouble, but if I don't snatch 'em up, Chapman over at the Redding Ranch is likely to hire 'em. I don't want to be caught shorthanded this year."

"I don't blame you." Evan motioned the young rancher to follow him inside the store. "Don't worry about the dust," he said when Matt removed his wide-brimmed felt hat and slapped it against his chaps before entering. "Can't seem to escape the dust, no matter how hard a body tries. Just like this infernal heat." Evan wiped the sweat from his shining head and strolled to the small cubicle behind the counter that served as the Madera Post Office. He reached into a pigeonhole and withdrew a fistful of envelopes addressed to Matthew Sterling, c/o Diamond S Ranch. "Sorry, Matt. Nothing from Dolores."

"Drat that girl," Matt muttered, swiping at the stubborn hank of black hair that hung over his eyes like a horse's forelock. He replaced his Stetson and sorted through the letters with a scowl. "Don't they teach young ladies to write at that fancy finishing school back east? You'd think Dori could send word to her only brother that she's alive and happy."

The postmaster made no comment.

Matt sighed. He missed little Dori. He missed her chatter. He even missed the silly, affected airs she put on when she wasn't happy with the way things were going out at the ranch. Sending her to school in Boston had been Solita's idea, not his. "Senor Mateo, you must let the senorita finish her education," the diminutive Mexican housekeeper had insisted. "She is unhappy here. Your mama and papa would have allowed it, had they lived. Since they are no longer with us, you must decide what is best for her, not what is best for you."

Matt had agreed, but he wasn't pleased about it. The white stucco, Spanish-style hacienda seemed huge and empty with the only remaining member of his family gone. He enjoyed these rare visits to Madera. Picking up the mail—a task easily done by any greenhorn ranch hand—was Matt's excuse to mingle with the friendly people of the small valley town.

Madera—*lumber* in Spanish—was the perfect name for the thriving little village that had sprung up all at once a few years back. The California Lumber Company had chosen this site along the Southern Pacific Railroad line as the terminus for their timber flume back in 1876. Six months later the town had been laid out, and building had commenced at a lively rate.

Matt often paused in the middle of the wide main street to take in the three hotels, three general stores, the drugstore, butcher shop, blacksmith shop, and livery. He thanked God each and every time for timber, flumes, and lumber companies. No longer isolated on his ranch ten miles east of nowhere, the rancher and his hands benefited from the influx of new businesses and the people who ran them. All in all, Madera was—in Matt's opinion—just about the prettiest and most wide-awake town in the entire San Joaquin Valley.

Matt gave Evan a curt good-bye and left the post office in ill humor. It rankled him that Dori, as usual, was probably caught up in her own affairs and wouldn't get around to writing her brother until Christmas. He stuffed the handful of envelopes into his saddlebag and sighed. "Sometimes I wonder why the good Lord made girls in the first place," he muttered. "Trouble. Nothing but trouble."

Matt shook himself free of musings. Thinking about Dori and her irresponsibility invariably made him remember Lydia Hensley. *Forget about her,* he ordered himself, clenching his jaw. *That's over. I'm free of her, and I won't waste the rest of a perfectly good afternoon reflecting on what went wrong between us.*

"Let's get on home, Chase," Matt mumbled to his horse. His trip to town, which he'd looked forward to all day, had turned into a disappointment. Now all he wanted was a bath, a clean set of clothes, and a tall, cool glass of Solita's lemonade—in that order. He untied Chase and glanced toward the elegant, two-story hotel that occupied the best lot in town. "I'll catch the captain later, I guess, though he'll probably give me what for for not stopping by."

Before he could mount up, the swinging doors to Dunlap's Saloon flew open. A wizened, bewhiskered man tore down the wooden sidewalk bellowing, "Somebody get the sheriff!"

Matt gave the old man a disgusted look when he stumbled across the street to where Matt stood beside his horse. The one blight on this town was the saloons that kept cropping up. He'd been glad when Captain Mace turned his saloon into a hotel a few years back, but another saloon just sprang up in its place—and another, and another, until there were more saloons than churches in Matt's beloved town.

"What's the trouble, Dan?" he asked the wheezing, wide-eyed man. "Can't Dunlap keep control of his customers?"

Dan Doyle reached out to steady himself against Matt's horse. "It's bad, Matt. Some wild-eyed, greenhorn kid came tearin' into the saloon yellin' that a two-legged skunk stole his horse. Like t'near started tearin' the place apart."

"Sounds like the usual scuffle. What's got you so fired up?"

Dan was breathing hard. " 'Cause he's just a kid, and it's Red Fallon he's accusin'."

Matt caught his breath. It sounded like this wasn't the usual fray that went on behind barroom doors. Red had a mean streak. He was an excellent cowhand, but the fiery redhead couldn't control his temper or hold his liquor—facts that kept him drifting from job to job. Against his better judgment Matt had hired Red on for the fall roundup. Now it already looked like he was going to regret it.

"I can't stay and jaw with you, Matt," Dan burst out. "I gotta get the sheriff quick, or there's gonna be a killin'. You oughta go over there and see if you can step in. Red's one of yer hands."

"I suppose you're right." Matt grimaced, set his jaw, and stepped into the street.

"Watch yourself, Matt." Dan gave a final warning. "Red's got a knife."

Matt grunted and hitched Chase to the rail again. A few long strides across the street and a mighty shove of the swinging doors put Matt inside the saloon—a place he only entered when he was obliged to round up some of his Diamond S hands after an occasional Saturday-night binge. The scene before him was one of wild confusion—just as Dan had described. Red Fallon towered over a stripling lad, knife in one hand, his other fist upraised. His steel gray eyes gleamed; a dangerous smile showed through his unkempt red beard.

The kid, who looked to be eighteen or nineteen, shook as he lay on the sawdust-covered floor. Matt sensed it was from rage, not fear. Blood poured from his nose. One eye was nearly swollen shut, and he was gasping for breath. His hand clutched his other arm, which told Matt that Red's knife had probably been busy. Clearly undaunted, the kid glowered at the hulking cowhand.

In spite of himself, Matt grinned. Although the kid was roughed up pretty bad, he didn't look beaten. Matt expected the boy to go after Red again at any moment. He could see it in the flashing blue eyes. *Down but not out. Thinks he can take on a grizzly bear! Just like Robbie.* In a flash the memory of Matt's little brother—much younger—going after Matt came to mind. His grin widened. A pair of cubs, neither of whom would admit defeat no matter what.

Matt was right. Uttering a shriek reminiscent of an Indian war cry, the youth sprang to his feet and lurched at Red, ramming his head into the big man's belly. With a surprised *oof*, Red reeled back, right into Matt's arms.

Chapter 6

"What's going on in here?" Matt demanded of the cowhand. He heaved Red away from the boy, who was stumbling around, flailing his arms, and trying to stay on his feet.

"I'll kill that little upstart!" Red bellowed, lunging past Matt with murder in his eyes. His knife flashed.

Quick as lightning, Matt lashed out and grasped Red's knife hand. A twist, and the knife thudded to the floor. Matt picked it up, brushed away the sawdust, and laid it on the bar.

Red glared at Matt. "This ain't your affair, Boss." He pointed a meaty finger at the kid. "This is between me and him." He took a step toward the youth, who backed away, still clutching his arm. Blood flowed freely between his fingers, but he didn't seem to notice.

Matt stepped between them. "I'll ask you once more, Red, and I want a straight answer. What in blue blazes is going on?"

"That's what I'd like to know," a deep voice said from the saloon door. Sheriff Meade elbowed his way past the onlookers and glowered at the two men in the middle of the room.

"I'll tell you what's going on," the bloody but unbeaten lad shouted. He pointed an accusing finger at Red Fallon. "He stole my horse and supplies two days ago. I had to hoof it here without food and water." The lad's dusty shirt, jeans, and boots gave credence to his statement. He shook his fist at Red. "Copper's hitched outside this very minute!"

"That's a mighty serious accusation, son," Sheriff Meade quietly said. "Can you prove it?"

"Naw, he can't prove it!" Red bawled. His nostrils flared. "I found that sorrel wandering around up near Raymond when I was going after strays the other—"

"Liar!" The boy leaped.

Matt caught him easily and steered him away from the enraged Red Fallon. "Take it easy, boy. No sense gettin' killed over a horse. Simmer down and let the sheriff get to the bottom of it." He looked into the kid's battered face, "What's your name?"

"Seth. Seth Anderson. And that ugly skunk is a lying horse thief." He made one more attempt to get at Red, then his eyes rolled back into his head, and he collapsed in Matt's arms.

Matt stared down at the unconscious youth. Seth's face was pale and gaunt beneath the dark bruises. Matt motioned to a couple of spectators. "Jake, you and Murray take this poor kid over to Mace's Hotel and ask Doc Brown to have a look at him. He's lost a lot of blood. I'll be along after a while." He gently placed Seth's limp body into the men's care and rounded on his erring cowhand. "There was no call to beat up that boy. Why'd you do it?"

"Boss, I don't take kindly to being accused of stealin' a man's horse and supplies. I tell you, I found that horse up in the foothills. There was nobody around." Red shrugged and spread his range-hardened hands. "Figured some feller met his end up near the mines. Why should I let a good piece of horse-flesh wander off?"

"When you found out the horse belonged to Seth, why didn't you just give it back?" Matt wanted to know. He frowned. Something didn't ring true with Red's story, no matter how plausible it sounded. Or how aggrieved and innocent the cowboy acted.

"Why, Boss." Red grinned and reached for his knife. "That wildcat kid burst in here madder'n a hornet, demanding to know who owned the sorrel gelding tied up outside. 'Course I told him it was mine." He examined his knife and slid it carefully into the sheath hanging from his belt. "He just lit into me after that."

"Yeah, Red. After you baited him," Charlie Dunlap piped up from behind the bar. He mimicked Red's voice. "Hey fellers, any of you missin' a sorrel? No kid like this one's got a horse like that, 'nless he stole him. Know what we do to horse stealers 'round here?" Charlie scowled. "Sure young Anderson pitched into you. No self-respectin' feller, kid or not, would take that guff—and I notice you took almighty pleasure in beatin' the stuffin' out of him!"

A murmur of assent swept through the onlookers.

The sheriff's disbelieving snort showed his opinion of Red's story and confirmed Matt's suspicions. "Let's take a look at the horse."

With Sheriff Meade in the lead, Matt, Red, and a crowd of interested bystanders left the saloon and approached the sorrel Seth had referred to as "Copper." The tired animal stood with drooping head, showing he'd been ridden hard. But his ears perked up and he whinnied when the sheriff laid a gentle hand on his mane.

Matt whistled softly. "Nice horse. No wonder the kid was upset to find him missing or stolen."

Red glowered at his boss at the word *stolen* but kept his mouth shut. Sheriff Meade opened a saddlebag and pulled out a change of clothes. "These look like they might fit young Anderson." He sighed. "But without more evidence, I don't know how I can just hand this horse over to some stray kid who claims the sorrel's his."

"What about this?" Matt asked from the other side of the horse. He held up a wrinkled and faded photograph. "It might be a picture of his family. One of them is a good likeness of Seth. The others. . ." His voice trailed off as he gazed at the faces of two women. One was an older woman who clearly resembled Seth. The other—

Matt held his breath at the picture of the. . .girl? No. Not a girl but a young lady. She was seated next to the woman he decided must be their mother. Matt was struck by the girl's clear, steady gaze and the look of quiet honesty on her young face. A pretty face. Innocent with a look of fun and laughter waiting to be set free. Not beautiful, but Matt had no interest in beauty. *"Favour is deceitful, and beauty is vain. . . ."* He'd learned that the hard way from Lydia Hensley a few years back. Quickly he passed the photograph to Sheriff Meade.

The sheriff gave the photo a brief glance and announced his decision. "Appears to me this sorrel belongs to Seth Anderson." He caught Red's baleful gaze, held up a weather-beaten hand when Red started to speak, and said, "Don't get your back up, Red. I want to hear the boy's side of this before I make any final judgment. He ain't up to talking and probably won't be for a while. I'm gonna overlook the beating you gave the kid—for now. But if that boy's injuries prove serious, I'm taking you in. This is the third cutting scrape this month, and I've had enough. Ben Hoder's still in jail waitin' trial for carving up Joe Mova so bad he died. You'll be joining him if you're not careful."

Red's face turned livid. "You can't arrest me for—"

"That's what you think." Sheriff Meade strode off, his boot heels clumping heavily on the wooden sidewalk outside the saloon.

"Get back to the ranch," Matt barked, "before I decide I'd rather go short-handed this season than put up with your shenanigans."

"Ain't got no horse," Red whined. "Sold him when I got the sorrel."

"A shame." Matt shook his head, not sorry in the least. "I suggest you go buy him back. Then get out to the ranch." He raised a warning finger at the man. "And I don't want this incident brought up again, is that clear?"

A curt nod was all Matt got for a response. The big cowhand turned on his heel and took off down the street.

A sigh of relief whispered through the crowd. The interested bystanders went about their business. Matt made sure Seth would be all right then mounted Chase and headed back to the Diamond S—thanking God he had chosen to ride into town this morning. His thoughts kept time to the rhythmic beat of the buckskin's hooves on the parched ground. Who was Seth Anderson? Where had he come from? Judging by his ragged, dusty clothing, he'd been on the trail for some time.

Were the woman and girl in the picture really the young man's mother and sister? Matt laughed. "Why should I care, Chase?" The gelding flicked his ears but didn't change his stride. "I do though. He's a game kid, just like Robbie." A pang went through Matt. "God, I miss Robbie so much. I don't know why he had to die so young." He forced his thoughts back to the present. "I hope Seth will be all right. I'd hate for anything to happen to him. He must be a pretty good sort, with a mother and sister like that. Looks like he could use some help. If he pulls through, I'll see what I can do."

Long before Matt reached the Diamond S, he had spun dreams of bringing Seth Anderson to the ranch and teaching him the tricks of the range—the same way he had once taught Robbie. Matt smiled. "Lord, if I'm a good judge of character—and I am—this tenderfoot kid will take to life on the Diamond S like Chase to a water trough on a hot day. He's as spunky as Dori, and with her off at school, it will be good to have someone like him around the place again." Stirrings of anticipation brought a laugh. "Oh boy, when she comes home, those two will liven up the ranch like fireworks on the Fourth of July!"

≈

Eighteen months later, Matt knew it had to be the good Lord who'd literally dropped Seth Anderson into his lap that dusty fall afternoon. After hearing from Doc Brown that the lad's injuries were not life threatening but merely a temporary annoyance, Matt had offered to free Captain Mace from having to care for the young stray. The tourist season was in full swing, and the captain had plenty to oversee. His hotel was crowded with guests waiting to take the Yosemite Stage and Turnpike Company's ninety-mile trip up ten thousand feet to enjoy the awesome grandeur of Yosemite Valley. In addition, the captain and his crew provided a hearty supper for the southbound passengers of the Southern Pacific Railroad when it stopped in Madera each evening. It was too much to ask the generous hotel proprietor to care for a boy who would need vigilant attention over the next few weeks. The Diamond S was the perfect place for Seth to recuperate.

Chapter 7

No one understood why Matt wanted to take on the still-wet-behind-the-ears kid.

"It's roundup, Matt. Are you loco?" the captain protested when Matt showed up with his wagon to transport the young man out to his ranch. "You've got no time to mollycoddle a greenhorn, especially one who probably won't be leaving his bed for the next month."

Matt couldn't deny that even without the beating from Red, Seth didn't look much like a candidate for ranch work.

"More like a shopkeeper," his foreman, Brett Owen, joked when he saw him.

Matt didn't explain why he wanted Seth out at the Diamond S. Or that something about the lad called out for help—help he hadn't been able to give his younger brother. So Matt brought Seth home to the Diamond S and placed him under the gentle, ministering hands of his family's long-time housekeeper, Solita. At once the round-faced, cheerful Mexican woman clucked and fussed over Seth as if he were a long-lost chick returning to the nest. *Perhaps he is,* Matt mused on more than one occasion. The more he became acquainted with Seth Anderson, the more the young man reminded Matt of his younger brother, Robert.

Robbie had worshipped the ground Matt walked on. He had followed him everywhere. Five years Matt's junior, Robbie tried to do everything his older brother did. The boy's desire to keep up with Matt often led him into trouble. Occasionally he lit into Matt in frustration when he found himself lacking the skills necessary to do whatever his brother did. Matt prayed for patience, took it all in stride, and tried to be the big brother he should be.

Unfortunately Robbie tried to keep up once too often. Matt, at twenty, had excelled at the ranching tasks he loved. His father, William, depended on Matt to help run the growing Diamond S spread. Matt could rope, ride, and brand just about anything on four hooves. He could break a colt gently or all at once.

Fifteen-year-old Robbie wanted to prove he could do it, too. Although forbidden to work with the green colts, he took it upon himself to try to break Skye—the wildest colt on the ranch. Matt found his little brother one afternoon—broken and near death. He lived two more days before passing quietly from Matt's arms into heaven.

Now, six years later—with his entire family either back east or in eternity—Matt saw in Seth a replica of the brother who had been snatched away from him too soon. Every day he grew closer to the plucky boy.

Fall roundup ended, and Matt devoted all his spare time to working with his newest cowhand. Seth healed rapidly and seemed anxious to please his benefactor. Although weak and shaky at times, the young man made up for his inexperience with the determination to conquer every task Matt set for him. The older and more seasoned hands watched in amusement and shouted good-natured barbs at Seth while their boss tried to teach him basic ranching skills.

"Ride 'em, cowboy!"

"Straddle that saddle, kid!"

Seth ignored the banter and raw jokes and focused every ounce of his willpower into mastering the various jobs on the Diamond S. To the astonishment of the skeptical Diamond S cowboys, Seth learned quickly. Even trail-hardened Brett Owen finally admitted—although not in Seth's hearing—"He's worth his salt." High praise indeed. It summed up the growing respect for Seth's hard work and stubborn determination.

By spring good food and steady exercise combined with the mild climate of Madera turned the stripling lad into a well-muscled and agile young cowboy. Once he proved himself adept at working with cattle and horses, haying, cutting fence posts, and the myriad of other duties a cowboy must do, Seth was welcomed into the ranks as a full-fledged cowhand, ready to pull his weight to make the Diamond S prosper. By summer he was one of the top hands.

During this time, Matt learned about his young friend's hardships back East. Often after church on Sunday afternoons, while the rest of the cowhands took the day off to head for town to court, cockfight, gamble, or take part in some other activity Matt preferred not to know about, he and Seth rode to Matt's favorite spot on the ranch—some distance into the Sierra foothills—and talked. The promontory that overlooked Matt's ranch offered both privacy and beauty. The entire valley spread out before them, dotted with dark clumps of the vineyards and orchards that were quickly springing up north of the San Joaquin River. Closer to their lookout, the rolling range was sprinkled with Diamond S cattle roaming freely.

A faint lowing sound drifted up to Matt's ears, and he sighed, perfectly content. "Must've been a hard thing to do, leaving your ma and sister back in St. Louis like that," he remarked, resting his long, lean body against the trunk of an old oak tree.

Seth lay down, settled his wide-brimmed hat over his eyes, and clasped his hands behind his neck. "Worse than you can imagine. But my mother knew I had no choice. She was hoping I could save enough money to bring Sarah out West someday." He peeked out from under his hat. "I showed you her picture, didn't I?"

Matt leaned forward and flopped his hands over his raised knees. He smiled patiently. "Often enough."

"Do you think she's pretty?"

"Oh yeah. Sure, kid," came Matt's distracted reply. This was dangerous territory. He didn't want to hurt Seth's feelings, but he really wasn't interested in thinking about whether the girl in Seth's wrinkled photo was pretty or not. He glanced at his friend, who had sat up and was rummaging through his vest pockets.

"I know I've got another picture of her around here somewhere," Seth muttered. "It's more recent. I sent my folks a letter back in July."

"Hmm," Matt answered, not really paying attention. Watching Chase graze, he thought how dry and unappetizing the late October grass must taste—even to a horse.

"I sent a picture of the two of us," Seth prattled on, "you know, when that fancy Eastern photographer, who set up shop next to Judge Barry's office, was offering a special during the Fourth of July celebration. It turned out real fine, and I sent it to my mother and Sarah—so they'd see I'm doing okay."

Matt didn't answer, but Seth persisted. "I got a letter yesterday from Sarah—and she sent another photograph. You want to see it?"

Matt yawned. "The picture or the letter?"

Seth gave Matt a disgusted look and passed him the photograph.

Matt sat up and glanced at the picture. Against his will his eyes widened. His pulse quickened. This young woman couldn't be the same girl he'd seen in the photograph he'd dug out of Seth's saddlebags the year before! She was more than pretty—she was striking. Her clear gaze—no doubt the same color blue as Seth's—riveted Matt. She seemed to be smiling just for him.

Stop it! he berated himself. *It's not like you to get moonstruck over a picture!* He swallowed and quickly handed it back to Seth. "Real nice, kid," he managed. "I sure hope you can get her out here, like your ma wants. From what you've told me, your sister's life sounds pretty rotten." If Matt ever saw that low-down sidewinder of a stepfather, he'd have a thing or two to say to him about the way a man should treat his wife and children!

Seth sighed. "I don't know if Sarah will ever come out now." He held up a well-handled piece of paper. "This letter says that my mother is in the family way. Guess I'll be getting a new little brother or sister sometime next spring." He shrugged. "No matter. I'll probably never see the baby—or Sarah, for that matter." He stuffed the picture and letter into his vest pocket and stared out across the valley, quiet all of a sudden.

Matt straightened up, suddenly ashamed for treating the photograph of Seth's sister lightly. He'd "adopted" Seth so completely that he occasionally forgot the young man had a mother and a sister whom he must love

41

dearly—just as Matt loved Dori. "Hey Seth," he apologized gruffly, "I'm sorry. Real sorry about the hard times with your family. As soon as your mother is settled with the new little one, no doubt Sarah will be able to come out to the Golden State." He smiled and punched his young friend lightly on the shoulder.

Seth didn't smile. "Sarah wrote that Mama will need her more than ever once the baby comes. She's fixed her mind on staying." He looked at Matt. Misery showed on his tanned face. "My stepfather will work her to death, most likely, or marry her off to one of his disreputable acquaintances." Seth clenched his fists and drove them into the ground. "And I'm helpless. Helpless to do anything but watch it happen. I almost dread another letter."

❧

Seth received no more letters. The following spring a telegram came to Seth, in care of the Diamond S Ranch, Madera, California. His sister had been born. But his mother and the baby had died.

Matt's heart ached with pity and the pain of remembering his own losses. Now the boy who had carved out a special place in Matt's heart would need his friendship more than ever.

"He will have it," Matt vowed one afternoon while returning from town. "For as long as he wants to stay, the Diamond S will be Seth Anderson's home." Comfortably slumped in the saddle, Matt gave Chase free rein and let his thoughts drift like a tumbleweed skipping along with the slight breeze. Feelings that had been growing ever since the telegram came surfaced then burst into full-fledged determination. They spilled into a prayer that hovered in the quiet air.

"God, if there's any possible way to get Sarah Joy Anderson out of her stepfather's clutches, please show me what it is. For Seth's sake," he hastily added.

Only for Seth's sake? a little voice whispered inside him. Matt tried to ignore it, but the face in Seth's photograph shimmered in the quiet air until Matt whacked Chase with the reins. The unaccustomed blow, light as it was, sent the startled buckskin into a gallop guaranteed to banish the mirage and bring any once-bitten, twice-shy rancher back to his senses.

Chapter 8

Nineteen hundred miles east of the Diamond S Ranch, Sarah wearily rose from her corn-husk mattress at the crack of dawn. She shivered in the early morning chill and hastily wrapped herself in her mother's old dressing gown. The tattered garment not only offered warmth but also the feeling of being enfolded in her mother's arms, comfort that Sarah sorely needed. Ever since Gus had sold her to Tice Edwards—being sold was exactly what it amounted to—Sarah's days had been filled with continued drudgery and her nights with fear. Nights in which she racked her brain to think of a way to escape.

So far none had appeared, in spite of her desperate prayers for God to make a way. Now she sighed and reached for her mother's Bible. During the final weeks of Mama's illness, Sarah had let her scripture reading fall by the wayside from lack of time and energy. "Lord, I'm stuck in St. Louis until I can figure out how to earn enough money to leave here," she whispered into her harsh pillow, careful not to disturb her sleeping half sister. If Ellie awakened, all chances of quiet time for Sarah would flee before the petulant child's demands.

Sarah knelt on the rough floor beside the window and stared out into a day as gray as her life. "I need the wisdom of Solomon to know how to endure Tice's unwelcome advances, God. He's made his intentions clear—he will court me briefly and then wed me."

Fierce determination surged through Sarah's body. She would not marry Tice. She would kick and scream and tear the wedding gown he had ordered made for her until everyone in St. Louis heard. Surely someone would come to her rescue!

Who? a little voice mocked. *Tice Edwards has this town, including the police chief and who knows how many others, in the palm of his hand.* Despair threatened to overwhelm her, but words her father had spoken long ago swept into her heart. Sarah could picture his face, haggard from illness, when he said: *"Seth, Sarah, you will be faced with many hard decisions throughout your life. There is only one way to choose rightly. First, consider all the possibilities and the likely consequences. Next, take them to the Lord in prayer. Finally, wait for His answer."*

He had raised his head with a look so loving and kind Sarah knew she would never forget it. *"Most importantly, once you make your decision, go straight forward, not looking to the right or the left, and carry it out. If it later needs to be altered, our heavenly Father will guide you."*

He hesitated a long moment, closing his eyes as if he needed to gather strength. When he opened them again, a smile lifted his lips, and the blue eyes so like Seth's and Sarah's twinkled. *"Most folks disagree, but I believe it's better to make a decision that may later have to be amended than refuse to make any decision at all."*

That is what Seth did, Sarah thought. A spurt of courage raised her spirits, but again, that dreaded word *how* sent them plummeting. She shifted her position and opened the Bible, which had been her parents' answer book to all their problems. A letter fell out. A letter with the words *Sarah Joy* inscribed on the envelope in her mother's handwriting. With a quick glance to make sure the rustling paper hadn't awakened Ellie, Sarah opened the letter.

Dearest Daughter Sarah, it began. A rush of tears blinded her, but she impatiently brushed them away and read on:

> *You may never see this letter. If everything goes well with my birthing, I will burn it. However, I can't help feeling that God may take me home—both me and your new little brother or sister. There are things I must say to you in case this happens.*
>
> *First of all, I know you will grieve for me, but you must also rejoice. My love for you and Seth has been my only joy for a long time. You have been everything a son and daughter should be. Your father and I chose our children's names long before either of you were born. Sarah—princess; Seth—anointed.*
>
> *I did a terrible thing when I married Gus. I knew he could never replace my beloved John, but he seemed sincere and a good Christian. I truly believed his promise to become a substitute father.*

Sarah stopped reading. Pity for her mother who had paid so dearly for her error in judgment warred with anger at Gus. Substitute father? Never! From the moment he said, "I do," Virginia Anderson Stoddard and her two children meant nothing to him but persons he could exploit. Sarah shook off the past. What was done was done. The important thing was what lay ahead. She returned to her mother's precious letter:

> *Sarah Joy, should it be that I cross over, I urge you to leave St. Louis as quickly as you can and never look back. Find Seth. Put yourself under his protection.*

"How?" Sarah murmured. "Long before I could earn any money, Gus and Tice will have me married and trapped forever."

Ellie stirred in her sleep, sending a warning chill through Sarah. She hastily read the final sentences of her mother's letter:

Tucked away in the bottom of the flour barrel is a small tin canister. In it you will find enough money to get away from St. Louis. I scraped and pinched to set aside a few gold coins for you. The gold wedding ring your father gave me is also in the canister. If the need arises, sell it. You must get away from Gus. There is no telling what he might take a notion to do.

Your Loving Mother,
Virginia Anderson

Sarah wanted to shout. Her mother had been a faithful wife, but Gus Stoddard wasn't worthy of having his name on Mama's last message. Sarah kissed it then swiftly and silently donned her old blue calico work dress and hid the letter inside next to her heart. The words of the "Old Hundredth" came to mind, written centuries before:

Praise God, from Whom all blessings flow;
Praise Him, all creatures here below;
Praise Him above, ye heavenly host;
Praise Father, Son, and Holy Ghost.

She silently whispered "Amen" and crept downstairs, avoiding the time-worn, creaking boards. Step by cautious step, she stole to the kitchen. Once there she raised the lid of the flour barrel with trembling fingers—then froze when a familiar, hated voice demanded.

"What're you doin', sneakin' around?" Disheveled and glaring, Gus Stoddard stood in the doorway watching her like a hawk watches baby chicks before pouncing.

Please, God, help me! If Gus finds the money and Mama's ring, I'm doomed.

Summoning the courage generated by her mother's letter, Sarah turned and said in a colorless voice, "Making biscuits. I woke up early." She reached into the barrel and filled the battered sifter with flour.

Some of the suspicion in Gus's face dwindled. An evil grin replaced it. "Sooooo," he drawled, "can't wait to see Tice, huh?"

Sarah shrugged, as if indifferent to the riverboat gambler and his intentions.

"I see you're gettin' used to the idea. Good. You make a fuss, and it will be the worse for you, missy," Gus warned.

Strength flowed into Sarah. She looked directly into Gus's face and managed to smile. "I won't make a fuss. I promise." Truth underlined every word, even though she mentally added, *I won't be here to make a fuss.* For the first time since Mama had fallen ill, happiness filled Sarah. No matter how long and hard the path ahead was, thanks to Virginia *Anderson*, her daughter would be free.

It was late afternoon before Sarah could retrieve the canister. Once emptied, it took its place on a kitchen shelf with nothing to indicate it had once contained treasure. Finished with her many chores for a few moments, Sarah opened her mother's Bible again. She riffled the pages and stopped at Matthew 10:16: "Behold, I send you forth as sheep in the midst of wolves: be ye therefore wise as serpents, and harmless as doves." It was underlined. Sarah resolved to take her mother's advice and secretly prepare to leave—all the while pretending to accept the inevitable future Gus and Tice had planned for her. Perhaps in that way she would throw them off guard.

Yet in spite of her determination, it was all Sarah could do to keep her fear and dislike of Tice Edwards from spilling out when he came courting. She had to admit that he never showed her anything but gentle, considerate attention. He took her for buggy rides and painted a glowing, wonderful picture of their future.

"You will love life on the *River Queen*," he assured her over and over. "Can't you just imagine gliding down the river and watching glorious sunrises and sunsets?"

Sarah nodded. She could imagine it all right—with horror, not anticipation.

Tice never let her forget him for more than a short time. He wrote flowery letters when he couldn't come in person. He brought her nosegays, not wildflowers but expensive bouquets from the best flower sellers in St. Louis. He arranged for the best dressmaker in St. Louis to fashion Sarah's wedding gown. Raging inside, she passively stood while the woman measured, cut, and draped. She must not arouse suspicion, even though she would rather wear faded calico all her life than spend one minute in the expensive gown Tice had selected.

He also bought her costly little trinkets. Sarah shrank from accepting anything from her would-be husband but privately gritted her teeth and stashed them away for her journey. Anything small enough to carry that she could sell would help. Between visits, Sarah continued her hard, monotonous tending of the house and trying to manage the children. In spare moments she started gathering the supplies she would need for her trip to California.

Sarah occasionally felt overwhelmed at the enormity of what she was attempting.

Nineteen hundred miles lay between St. Louis and the Diamond S Ranch near Madera, California. Nineteen hundred mind-staggering miles filled with unknown dangers. At those times Sarah took comfort in rereading Seth's letters, which soon became ragged. Countless times she looked at the photograph he'd sent and imagined life in the West. Against her better judgment her imagining always included the dark-haired stranger with Seth.

Her brother surely couldn't be wrong about Matthew Sterling's character. If only Tice were the man the young rancher appeared to be!

She laughed bitterly. Despite his suave sophistication, Tice Edwards was no better than Gus Stoddard. Marrying him would be like the old saying, "Leaping out of the frying pan into the fire."

"Never," Sarah vowed again and again, thanking God for her mother's far-reaching wisdom and attention to her daughter's need to escape when she was gone.

During one of the times of fanciful musing and the inevitable comparison between Matt Sterling and Tice Edwards, the children swarmed up the stairs, screaming for Sarah's attention. A few of Seth's letters and the photograph scattered to the floor. Sarah hastily gathered them up and shoved them into her reticule.

⋙

Sarah's precarious tightrope walk between appearing submissive and secretly plotting her escape ended long before she felt ready to steal away.

Her plans shattered one morning when Gus shuffled into the kitchen. His wide grin and triumphant expression set Sarah's nerves jangling. Tice was right behind Gus, wearing a look of satisfaction that chilled Sarah to the marrow.

"By tomorrow night you won't be doin' this, missy," Gus announced with a smirk. "Tice here says he's waited long enough and done enough courting. You'll be married tomorrow afternoon. Right, Tice?"

"Yes." Twin devils danced in the gambler's wicked black eyes. "I've been pining away for you long enough, Sarah."

She dropped a frying pan. It splashed soapy water on her apron and the floor, giving her time to hold her tongue instead of screaming and rushing out the open door. She started cleaning up the mess, desperately searching for words. Psalm 50:15 came to sustain her, as other familiar verses had done in the past few weeks: *Call upon me in the day of trouble: I will deliver thee, and thou shalt glorify me.*

"Tomorrow? I hardly think that is possible," she began.

"It's your own fault," Gus growled. "Tice says you won't even let him kiss you until you're married."

It took every ounce of self-control to keep from shuddering. Kiss Tice Edwards? She'd sooner kiss a copperhead!

The two men took her silence for consent and strode out, slapping each other on the back and jesting in a crude way.

But Sarah bit her lip until it bled. Ready or not, she must slip away that night.

Chapter 9

From the time he was old enough to straddle a pony, Matthew Sterling's favorite season on the Diamond S had always been spring. For a short time a green carpet covered the brown and barren hills. The mud and rain took a break. New calves and foals and baby chicks appeared almost overnight. How Matt loved to see the colts and fillies kick up their heels in the pasture then flee to their mamas when startled.

Spring also had sounds of its own: the peeping of baby chicks, music to a child's ears. The clang of the triangle outside the cookshack and the stentorian command "Come and git it before I throw it out" that roused grumbling hands from their beds earlier than they had grown accustomed to rise during the slower winter months.

Whenever young Matt could escape his parents' watchful eyes, he delighted in sneaking out in his nightshirt to eat breakfast with the cowboys. He later laughed at the childhood glee he had felt at outwitting his parents. He hadn't found out until he was ten years old that he hadn't put anything over on them. William and Rebecca Sterling had recognized their son's need for independence even at that early age. Besides, no harm would come to Matt in either the cookshack or the bunkhouse. The hands adored the plucky little boy who manfully tried to ride everything that moved, including uncooperative cows, squealing pigs, and even a turkey whose tail came off in Matt's futile grab to keep from sliding off. If a laughing, hip-slapping cowboy hadn't rescued the youngster, Matt would have been in danger of being seriously pecked by the irate, partially denuded fowl. With Matt's penchant for mischief, it wasn't the last time a ranch hand came to his rescue.

The Sterlings' carefree life ended with the death of Matt's mother when he was only fifteen. Yet God had not forgotten the family, which had grown to include Robert and Dolores. In the midst of their sorrow, God sent Solita, whose name meant *little sun*. The round-faced Mexican housekeeper and cook more than lived up to her name. She not only brought sunlight back into the grieving family's dark world, but she also became a substitute mother. She spoiled the children rotten, especially "Matelito." But when Matt took his position as head of the family after his father's death, he became Senor Mateo to Solita, and she became his confidante and guiding light. Matt loved her dearly and was never too proud to seek and heed her advice.

The second spring after Seth Anderson came to the Diamond S meant that Matt, Seth, and the rest of the hands spent every waking moment outdoors as the ranch swung into full operation. This particular year, the amount of work was heavier than ever. A deep frown creased foreman Brett Owen's leathery face when he approached Matt and Seth, who were leaning on the corral fence, watching a frisky colt.

"This spring is fixin' to be the driest in years," Brett predicted. "How about drivin' the herd up to the high country early this year?"

"Good idea," Matt agreed. "The grazing down here is already getting mighty poor."

"Yippee-ki-ay. Up to the high country!" Seth leaped into the air, clicked his heels together, then reddened and looked sheepish. "Sorry, Boss. Sometimes I forget I'm not still a kid."

Brett shook his finger at Seth. "You ain't so all-fired old," he admonished. "And you'll live to be a lot older if you don't tangle with rustlers or all the other confounded trouble a feller meets while herdin' ornery cows." He turned on his heel and stomped off, but a loud *haw haw* floated back to the corral.

"He's right," Matt said quietly. "A man mean enough to steal another man's stock is either a coward or crazy. Either can be dangerous in the right circumstances." He lightly punched Seth's shoulder. "Let's go tell Solita we're going on a roundup." He grinned, knowing it was all Seth could do to restrain himself from yippee-ki-yaying again. For the hundredth—no, the thousandth—time, Matt thanked God for sending the young man so like Robbie to fill the empty spot in his life. Seth was totally absorbed in what he considered the best profession on earth: ranching. He was also loyal and true, a boy after Matt's own heart.

Seth had only one fault: the desire to draw Matt into the social doings of Madera. Although Matt enjoyed socializing with the townsfolk, he drew the line at getting involved with the fairer sex. He steadfastly declined Seth's invitations to any entertainment that would force him into their presence and compromise his stance.

"Why?" Seth wanted to know.

One day, Matt, in a fit of exasperation, blurted out, "When I was about your age, I met a girl I thought was an angel straight from heaven. She wasn't."

"Oh?" Seth cocked an eyebrow, obviously waiting for Matt to continue.

He didn't. Instead he walked off, feeling Seth's gaze bore into his back. But those few words opened a floodgate of memories that began five years earlier, memories Matt had thought were banished forever. . . .

Lydia Hensley was the daughter of the supervisor for the California Lumber Company from Chicago, sent out west to prepare for laying out the new town of Madera and the sale of the lots. Lydia was lonely, so far from home, so Matt received permission from her father to escort her to social engagements in Fresno—twenty-two miles south.

Lydia hit the San Joaquin Valley like a tornado. She created havoc among the young men and heartburn among the girls. Matt fell head over heels for the young miss the first time he saw her—a vision in a soft pink gown, white skin shaded by a ruffled pink parasol. She was the prettiest and brightest girl Matt had ever met. Time after time he wondered why he had been so fortunate to be chosen as her escort from the dozens of swains who flocked to her doorstep. Lydia's green eyes flashed with mischief or softened into languishing glances, depending on her mood. Not a single ash-blond hair ever seemed to be out of place.

The smitten Matt escorted Lydia to parties and dances all spring and summer. He sat by her in church. He took her on picnics, little realizing he'd been chosen to be the favored one not only for his good looks but because he owned the Diamond S and was considered a catch.

Lydia led Matt on, driving him to distraction. He lost interest in the ranch, left its running in Brett Owens's capable hands, and spent most of the season calling on Miss Lydia. He dreamed of making her queen of the Diamond S.

Love's young dream ended six months later when the surveying ended. Hensley and his daughter packed up to head back to civilization. Lydia's parting with Matt was a disaster. He managed to extricate her from the young people who had gathered for a farewell party and led her to a secluded alcove.

Heart beating double-time, Matt went straight to the point. "I can't let you go, Lydia. Will you marry me?" He held out a diamond ring the size and brilliance of which was unknown in the valley.

Lydia stared at the beautiful ring as if unwilling to let such a treasure slip through her white fingers. She stroked his lean face with a well-manicured hand and looked deep into his eyes, the sign of affection she often employed. An incredulous smile crossed her face. "Matthew Sterling, you don't really expect me to stay out here? I belong in Chicago where it is civilized. I do appreciate your asking me though." She glanced down then back up with the appealing look that brought suitors to their knees and subject to her will. "If you want me to take the ring to remember my Westerner, I'll be happy to do so."

Disillusionment swept through Matt like the San Joaquin River in flood. "Your Westerner, Lydia? Have you only been amusing yourself to pass the time?"

She had the grace to redden but tossed her head. "It was fun while it lasted. You'll have to admit that." She gave him the smile that had formerly bewitched him and now left him as cold and hard as the diamond in the ring he had so carefully selected. "About the ring—"

Scales fell from Matt's love-blinded eyes. He saw Lydia for what she was: a selfish, greedy girl out for all she could get. Brokenhearted he raised his head in a gesture that would have impressed anyone with the sensitivities of a turnip. Then he slipped the ring into his pocket and said, "You will have no keepsake to remember me by, Lydia." He marched out, head still high, like a one-man army with flags waving. And he vowed the San Joaquin River would run dry before he ever again trusted any girl or woman except Solita.

Matt had faithfully kept that vow until the wrinkled and much-handled picture of Sarah Anderson, taken just before her brother left home, kindled a spark of interest and admiration. Such an honest and steady gaze in the young girl's face. The delicate way her hands were clasped. Her eyes radiating love for her Seth and her mother. And all that beautiful hair, long and rippling to her waist.

The second picture threatened to undo the weeks, months, and years Matt had spent locking up his heart and throwing away the key. It didn't help when Seth asked Matt to take the picture as a favor.

"Maybe you could look at it occasionally and say a prayer for her and my mother. I worry about her constantly."

"I will, but I don't need the picture," Matt protested. Yet when Seth insisted, Matt's hands turned sweaty, and his heart beat unnaturally fast. He slipped the picture into the pocket inside his vest "as a favor to Seth," he reminded himself, and was never without it.

The image of Sarah's honest face rode sidesaddle with Matt across the California range even when he wasn't looking at it. In spite of his unwillingness to admit the rusty hinges of his heart were creaking open, the image of Sarah's sweet face was like oil to a long-unused lock. Over and over, Matt wondered how any man could treat an innocent girl the way Gus Stoddard treated Sarah. He found himself wishing he could intervene, "for Seth's sake, of course," he reminded himself.

Just before spring roundup, the town of Madera planned a money-raising event. Seth Anderson was wild to go. Matt was sitting in the kitchen watching Solita toss tortillas when Seth raced in. "What time are we leaving?"

Matt gave him a puzzled look. "Leaving for where?"

"To Madera. This Saturday. There's gonna be a baseball game and stuff for the little kids and a box social. I've never been to one. Gus didn't cotton to such, so even though he took us to church, we didn't get in on the fun. I've been saving my money to bring Sarah out West, but Solita can pack me a lunch. It will be fun to watch you bid on a young lady's box."

"Me!" Matt's stool tipped and threatened to spill him on the floor. "A box social is the last place I intend to go."

"You gotta go, Boss. It's to raise money to repair the church roof."

Matt stood. "I'll make a contribution."

Seth looked so disappointed that Matt relented. "Tell you what. I'll go to the game, and I'll give you some money to bid."

"It won't be half as much fun without you."

Seth's disappointed response convinced Matt. "Well, if it means that much to you, I suppose I could go and watch. But don't expect me to bid, no matter how fancified the boxes are or how much they smell of fried chicken and chocolate cake."

"Is that what they put in them?" Seth licked his lips. He staggered out holding his stomach, leaving Matt wondering why he'd agreed to appear at the social.

Solita told him, "It is good that you are going, Senor Mateo. There are many nice senoritas in Madera who will be glad."

"I am not going to make senoritas glad," Matt mumbled. "Did you cook this up with Seth?"

Solita placed her hands on her apron-covered hips. "Would I do such a thing?" she demanded, but Matt noticed she didn't deny his charge.

For the rest of the week, Matt felt like a trapped bobcat. On Saturday he reluctantly donned his best plaid shirt, tied on a red neckerchief, and crammed his Stetson down to his ears, feeling like he was headed to a hanging. By the time he and Seth reached Madera, the boy had lost some of his high spirits. With a pang of regret for being surly, Matt suggested they volunteer for the ball team.

Seth immediately perked up and showed a surprising amount of skill.

The dreaded box social finally began. Matt had never seen such an array of ribbons, ruffles, and flowers as adorned the boxes, but he kicked himself for coming.

Evan Moore, Madera's portly postmaster, made a fine auctioneer. "Who'll start the bidding?" he called, holding up a box and sniffing it. "Smells like fresh-baked apple pie."

"Two bits."

"Two bits?" Evan looked outraged. "Twenty-five measly cents for this lovely basket? What kind of miser bids two bits?"

The crowd roared.

The bidder quickly raised his hand. "Sorry, I meant to offer six bits."

"Not good enough. This is worth at least a couple of good ol' American dollars. Dig deep, folks. None of us want to be dripped on next winter 'cause the church roof leaks."

One by one, the baskets sold. Seth bid twice but dropped out when others "dug deep." Only a worn shoe box tied with string remained. Evan held it up. "Almost through folks. What am I bid?"

Stone-cold, dead silence greeted his plea.

Evan cast an imploring glance toward Matt. Despite his resolve to have no part in the social, Matt's heart ached for the owner of the unattractive box. He opened his mouth.

Seth beat him to it. "I bid a half eagle." He fished a five-dollar gold piece out of his pocket and held it up. "It better be enough. It's all I've got."

The crowd gasped. Only one or two of the fancy boxes had sold for that much.

"Sold!" Evan shouted. "What lucky lady gets to eat supper with Seth Anderson?"

"Me. Bertha Bascomb." A wispy, white-haired old lady hobbled forward.

Seth led Bertha to a nearby table. When he opened the box, a sour smell rushed out.

Matt's heart sank. Not only were the bread and cheese ancient, but Bertha was proudly lifting out the sorriest excuse for cake Matt had ever seen. If it hadn't been so pathetic, it would have been hilarious. Matt quickly said, "Mrs. Bascomb, I missed out on a box. Is there enough for three?"

"If you ain't too big an eater," she grudged. "I don't want to skimp on this young man."

Seth remained gallant. "My boss and I had a big dinner so there should be enough."

The two men somehow choked down the terrible meal, amid grinning townsfolk and cowboys. Looks of respect showed that Seth Anderson's kindly bid had endeared him to Madera.

Matt's stomach had barely recovered from the box social when a few days later a young lad galloped up to the Diamond S corral where Matt and Seth were leaning against the fence. He reined in his horse and leaped from the saddle.

Matt blinked in surprise. "What are you doing here, Johnny? And how come you're in such an all-fired hurry?"

Johnny rubbed a grimy hand over his freckled, sweaty face. "Telegram. Mr. Moore said I was s'posed to get it here pronto."

Matt's heart lurched. A lump as solid as Bertha Bascomb's sour bread and heavy cake formed in the pit of his stomach. He hated telegrams, especially since Dori had gone back east. Had something happened to her? Matt shook his head. It was far more likely that his impetuous sister had been expelled from the eastern academy she attended. Matt had received previous warnings about Dori's conduct. Her shortcomings had only been tolerated by the grace of God and several generous contributions to the prestigious Brookside Finishing School for Young Ladies in Boston.

Matt reached for the telegram.

Johnny shook his head. "It ain't for you, Matt," he said. "It's for Seth." He tossed a soiled envelope to the younger man. "From St. Louis."

Seth's face went paper white.

Alarm shot through Matt as Seth ripped open the message. "Is it about Sarah?" he demanded. "Bad news?"

53

Seth looked stricken. *"The worst."*

"Well?" Matt's question cracked like a bullwhip.

"Read it for yourself." Seth thrust the telegram at Matt, eyes filled with pain and hopelessness.

Matt snatched the message and read:

SARAH DISAPPEARED *STOP* MAY COME TO MADERA *STOP* HOLD FOR FIANCÉ TICE EDWARDS AND ME *STOP* GUS STODDARD

The words slashed at Matt's heart like a hunting knife, cutting and tearing until he could barely breathe. Sarah engaged to be married? "Who is this Tice Edwards fellow?" he demanded.

Seth looked defeated. "A real rat. Everyone in St. Louis knows him. He owns a riverboat where folks go to gamble."

Matt caught his breath. Such a monstrous thing couldn't be true. Not when he had fallen in love with her picture. How could such a sweet and innocent-looking girl be promised to a riverboat gambler?

Chapter 10

The news that Tice planned to wed her the following day sent Sarah into a panic. She must disappear. Tonight. But how? At least Gus and Tice hadn't waited until evening to spring the bad news. By midnight the children would be asleep, and the two men she hated and feared most would probably be having an early celebration: Tice, knowing tomorrow he would have her in his control, and Gus, ecstatic at having his six-thousand-dollar debt forgiven and at receiving unlimited gambling privileges.

Sarah checked the time. It wasn't quite six. No wonder Gus had been grumpy. After his nights of gambling and carousing, he tended to sleep much later. "Lord," she whispered while beating the biscuit dough until it threatened to fight back, "I have eighteen hours. If I fly around and finish my chores quicker than usual, I should be able to make it."

A single glance around the shack sent hope plummeting to her toes. The place had never looked worse. How could she accomplish everything from washing the streaked windows to scrubbing the worn floor? She also needed to bake and wash clothes. Gus would rage if, on what he considered a special day, things weren't spick-and-span. Sarah set her jaw in a manner that boded no good. If she did all that needed doing, she wouldn't have a smidgen of time for herself. She would not bake bread. She would not wash clothes. They could wait until tomorrow—and by then she'd be gone. Fleeting pity for the burden soon to fall on Ellie's eight-year-old shoulders stirred Sarah, but she shrugged it off. Let Tice hire someone to help. Or as Gus had said, he could always get a woman to replace his long-suffering wife.

Sarah patted out her biscuits with well-floured hands, planning as she worked. *If I can catch Timmy alone and offer him a cookie he might help me,* she decided. *There's no use asking the boys or Ellie for help, even if they were around. They'd make a worse mess just to be ornery.* Her fingers itched to get started sweeping and cleaning instead of cooking mush and setting out butter and jam. Thank goodness they were out of bacon and eggs. Gus would roar, but when she'd asked for money to replenish the larder, he'd refused to give her any.

The ticking clock counted off the racing minutes until seven of Sarah's precious hours had been swallowed up in hard work. Sarah grew so frustrated she wanted to stomp her feet and throw a tantrum like Ellie did when she didn't get her own way. Hindrance after hindrance continued to rise, as if conspiring against her. Instead of staying away with his cronies as usual, Gus popped in and out of the house, commenting on how well Sarah was doing for herself by marrying Tice. She longed to hurl bitter words at him but bit her tongue and reminded herself that, by this time tomorrow, she'd be shut of him.

Not so for Ellie and Timmy. The older boys could fend for themselves, but the younger children would be at Gus's mercy. Sarah was almost glad when the youngsters acted up worse than ever before, fighting and demanding her attention. The last straw was when Sarah forcibly separated them and ordered them outside.

Ellie shrilled, "You ain't our ma. I hate you, and I'm glad you're going away. We don't have to do what you say. We're gonna get a new ma. Pa said so."

"And she ain't never, ever gonna tell us what to do," Timmy piped up, his face contorted with rage. He was so unlike the little boy who crept to Sarah for comfort it eased her guilt over leaving them, even though she could not stay.

"I feel like Job's granddaughter," she muttered to herself. "The way I've been plagued, the devil himself must be in league with Tice and this family today." She washed her hands and hot face, smoothed her hair, glanced around the cottage, and sighed. The place looked as good as she could make it, considering its shabby condition. Pale sunlight poured through the freshly washed windowpanes. Sarah had even washed the bedraggled calico curtains, and the floor smelled of the strong lye soap she'd used to scrub it to within an inch of its life. She'd relocated stacks of old newspapers and soiled clothing dropped at will by simply tossing them out of sight.

Reheated leftover stew and more biscuits had made up dinner an hour before. Sarah racked her brain to think of something for supper. Baked potatoes, maybe, and there was enough buttermilk. She'd make corn bread, open one of the last jars of fruit she had canned last fall, and serve the few cookies she had hidden from the children. Gus would complain, but she didn't care. It would be the last time she'd have to hear him rant and rave.

The clock struck one. It was time for her to go for the final fitting of her wedding dress.

Sarah sighed again. In spite of rushing, she wasn't one inch closer to being ready to steal out in the dead of night than she had been seven hours earlier. Now she had to spend precious time in a final fitting of the elaborate wedding gown Tice had selected for her. Sarah hated every inch of fancy lace, every tuck, every thread of the fine satin dress. She hated the cloud of a veil held by orange blossoms that would shroud her until her husband-to-be lifted it. Most of all she hated the imagined stares of those who came to gawk at her in her bridal white, the knowing glances exchanged between men as vile as Tice himself.

By supreme self-control Sarah refrained from tearing the wedding garments from her body and throwing them in the dressmaker's smug face when the woman purred, "What a beautiful bride you will be, *ma cherie*" in an accent as artificial as her smile. Sarah turned away. She had avoided looking at her mirrored image, but curiosity got the better of her. How would she look in bridal white should God someday send a man to love, honor, and cherish her? Not married wearing this lavish, pearl-beaded gown but in a modest white dress that did not silently shout its cost.

Sarah faced the full-length mirror. Her mouth fell open. Costly the gown might be but how it flattered her strawberry blond hair, shining blue eyes, and the color in her blazing cheeks! A small smile trembled on her lips, adding the one factor needed to make the vision perfect. If only Matthew Sterling could see her in this gown!

Sarah closed her eyes and allowed herself the luxury of a dream. What would it be like to walk up the aisle of a church in Madera in step with her brother? To see dark-haired Matthew Sterling, tall, strong, and straight, waiting for her? To watch love and wonder spring into his eyes when he first caught sight of her—the same love and wonder that filled her heart and overflowed into the joyous occasion? To hear the time-honored words, "Dearly beloved, we are gathered here today to unite this man and this woman in holy matrimony. Marriage is ordained of God...."?

Not this marriage!

Had she spoken aloud? No. The dressmaker was busily straightening a fold of the ostentatious train of the gown.

Sarah shuddered, but the picture of what a wedding could and should be had started a train of thoughts that could not be derailed. How she would welcome the opportunity to love and cherish a man such as Matt Sterling! Like Ruth in the Bible, she would unhesitatingly say, *"Intreat me not to leave thee, or to return from following after thee: for whither thou goest, I will go; and where thou lodgest, I will lodge: thy people shall be my people, and thy God my God."* Unlike marriage with Tice, she would not be unequally yoked. What she'd learned about Matt from Seth's secret letters had convinced her that Matt Sterling was a true Christian.

Her thoughts trooped on, repeating the majestic promises in the wedding service:

"For better. For worse. For richer. For poorer. In sickness. In health. Mutually agreeing to be companions. Forsaking all others. Keeping themselves for each other as long as they both should live." And finally *"Whom God hath joined together, let no man put asunder."* How did anyone dare take those vows lightly, only to break them as Gus had done. . .and as Sarah knew in her heart Tice would do?

"Does *mademoiselle* wish me to remove the gown?"

The dressmaker's question jerked Sarah from her wool-gathering. Her dream crumpled. It was highly unlikely that Matthew Sterling or someone like him would ever see Sarah Joy Anderson in a wedding dress. Worse, if her escape plan failed, only her miserable stepfamily, Tice Edwards, and his cohorts would gloat over the vision she had seen in the mirror. Depression filled her. Was this how maidens of old felt when forced into loveless marriages by domineering fathers desirous of forming strong alliances? Sarah's heart ached for all those denied the chance for true love and sacrificed on the altars of greed.

"Please take the dress off," she quietly said, ignoring the woman's babble and wishing only to slip into her own clothing.

When Sarah reached home, another two hours had passed. Now only nine of the eighteen remained. The relentless *tick tock, tick tock* of the clock greedily nibbled away at the day. It reminded Sarah of the "Grandfather's Clock" song that had come out a few years earlier. The chorus rang in Sarah's head:

Ninety years without slumbering, tick tock, tick tock,
His life seconds numbering, tick tock, tick tock,
It stopp'd short, never to go again, when the old man died.

"I won't be ninety, and my body won't die if I have to marry Tice Edwards, but my life will stop short," Sarah grimly told herself. "I feel like my seconds are being numbered, just like the grandfather's were."

Matthew 6:34 popped into her mind: *"Take therefore no thought for the morrow: for the morrow shall take thought for the things of itself. Sufficient unto the day is the evil thereof."*

In spite of her troubled heart Sarah couldn't help smiling. Today's evil was more than sufficient! The scripture cheered her up, and she resumed her duties with a lightened heart—until someone knocked on the door. Now what?

The "what" proved to be two fashionably dressed, strange women.

"Miss Anderson, we just *had* to come and call," one gushed.

"Yes," said the other. "Dear Mr. Edwards said you might appreciate our help, since you lost your dear mother so recently. So sad, just before your wedding." Her laugh grated like broken glass.

"Mama isn't lost," Sarah quietly said. "She's gone to heaven." She swallowed the words: *And there would be no wedding if she were here.*

The women gasped as if Sarah had shown bad taste in speaking so. "Oh yes, of course," the gusher said. "Now what can we do? Last-minute arrangements and all that."

Sarah laughed. What would they think if they knew her "last-minute arrangements" consisted of packing what she could carry and fleeing from "dear

Mr. Edwards" like a rabbit from a hound? "You're too kind." *As in kind of nosy.* "Thank you for coming, but things are in control." *In control of my heavenly Father.* "Now if you will excuse me. . ."

"Oh, to be sure. Come, Estelle." Clearly disappointed, the gusher took her friend's arm and sailed across the unkempt yard with a disapproving sniff that showed what she thought of "dear Mr. Edwards's" choice of a wife.

Sarah closed the door, leaned against it, and laughed until tears flowed. Taking advantage of an empty house, she raced to the attic. Gus and the children, perhaps even Tice, might appear at any time. She didn't know where they were, and she didn't care whether they were in school or playing hooky. Either way, one more day wouldn't make a difference.

She hastily gathered her things. The need to leave Seth's "treasures" behind saddened her. Sarah discarded most of her own as well—but not all. She took the tattered copy of *Little Women* Seth had found on the docks and her mother's worn dressing gown. The little wooden pistol Seth loved went into her reticule. She and her brother would at least have those reminders of their once-happy home.

Sarah feared the money her mother had hoarded for her wouldn't be enough for a quick trip west by rail. It seemed unwise to plunk down all she had in the world. She must count her pennies carefully, even if it took weeks or months to reach California. Perhaps she could find work along the way. She was pretty sure her stepfather would have no idea where she was headed. Sarah and her mother had taken great pains to keep Seth's location a secret.

When the clock struck midnight, Sarah slipped from her cot, praying the rustle of husks wouldn't awaken Ellie or the boys. The plan of escape hinged on Sarah's being able to sneak out undetected. With a silent prayer she began her long journey to freedom.

Chapter 11

Sarah crept down the ladder from the loft and into the brooding St. Louis night, thankful when it closed around her and muffled her light footsteps. She started down the road toward Jefferson City, clutching her heavy carpetbag in one hand, her reticule in the other.

It was the longest night of Sarah's life, a night that taught her the true meaning of 1 Thessalonians 5:17: "Pray without ceasing." She jumped at the slightest sound. Passing hoofbeats drove her into hiding every few hours. "Lord, I know this is what You want me to do," she whispered. "I know You will be with me. But I'm still frightened. It is so far to California. Please help me be strong and not afraid."

The rising wind whisked away Sarah's prayer and fluttered the long cloak she had donned over her mother's worn, but still serviceable, Sunday-go-to-meeting dress. Sarah shivered and pulled the cloak closer, thankful both it and the dress were dark blue. With dark gloves, Virginia Anderson's old black hat pulled low, and a thick dark veil hiding her face, Sarah was next to invisible. Why, then, did concern over what Gus would do if he realized she had escaped haunt her? Every shifting shadow, every night noise set her heart pounding until it felt like it would burst.

A horrible screech from a nearby tree sent Sarah into a panic. She began to run, thankful for the few stars that broke through the murk to light her way. The unseen culprit screeched again. This time the flapping of wings followed.

Sarah stopped short. "You noisy bird," she told the owl that glided over her head. "Go on with your hunting. I'm too big to be your prey." She laughed softly. "Sarah Joy Anderson, if a stupid bird can scare you, how will you ever survive in California? There will be a lot more terrifying things there than a silly old hooting owl."

Not as terrifying as staying in St. Louis.

The thought dried up Sarah's laughter like drought parched a prairie. Nothing the unknown West might have in store for her could be more threatening than the horror of having to marry Tice Edwards.

Step-by-step, Sarah's shabby shoes carried her away from the gambler and her stepfather. In an effort to stem the nightmare image they conjured up, she began repeating scripture. A wave of gratitude filled her once more, as it had done all through her ordeal. Gratitude that John and Virginia Anderson had instilled in their children a love for the Bible and its promises from the time Seth and Sarah were born. Each verse from the psalms that Sarah murmured in the semidarkness quieted her troubled spirit. She ended by reciting: " 'In my distress I called upon the Lord, and cried to my God: and he did hear my voice out of his temple, and my cry into his ears.' "

When no more verses came to mind, Sarah fought the darkness surrounding her by softly singing hymns. Each brought comfort, most of all the hymn her mother had always sung when things with Gus became unbearable. Now, although Sarah kept her voice so low it didn't even carry to the treetops, the much-loved words came straight from her heart:

He leadeth me! O blessed tho't!
O words with heav'nly comfort fraught!
What-e're I do, wher-e're I be,
Still 'tis God's hand that leadeth me.
Sometimes 'mid scenes of deepest gloom,
Sometimes where Eden's bowers bloom—

Sarah's voice broke. A river of tears crowded behind her eyes. Eden itself could be no more wonderful than reaching California and Seth. Her heart swelled, and she bowed her head. "There's a long, hard road ahead of me before I get to Madera. Please go before me and open the way." She took a deep breath. "I want to trust You, no matter what happens."

No peal of thunder answered Sarah's prayer. No bolt of lightning illuminated the road. But a still, small voice whispered deep inside, *I will not only walk before you, Sarah Joy. I will walk beside you: your Savior, companion, and friend.*

Tears gushed. "Thank You, God," she fervently said. "I needed to be reminded like Elijah in the Bible. Your presence wasn't in the strong wind or the great earthquake but in the still, small voice." The still, small voice that spoke to Sarah's heart did what nothing else could accomplish. It increased her determination to throw herself totally on God's mercy and let Him take charge. Each step took her farther from Gus and Tice. Each hour meant that much more time before they raised a hue and cry over her absence.

By morning Sarah had traveled a goodly piece. However, lack of sleep had begun to take its toll. She ate sparingly from her small supply of food and drank from a nearby spring. A little later a farmer in a mule-driven wagon stopped beside her.

"Need a ride, miss?" he called.

Sarah looked into the farmer's kindly face. The steadiness of his faded blue eyes and the creases many years of living had etched in his trustworthy face reassured her.

"Yes, thank you." She climbed into the back of his wagon. She felt badly about not removing her veil but decided to leave it on. She *must not* be recognized in case Gus or Tice ever crossed paths with the old man. Surely they were searching for her by now, determined to make her go through with the wedding! Still, how could they know where she was? She had confided in no one and left no trace of her destination. Thankful that, although the farmer looked curious, he asked no questions about why she was alone on the road at such an early hour, Sarah gratefully dozed off and didn't rouse until he said, "Wake up, miss. This is where I turn off the main road." He pointed. "My farm's a mile or so down the lane."

He paused and looked worried. "Wish I could take you farther, but lots o' folks travel this way. You're sure to get another ride soon."

It seemed shabby not to give any explanation so Sarah said, "Thank you for the ride. I'm going to see my brother." Somewhat refreshed from her nap, she jumped from the wagon and reclaimed her meager possessions.

Relief settled over the old man's face. "That's good. Mighty good. There's nothin' like kinfolk." He took up the reins and clucked to the mules. "I better get along home. My old woman will be waitin' for me."

Sarah watched him until a bend in the side road hid him from sight.

Thank You, God, for sending him. I was so tired.

It wasn't the last time Sarah thanked God for providing for her needs. Other helpful people offered assistance and food. Sarah fought the dread of being overtaken every mile of the way, heartbeat quickening each time hoofbeats sounded behind her. She continued to be vigilant, but when no one showed undue interest in her cloaked, heavily veiled figure, she began to believe her goal of reaching California in one piece was actually possible. However, arriving in Jefferson City two weary days later convinced Sarah her arduous journey had just begun. She realized her only hope of reaching California before Judgment Day was to find a faster mode of transportation. Using extreme caution, her mouth dry from fear, Sarah wrapped her long dark veil around her head, bent forward and shuffled up to the ticket window in the Jefferson City train station like an aged woman. In a cracked voice she purchased a railway ticket to Denver. It was all the money she dared spend.

Once on the train Sarah remained wary of strangers and kept strictly to herself. Heart thudding she hid behind her veil each time the train stopped. She cast furtive glances at every man who boarded—and heaved great sighs of relief when she recognized no one and the train continued its journey.

In spite of keeping up her guard, the ever-changing landscape that rushed outside the train window fascinated Sarah. From cornfields to rolling hills and, at last, distant snow-covered peaks, it was unlike anything she had ever seen.

Sarah also comforted herself by rereading Seth's letters and reflecting on what a good man Matthew Sterling must be. She often lapsed into daydreams about meeting Seth's idol. Her heart beat fast beneath her worn traveling gown, and she blushed, remembering her fantasy about walking down the aisle of the Madera church to become Matt's bride.

"Why are you allowing a man you have never met to win a place in your heart?" Sarah chided herself. "Matthew Sterling is so far beyond your reach that it is foolish to allow him in your thoughts." Sarah sighed. Why couldn't Tice Edwards have been as honest and kind as Seth said Matt was? What a contrast! Despite reprimanding herself, every time Sarah looked at the faded photograph, she couldn't help wondering if God might be leading her toward happiness in the far West.

Yet scrunched up in her seat in the dark hours of the night, common sense mocked her. *Why would anyone as important as Matthew Sterling be attracted to a runaway girl whose education is limited to what her mother taught her and a love of books? A girl whose skills are better suited to drudging in Gus Stoddard's household than being mistress of a great ranch?* The cruel taunt plunged Sarah's spirits to the toes of her shabby shoes, but the coming of morning and whispering, "Get thee behind me, Satan," brought a measure of comfort.

The evening before the train reached Denver, Sarah sustained a terrible shock. When she took out her letters from Seth, she discovered one was missing! She felt the blood drain from her face. Impossible! Surely she would have noticed before now. She frantically searched her carpetbag to no avail. Her reticule. Her seat and the floor around her. Between the pages of her mother's Bible.

It was no use. The letter was gone.

Sarah tried to think what might have happened to it or where she may have lost it. A heartbeat later the truth hit her like two locomotives colliding head on. It painted a chilling picture in her mind. Once in the attic while musing and comparing Matt Sterling with Tice Edwards, she had been interrupted by the children swarming up the stairs, screaming for her attention. All Seth's letters and the photograph scattered to the floor. Sarah had hastily gathered them up and shoved them into her reticule.

Sarah swallowed the terror that threatened to overpower her and buried her face in her hands. *Lord, when I dropped the letters, one must have gotten pushed under my bed. Otherwise I would have noticed it my last night at home while I was frantically gathering my things.* What little sense of security she had been able to muster between spells of panic fled. Gus and Tice must know her destination, a truly alarming twist.

Sarah harbored no hope that they would give up and leave her alone. Gus still had his debt. Tice had his pride. The owner of the *River Queen* would never stand for being made a laughingstock. By now all of St. Louis must be buzzing about Tice's being practically deserted at the altar. Any feelings he ever had for Sarah would have changed to hatred and the desire for revenge.

Tice would never let her go. He and Gus would dog every step of her way until they found her.

Sarah groaned. When they did, Gus would swear on a stack of Bibles as tall as the snowcapped peaks of the Sierra Nevada that he was her legal guardian and had the right to return her to Missouri. The false documents he and Tice had illegally procured would convince the authorities. Her only hope was to reach the Diamond S before they caught up with her. Seth would fight to the death before allowing Gus and Tice to take his sister. And if Matthew Sterling was half the man her brother thought he was, he would protect her for Seth's sake.

During the remainder of the trip to Denver, every time the train stopped, Sarah shrank lower into her seat and fervently prayed. She asked just one thing: that she not look up and see Gus's ugly face leering at her. Or Tice Edwards's eyes filled with anticipation of the punishment he would surely inflict on the girl who hated him but would soon be in his power.

Chapter 12

Denver, Colorado, at last.

Long before the train that carried Sarah Anderson away from a fate worse than death and into an unknown future reached the Mile-High City, she had gazed out the window in awe. Colorado was a far cry from St. Louis. Or the Great Plains. The rolling land ended abruptly at the foot of the mighty Rocky Mountains. Snowcapped peaks reached toward heaven and provided a spectacular backdrop for the city. Sarah rubbed her eyes to make sure she wasn't dreaming. An abundance of wildflowers added to the charm. *Thank You, God, for all this beauty. And for bringing me safe this far, even if I only have mere pennies left,* Sarah silently prayed.

Thoughts of her financial straits dampened the spirits that had soared at the grandeur of the Rocky Mountains. Sarah sighed and continued her prayer. *I'm less than halfway to Madera, Lord. Once I get off the train, I don't know where to go or what to do. Please help me.*

The monotonous *clackety-clack* of the train's wheels slowed. The grinding screech of brakes signified the "iron horse" would soon stop. Sarah gathered her meager belongings, leaving Seth's wooden pistol and her few valuables in her reticule. Should someone attempt to rob her, she could hang on to the reticule better than her heavy carpetbag. She stood and grimly muttered, "'I will fear no evil: for thou art with me.'"

"Did you speak, miss?" the conductor asked.

Sarah felt herself redden. Although reticent about who she was and where she was going, she had found the white-haired conductor to be kind to her on the journey. Perhaps he would help her now. "I'm not familiar with Denver," she confessed. "Could you direct me to a boarding place for young ladies?"

The conductor's bushy white eyebrows rose almost to his cap. "A nice young lady like you shouldn't be running around alone," he advised. "Denver can sometimes be a rip-roarin' town." The eyebrows drew together. "Isn't anyone meeting you?" Disapproval oozed in every word.

"Not right away." Sarah fought back tears. It was true. Seth wouldn't be meeting her right away. More than a thousand miles lay between them. In the meantime she had to find a place to stay and some kind of employment.

The conductor's keen blue eyes reflected surprise before he gruffly said, "I take it you don't want any place fancy?"

Sarah nodded and swallowed the lump in her throat. Once she left the train and the kindly conductor, she would be on her own. No, not really alone. One person with God was a majority.

The conductor patted her on the shoulder and pulled a pencil and pad from his pocket. He wrote something, tore the page off, folded it, and wrote more on the outside. "I figured as much. Don't worry, miss. Take this to Miz Hawthorne's. This is her address. It's just a few blocks from here." He pointed. "She's a good Christian woman and will take care of you. If I had a daughter, my mind would be at rest if she lived at Miz Hawthorne's."

He paused then added, "It's best for you to put your veil over your face. Lots of first-rate folks here but some that ain't." He sent a significant glance at the crowded station platform. Sarah obediently pulled down her veil but choked up. "Thank you." It was like losing a friend when the conductor helped her down the train steps. He swung back up the steps, paused to wave at her, then disappeared into the railroad car that had come to feel like home. Clutching her reticule in one hand and her carpetbag in the other, she turned to face the station platform.

Sarah had run the gauntlet of admiring male eyes the few times she had been forced to visit the docks in St. Louis. Now, securely masked from curious stares by her heavy cloak and veil, Sarah thrilled at the sight of the men who lounged against the station walls: cowboys like she would find on the Diamond S. Some looked to be still in their teens. Garbed in checked or plaid shirts and high-heeled boots similar to those Seth and Matt Sterling wore in the picture Seth had sent, their hats looked wide enough to shade a city block. A few wore buckskins or woolly chaps. Sprinkled in the crowd gathered to meet the train were Indians in blankets and Mexicans in brightly colored clothing. A few women, who at first glance appeared not of her kind, stood nearby. Fewer children but several dogs.

Sarah took a deep breath. In spite of the warm day she pulled her cloak close around her, raised her chin, and briskly set out in the direction the conductor had pointed. Conscious of stares boring into her back, she felt grateful for the cloak that disguised her slender, girlish form.

When Sarah reached the hastily scrawled address, dismay filled her. Nothing at the white picket gate or on the door of the modest two-story white house indicated its owner took in boarders. Had the conductor been mistaken? Had "Miz Hawthorne" moved? If she still lived here, had she stopped welcoming strangers into her home? Sarah peered at the written address, wondering if she had misread it. No. The numbers matched those on the house.

Tired from travel and wanting to cry, Sarah considered leaving. She shook her head. Where could she go if she did? The house was obviously well cared for. Even if Miz Hawthorne no longer lived there, surely whoever did could recommend a place where Sarah might find rest.

The weary girl resolutely opened the gate and walked up the flower-bordered path to the front steps and onto a hospitable, vine-clad covered porch. If only she could sink into one of the chairs that invited weary bodies to tarry! She couldn't. She must find safe shelter before nightfall.

Heart thumping, Sarah threw back her veil and knocked on the frame of the screen door. She noticed the inner door stood partly open. Good. At least someone was home. A moment later footsteps sounded. The inner door opened then the screen door, so quickly Sarah had to step back to avoid being struck. A round face framed with white hair and a cap that was askew appeared.

"May I help you?"

"I hope so," Sarah faltered. "Can you tell me where I might find Miz Hawthorne?"

Laughter bubbled up from deep inside the jolly woman. "I'm Miz Hawthorne, child. What can I do for you?"

"Do you still take in boarders?" Sarah clutched her reticule and carpetbag until her knuckles whitened. "There's no sign." She held her breath, hoping against hope she had found a refuge.

Blue eyes opened wide. "I've no need of a sign, dearie. Folks 'round here all know me. Besides, I don't take in just anyone. Only those my friends recommend." She cocked her head to one side. "Who sent you to me?"

Sarah sighed with relief. She dropped her carpetbag and searched in her reticule. "The conductor on the train. He said to give you this."

Miz Hawthorne barely glanced at the passport to her boardinghouse and tossed it onto a small table in the cool entryway. "Come in, come in, child. Welcome. Joseph wouldn't send me anyone who isn't all right. Lay off your wraps. I'll bring some cold lemonade."

Thank You, God, Sarah silently breathed. She removed her voluminous cloak, hat, and veil but wondered what the conductor had said to open the door of Miz Hawthorne's home so quickly. Sarah had scrupulously refrained from reading the note, but curiosity now overcame her. Feeling guilty she tiptoed to the table. With a furtive glance toward the door through which Miz Hawthorne had disappeared, she snatched up the missive. The message was short and to the point:

> *Here's a little lost lamb, Miz Hawthorne. Something's troubling her. Open your home and your heart. She can't pay much but needs help.*
>
> *Joseph*

Gratitude flooded through Sarah. A verse from Isaiah came to mind. *"And it shall come to pass, that before they call, I will answer; and while they are yet speaking, I will hear."* Even before she asked God to guide her as the train approached Denver, He had already prepared Joseph's heart to give aid when Sarah needed it most.

Over lemonade and cookies she threw caution to the winds and told Miz Hawthorne who she was and why she had fled St. Louis. "I'm down to almost nothing," she confessed. "I must find work. Do you know of anyone who can use me? I am strong and willing to do anything that's decent."

Miz Hawthorne shook her head. "I don't know of anything. If you're willing to help me out here, I can give you room and board, but that won't get you to California."

"I can sell my mother's wedding ring if I have to," Sarah told her. "But it's my last resort."

"Indeed it should be!" The old lady snorted. "Before you do anything like that, let me see what I can find out."

A few days later, after Sarah had pounded the streets looking for work and found nothing, her landlady bustled into the kitchen where Sarah was finishing a mountain of dishes. She triumphantly waved a piece of paper. "A friend gave me the address of an employment office not far from here." She beamed. "There's a GIRLS WANTED sign in the window. Hurry yourself on over there before the positions are filled."

Sarah quickly changed from work clothes into her mother's Sunday-go-to-meeting dress. She plaited her red-gold hair, wound the braids around her head, and topped them with her mother's old black hat. Heart beating with anticipation, she ran to within a block of the employment agency then slowed and regained her composure. It would never do to burst into an office red-faced and out of breath. "Please let the sign still be there," she murmured when she reached her destination.

It was. The door stood open. Should she knock or just walk in? Sarah had never faced this situation before so she tapped lightly and hesitated on the threshold. A masculine voice called, "Don't just stand there. Come on in."

A twinge of annoyance straightened Sarah's spine. A rather discourteous way to greet one. She lifted her chin and walked inside. Once she had a job, there would be no call for her to put up with such rudeness.

A well-dressed man about Tice Edwards's age sat with his feet propped on an untidy desk. He stared at her then stood. His belly bulged over a fancy, too-tight belt. "Well, and what have we here?" His teeth gleamed in the travesty of a smile. "Sit down. Sit down."

The look in his eyes reminded Sarah of Tice. It made her uncomfortable, but the need for a job overrode her desire to turn and run. She had outwitted a riverboat gambler. Surely she could put up with rudeness. Sarah poised on the edge of a chair facing the desk, still clutching her reticule. "I am looking for a position." It sounded better than *job.* "I can cook, sew, tend children, clean, or wait on tables."

The man looked her over and smiled again. "Take your hat off and let your hair down."

"I beg your pardon?" Sarah said in the icy voice with which she'd refused to marry Tice.

"Your hair. I can find you a better job than household drudge. The starting salary is—" He named what sounded to Sarah like a princely sum.

"What would I have to do, and why do you want my hair down?" Sarah demanded.

The man gave a long-suffering sigh. "Do you want a job, or don't you? You look like someone's sainted aunt with your hair like that. People who come to my club want to be served by girls who are lively and attractive. In the right clothes and with that hair, you can be a raving beauty. You'll make more just in tips than you can imagine."

A warning bell sounded in Sarah's brain. She remembered her father saying, "*If something sounds too good to be true, it probably isn't true.*" "Club? Do you mean a restaurant?"

He guffawed. "Hardly. I run the Golden Peaks Men's Club. High-class entertainment. Can you sing? Ace Hardin's girls have to do more than serve food and drinks." He leered. "A lot more."

Sarah stood so quickly that her chair crashed to the floor. She felt her face flame. "I will neither sing nor serve food and drinks in your Golden Peaks or any other club. Such places are unholy and lead men to destruction. They are an abomination to God and to decent people." She whipped around and started for the door.

Hardin sprang with the speed of a panther. He grabbed Sarah by the shoulders and kicked the door shut. "No one talks to Ace Hardin like that. You came in here of your own free will, missy." He began dragging her to an open door in the back of the room. "I'll lock you in the storeroom and let you reconsider. You're just the kind of girl who will bring customers to my place. I'm not passing up a chance like this."

Filled with horror Sarah slumped. Only Hardin's cruel grip kept her from falling. The next instant she began kicking and scratching with all her strength. She opened her mouth to scream, but Hardin let go with one hand and put meaty fingers over her mouth. "Shut up, you hellcat," he commanded.

It was the opportunity Sarah needed. She wrestled her right arm free and snapped open the reticule still hanging from it. She pulled out Seth's wooden gun and shoved the muzzle into the man's stomach so hard he let out a huge wheeze.

"Stand back!"

Hardin's mouth fell open. His skin turned a sickly green, and his hold on her loosened. "You—you're not going to shoot me, are you?" He took a step back.

Sarah pushed the gun farther into the overhanging belly that hid the carved pistol. "Put your hands in the air and walk backwards to the storeroom door," she ordered.

Step-by-step they crossed the room with Sarah's hand firm on Seth's toy. "Reach behind you, and open the door. Step inside and don't try any tricks. I won't say what might happen if you do." It wasn't a lie. If her bluff didn't work, she was a goner.

Hardin did as he was told.

The door closed behind him.

Sarah turned the key in the lock and fled from the employment office as if pursued by Gus Stoddard and Tice Edwards.

Chapter 13

When Sarah fled from Ace Hardin's employment office, she headed straight for Miz Hawthorne. She flung herself into the good woman's arms and sobbed.

"My goodness, child," the old lady gasped. "Whatever is the matter?"

"I should have left when I first felt something was wrong, but I need a job so much. I didn't know that he—" A fresh torrent of tears came.

Miz Hawthorne's arms tightened. "Who? What did he do to you?"

"He said to take down my hair and asked if I could sing." Fury dried Sarah's tears, and she sat up straight. "He said 'his girls at the Golden Peaks had to do more than serve food and drinks—a lot more.' I told him such places were terrible and started to leave. He grabbed me and said he'd keep me in his storeroom until I changed my mind!"

"How did you get away?"

The absurdity of Sarah's escape sent her into peals of laughter. "I threatened him with a wooden pistol!"

"You *what?*" Miz Hawthorne stared as if she couldn't believe her ears.

Sarah chortled. "I really did." She groped in her reticule and brought out her weapon of defense. "I stuck the muzzle right in his fat belly and backed him into the storeroom. He thought I was going to shoot him!"

After a moment of stunned silence Miz Hawthorne said, "Well, I never!" and burst out laughing. When she could control herself, she wiped her eyes and pushed Sarah away. "We have to tell our sheriff about this right away. The idea, recruiting young girls to serve in such a place. The sheriff will put a stop to that."

"No," Sarah cried. "I'd have to sign my name on a complaint. It would become public knowledge. Please, Miz Hawthorne, don't tell anyone what happened." A new, terrifying thought struck her. "You don't know Tice Edwards. He has the chief of police in St. Louis under his thumb. If Gus found Seth's letter, Tice may already have had the authorities in St. Louis send telegrams to sheriffs along the train route." She finally convinced her landlady the best thing to do was for the runaway to lie low for a few days and see if there were repercussions from the fiasco, although Mrs. Hawthorne doubted there would be.

"I don't know this Ace Hardin, but if word ever got out that a slip of a girl had gotten the best of him with a toy pistol, the scoundrel would be the laughingstock of Denver." Her eyes twinkled. "After you leave, I'll tip off a deputy sheriff friend of mine. He's an honest young officer. If anything can be done to put Hardin out of business, he will see to it."

"You won't mention my name, will you?" Sarah pleaded.

"Oh no. I'll just say Hardin and the Golden Peaks Men's Club need looking into."

For the next week Sarah seldom went out, even to look for work. Miz Hawthorne guarded her as a mother cougar guards her cubs, and the few young ladies staying with her at the time knew nothing except that "Miss Joy" would soon be leaving. Yet Sarah no longer felt secure in Denver. Destitute and dependent on her landlady's kindness, the thought of being followed and dragged back to St. Louis against her will prompted her to forget about employment—especially after being nearly frightened to death when she saw a man who closely resembled Tice Edwards.

The next day she tearfully got out her mother's wedding ring and without a qualm gathered together the trinkets Tice brought while courting her and prepared to leave Denver. However, the pathetic amount she received from their sale left her without enough money for a quick ride to Madera. Although it would take much longer, she would have to make the last leg of her journey by stagecoach. Miz Hawthorne wanted to make up the difference, but Sarah refused.

"I won't be beholden to you, Mrs. Hawthorne. I can make it on my own the rest of the way. I have enough to purchase passage on the stage to Madera and pay for what little food I'll need and lodging at the stage stops. Once in Madera I'll be safe with my brother. The Diamond S Ranch is close by."

"I hate to see you go, child, but go you must," Miz Hawthorne told her. "Godspeed, and I'll be praying for you. Always remember: He cares for His own."

"I know." Sarah embraced her. "I'll never forget you. I'll send word when I get to California." *If you ever do,* an inner voice mocked.

Sarah didn't listen. God had delivered her from Gus Stoddard, from Tice Edwards, and from Ace Hardin. He knew what lay ahead and would prepare ways of escape.

❧

Sarah traveled the endless miles from Denver to Madera in a rocking coach. She shrank into a corner and looked over her shoulder at every stage stop. She kept her veil over her face much of the time, a shield against bold stares, even though it almost gave her heatstroke. She rejoiced when other women or families came aboard or clean-cut cowboys who glanced at her then respectfully looked away. If it became necessary to identify herself, she gave the name *Miss Joy,* which she'd used to take passage.

Not all the trip was unpleasant. Sarah marveled at the ever-changing landscape. Towering forests. Deep canyons with silvery streams rushing from their mountain birthplaces to their final destination: the Pacific Ocean. Huge rocks ranging from frowning granite walls to grotesque red peaks and columns. Stretches of desert with little shade. Pungent sagebrush. Giant tumbleweeds. Long-eared rabbits the loquacious driver called *jacks*. Deer and antelope. Sheep and cattle and horses.

Sarah learned from listening to California-bound ranchers who boarded the stage that there would be no sheep on the Diamond S. "Scourge of the earth," one weather-beaten man declared. "Those stinkin' sheep crop the grass so close our cattle starve, along with drivin' folks crazy with their *baa baa*."

Weary beyond description Sarah reached Madera travel worn and near penniless. She was tired of looking at flat land. Even glimpses of the snowcapped Sierra Nevada in the distance had palled—and if she never saw another stagecoach, it would be too soon. Thoughts of a real bath sent a pang of longing through her body. She sighed. Baths cost money she didn't have.

The stagecoach door swung open. Stiff from her long ride, Sarah carefully lowered her veil and accepted the driver's helping hand. She clutched her precious reticule and stepped out of the coach. The driver swung her carpetbag to the board sidewalk nearby. His team snorted and stamped, obviously eager to reach the large water trough in the middle of town. Their hooves stirred up a cloud of yellow dust. Sarah quickly reached for a handkerchief and held it over her nose, wondering what to do next.

The driver pointed toward the wooden sidewalk and a portly, bald man standing in front of a building identified as MOORE'S GENERAL STORE, MADERA POST OFFICE. "Set yourself down in the shade of the store. Our postmaster will take care of you."

The jolly-looking man laughed. "I sure will, miss, or my name's not Evan Moore. Would you care for some lemonade? It's fresh made."

The friendly welcome unknotted Sarah's nerves. She threw back her veil, dropped to a bench, and fervently said, "I can't imagine anything I'd like more."

The postmaster's eyes twinkled. "Fine. Would you like to come inside or stay here in the shade? My 'post office' is actually just a cubbyhole behind the counter in my general store. It has enough pigeonholes for the mail."

Sarah smiled at him. "I'm too tired to move, Mr. Moore. If you don't mind, I'll see your post office—and the store—some other time."

"Fine. Fine." He rubbed his hands together and stepped inside. When he returned, carrying large glasses of cold lemonade, he sat down beside her. Sarah thanked him and timidly said, "I'm Sarah, Seth Anderson's sister. How can I get word to the Diamond S that I'm here?"

"Well, I swan! I shoulda known." Evan slapped his leg. "You resemble him some. Say, does he know you're coming?"

"No." Not sure how much to tell, Sarah said, "I wasn't sure when I'd arrive."

Evan scratched his bald head and looked troubled. "Last I heard, the Diamond S were driving the cattle up to the high country. I'm not sure when they'll be back. Do you want me to get someone to carry you out to the ranch?"

Bitter disappointment filled Sarah. What should she do? Except for a lone ten-cent piece, her coffers were empty. Pride warred with necessity—and won. "I can't just show up and beg to be taken in until Seth returns," she whispered.

"Any sister of young Anderson would be welcome on the Diamond S," the postmaster reassured her. "That's how we do things 'round here. By the way, call me Evan. Mr. Moore was my dad, God rest his soul. Anyway, if going to the ranch isn't to your liking, you bein' an Easterner and used to different ways and all, 'tain't no problem." He called to a freckle-faced boy kicking up dust with a worn boot, "You there, Johnny, get over here. This lady's Seth Anderson's sister. Ride out to the Diamond S, and tell them to send word to Matt and Seth that she's here."

Johnny grinned. "Sure, Evan. Whatever you say."

Sarah took the last of her money from her reticule and held it out. "Thank you, Johnny."

He drew back, and his face turned red. "Aw, you don't have to pay me. It's only ten miles."

How unlike the Stoddard children, Sarah thought. *This boy must be about Peter's or Ian's age but what a difference! Neither would walk across the street on my behalf, let alone take a hot, dusty, twenty-mile round trip without being well paid.* She pressed the dime in Johnny's unwilling hand. "Please. I'll feel better if you take it."

"Well, all right. Thanks." He pocketed the ten-cent piece and sped down the street toward the livery stable hollering, "Hey Pa, I gotta ride out to the Diamond S. Seth Anderson's sister's here, and he don't know it. She's real nice, Pa—and purty."

Evan laughed outright, and Sarah felt warmed through and through. Never before had she been more aware of God's loving care and His promise in Isaiah: *"No weapon that is formed against thee shall prosper; and every tongue that shall rise against thee in judgment thou shalt condemn. This is the heritage of the servants of the Lord, and their righteousness is of me, saith the Lord."* God had cared for her every step of the way. Surely He would provide for her in this strange land that oddly enough didn't feel strange at all but as if she'd come home. She impulsively turned to Evan.

"Mr. Moore—Evan, I just gave my last dime to Johnny. I need a place to stay until Seth comes and a way to pay for it. It will take time for him to get back from the high country, won't it?"

"You can bet your bottom dollar on that. Don't fret, Miss Sarah." Evan stood and offered her his arm. "We'll just mosey on down to the Yosemite Hotel and see what the proprietor says. The captain took care of Seth when the boy was hurt. He thinks a powerful lot of him." Evan coughed. "We all do. Especially Matt Sterling. Seth reminds him of Matt's kid brother, who died a few years back."

If Sarah had been able to choose someone to enlighten her about Madera, she couldn't have found anyone better than Evan Moore. He proudly escorted Sarah to the Yosemite Hotel, talking while she observed. A wide main street, typical of other western towns she'd come through, stretched on either side of Evan's store and post office. The friendly man's face wreathed with smiles when he said, "We've got ourselves three hotels. Three general stores. A drugstore, a butcher shop, a blacksmith shop, and a livery." He laughed. "And according to Matt Sterling," he said impressively, "'just about the prettiest and most wide-awake town in the entire San Joaquin Valley.'"

Sarah stifled a yawn. After the hustle and bustle of St. Louis, Madera seemed more sleepy than wide awake, but unwilling to offend she kept her opinion to herself.

After running out of information about the town Evan obviously loved, he said, "We've got some mighty fine folks here, Miss Sarah. Captain Perry Mace is one of them. He's been 'most everywhere and done 'most everything. Funny. The Mexican War's been over for ages, but he's never been called anything but 'the captain.' Wears a top hat all the time. Well," he added in a droll voice, "maybe not to bed."

Sarah rewarded him with a smile, but her heartbeat quickened. God sometimes led His children by strange paths. Would He use this eccentric adventurer to help her as he had helped Seth? It could be days before her brother was able to reach her.

On hearing Sarah's plight the captain promptly said, "Sho, you'll stay right here in my hotel until Seth comes." He waved an expansive hand. "You're more than welcome."

The kindness and western hospitality Sarah had encountered ever since she reached Madera brought a lump to her throat. She swallowed hard. "Thank you, sir. I appreciate it, but I will only accept on one condition. I'm no stranger to hard work and can earn my keep."

An approving look brightened the captain's keen eyes. "Spunky, just like that brother of yours. Good. If you want to work, it's fine with me. I can always use another girl to help wait tables." He glanced at her hot, dark traveling outfit. "You'll need a lighter dress though."

Would lack of proper clothing mean she wouldn't get the job? Even so, she had to be honest. "My few calico work dresses are pretty worn."

The captain waved aside her stumbling confession. "Your dress doesn't much matter as long as it is clean. The girls wear aprons that cover them from their necks to the tops of their shoes. I'll have Abby show you to a room and fix you up."

Sarah still wasn't satisfied. Even if she only worked for a few days, the captain must know the whole truth. "I've never waited tables, but I've cooked and scrubbed and taken care of a mean stepfather and his four ornery kids," she burst out.

"If you've done that, then I reckon you'll feel right at home waitressing." He shook Sarah's hand until her fingers tingled. "Thanks for bringing her over, Evan. Unless I'm a piker and not Captain Perry Mace, Miss Sarah's going to be a mighty fine gal to have around."

❧

Several long, uncertain days passed with no sign of Seth. Although longing to see him, Sarah concentrated on her new job and quickly caught on. Her eagerness to always do more than her share endeared her to the other girls. It also won the captain's approval.

"I just wish I could keep you on permanently instead of just until your brother comes," he grumbled. "We're going into the busiest season of the year."

Sarah just smiled, but in the dark hours of the night, a daring thought took root in her mind and refused to be banished. *Why not keep working at the hotel after Seth comes?*

Another thought set Sarah's heart thundering. She wanted Matthew Sterling's approval as much as she'd ever wanted anything. If she kept her job, Seth would rage—but surely the hardworking rancher would respect and admire her a lot more than if she landed flat broke on the Diamond S.

Chapter 14

That's the last of them, boys." Brett Owen's stentorian yell brought a roar of approval from the Diamond S cowboys. Grimy and tired from long days of chasing ornery cattle that preferred hiding in draws over being driven up to the high country, the thought of real beds instead of bedrolls on the hard ground gave Matt and his outfit reason to rejoice.

"First thing I'm gonna do when we get back to the ranch is sleep for a week," one of the hands announced. A murmur of assent rose, but Matt Sterling just laughed and turned to Seth Anderson.

"What's the first thing you're going to do?"

"Ride to Madera, and see if there's a letter from Sarah."

The poignant look in Seth's blue gaze hit Matt straight between the eyes. Ever since the telegram came from Gus Stoddard with the shocking news that Sarah had disappeared and might be on her way to California, Matt and Seth had waited in vain for word from the missing girl. Seth had grown quieter with each passing day. Matt's best efforts to cheer him up hadn't stemmed his worry—or Matt's.

"Gus and Tice won't give up," Seth said. "They'll hound her until they find her. I just pray to God it won't be before she gets here if she's coming. Once she does—"

Matt set his jaw. "Once she does, she's safe. Any trumped-up claim Gus Stoddard may have won't be worth a snap of his fingers. You're of age now and your sister's natural protector."

Some of the shadow left Seth's eyes, but Matt had more on his mind than Sarah's whereabouts. According to Gus's telegram, Sarah was engaged. The thought of the innocent girl tied for life to the kind of man her stepfather would choose made Matt grind his teeth. Yet how did he know she hadn't given her promise to marry? No. If she had, she wouldn't have run away.

Heedless of Seth's presence, Matt bowed his head. "Please help me, God," he prayed. "I love Sarah, but she's already committed to someone else. You've commanded that we should not covet our neighbor's house, his wife, or anything that belongs to him." Rebellion flared, and he burst out, "Surely that doesn't mean a Christian girl in danger of having her life ruined by marriage with a rotten, no-good polecat, does it?"

"Amen to *that*," Seth echoed.

Matt raised his head and clenched his hands. It took all his will to say, "Help me be honorable, Lord. May Your will be done in Sarah's life and in mine." But his traitorous heart silently added, *I hope Your will is for us to be together.*

❧

The closer the outfit got to the Diamond S, the faster Matt's pulse beat. If only Sarah would write! She should have reached Madera by now—if that was her destination. Matt's spirits dropped to his trail-worn boots. Perhaps she had never left St. Louis. Perhaps friends had taken her in and hidden her. He shook his head. It didn't seem likely. As determined as Seth said Gus and Tice Edwards were, they'd have scoured St. Louis raw to find Sarah.

Hours later the outfit reached the Diamond S. The hands unsaddled and headed for the bunkhouse. Matt and Seth turned Chase and Copper out to pasture. Any riding into Madera for the mail would require fresh horses.

A small, colorful tornado burst from the ranch house door. "Senor Mateo. Senor Mateo." Solita ran to them, waving a wrinkled piece of paper. "Senorita Anderson is in Madera! The message came more than a week ago." Tears glistened in her dark eyes. "The *muchacho* Johnny rode out the day the stagecoach bringing the senorita arrived."

Seth sagged against the corral fence. "Thank God!"

Matt silently added *Amen* then furiously said, "More than a week ago? Solita, why didn't you send word to the roundup?"

Wet streaks marred the housekeeper's smooth brown cheeks. "I myself ordered the lazy peon you hired just before leaving to take it to you. He said *sí* and rode away. Only today did I find the paper by the barn. I pray to *Dios* that you will forgive me."

"Don't cry, Solita. It's not your fault."

She sniffled. "But where is Senorita Anderson? What must she think of us?"

A chill went down Matt's spine in spite of the hot day. "That's what we're going to find out." Matt wheeled and hollered to a stable boy. "Emilio, saddle two of our fastest horses. Pronto!"

Solita wiped her eyes with her voluminous apron. "Senor Mateo, shouldn't you take a buggy for the senorita? She may not be used to riding horses."

Seth laughed, the first real sign of mirth he'd shown since Gus Stoddard's telegram had arrived. "Sarah can ride. She had a chestnut gelding named Pandora before our father died. He had to be sold."

"Pandora for a *gelding*?"

Seth nodded and rolled his eyes. "That's what Sarah named him."

Matt chuckled but silently determined to search for the most beautiful chestnut gelding he could find. Sarah might be unwilling to accept it from him but would have no qualms if it came from Seth.

"We can get a horse for Sarah from the livery stable," Matt said. He rue-fully looked down at his dust-encrusted garb. "What say we clean up before going?"

Seth looked ready to mutiny. "You can if you want to, Boss. I'm going to find my sister."

His belligerence took Matt by surprise, but he nodded. "All right. It won't be the last time she will see trail dust." He followed Seth to the horses Emilio held and vaulted into the saddle. "Make tracks," he told his mount, and they headed for Madera.

The ten miles to town felt more like a hundred. Only Seth's excited chatter and the anticipation of meeting Sarah in person kept Matt from goading his horse into a dead run. Would Sarah live up to her picture? Had her troubles taken a harsh toll on her spirit? More importantly could she ever feel the way about Matthew Sterling that he already felt about her?

At last they reached town. They permitted their horses to drink sparingly from the water trough then tethered them to the hitching post nearby. A moment later Evan Moore burst from the store/post office. "Where in blue blazes have you two been?" he yelled.

"Keep your shirt on," Matt snapped. "Where's S—Miss Anderson?"

"Workin' at the Yosemite Hotel. The captain told her she could stay until you came." He rubbed his glistening bald head. "She agreed only if she could work. She's been—"

Matt's and Seth's boot heels drummed on the wooden sidewalk and drowned him out. "Thank God she's safe," Seth muttered when they reached the hotel.

"Yeah. Now beat some of the dust off your jeans and wipe off your boots," Matt told him. "The captain runs a tight ship, and we look like a couple of scarecrows from a cornfield." Seth obeyed, then—heart thudding out of all proportion—Matt led the way into the hotel dining room.

He didn't need Seth's joyous cry, "Sarah!" to identify the girl whose picture he carried. Her red-gold hair lay braided across her head. Her lake-blue eyes matched the sleeves of the sprigged calico gown peeping from beneath a white apron that enveloped her from the base of her neck to the top of her shoes.

Her heavily laden tray tipped and would have crashed to the floor if Seth hadn't sprung forward and caught it. "Seth. Oh Seth!" The heartfelt cry and expression on her face told the story of what Sarah Joy Anderson had been through.

Seth laid the tray on a nearby table and wordlessly caught Sarah in his arms, but Matt hung back. Not for all the gold in California would he in-trude on the long-delayed reunion. Instead, as skittish as a colt under his first saddle, he riveted his gaze on Sarah. Even the second photograph had not done her justice. She was the most beautiful young woman Matt had ever seen, with nothing but purity and honesty in her eyes. How different from Lydia's coquetry! Thank God, Sarah was nothing like the haughty girl who turned him down.

"Boss, this is Sarah," Seth said after what felt like an hour but was only a few minutes.

She extended a small, shapely hand and curtsied. "Mr. Sterling, I thank you for what you've done for my brother. I can never tell you what it means to me."

He smiled. "Call me Matthew. Or Matt. We're not much for 'Mistering' folks out here. Anyway, Seth carries his weight. You'll see how much when we get to the ranch."

"I'm sure I will when I come to visit." Her eyes sparkled. "And please call me Sarah."

"What do you mean, visit?" Seth sounded outraged "You're going home with us today."

"No. I've accepted a full-time position waiting tables for Captain Mace. The road to Yosemite has opened; the tourist season is in full swing. I can't impose further on your kindness, Mr. . . .uh. . .Matthew. You've done enough for the Andersons, and I'm perfectly capable of making my own way."

Matt was shocked speechless. Not take Sarah to the Diamond S? His plans to have her close by and try to win her love hit the floor with a thud. He started to protest. Instead the question that had burned in his soul ever since Gus Stoddard's telegram arrived came out. "Sarah, are you promised in marriage?"

The next instant he felt like kicking himself to Fresno and back. But relief filled him when Sarah's eyes shot sparks and she said, "Promised? God forbid! Gus sold me to Tice Edwards to pay back six thousand dollars in gambling debts, but I never agreed to marry the scoundrel." Fear crept into her eyes. "I'm just afraid they will follow me. I dropped one of your letters, Seth."

Seth glanced at Matt and reluctantly admitted, "He sent word you had run away and—"

Sarah's face turned paper white. "He said he and Tice were coming, didn't he?"

Matt couldn't stand the agony in her sweet face. "Don't worry about it. Folks out here have a way of getting rid of varmints. If Gus and Tice come, Sheriff Meade and the Diamond S boys will kindly advise them this part of the country isn't healthy for St. Louis gamblers and their toadies."

Red flags flew in her cheeks. "Thank you. That makes me feel better. You can't know how hard it is to be alone with no one to help you."

"Come back to the ranch with us then," Seth insisted.

Sarah held her ground. No matter how hard Seth and Matt tried to talk her into staying at the Diamond S, she stubbornly refused.

Late that evening, after returning to the ranch empty-handed, Matt headed for the rise overlooking his spread. The full moon hung over the range. Stars dusted the vast expanse. Cattle lowed in the distance, and the soft cries of night birds filled the still air. "Lord, Sarah is everything Seth said and more. I feel like I've been run over by a stagecoach." He threw his head back and laughed. "Just think. I once thought I was in love with Lydia Hensley!"

&

After Sarah saw Matt Sterling in person, she had more reason than ever to keep her job at the Yosemite Hotel. Her feelings of attraction had multiplied until she was secretly afraid to be near Matt on the Diamond S. Sarah knew she was falling deeper in love with the young rancher, but she didn't fully trust her feelings. Her experiences with Gus and Tice kept her wary of giving herself to someone she hardly knew, even in the unlikely event Matt could someday care for her. It was best for her to stay far, far away from him.

She did, however, accept enough money from Seth to buy some decent clothes. The capacious aprons covered a multitude of deficiencies, but Sarah felt self-conscious wearing gowns with frayed collars and cuffs. One of the general stores carried ready-made dresses, so she selected two lightweight work gowns and a white muslin for church. Her mother's dark blue was just too hot.

Sarah continued to make friends with her co-workers at the Yosemite, especially Abby Sheridan, who was a well of information about dark-haired, blue-eyed Matthew Sterling.

"He's truly the most eligible bachelor in the entire county, maybe in the entire valley," Sarah's new best friend said during a break between customers. "His character and principles are above reproach."

Sarah's heartbeat quickened. "It's sure good to know there are still honest men in the world," she replied. But when she heard Matt's praises sung over and over, against her will and common sense, Sarah began to daydream about the popular rancher once more.

One of the best things about working at the hotel was the opportunity for Sarah to live her Christian faith, planting seeds in the hearts and minds of her co-workers—especially Abby. Sarah's quiet but fun-filled personality soon made her a favorite with both regular customers and her fellow workers. At times she even forgot Gus and Tice.

Her idyllic world shattered whenever Red Fallon swaggered into the dining room. Matt had fired him after the spring roundup, tired of trying to keep him and Seth apart. In spite of being a top hand, Red was more trouble than he was worth.

Rumor had it that Red held a grudge against both Matt and Seth. It made Sarah shiver. From the first time Red saw Sarah, he dogged her steps. His bold gaze followed her every minute he was in the hotel dining room. He tried to walk with her on the street, paid her numerous compliments, and did all he could to get her to notice him.

Sarah actively disliked the obnoxious cowhand. She knew her rebuffs to Red's advances stung his pride, and she avoided waiting on him whenever she could. His biding-my-time look frightened her.

One Saturday after supper Sarah looked around the dining room and gave a contented sigh. The room was deserted. A medicine show had set up across the street from the hotel, and folks of all ages had hearkened to the *boom, boom* of the big brass drum.

She glanced out the window and smiled. The crowd looked tantalized by whatever entertainment the hawker was offering—probably an elixir that would cure everything from warts to summer complaint.

No matter, she thought. *The medicine show will allow me to finish my work earlier than usual.* Seth had promised to come see her, and she was looking forward to spending precious time with her brother.

"Go ahead," Sarah told Abby, who was helping her tidy up. "I'll finish here. I saw plenty of medicine shows in St. Louis and don't care about going."

"Are you sure?" Abby whispered with a pointed glance at Red, who was lounging in the doorway.

"Don't be silly," Sarah whispered back. "Bullies like Red waylay girls in alleys, not in hotel dining rooms. Besides—"

"Besides," Abby mimicked, "just maybe a certain Diamond S rancher will drop by like he often does on Saturday nights."

Sarah felt herself blush, but she laughed and retorted, "And just maybe you think my brother might be in town and at the show."

Her pretty, dark-haired friend grinned impishly. "Tit for tat. Thanks. I'll freshen up first." She disappeared through a side door into the hall, where a stairway led to the second-story rooms.

Before Abby's footsteps died away, Red strode into the dining room and started in with his usual effusive compliments.

Sarah ignored him. She took a deep breath and concentrated on a final tidying of her assigned tables. But she couldn't still her shaking hands.

"You and me oughta get hitched," Red insisted, coming up behind her. "No sense for a purty little gal like you to slave away here when you could be takin' care of me." He reached out and touched her shoulder.

Sarah whirled at his touch. She slapped Red's hand away and fixed him with a haughty gaze. "Keep your hands away from me, Mr. Fallon. I like my job here and intend to keep it. Now, get out."

Red's face turned a dusky red. "I'll teach you!" he raged. "Just like I'da taught your brother if Matt Sterling woulda kept his nose out of my business." He grabbed Sarah's shoulders and tried to pull her to him.

Biting pain and Red's reference to Seth and Matt freed Sarah from the horror of the moment. Horror she'd too often felt when Gus jerked her around. Fury gushed through her veins like water from a broken dam. Never again would Sarah allow any man to lay rude hands on her.

She jerked one arm free and swung at him with all the strength gained from hard work.

Crack!

The open-handed slap staggered Red and etched her fingerprints on his dangerously red face.

Chapter 15

Sarah's ringing slap was not meant for Red alone. The rage behind it was payback for the mistreatment she had received from Gus Stoddard.

Naked hatred sprang into Red's steel-gray eyes. A curse made Sarah want to clap her hands over her ears. He lunged for her, arms extended and fingers curled into fists.

Sarah was too quick for him. She scurried around the table she'd just finished tidying. Regardless of the white cloth, shining cutlery, plates, bowls, and glasses set up for breakfast, she shoved the heavy table with all her might. It crashed into Red, hitting him in the stomach. He groaned and doubled over. His clawlike hands flew to his belly.

"How does it feel to be bested by a girl?" Sarah taunted. "You're a yellow coward and a bully, Red Fallon. No wonder Matthew Sterling fired you. After folks hear about this, you won't be able to get a job on any ranch in the valley." She regretted the words as soon as they left her mouth. Why hadn't she controlled her unruly tongue and kept still? The anger in Red's eyes showed he was not only obnoxious but downright dangerous as well.

"You wildcat!" He sprang around the overturned table but groped thin air.

Always quick stepping, Sarah knew her fury lent wings to her feet. *Why doesn't someone come? I need help.* Her heart sank. With all the commotion in the street, there was little likelihood anyone would hear the noise in the dining room. Sarah skipped behind another table and sent it flying.

Red stepped out of the way. Before she could barricade herself again, his long legs strode toward her. His face darkened into an ugly scowl. He let loose a string of oaths reminiscent of Gus Stoddard at his worst. Then he backed Sarah against the wall. When she tried to scream, Red put a huge paw over her mouth and gloated at her futile attempts to free herself. Triumph shone in his contorted features. "I've got you now!"

Never had Sarah known such terror, not even when she faced down the saloon owner in Denver with Seth's wooden pistol. Her slender frame was no match for the hulking cowhand.

❧

Earlier that afternoon Matt Sterling and Seth Anderson rode in from the range and dropped into comfortable chairs on the shady ranch house porch. Seth grinned. "Sure feels good to sit on something softer than Copper!"

"Or Chase." Matt stretched and yawned, glad for the chance to relax. "We rode farther than we'd planned." He glanced toward the west. "Sun's going down in a hurry this evening."

Seth bounded to his feet.

"What's the trouble?" Matt asked, suppressing another yawn.

"I promised Sarah I'd ride in and see her today." Seth replied, shamefaced. "I've gotta clean up and get to town."

Matt searched for an excuse to go along and fell back on the tried and true. He stood up and said, "Think I'll mosey along with you and get the mail."

"Glad for the company." A grin spread across Seth's face. "Won't be surprised if Sarah will be, too." With a mocking laugh he headed off to get ready, leaving Matt with his mind miles away.

When Matt and Seth reached town, they watered their horses and hitched them to the rail in front of the Yosemite Hotel. Matt shook his head in amusement at the crowd of folks gawking at the medicine show.

"Nice weather brings the hawkers out more than usual," he commented. He fell in step with Seth as they climbed the porch stairs to the hotel.

"I thought you were going for the mail," Seth reminded him.

"Plenty of time for that," Matt replied sheepishly.

The two men stepped into the hotel's dining room and stopped short. The room looked like it had come through a war. Overturned tables, cutlery, smashed dishes, and glasses littered the floor.

"What's carrying on in here?" Matt thundered, scanning the debris.

A muffled shriek drew his attention across the room. His eyes widened in horror. *Sarah!* And Red! The rough cowhand had Sarah backed against the far wall and was shaking the living daylights out of her.

Seth gave a low groan and leaped for the pair.

Matt yanked Seth back. Roaring, he flew over the tables and dealt a hard left to Red's jaw. Then he tossed him halfway across the room with one powerful heave. Red lay unmoving where he landed. Was the ruffian dead? At that moment Matt didn't care.

"Oh Matt, thank God you're here!"

Sarah's agonized cry sent an arrow straight to Matt's heart. He reached her in a single bound and knelt beside her, wishing he had the right to hold her close.

The thud of heavy boots heralded Seth's approach. "Sarah, are you all right? Did that lowdown skunk hurt you?" Without waiting for an answer he jerked his chin at Red. "Is he dead?"

"Naw, I ain't dead." Red groggily sat up and rubbed his jaw.

Blue murder flashed in Seth's eyes. "If you've hurt my sister, you will be!" He sprang toward Red, hands balled into fists.

Matt leaped up and restrained the young man for the second time. "Let's leave Red for the law." His quiet command halted Seth's progress, but it didn't restrain Seth's tongue.

"Red Fallon, I'm gonna nail your ugly hide to the barn door if you ever get near Sarah again," he threatened.

"And I'll hand him the hammer and nails!" Matt paused. "That's not all. One more stunt like this, and we'll sic the Diamond S on you. Brett and the boys think a powerful lot of Sarah. They've had a craw full of you and your shenanigans. Some of the outfit's already rarin' to take a piece out of your hide." Matt's voice grew deadly. "I can't rightly say I could stop them if they made up their minds to have a necktie party—with you as the guest of honor."

"Yeah," Seth Anderson put in. "There's this big ol' cottonwood just out of town. A great place for a hanging."

Red's face turned a sickly yellow. He reached for his gun, but Matt nimbly kicked it out of his hand. "Seth, go fetch Sheriff Meade." Matt knew he'd better keep his young friend as far away from Red Fallon as he could for now.

❧

From her position across the disturbed room, Sarah felt torn between relief that the sheriff would come soon and a horrid fascination with the explosive situation. Did Matt and Seth mean the cowboys would *hang* Red? Seeing their wrath, she believed it could happen. Even in the short time she had been in Madera, Sarah had learned about the code of the West. The unwritten law carried harsh consequences. According to articles in the *Expositor* newspaper, it could even mean a death sentence for men who insulted decent girls and women as Red had insulted her.

"Not all the varmints out here are four-legged," Abby had warned. "The code of the West is what protects girls like you and me from the two-legged kind."

A new thought struck Sarah. Would Matt and Seth's Christian principles, especially the commandment *"Thou shalt not kill,"* be able to deter the two men she loved if Red transgressed again?

Will yours, an inner voice demanded, *when the pain Red inflicted and the fear of it sometime happening again make you want to shout, "Hang him! I'll get the rope!"*

Sarah had been angry and helpless when Gus ill-treated her, but she'd never wished him dead. Now the realization of what she was capable of thinking appalled her. For the first time she realized the wickedness of feelings generated by hate. Feelings she wouldn't have dreamed possible lurked beneath her calico gown.

Jesus, forgive me. You said, "Whosoever hateth his brother is a murderer: and. . . no murderer hath eternal life abiding in him." I am so sorry!

Sick at heart from learning what lay hidden in her soul, Sarah was still aware when Sheriff Meade arrived and handcuffed Red. She roused from her misery when the sheriff said, "You can cool your heels in jail, Red. This time you've gone too far." He wheeled toward the distraught girl. "I'll need you to sign a statement, Miss Sarah. Once you do, this skunk won't bother you again. There's not a jury in the state that won't hand down a guilty verdict when they hear how he roughed you up."

The vision of a lifeless figure hanging from the limb of a cottonwood tree made Sarah shudder. She licked suddenly dry lips. If a jury sentenced Red to death, he would leave this world and enter into a greater punishment than she could bear, no matter how much he deserved it. "Just make him go away," she whispered. "I don't want his blood on my hands."

Seth gave a murmur of protest, and Sheriff Meade's eyebrows shot skyward. "You won't press charges?"

She mutely shook her head.

"But Sarah—"

"No, Seth. Let him go." She looked from her brother to Matt, who stood as if turned to stone. His dark blue gaze bored into Sarah. She unflinchingly met it, knowing he held Red's life in his hands. Even if she didn't press charges, Matt's testimony of what he had seen would condemn the cowboy. A minute passed. Two. Sarah's heart pounded like cannon fire.

What felt like an eternity later, Matt took a ragged breath and whirled toward Red. "She's saved your bacon, Fallon. Get out of the valley, and don't come back."

Some of the color returned to Red's face. He rubbed the darkening bruise on his jaw and silently stalked out past the sheriff, leaving Sarah haunted by his venomous look. It shouted more clearly than words: *This ain't over. Not by a long shot.*

☙

Summer passed, then September. Although vigilant as ever, Sarah began to relax. There had been no sign that Gus or Tice was anywhere in the area. Red had mercifully disappeared, at least for the time being. Sarah liked her job, her co-workers, and especially the warmhearted Captain Mace. She felt she had found a home in Madera.

Matt Sterling dined at the hotel more often than he did at home. Soon the entire town suspected he had fallen for pretty Sarah Anderson. She endured the teasing from her fellow workers, yet the blush that colored her cheeks each time the faithful customer entered the dining room was more than mere embarrassment. So was the swift beating of her heart when Matt sat down at her table. The only real embarrassment was the size of his tips. Sarah finally accepted an invitation from Matt to walk her home from church services one Sunday. Just maybe it would be God's plan that she become part of Matt's life.

Late that fall while the Diamond S crew was out rounding up strays, shots rang out and Seth slumped over in his saddle. He had been seriously wounded by an unknown assailant. Matt thought his heart would break when Brett and the boys packed Seth in. *Oh God, please save him,* Matt prayed. *This is like losing Robbie all over again. How can I tell Sarah? I'm responsible for her brother. She trusted me to take care of him. Now Seth may die because he's working for me. Even if this is Red Fallon's revenge, it can't be proved. No one's seen hide nor hair of Red in weeks.*

Seth's injuries were so dangerous that when Doc Brown arrived from Madera and examined the young man, he flatly stated, "He's in no condition to be moved to town. The trip would kill him. Go get his sister. He needs to be cared for here."

Dreading the confrontation with Sarah, Matt rode as he had never ridden before. When he reached the Yosemite Hotel, he told Captain Mace what had happened and asked him to summon Sarah. Her puzzled expression when she entered the office quickly changed to fear when Matt said, "I have some bad news. Seth has been. . ." He paused and considered his words. "Hurt," he finished.

Her lips quivered then set in a straight line. "How badly?"

"Enough for you to take a leave of absence and come out to the Diamond S to help Solita and me care for him," he told her bluntly.

Captain Mace wholeheartedly agreed. "The road to Yosemite will be closing soon for the winter, so I won't need you. Take good care of Seth. Your job will be waiting for you when you return in the spring."

If she returns, Matt thought. *If I have my way, Sarah Joy Anderson will be Mrs. Matthew Sterling by the time the road opens again.* He wisely kept his thoughts to himself. With Seth so badly hurt, this was no time to openly pursue Sarah.

"It won't take me long to pack," she said. "I can't wait to see Seth. He's not going to die, is he?" Terror darkened her blue eyes.

Matt wouldn't lie, so he merely said, "He's sure to get better when he sees you," and let it go at that.

❧

On the way to the ranch Sarah hunkered down in the carriage and announced, "I will earn my keep by helping Solita when I'm not needed to nurse Seth. That's how it's going to be. Period." The tilt of her sturdy chin showed she meant what she said.

"Did anyone ever tell you you're as stubborn as a mule?" Matt asked. To his amazement Sarah burst out in a chime of laughter that made the high-stepping horses' ears prick up.

"Oh yes—a *Missouri* mule!"

Matt grinned, outwitted and more in love than ever. God willing, that was where she would always be: close beside him for the rest of their lives.

Chapter 16

A pall lay over the Diamond S equal to when first the elder Sterlings then young Robbie died. Now Seth Anderson's life hung in the balance. Everyone on the ranch had learned to admire and respect the plucky tenderfoot who made good. Under the capable direction of Brett Owen, life went on but not as usual. The outfit walked softly, hoping and praying for Seth but knowing how little likelihood there was of him recovering. One of the bullets that felled Seth had lodged close to his heart. The ranch held its collective breath until Doc Brown dug it out.

The rejoicing was brief. The operation took far longer than even Doc Brown expected. Seth pulled through but remained unconscious. The shock of the surgery to his body and the loss of blood he'd sustained had left him so weak even Sarah wondered if he would live. Once the doctor operated—ably assisted by Matt and Solita, with Sarah hovering outside the bedroom-turned-operating room—Sarah refused to leave Seth's side. Only when her body refused to keep vigil and forced her to her room for a few hours of uneasy sleep would she desert her post.

Haggard from worry, Matt faithfully remained on duty as well. He and Sarah spent hours with Seth, asking God to spare the life of the boy they loved. They soon noticed Seth's fingers stopped plucking the sheets at the sound of their voices in prayer. "Try quoting scripture to him," Matt suggested.

Sarah again blessed her parents for instilling in their children the truths of the Bible. If Seth could hear her voice, he would surely recognize the verses, perhaps even receive comfort from them. Besides, Doc Brown admitted no one knew how much an unconscious person grasped.

"I've read about cases where patients came out of a coma and repeated things they'd heard, even when they couldn't speak," he gruffly told them. "Anything that quiets Seth is good."

So while her brother hovered close to death's door, Sarah held his hand and quoted scriptures, praying they would reach through the curtain that kept Seth from awakening.

" 'In the world ye shall have tribulation: but be of good cheer; I have overcome the world.'

" 'Let not your heart be troubled: ye believe in God, believe also in me.'

" 'Peace I leave with you, my peace I give unto you. . . .' "

89

When Sarah's voice threatened to give out, Matt took over. The weary girl rested her head on one hand and let the stories of those whom Jesus had made whole flow over her like a healing stream. She prayed for Seth to hear them—especially the story where Jesus commanded the man with the palsy to take up his bed and walk.

Matt finished reading, bowed his head, and said, "Lord, we know that You love Seth even more than we do." He reached across the bed and took Sarah's hand in one of his own. "We ask You to spare our brother's life." He paused, as if struggling to go on. When he did, his voice broke. "Nevertheless, Thy will, not ours, be done." The last word was barely audible.

Sarah felt a lump the size of a windmill leap to her throat. The agony in Matt's voice showed how much it cost him to relinquish Seth into God's care. *Matt is stronger than I am,* she thought. *Seth is my sole remaining link to our once-happy home. I'm sorry, God, but I just don't want You to take Seth. He's all I have left.*

Sarah's confession brought relief, but she added, *If it is Your will, Lord, please make me willing to accept it. That's as far as I can go right now.*

Seth lingered between life and death for several more days. Then one afternoon, the overworked Doc Brown told Matt, Sarah, and Solita, "He's going to make it. His fever's gone, and he shows signs of regaining consciousness. Don't thank me," he barked when Sarah started to speak. "I'm just a rough old sawbones. The Almighty had a hand on Seth, or he wouldn't still be alive. I've a sneakin' hunch all the prayin' and readin' from the Good Book did their part, too."

Doc cleared his throat and shook a bony finger at the three. "Once awake, Seth will want to get up. Keep him in bed if you have to hog-tie him! He's going to need the same watchin' over he's been getting."

Too overcome with hope and joy to reply, Sarah felt tears of relief spill down her cheeks.

Not so for Matt and Solita. Matt's quick "Don't worry, he'll get it" was drowned out by the Mexican housekeeper's fervent "Dios be praised! I will care for Senor Seth the way I cared for Matelito and Dolores." A flood made glistening tracks down her round brown face.

"You'll probably spoil him rotten," Matt told Solita. His obvious attempt to lighten the moment and drive away the shadows that lurked in Sarah's eyes brought a look of gratitude and a small smile. How would she have lived through the ordeal without him?

"No wonder Seth idolizes Matt," she told herself after Doc Brown ordered her away for a sorely needed rest. She fell into the deepest, most refreshing sleep she had known since she arrived at the Diamond S and didn't awake until Solita shook her hours later.

"Come quickly, senorita." The housekeeper's face shone like a brown full moon. "Dios is good. Senor Seth is awake!"

Sarah sprang from her bed and barreled into Seth's room. Matt stood by the bed, one hand on her brother's shoulder. "Don't try to talk," he advised the groggy young man. "You were shot. God and Doc took care of you. Now you need to rest. There's plenty of time to talk later."

Seth looked from Matt to Sarah. A wan smile crossed his pale face, and his eyes closed again. But Sarah dropped to her knees beside his bed and thanked God.

With the good news about Seth, joy descended on the ranch like rain from heaven. The Mexican workers played their guitars and sang again. The cowboys let off steam in a dozen different ways: playing tricks on one another and bragging, "Sho, we knew all along that Seth wouldn't die from any ol' bullet. He's too tough to let a little thing like that get him down."

Their antics delighted Sarah and showed better than anything else could have done in what high esteem the outfit held her brother.

Seth grew stronger with each day. For the first time, Sarah had time to appreciate the ranch. Compared with life in St. Louis, Sarah had considered living in Madera close to heaven. Now she discovered life on the Diamond S was even better. She fell in love with everything about the ranch: the grinning cowboys who surreptitiously eyed her then blushed when she caught them; the dark eyed vaqueros; the horses in the corral; the distant Sierra Nevada. Most of all, Solita. Sarah loved listening to the housekeeper's warm tales of Matt's little sister, Dori, and his brother, Robbie.

One day Solita rolled her expressive eyes and pounded down a huge mound of bread dough. "Dolores means *sorrowful*. She brings sorrow to those who displease her or stand in the way of what she wants. She is not bad," Solita hastily added, "just filled with mischief. I am to blame. She is like my own *muchacha* and so beautiful it is hard to deny her anything." She sighed, and her hands stilled. "Dori saw an advertisement in a magazine for Brookside Finishing School for Young Ladies in Boston. She pleaded and cried. I reminded Senor Mateo that Senora Sterling would be glad for her daughter to attend such a school." Solita sighed. "He spent much money getting a place for her, and I almost wished I had not urged him to do so. Our casa seemed empty until Senor Seth came. Then Senor Mateo and I, we laugh again." She shot a keen look at Sarah and innocently added, "He also laughs much now that you come to California, senorita."

Sarah felt a blush rise from the modest neckline of a sprigged cotton dress she had bought in Madera. She fingered the crisp white trim on the cuffs and quickly changed the subject. "I would have loved to go to such a school," she said in a small voice. Hating the "poor me" tone of her voice, she asked, "Does Dori like it there?"

Solita grunted. "Who can say? She would be too proud to admit it if she does not." Solita lowered her voice. "Dori has been in what Senor Mateo calls 'scrapes.' It is a wonder she has not been sent home in disgrace. I think Senor Mateo has had to pay *mucho dinero* to keep her there." Sarah saw how disturbed the housekeeper was over Dori, so she said, "Tell me about Robbie, please."

"It is a sad story. He wanted to prove he could do everything Senor Mateo did—but Roberto was too young." She sighed. "I think Senor Mateo's heart broke in two pieces when Roberto died."

Sarah couldn't hold back a question she'd wanted to ask for a long time. "Did no one try to heal it?" She felt guilty for asking but blurted out, "The girls at the Yosemite Hotel said Matt had been engaged to a girl named Lydia Hensley. . . ." Her voice trailed off.

"Sí." Solita's face clouded up like the sky before a thunderstorm. "That one was no good." She pounded her dough again as if taking out her disgust with Miss Hensley. "Senor Mateo vowed to never again trust a girl or woman. Senorita, he kept that vow until he saw your picture."

Sarah sat bolt upright. Heat raced through her veins. "What do you mean?"

"It is true. Senor Seth told me that since he gave the picture to Senor Mateo, it has ridden in Senor Mateo's shirt pocket."

Sarah couldn't doubt Solita. So Matthew Sterling carried her picture. Did he look at it as often as she did the one she had of Seth and him? She gulped. "I don't understand. Why would Seth give him my picture?"

Solita quietly said, "Both senors were worried about you and praying for you. We all were." The sweetest smile Sarah had seen since her mother died brightened Solita's face. "Every day I say *gracias a* Dios, thanks to God, who brought you safely to us."

Sarah knew she'd be bawling if she didn't get away. She hugged the diminutive housekeeper and escaped from the kitchen—but not from the effect of Solita's disclosure. Imagine. The girl-shy Matthew Sterling carrying her picture!

A few days later Matt stunned Sarah by presenting her with a beautiful chestnut gelding.

"Why, he looks just like Pandora, the horse of my childhood," she cried in delight. "Seth must have had a hand in the selection. But I can't take him."

"Of course you can. He's a gift from Seth and a bribe from me," Matt told her.

"What kind of bribe?" Sarah suspiciously demanded.

"You need to get out of the ranch house and into the fresh air and sunshine to keep healthy," Matt said. "Not just for your own sake but for Seth's. You've been cooped up too long. Now that he is recovering, you have to think of yourself. You've gotten thin and peaked looking. A good dose of the outdoors is just what the doctor ordered. You'll also have more to tell Seth when you get back."

"Did Dr. Brown ask you to take me riding?" Sarah held her breath and waited.

"Hardly!" Matt's eyes lit up. "My own idea, but I'm sure he'd have prescribed it if he'd thought of it."

The afternoon rides quickly became part of Sarah and Matt's routine. While Seth napped, was pampered by Solita, and grew strong, Sarah and Matt explored the vast holdings that made up the Diamond S. She loved every inch of the place.

Late one golden October afternoon Matt took Sarah to his special place overlooking the ranch. The promontory offered both privacy and beauty. The entire valley spread out before them, with its vineyards and orchards, its cattle and horses. They dismounted and gazed down into the valley for a long time. Sarah passionately wished she could stay there forever.

Matt wheeled from the view. He drew Sarah close in his strong arms. "I love you, Sarah Joy Anderson," he said. "I want you to marry me and never leave the Diamond S. You don't need to answer right away, but no one on this earth can ever love you as much as I do."

Shaken by his intensity and the beauty of the moment, Sarah longed to respond to the gentle invitation in his eyes. She hesitated then faltered. "Matthew, I admire and respect you with all my heart, but..."

"But you don't know if you love me." Disappointment cast a shadow over his strong features, but it vanished the next moment. "I'll settle for your admiration and respect—for now—and leave the future in God's hands. Don't worry about it." He leaned forward and kissed her forehead. "I understand."

Sarah felt torn. How could he understand when she didn't? Before she pledged herself to this fine man, she must settle something forever: Were her feelings really love? Or were they hero worship mixed with gratefulness for everything he had done for her and Seth? She must be sure. "I need time to think," she whispered.

"Take as long as you need," Matt offered. He released her and raised an eyebrow. "I can afford to be patient. I intend to live to be an old, old man." His eyes sparkled. "I'll bet my bottom dollar that someday you're going to walk up the aisle of our Madera church on Seth's arm, all gussied up in a fluffy white dress and ready to become Mrs. Matthew Sterling."

Sarah gasped and stared at him. Impossible as it seemed, the scene Matt described was identical to the one she had conjured up while being fitted for the hated wedding dress months before—the dress Tice Edwards had paid for but had never seen her wear.

Chapter 17

Now that Seth was rapidly improving, Sarah's worries should have been over. They weren't. She was faced with a dilemma that had nothing to do with her brother's health. Captain Mace had promised she could return to waitressing at his hotel, but his trade depended heavily on the Yosemite Stage and Turnpike Company, which daily transported tourists from Madera to the Yosemite Valley. The visitors remained overnight before returning home the following day. The stage line, however, had ceased operation for the year and would not resume until spring. This meant that the captain could only keep a limited number of girls working during the winter, and Sarah was the newest employee.

On a beautiful Indian summer morning while Matt and the boys were busy away from the ranch house, Sarah saddled the chestnut gelding she had already learned to love and rode out alone. John Anderson had taught his daughter well, insisting that she learn to saddle and care for the first Pandora before he allowed her to even ride to the borders of their small farm.

Riding Pandora II brought back so many happy memories! Sarah giggled, remembering the look on her father's face when she announced she wanted to name her new horse Pandora. A twinkle crept into his blue eyes, and his lips twitched.

"Pandora?" He scratched his head and looked puzzled. "Seems to me Pandora was not only a gal but one who caused a heap of trouble. She opened a box she'd been told not to and let loose a passel of evil on the world—including sickness. Are you sure you want that name?"

Sarah stubbornly shook her head. "No. It said in a book that Pandora means *all gifts*, and he's a gift. Besides, my horse wouldn't ever do anything bad. It doesn't matter if he has a girl's name."

"Then Pandora it is," John Anderson said. "You are responsible for taking care of him. That means feed, water, muck out his stall, brush, and curry him."

"I will, Pa."

Sarah had faithfully kept her promise until the awful day she watched a stranger mount the gelding and ride away. "If Pa had lived, we would never have had to sell Pandora," Sarah told her mother.

"I know." Mama looked as sad as Sarah felt. "We can't stay on the farm. It no longer belongs to us. You know we need the money to get to St. Louis."

"I know, but Seth gets to keep Copper!"

"Would you have me sell Copper in order to keep Pandora?"

Sarah felt ashamed. Seth had raised Copper from the time he was weaned. Selling him would almost be like selling Seth. "No, but I will miss Pandora *so much.*"

"We all will." Mama hugged Sarah. "Someday if we have enough money, I hope you can have another horse."

Now, years later and nineteen hundred miles from the farm, Sarah had another Pandora. A wave of gratitude toward Matthew Sterling flooded through Sarah's body. "Lord, what would Mama and Pa think of me now?" she prayed. "And of Seth?" Love for the brother whose life God had spared settled into Sarah's heart. How could she help loving Matt when he had been so good to Seth and her?

"That's the problem," she told Pandora. "He's everything I ever dreamed of, but I have to be sure of my feelings. I don't want to marry Matt out of gratitude. Or because I see him as the answer to my worries about Gus finding me. Or being forced to wed Tice. It wouldn't be fair to either of us." A new and horrid thought rushed into her mind.

"I didn't actually read the papers Gus waved at me." A chill went through her. "What if Gus had copied Mama's handwriting and wrote a letter naming him as my legal guardian in case anything happened to her?"

The thought was so appalling that Sarah nudged the gelding into a canter in order to escape. Pandora settled into the easy stride that ate up distance like a visiting preacher gobbling down fried chicken. At the foot of the hill that sloped up to the promontory offering solitude—Sarah's favorite thinking place—Pandora slowed for the climb, but he wasn't even winded when they reached the top.

Sarah loved the spot for itself and not just because she had spent happy times here with Matt. Nothing disturbed the quiet except the sound of cattle lowing in the distance, the occasional cry of a hawk, Pandora's occasional gentle whinny, and a breeze rustling through the manzanita. A carpet of needles beneath a pine offered a soft place to rest and ponder knotty problems.

Sarah sat down and clasped her hands around the knees of her divided riding skirt. No sidesaddle for her. Back on the farm, she'd ridden in Seth's britches when they got too small for him.

However, Solita had raised her eyebrows in horror at the idea and produced a riding skirt Dori had left behind when she went back east. "Senor Mateo would not like you to dress so," she protested when Sarah came into the kitchen clad in trousers and ready for her first ride with Matt. "Senorita will wear this. *Mucho mejor.* Much better."

"Didn't Dori ride in pants?" Sarah asked.

The corners of Solita's mouth turned down. "Only when Senor Mateo was not here to stop her."

Sarah snatched the skirt and went to her room to change. From then on she scrupulously dressed to go riding according to Solita's decree.

Sarah always felt close to God on the promontory. It offered the opportunity to seek Him and lay her concerns at His feet. The hustle and bustle of a busy ranch didn't always offer the opportunity to be alone and quiet. She had always treasured the scripture *"Be still, and know that I am God."* Nowhere else could she find a better setting to obey His command.

Today another verse came to mind. The advice from James was as applicable for Sarah as for those to whom they were originally directed: *"If any of you lack wisdom, let him ask of God, that giveth to all men liberally, and upbraideth not; and it shall be given him. But let him ask in faith, nothing wavering. For he that wavereth is like a wave of the sea driven with the wind and tossed."*

Sarah pondered the timeless admonition then stared unseeingly across the valley. "Lord, I thank You for bringing me to this place. I thank You for Your loving care and that Gus and Tice have not followed me. Yet I feel they will come. Neither will give me up without a fight." She shivered and hugged her knees tighter.

"In the meantime I need a job. Should I go to Fresno and look for work? It's a much bigger town, and Captain Mace will surely give me a good recommendation." She shook her head, and dread crept from the tip of her toes to the crown of her head. "I don't know anyone in Fresno. I would have to pay for my room and board. If Gus and Tice come, I'll have no one to protect me." She hastily added, "You can, of course, but is it really Your will for me to leave the Diamond S?"

Emotion surged through her. Leave Seth? Matt? Solita? The cowboys who respectfully tipped their Stetsons to her when she passed by? This promontory where she felt God's presence in every stirring breeze, every bird's song? No—yet how could she stay? If only there was something she could do at the ranch.

"I'll be glad to do any kind of work, Lord," she promised. "I just don't know what. When I try to help Solita, she shoos me away and tells me to go amuse Senors Seth and Mateo. The maids who help her giggle and shake their heads when I offer to make beds or dust. It feels like a conspiracy."

She jumped up, smoothed out her riding skirt, and mounted Pandora. "Do you know what I am going to do, my fine, four-footed friend? I am going to tell Matt Sterling point-blank that either he puts me to work, or I'll go where I can work."

With a prayer in her heart that she wouldn't have to leave, Sarah left her trysting place and headed home—the first real home she and Seth had known since their father died.

God answered Sarah's prayer in a way she wouldn't have suspected if she lived to be older than Methuselah. That same evening, Matt, Seth, Solita, and she gathered in front of the huge rock fireplace in the spacious ranch house sitting room. Dancing flames turned Seth's hair to glistening gold. The crackling fire targeted the brilliant colors of the beautiful Mexican tapestries on the walls and glinted off the silver belt buckle Seth sat polishing.

Sarah took a deep breath. It was time to state her own little declaration of independence. "I need a job."

A stick of dynamite exploding in the quiet room couldn't have had a more startling effect. Solita's mouth dropped open. Seth stared then burst into a loud "Haw haw!"

Matt sat up straight in his hand-hewn chair and gave Seth a quelling look. "What would you like to do, Sarah? I have enough cowhands. You're a good rider, but I don't think you could tame wild mustangs."

Sarah sprang to her feet and clenched her fists. For the first time since meeting Matthew Sterling, she was thoroughly angry at him. "Don't make fun of me," she cried. "You don't know what it's like to be beholden." Tears of fury fell. "I mean it, Matt. Either you give me worthwhile work to do here on the ranch, or I'm going to Fresno and find a job."

He looked stricken. "I'm sorry, Sarah. I was only teasing you. If you want a job, I have one for you. I've been meaning to mention it, but what with Seth being shot and all, it slipped my mind."

Sarah cocked her head to one side. "What is it? Some made-up something that isn't important?"

Matt gave her a smile. "Not at all. Some of our Mexican workers have children. They help with crops and in the orchards, but are at a great disadvantage because of the language barrier. Do you think you could teach them to speak English? Winter is the perfect time."

Sarah's knees gave way, and she dropped to a nearby settee. "Why, I—"

"Solita will help you," Matt assured her.

"You can do it, Sarah," Seth interrupted. He let out a cowboy yell. "Miss Sarah Joy Anderson's gonna be a schoolmarm!"

Speechless, all she could do was stare. Yet her mind raced like Pandora. She had asked God for work. Matt had offered work that was truly worthwhile. How could she refuse? She closed her eyes and pictured young brown faces turned toward her, shining dark eyes showing eagerness to learn. *Thank You, Lord.*

"How many children will I have?" Sarah asked. "I will need supplies. Slates and chalk and a blackboard so I can draw pictures."

"Only a few families live here year-round. There's fewer than a dozen children right now, ages five to fourteen, in addition to the toddlers and babies.

Evan will order whatever supplies you can't find at the general stores. Seth can take you to town tomorrow." Matt grinned. "If it's not too hard a trip for our invalid."

Seth snorted. "Are you crazy? I can't wait to straddle a cayuse again."

"Hold your horses, fire-eater. No cayuses. Take the carriage. You'll need it to bring back Sarah's stuff." Matt stood, crossed the room, and held out a calloused hand. "That is, if it's a deal."

A dozen children? Could she do it? She had to. The only other alternative was a lonely boardinghouse in Fresno where she would never feel safe. "Yes." Sarah put her hand in his. "I don't know how good a teacher I will be, but I promise to work hard."

"That's good enough for me." Matt squeezed her hand then dropped it, but not before Sarah caught a satisfied gleam in his dark blue eyes. "About your salary. . ."

Sarah felt herself redden. "I just need enough for room and board."

"Not on the Diamond S," Matt quietly told her. "Everyone works. Everyone gets paid. You won't make what a regular teacher makes because it will only be for an hour or so a day." He raised his hand when Sarah started to disagree. "No argument. The children have chores, even in winter."

The new schoolmarm subsided. Solita had long since warned her there was no use arguing with Senor Mateo once he made up his mind.

Oh dear! In the discussion with Matt, Sarah had forgotten Solita. She turned to the housekeeper. Her heart thudded to her toes. Solita sat with bowed head. Did she feel it was an insult to the Mexican children to have a girl only a few years older than some of them become their teacher? Sarah rushed to her. "Solita, what is the matter? Don't you want me to teach the children?"

The housekeeper raised her head and blinked back tears. "Sí! It will make them so happy." She caught Sarah's hand and kissed it. "*Gracias*, senorita. Dios will bless you for your goodness."

Matt said nothing. But his expression when he bade Sarah "Good night" spoke volumes.

Chapter 18

Two days later Sarah became a teacher. The outfit had turned a vacant storeroom into a schoolroom. Sarah surveyed it with satisfaction. Everything she needed—including her mother's Bible. She tingled with anticipation. After she taught the children to speak English, perhaps she could teach them their *ABC*s.

At nine o'clock sharp, ten excited children took their places. Sarah smiled from behind her new desk, loving the smell of the freshly sawed lumber. "Most of you already know that I am Miss Anderson, but I don't know all your names yet. Tell me so I can write them on the blackboard."

Solita translated into Spanish.

A chorus followed. "José." "Carmelita." "Rosa." "Jorge." "Mateo."

"Mateo?" Sarah eyed the tallest boy suspiciously.

"Sí, senorita," he proudly told her.

"His name honors Senor Mateo," Solita explained.

Sarah disciplined a smile and wrote down the rest of the names. Then she picked up her mother's Bible. "Solita, I want to start each day with a Bible story. You will translate."

The housekeeper nodded. "Sí. I will make the English words Spanish."

Sarah thrilled at the interest in the attentive faces as she spoke and Solita translated after each sentence.

"David was only a shepherd boy, but God chose him to be a king when he was still a lad, probably no older than you are now, Mateo."

A delighted murmur rippled through the group.

Sarah continued. "God knew that David would one day become a wise king. God may never choose you to be kings, but He has something special for each of you to do. For now it is learning to speak English. Let's bow our heads and pray.

"Dear God, we want to be like David, so we can be whatever You want us to be. In Jesus' name. Amen." A collective *Amen* followed Solita's translation.

"Now we are going to have some fun," Sarah said. Through a combination of gestures and pictures Sarah had drawn on the blackboard, the children learned their first English words. By the end of the first session, the students could understand a few simple instructions such as "stand up" and "sit down."

She could scarcely believe it when Matt stepped inside the open door and said in Spanish, which Solita repeated in English, "Ten o'clock. School's over for today. Did you like it?"

A chorus of, "Sí, sí! Gracias, senorita. Gracias, senor" left no doubt. Sarah's first day as a teacher was a smashing success. The children clustered around Matt, proudly reciting the English words they had learned.

"That is good. *Adios*," he told them. "You have chores to do before dinner." Solita shooed them out, and Matt turned to Sarah. A wide grin split his tanned face. "Well? How do you like being a teacher?" he asked in English.

She sank into the chair behind her desk, still excited but suddenly tired. She hadn't fully realized until now how much she wanted to make good in her new job. "I love it. The students—they are so. . ." She couldn't find the words.

Understanding shone in Matt's eyes. "They are God's precious children." He ducked his head and idly made circles on the floor with the toe of his boot. "I have a confession. I eavesdropped."

"You did?" Sarah sat bolt upright. Her pulse quickened.

"Yeah. Good choice of story." A poignant light crept onto his face. "These children need to know they are special." He cleared his throat. "The Diamond S treats them that way, but I can't say the same for everyone in Madera."

Matt's words haunted Sarah long after he left. Head bowed, she prayed, "Dear Lord, please use me to touch the lives of these children. Help me to show how much You love them, so much You sent Your Son to die on the cross for them." A gentle breeze wafted into the silent room like a heavenly benediction—and Sarah rejoiced.

❧

If Matthew Sterling hadn't already been fathoms deep in love with Sarah, the sight of her conducting school in his home would have sent him head over heels. After eavesdropping on "Sarah's School," as Brett Owen and the hands dubbed it, Matt breathed a prayer. *Someday, Lord, if it be Your plan, Sarah Joy Anderson will be telling Bible stories and pointing our own children to You.* The thought set his heart pounding. The sparkle in Sarah's luminous blue eyes when he asked if she liked teaching was enough to drive a man loco. The vision remained with Matt long after the triangle outside the cookshack clanged, calling the hands to dinner.

That afternoon Matt rested his hands on the top rail of the corral and watched Sarah lead Pandora out of the barn for their usual afternoon ride. Chase was already saddled and waiting. Matt started toward Sarah, but his three youngest cowboys—all just a little older than Seth—beat him to it. Matt frowned. What were Curly, Bud, and Slim up to?

The trio doffed their Stetsons, then Curly respectfully asked, "Beggin' your pardon, Miss Sarah, but has the boss slapped his brand on you?"

Sarah stared at him as if unable to comprehend. She opened her mouth, but no words came out. Before Matt could bellow at the boys, Bud added, "The reason Curly's askin' is, if the answer's no, then we'd like to carry you to the big doin's in town this weekend."

"Yeah," Slim chimed in, "there's a rodeo an' a square dance an—"

Matt gritted his teeth, but Sarah said, "Carry me? What do you mean?"

Curly whacked his hat against his leg. "Don't pay Bud no mind. He's from Virginny. They talk funny back there. If he were better eddicated, he'da said, take you. Or *es*-cort you. That's more high-toned."

Matt saw Sarah's lips twitch. In spite of his annoyance, he also wanted to laugh. What would the lovable but unpredictable boys do next? More importantly, what would Sarah do?

"Am I to understand all three of you want to escort me?" she demanded.

Astonishment swept over all three faces. Curly—evidently elected spokesman for the group—said, "Why, shore. We're gonna be the three most important fellers there. I'm the best rider and aim to give the boss a run for his money in the men's race. Bud's sure to win either the calf ropin' or the bull ridin'."

Sarah let out a silvery peal of laughter. "What about Slim?"

"He's the modest kind. Don't like to brag, but he's the best square dancer in the outfit," Curly explained. "So, Miss Sarah, are you free to accept our 'nvitation?"

Matt found his tongue. "She is not. Seth and I'll do any *es*-corting there is to do."

Bud stood his ground. "Aw, Boss, we'd be mighty proud to carry her," he protested. " 'Course, if it's hornin' in on you, just say so."

Matt felt trapped between a rock and a hard place. If he said the cowboys were horning in, it would embarrass Sarah. Keeping silent would put her in a tough position. Inspiration hit him. "It's like this, boys. If Sarah comes sashaying in with the three of you, it will get her in bad with the other girls, especially those who came all by their lonesome. We don't want that to happen, now do we?" The crestfallen escorts looked at each other and shuffled their feet. "Reckon we never thought of that," Curly admitted. A smile broke through the sudden gloom. "Can we at least dance with her?"

Matt laughed. "That is up to the lady."

Three pairs of hopeful eyes turned toward Sarah. She blushed, mounted Pandora, and rode off, but she called back over her shoulder, "The lady says yes."

"*Yippee-ki-ay!* The Diamond S is gonna ride high, wide, and handsome come Saturday," Curly shouted. "Say, Boss, Miss Sarah stays in that saddle as if she'd been born there. Why'n't you get her to ride in the ladies' race? Since the outfit's bent on winnin' all the rodeo prizes, we might as well get one more."

101

"Good idea, Curly." Matt swung into the saddle and headed in the direction Sarah had taken.

&

Later that afternoon, Sarah persuaded her brother into taking a walk with her on the pretense she needed to consult him about something. When they stopped beneath a tall cottonwood, she gleefully related her invitation to the "big doin's."

Seth thought it was hilarious. "Those three are my favorites of the outfit, except for Brett Owen. They're such pardners they should have been triplets!" He laughed but quickly sobered. His keen gaze bored into her. "They weren't disrespectful, were they?"

"Oh no! They were polite, funny, and *very* determined to find out if I was wearing Matt's brand. What does that mean, Seth?"

"Out here, an engagement ring stands for a brand—a mark that a girl or young woman is spoken for. Kind of like a No TRESPASSING sign." Seth hesitated. "Sarah, I don't want to pry, but is Matt going to someday be my real brother?"

"Would you like that?" Sarah held her breath.

"He's the only man I've ever known who is good enough for you. And," he loyally added, "I'll bet my bedroll you're the only woman good enough for him." His face darkened. "Be careful, though, Sarah. Lydia Hensley did a lot of damage to Matt's pride. He thinks a powerful lot of you, and the last thing he needs is to be let down a second time." Seth patted her hand. "Just take your time and be sure." He cleared his throat and changed the subject. "I figured that Gus and Tice would follow you. Wonder why they haven't?"

Sarah shook her head. The fear that lay hidden within her and was sometimes temporarily forgotten flared up like a brush fire. "I don't know."

"If they do come, it probably won't be until spring," Seth comforted. Mischief sprang to his eyes. "Who knows? By then you may have a husband as well as a brother to protect you. What Matt did to Red Fallon isn't a patch on what he'd do to anyone who *really* tried to hurt you."

Sarah grimaced but she kept her thoughts to herself.

&

Sarah had never been to a rodeo and had no idea what to expect. As usual she sought out Solita. "I know what horse racing is, and calf roping must mean the cowboys are going to rope calves, but why would anyone want to ride a bull?"

Solita's merry laugh bounced off the ceiling of the large, cool kitchen. "You have much to learn if you are to be a rancher's wife, senorita!" The housekeeper's laughter died, and she rolled her expressive dark eyes. "Vaqueros, they are all alike. They ride anything they can straddle, especially bulls. The meaner the better. It is dangerous, very dangerous."

Sarah's mouth dried. She ignored Solita's comment about being a rancher's wife and asked, "Does Matthew do that?"

Solita shook her head. "He only rides in the horse races, and usually he wins."

Sarah sagged with relief. The thought of Matt being trampled by an enraged bull was more than she could bear. She shuddered. "Curly said Bud would either win the calf roping or the bull riding."

"Sí. He has won before." Solita patted Sarah's shoulder. "Do not worry, *querida*. We will pray for Senor Bud's safety."

"Matt and Seth want me to enter the ladies' race. Should I? They say Pandora is fast enough to beat almost any horse that runs, but surely there are western girls who ride better than I do."

Solita shrugged. "Perhaps, but you will have fun." She laughed again. "Our Dori won the ladies race when she was fourteen. You will look beautiful in her riding clothes."

Sarah capitulated when she saw the outfit. The expensive riding skirt and vest, high boots, blue silk blouse, and white Stetson fit as if they had been designed for her. And the way Matt looked when he saw her made Sarah feel beautiful.

The rodeo brought out everyone's brightest clothing. The cowboys donned fancy shirts and highly colored neckerchiefs. They polished their boots until they shone, regardless of the fact they would soon be dusty from the events. The ladies decked themselves out in their best gowns. Some carried parasols.

Sarah was delighted to discover her friend Abby from the Yosemite Hotel was going to ride in the ladies' race. "It is so good to see you," the attractive young woman said. "Everyone is glad to know Seth is much better." She cast a furtive glance both ways then leaned close to whisper, "Keep your ears open and your eyes peeled. I heard Red Fallon plans to be here today. He never misses a rodeo."

Sarah gasped. "Surely he wouldn't come after everything he's done!"

"You don't know Red Fallon," Abby warned. "He's likely to turn up anywhere. Besides, even though folks suspect him of shooting your brother, there's no proof." She sighed. "I just wish Sheriff Meade would get some positive evidence that would send Red to the penitentiary!"

The disturbing news cast a cloud over Sarah's day. She alerted Matt and Seth to what she'd learned, but Red didn't appear until the calf roping. To Sarah's disgust he leaped from the saddle of his black stallion, expertly roped and tied the calf, then jumped up with a smirk and threw his hands into the air. A few minutes later, however, Sarah clapped until her hands stung. Bud's time was a few seconds less than Red's. The swaggering cowboy sullenly had to accept second place.

To Sarah's relief Bud didn't enter the bull riding event. "Stove up my ankle when I hit the ground durin' the calf ropin'," he growled.

"You beat Red," she reminded.

"Yeah." A triumphant gleam shot across Bud's disconsolate face. "Now either Curly or the boss needs to win the men's race. If you win the ladies' race, it'll be frostin' on the cake."

"I'll try," she promised and mounted Pandora for the race. When the horses took off, Sarah bent low over the gelding's neck and screamed encouragement into his ear. Never had he galloped faster. Wind burned Sarah's face and sent her hat flying, along with the hairpins which secured her braids. Her red-gold hair streamed behind her like a flame, and the roar of the excited crowd dinned in her ears. On the homestretch Abby's palomino mare kept pace with Pandora. A few yards from the finish line, they surged ahead just enough to win.

"No hard feelings?" Abby asked when they slowed their horses.

"Oh no!" Sarah attempted to smooth her disheveled hair. "That was exciting. But I challenge you to another race sometime."

Abby laughed and held out a gloved hand. "You're on. You're not bad for a tenderfoot. Let's go get our prizes. It's almost time for the men's race."

Chapter 19

I t was not Red Fallon's day. He and his black made a strong showing but only placed third in the men's race. Top honors went to Matt Sterling on Chase and Curly on his favorite buckskin. They were neck and neck all the way and crossed the finish line at the exact same moment.

Red yanked at his horse's reins and gave the winning pair a menacing look that frightened Sarah. So far the Diamond S outfit had studiously avoided him like the plague, but could it last? What if Red showed up at the square dance? There was no telling what might happen.

To Sarah's great relief, Red didn't come. Curly, Bud, and Slim got their turns dancing with her, but most of the time Matt fended off would-be partners by whirling her away. Yet all through the happy evening, a bad feeling niggled at Sarah. Red Fallon was not out of the picture. As the cowboys would say, "Not by a long shot."

❧

One beautiful evening shortly after the rodeo Matt told Sarah there would be no school the next day. Everyone was needed to prepare for a special fiesta in honor of Seth's miraculous recovery.

"What can I do to help?" she inquired.

"Nothing." Matt grinned, the maddening expression that always left her feeling unsettled and wondering what he was thinking. "Why don't you take tomorrow off and do something you really want to do?" He gave her a mock glare. "That does not mean helping Solita!"

Instead of sticking to her guns and reminding Matt she was there to work, as she often did, Sarah obediently said, "All right," then laughed at his look of surprise. She stared west toward a spectacular sunset. Crimson, scarlet, gold, and purple set the skies on fire. "The Bible says red sky in the evening means a fair tomorrow. If it's all right, I will borrow a horse and buggy and go to Madera. I've been wanting to tell Abby and the other girls at the Yosemite Hotel how good God was to spare Seth. There was no chance for a serious talk when I saw them at the rodeo."

Matt looked regretful. "Sorry I can't take you, and Seth's nursing a bum ankle. But one of the boys will be glad to drive for you." Mischief sparkled in his teasing blue eyes. "All of them are more than willing, especially Curly, Bud, and Slim. Of course, choosing one over the others means we will probably have a range war on our hands."

Sarah just laughed and waved away his suggestion, but her pulse quickened. "Actually I was teasing," Matt said. "One of the men will escort you to town. Just because your stepfather and that gambler haven't showed up yet is no reason to believe they won't—sooner or later."

The next morning, Sarah dressed in her best, blue-checked gingham dress, donned a wide-brimmed hat, and climbed into the buggy Matt had ready and waiting. Curly, clad in a blinding plaid shirt and neckerchief, beamed at her from the driver's seat. "My pards and I tossed a coin to see who got to drive you. I won," he bragged. Sarah couldn't help laughing at his triumphant expression—and at the obviously disgruntled Slim and Bud, who stood nearby.

"Take good care of her, Curly," Matt called when they started off. "*Vaya con Dios*, Sarah, and hurry home."

Go with God. Hurry home. What a beautiful blessing! "We should be home early in the afternoon," Sarah promised. "Don't eat up all the tamales and enchiladas at dinner." She waved, and they drove away.

Matthew's blessing perched on Sarah's shoulder on her trip to Madera. An occasional lazy hawk circled in the Indian summer sky. A few long-eared jackrabbits with bulging eyes peered at her from beside the road. After Curly made a few unsuccessful attempts to start a conversation, he gave up. It provided the perfect opportunity for Sarah to think and silently talk with her heavenly Father.

Who would have thought the frightened girl who fled from St. Louis would be teaching school on a cattle ranch in California a few months later?

Sarah smiled to herself. Her original ten students had grown to sixteen. After the first few sessions, Carmelita's mother had shyly asked Senor Mateo if "the good Senorita Sarah, who so kindly teaches the muchachos, will also teach the senoras English?" Sarah was aghast. Teaching children was one thing. Teaching their mothers was a different story. Yet the eagerness in the brown-skinned faces awaiting her answer went straight to Sarah's tender heart. These Mexican women were God's children, too. How could she deny them the joy of learning?

She swallowed a lump in her throat and nodded. "Sí." All the electric lights that glowed in St. Louis couldn't match the brightness in the women's faces—but the greater reward was Sarah's. The scripture from Luke 6 rang in her ears each time she saw the women struggling to master English and saw their toil-worn fingers painstakingly copying words on the extra slates Matt provided: "*Give, and it shall be given unto you. . . . For with the same measure that ye mete withal it shall be measured to you again.*"

When she mentioned it to Matt, he quietly said, "We can never out give God, Sarah." He smiled with such obvious approval and love that Sarah felt warmed through and through.

Now as the buggy neared Madera, she silently prayed, *Lord, I am so glad I was able to sow seeds of Christianity during the time I worked at the Yosemite Hotel. I pray they will begin to bear good fruit in the lives of my new friends.* She reflected on how much she had learned to love the country and how much Matt had come to mean in her life. A small smile crept up from her heart. *Thank You, God, for bringing me to California.* She turned to Curly with a bright remark, and they visited the rest of the way to Madera.

Once there, Sarah could hardly wait to see her friends. They left the buggy in a shady grove at the edge of town and agreed to start home around noon.

❧

The din of the metal bar drumming on the triangle announcing the midday meal sounded shortly after Matt rode in from several hours of checking fences.

"About time," Seth complained. "My stomach feels so empty it thinks my throat's been cut."

"Good sign." Matt slapped his dusty Stetson against his boot tops. "If I don't get cleaned up before dinner, Solita will clean my clock." He strode up the wide steps. "Sarah back yet?"

"Naw." Seth raised one eyebrow. "She probably couldn't get away from the girls at the Yosemite Hotel."

"Probably," Matt agreed. But when two o'clock came, he lounged on the shady porch and stared at the road to Madera, nervous as a Mexican jumping bean. Seth had long since settled down for an afternoon siesta, obviously untroubled by his sister's absence.

"Don't be stupid," Matt told himself. "Nothing can happen to Sarah when Curly's with her." It didn't help. And when a lathered horse and wild-eyed rider charged into the yard, Matt cleared the porch steps in one leap.

"Doc Brown says you gotta come quick!" Freckle-faced Johnny Foster gasped for breath. "Curly's hurt bad. He was found knocked out cold in an alley. Nobody knows how long he'd been there."

Heart thundering, Matt grabbed Johnny's shoulder. "What about Sarah?"

"Seth's sister?" Johnny looked surprised. "I don't know anything about her."

In the time it took to saddle Chase and a fresh horse for Johnny, something inside Matt died.

Every pound of the horses' hooves on the way to Madera echoed the beat of his worried heart. "Lord," he prayed, low enough that Johnny couldn't hear, "You know my life will be meaningless without Sarah. Please be with her, wherever she is."

It seemed like a century before they reached Madera and Doc Brown. Curly had just regained consciousness, face pale beneath a heavy bandage around his head.

"Where's Sarah?" Matt challenged.

"Sarah?" Curly groggily shook his head and winced. "Probably still at the hotel. I remember starting to meet her before noon. I passed an alley and woke up here in Doc's office...."

Matt was already rushing for the door, heart in his throat. *God, is Sarah at the hotel? If so, surely she would have heard about Curly and gotten word to me!* Fortunately Abby was on duty.

"Sarah? She went to meet Curly just before noon," Abby said. "Maybe they stopped off to see someone."

Fear spurted. "Who does Sarah know?" Matt demanded.

Abby laughed. "Everyone knows and loves Sarah. She could be at the post office or the minister's or—"

"Thanks," Matt cut in. He forced a smile over the rising suspicion that something was terribly wrong. Not everyone loved Sarah. He could name three without thinking: Gus Stoddard, Tice Edwards, Red Fallon. Well, Stoddard and Edwards were far away, but Red might still be around.

Matt felt sick. He turned on his heel and headed for the sheriff's office. "Whoever knocked Curly out did it for a reason," he told Sheriff Meade. "I'm dead sure that reason is Sarah."

A thorough search of the small town turned up no sign of the young woman or the buggy. The sheriff hastily organized a posse. The questioning of citizens began in earnest. No one had seen or heard a thing about Sarah.

Helplessness fell on Matt like a saddle blanket on Chase's back. There were no clues to Sarah's disappearance. Matt only knew she hadn't taken the road back to the ranch. He would have passed her on his way to Madera. Sick at heart, he bowed his head. His anguish-filled mind repeated over and over, *Where is Sarah?*

ঽ

Sarah had a wonderful time visiting with her friends at the Yosemite Hotel, including Captain Russell Perry Mace. The captain's hints about what an exemplary man Matthew Sterling was and the assurance her job would be open in the spring "if she needed it" failed to get a commitment from Sarah. His words did, however, make her anxious to get back to the ranch. Her reflections during her ride into town had helped Sarah realize her feelings for Matt were genuine and did not spring from a desire to escape from Tice. Her prayers had led her to believe that Matt was the man with whom God wanted her to spend the rest of her life. Matthew had patiently given her the time she requested to be sure, but now she couldn't wait to tell him she had never been more certain of anything in her life. Her heart felt lighter than a spring morning. Was any woman ever so blessed as she?

When Curly didn't come for her at the appointed time, Sarah figured he must have misunderstood their meeting place and would be waiting for her at the buggy. She strolled to the grove of shade trees at the edge of town. The buggy sat waiting. The carriage horse, tethered so he could graze, nickered a welcome, but there was no sign of Curly.

Sarah laughed and hitched the horse to the buggy. "Curly probably ran into a friend and lost track of time," she mused. "He will be along soon." She sat down in the shade and closed her eyes, lost in anticipation of seeing Matt soon.

Her joy was short-lived. All too soon, a coarse voice interrupted her reverie. "Well, lookee who's here."

Sarah's eyes jerked open. Red Fallon grinned down at her from atop his black horse. There was no mistaking his coarse red hair, beard, and leering face.

Sarah's ballooning spirits fell to the ground as if punctured.

"I want a word with you."

A spurt of fear shot through Sarah. She looked around for help, but no one was in sight. "I have nothing to say to you." She stood then sprang into the buggy. Lightly flicking the horse with the reins, she urged him forward.

Her attempt to escape was futile. Red vaulted to the ground and onto the buggy seat in two gigantic leaps. Then he pulled a pistol. "None of that, missy. I'd as soon knock you out as look at you." He snatched up the reins with his free hand, leaving his mount to follow behind. "I reckon I'll ride a piece with you."

Red whipped the horse, and they sped away from town—at far too fast a pace for Sarah to risk jumping from the rig.

When Sarah could find her voice, she summoned her iciest manner. "I demand an explanation. Why are you doing this?"

Red smiled wickedly. "Just doing my job," he mumbled.

Doing his job? A horrid feeling engulfed Sarah. It couldn't be! Surely Gus and Tice were not involved in her abduction. Here? After all these months? It seemed impossible that they would have followed her all the way to Madera and then been able to keep their presence a secret.

Determined to learn the worst, Sarah pushed for the truth. "And just what is this job?" she demanded.

"I met some men from St. Louis, old friends of your'n, in Fresno," he bragged. "Yore daddy and your heartbroken fiancé—Edwards, isn't it? What'd you mean runnin' off like that?" He didn't wait for a reply but rambled on, obviously getting perverse pleasure from the situation. Every word from his cruel mouth brought despair.

"No one makes a fool outa Red Fallon," he sneered. "I alwuz git even." He whipped the horse into a dead run, and his eyes gleamed.

A few miles south of Madera, Red halted the buggy. Standing in the middle of the road was a horse-drawn coach and two men: Gus Stoddard and

Tice Edwards smiling in a way that curdled Sarah's blood.

Tice yanked her out of the buggy. "I've lost a lot of time and money tracking you down," he shouted, "more than you're worth."

Sarah felt sick. Her heart fluttered in fear. "How did you find me?" she whispered.

He sneered. "Gus found a barely legible letter from Seth under your bed." Sarah gasped. Seth's missing letter!

Tice cursed. "Unfortunately there were no clues to his whereabouts. Worse, the postmark was so blurred that all we could make out was *M-a-something, California.*"

Tice shook his fist in Sarah's face. "Have you any idea how much it costs to send telegrams to 'Seth Anderson,' in care of every post office in California that starts with the letters *M* and *a*?"

He blew out a breath as putrid as himself. "None of them did any good. We've spent weeks crisscrossing this rotten state. If we hadn't run across Fallon when we stopped at a saloon in Fresno on our way here, we'd still be looking for you. When we're back in St. Louis, you'll pay, Sarah Anderson!"

She shuddered. Any true feelings the man might have had for her had clearly worn away over the past months. Only Tice's pride and Gus's outstanding gambling debt had kept them searching for the ungrateful girl. Clenching her fingers until the nails bit into the palms of her hands, Sarah defied them. "I am not going back to St. Louis. And I will never be your wife."

"Oh, I think you will," Tice said silkily. He reached into his waistcoat, brought out a goodly amount of money, and thrust it at Red. "Here you are. If anyone asks what's become of Sarah, tell them her father and her husband came to get her."

Red's jaw dropped. "Husband! And her carryin' on with Matt Sterling? Well, whadda you know!"

"Oh yes." Tice took out a paper and flourished it before Red's amazed eyes. "See? A marriage certificate, all signed and proper. Wonder what your Matt Sterling's going to say when he hears he's been courting a married woman?"

Chapter 20

Tice Edwards waved the sham marriage certificate under Sarah's nose. Triumph and hatred made his eyes more snakelike than ever. "Did you hear that, *Mrs. Edwards?* You think you're such a high and mighty Christian, better than honest men like your daddy and me. Bah!" He spat in the dusty road. "According to Fallon here, you've been acting all sweet and *available*, all the while being my wife." He donned a pious expression that made Sarah's stomach lurch. "Good thing Gus and I found you when we did. Sounds like we got here just before you up and married this Sterling in spite of already having a husband."

Gus Stoddard let out a coarse "haw haw." The delight in Red Fallon's gloating face was enough to send arrows of fear winging into Sarah's heart. Never in her life had she encountered such evil. Yet part of her wanted to shriek with laughter at Tice's hypocrisy, although the knowledge that his slick tongue could charm a den of rattlesnakes added terror to her situation. What should she do? She was no match for even one of these wicked men, let alone the three together in cahoots against her.

A heavily marked verse in Virginia Anderson's Bible flashed into Sarah's mind: *"Submit yourselves therefore to God. Resist the devil, and he will flee from you."* It was so strong it swept away some of Sarah's fear. Isaiah 54:17 quickly followed, the beloved verse Sarah had relied on in her wild flight from St. Louis to Madera: *"No weapon that is formed against thee shall prosper. . . . This is the heritage of the servants of the Lord."*

A silent prayer shot skyward. *God, I have submitted myself to You. I am Your servant. I claim Your promise, which is my heritage. I don't know how You are going to free me, but I trust that You will. Perhaps even now Matthew and the outfit are looking for me. In the meantime. . .*

Tice roughly grabbed Sarah's shoulder. "Well?" The word cracked like a rifle shot. "What have you to say for yourself?"

Red Fallon cackled. "More like a mountain lion when you get her riled." He rubbed the cheek that had worn the prints of Sarah's fingers.

Tice's eyes gleamed with anticipation. "All the better. More fun to tame her that way."

The men's suggestive laughter sent fury cascading through Sarah. She tore herself away from Tice's painful grip, opened her mouth to shrivel them with

111

words then stopped. A plan had popped into her head with the speed of a bullet. There was a far better way. She turned her back on Tice and Red. If the idea were to work, it must be through Gus. He loved money more than anything in the world. Could she play on his greed?

"I know I've caused you a lot of trouble," she told him.

Gus's mouth gaped, disclosing his stained teeth, but she rushed on.

"I can make it up to you, Gus."

Her stepfather's disbelieving snort boded no good for Sarah's plan. "You can make it up to me by marryin' Tice. You shoulda done it in the first place 'nsteada runnin' off out here."

Sarah drew herself to her full height. "Matthew Sterling is the owner of the Diamond S Ranch, the biggest spread in the valley. He's rich and the most respected man in this part of the state. If you release me, he will pay you far more than Tice will ever give you. I promise you that."

Tice bellowed with rage, but Sarah saw the telltale avarice spring to Gus's eyes. "What makes you think this rancher would do that for the likes o' you?" he said suspiciously.

"Matt will do whatever it takes to get me back." Knowledge it was true rang in every word. If it took everything Matt Sterling possessed, he would gladly give it away to free her.

Gus turned to Tice. "If he's that rich, it might not be a bad idee," he tentatively said. "You can get any woman you want, and we wouldn't have a kidnapping charge hangin' over our heads."

"Kidnapping!" Red Fallon cursed. "You didn't say anythin' about this bein' a kidnapping. Is she your wife or ain't she?"

"Sure she is," Tice lied. "Can't you tell she's just trying to work us against each other? She's having pipe dreams about Sterling. Besides, if he's all that respectable and looked up to, he's not going to pay out good money when he finds it's for another man's wife."

A surge of courage caused Sarah to say, "Don't believe him, Red. It's a wicked lie. I am not his wife, and Gus Stoddard isn't my father. He sold me to Tice to pay his gambling debts."

Her hopes of enlisting Red's aid died aborning. He raised one eyebrow and said, "I reckon I'll believe the feller what paid me for helpin' him." He held out a soiled paw and solemnly shook Tice's smooth hand then smirked at Sarah. He quickly mounted the black horse that had followed behind Matt's horse and buggy. "So long, Sarah Anderson Edwards. I'll make sure to announce yore marriage," he mockingly called as he rode back the way he had brought Sarah.

Sarah was aghast. With him went all hope for escape. Even if Gus believed Matt would pay a ransom for her, he was too weak to stand up against Tice. Once they got to Fresno, Gus and Tice would hustle her aboard the train. All would be lost. If she tried to enlist help, they would produce the forged marriage certificate and make up some plausible story about her not being well and unable to know what she was saying.

"We better get outa here," Gus muttered, peering fearfully into the rapidly falling shadows. "If Sarah ain't lyin' about Sterling, we may have a posse on our trail."

Tice shoved Sarah inside the coach, waited for Gus to climb aboard, then jumped to the driver's seat and urged the horses faster and faster through the darkening evening. The two lighted lanterns barely gave enough light to penetrate the growing gloom that hovered between sunset and the appearance of moon or stars, but Tice didn't slow the horses. He whipped them unmercifully and swore when they could run no faster.

Sarah clung to the side of the rocking coach to keep from being tossed about. Where would it all end? They rounded a sharp turn. Sarah screamed.

A deer stood in the middle of the road, transfixed by the lantern light.

The horses whinnied and reared. "Get out of the way, you—" A string of curses followed. Tice lost control of the carriage. It slammed into a boulder at the side of the road and overturned.

Sarah's last conscious thought as she was hurled from the coach was a silent cry: *This is the end, God. At least You saved me from Tice. I'm just sorry I never got to tell Matt how much I care for him.*

᷺

Earlier that day Matt and Sheriff Meade and his posse had conducted a thorough search for Sarah. It was no use. She had vanished as if spirited away by the wind. Tired and discouraged they turned back to town.

While they were riding down the street, Evan Moore rushed into the street and waved them down.

"Red Fallon's in the saloon. He's spinning a yarn about getting even with you and the tenderfoot you took in." Dread etched deep lines in the postmaster's face. "I'm afraid it might have something to do with Miss Sarah being missing."

Matt leaped from Chase. "It had better not. If Red's up to his old tricks, I'll break every bone in his body!" His long strides took him down the street ahead of the others and into the saloon with a crash of the swinging doors. "Fallon?"

"Right here." Red gave a drunken laugh and jingled a handful of money, more money than he should have on him this far from payday.

Matt collared him and bellowed, "Do you know anything about Sarah Anderson?"

Red crowed with glee. "A lot more than you do, Matthew Sterling. All this time you been sparkin' her, she's been married!" He gave a fiendish laugh and pointed an accusing finger. "I reckon that'll tie a knot in your lasso. She ain't

Miss Sarah Anderson a'tall. She's *Mrs. Tice Edwards!*"

"That's a rotten lie," Matt shouted. "Who told you such a monstrous thing?" Red burst into laughter again. "Her daddy and her husband. That's who!"

A collective gasp went up from the hangers-on in the saloon. Matt, although shocked to the core to learn Tice Edwards had found Sarah, kept a tight rein on himself. If he could string Red along, perhaps the despicable cowhand would spill his guts with more details—especially the whereabouts of Sarah and her companions. "How'd you happen to make the acquaintance of Tice Edwards?"

Drunk as much with success at finally besting Matt as by being "likkered up," Red was triumphant. "Met him an' Gus Stoddard in Fresno. Gossip had it they were tryin' to find Sarah. I told 'em for a consideration I'd help them. They were all torn up over her havin' run away from home."

Matt could barely breathe. "You helped kidnap Sarah?"

Red's face flamed, and he shook himself free from Matt's clutch. "Naw! There was no kidnapping to it! I just took Sarah to her daddy and her husband. There's a real happy endin'. Right now they're in a coach bigger than yours, on their way back to St. Louis." Red guffawed. " 'Course that cuts you out, Matt. Lady Luck ain't very good to you when it comes to love, is she? This is the second time a little ol' gal has made a fool of you!"

After getting a fuller description of the coach from Red, Matt had heard all he needed to know. *Crack*. A well-placed punch left Red sprawled on the saloon floor. Matt towered over him. "Listen, Red, and listen hard. Either you leave the valley for good, or I'm swearing out a warrant for kidnapping." He ignored Red's protest. "Sarah Anderson is not and never has been married to Tice Edwards. If she'll have me, I aim to make her my wife. Even if she were married, your waylaying her could send you to jail for a long time. Right, sheriff?" He turned to Sheriff Meade, who had arrived in time to see Red hit the floor.

"That's right," the sheriff seconded. "You've plumb wore out what little welcome you ever had in Madera. Now git up, and git before I run you in!"

Red slunk out but not before giving them both a baleful look.

❧

Now that Matt knew Gus and Tice's destination, he rode toward Fresno as if pursued by a thousand howling devils. Chase fully lived up to his name. The buckskin gelding had never run faster or more smoothly. They reached the buggy in which Sarah and Curly had driven to Madera. The horse was still in the traces. Matt freed him but didn't attempt to lead him. He would only slow Chase down. Instead Matt staked him out by a patch of nearby grass. He'd retrieve the horse and buggy after he found Sarah.

Daylight gave way to growing darkness, but there was still no sign of the girl Matt loved. He slowed Chase and gave thanks for the multitude of brilliant stars that lighted their way. Then, around a bend in the road, Matt came across a gruesome scene: an overturned coach, with the horses still in their harness. The driver sprawled across the seat. Dead. The coach fit the description he'd gotten from Red.

Matt yanked the coach door open. A battered and bleeding older man—Gus Stoddard, no doubt—fell into his arms. The coach was empty. Matt's world turned black. "Where's Sarah?" he demanded, torn between rage and a reluctant pity for the injured man.

"I don't know." Gus was incoherent. Blood flowed freely, but a quick examination showed his injuries didn't appear to be life threatening. Gus Stoddard would live to return to his family.

Matt gave a cry of despair. "Sarah, where are you?"

The silence was so profound Matt could hear his breaking heart thunder in his chest.

Chapter 21

Matthew Sterling fell to his knees beside the coach and faced his own personal Gethsemane. How could God take Sarah and let worthless Gus Stoddard live? From the looks of the overturned coach, it had been traveling at a terrible pace. He would find Sarah somewhere in the darkness, lifeless and broken. Despair descended like a woolen blanket, smothering Matt until he wondered if he would survive. He beat his fists on the ground. Guilt tormented him. He had promised Seth to protect his beloved sister—and failed. "I should have taken Sarah to Madera and let the ranch chores go hang," he cried out.

Memories rose to haunt him: Sarah as a young girl in the picture in Seth's saddlebags. Sarah miraculously transformed into the woman whose picture Matt carried just over his heart. Sarah at the Yosemite Hotel, eyes filled with gratitude for what Matt had done for her brother. Sarah on Pandora. Sarah with Seth. With Solita. With Curly, Bud, and Slim, who were outspoken in their admiration. The courageous girl repelling Red Fallon's advances. Finally Sarah teaching the Mexican children and their mothers, face alight with the joy of giving.

Matt had thought he loved her beyond description, praying she would be God's choice to complete his life. Yet those feelings were nothing compared with what he now felt—when it was too late. She had asked for time to be sure of her own feelings. He had given it to her. She must not marry him out of gratitude or the need for a protector. She must explore her heart before she wore the gold band of wifehood.

Now there was no time for Sarah to learn to love him the way he believed she had begun to do. No time to place the sparkling engagement ring that had belonged to Matt's mother on Sarah's finger—the ring he had never considered offering to Lydia Hensley. Matt groaned, the sound loud in the quiet spot. "Why, God?" The night remained still, as if holding its breath, waiting for an answer or silently mourning a life snatched away by lust and greed. A rustle of leaves came, and a low cry as soft as an angel's wing.

"Matthew? Thank God. I knew you'd come!"

Matt leaped up, snatched a lantern, and strode toward the sound of Sarah's voice. She lay in a crumpled heap in the shadows at the side of the road, dirty and disheveled. One sleeve of her blue-and-white gingham dress was torn.

A dark bruise and a trickle of dried blood on her forehead showed in the flickering light.

Matt set the lantern down and peered at her. How badly was she hurt? *Please, God, don't let her have broken her back when she was thrown from the coach.* "Can you move your legs and arms?" he asked.

"I think so." She struggled to a sitting position and smiled weakly.

Relief gushed through Matt like water through a sieve. He caught Sarah in his arms and held her against his out-of-control heart. "I thought I'd lost you!"

A dirty but sturdy hand stroked his tear-stained face. "You won't have to, Matthew. When Tice lost control of the coach, I knew I was going to die. My last thought was regret that I didn't have the chance to tell you I've come to love you with all my heart."

Too overcome with emotion to speak, Matt tenderly kissed her and thanked God.

a.

Any lingering doubts Sarah may have had about her love for Matt vanished forever with their first real kiss. She returned it with all her heart then nestled in his arms, feeling like she had come home after a long, arduous journey. "How did you find me?"

"I had a little talk with your old friend, Red Fallon."

Sarah gasped. "What did you do to him?"

"Gave him a quick punch to remember me by then told him to pack up and leave Madera or get jailed for kidnapping."

A moan brought Sarah back to the present. Filled with dread, she quavered, "Gus? Tice?"

Matt placed his hands on each side of her troubled face. "Gus isn't seriously hurt, but Tice is dead."

Sarah slumped against him, feeling she had received a stay of execution. Never again would the riverboat gambler have power over her, even false power granted by those in high places who were as unscrupulous as himself. "Was he killed instantly?"

Matt sounded reluctant to tell her when he said, "It appears Tice's neck was broken when the coach turned over."

Sarah shuddered and grasped Matt's strong hands. "The last thing I heard before Tice lost control of the carriage and it slammed into the boulder at the side of the road was him cursing the horses. Would he have had time to ask for God's mercy before he died?"

"We'll never know," Matt quietly told her. "I hated Tice, but God help the man if Tice carried his sins into eternity." Matt cleared his throat. "We need to head home. The coach is no use to us. We'll ride Chase double. Gus will have to ride one of the coach horses. When we reach the place where Red

Fallon left the horse and buggy, we'll be right as rain."

Sarah jerked her attention from Tice Edwards's fate to the present. She hadn't told Matt that every bone in her body hurt. Could she ride, even surrounded by Matt's protective arms? She had to. *"I can do all things through Christ which strengtheneth me,"* she silently quoted, trying not to limp when Matt helped her to her feet. She needn't have worried about him noticing. He stepped toward Gus, who lay moaning and cursing where Matt had left him earlier.

"Don't stand there like a blitherin' idjit, girl. Git over here and help me!" Gus barked. Another string of curses followed.

"Shut your dirty mouth, or I'll gag you and leave you here," Matt threatened. "The only reason you'll get any help is so I can turn you over to the sheriff. And you'll get no help from Sarah, ever again." He hoisted Gus to a standing position.

"I didn't do nothin' wrong," Gus whined. "Who're you, anyway, to interfere with a man and his daughter? I come all the way from St. Louis to fetch Sarah home. By all that's holy, that's what I'm gonna do." He put on an innocent air that sickened Sarah. "Tice is dead which means I ain't owin' him anything. Sarah, you've got no reason for not comin' home. Your daddy and the young'uns need lookin' after."

The relief Sarah had felt when she heard the miserable wretch was still alive changed to outrage. "Gus Stoddard, you aren't my father, and you know it! Never in this world would my mother have put you in charge of me." Contempt for the pitiful excuse of a man underscored every word. "Your trumped-up claims are more worthless than Confederate money." She paused, caught her breath, and drew herself to her full height. "This is my betrothed, Matthew Sterling. He has Sheriff Meade and half the men in Madera out looking for me."

Gus sneered. "What'd that good-for-nothin' Fallon do? Spill his guts?"

"Oh yeah," Matt told him. "Mighty proud he was of helping Sarah's 'brokenhearted daddy and fiancé' find her. You must have been mighty convincing, but you don't sway me. You'll have a snowball's chance in August of making Sheriff Meade swallow your yarn. This is the last time you'll stalk Sarah, Stoddard. Try it again, and I'll see that you get everything that's coming to you. If Edwards had lived, he'd have found out how the code of the West deals with citified dandies who bother our women."

Gus cringed, as if each word were a heavy blow to his hapless head. *How quickly he lost his false bravado when confronted by a real man,* Sarah thought.

Matt freed the horses still harnessed to the overturned coach and quickly fashioned crude hackamores from the reins. "Time to be on our way."

"I can't ride no horse bareback," Gus grumbled.

"Quit bellyaching and suit yourself. You can either ride bareback, or I'll tie you." Matt reached for the lariat coiled on Chase's saddle.

Gus glared at him, face sullen in the dim light. "No one's ropin' me to a horse." Groaning and complaining, he managed to get astride one of the coach horses and cling to the rude hackamore. He mercifully fell silent when they got to the Diamond S horse and buggy and clambered in for the ride back to Madera, which was closer than the ranch. Matt drove, leaving Chase and the other horses to tag along behind. But the moment the first lights of town became visible, Gus vaulted from the buggy and disappeared into the night.

"Shall I go after him?" Matt asked Sarah.

She sighed. The thought of Gus being in California left her shaken, but— "Let him go. He will find someone to fleece or lend him money enough to go back to Missouri. He'll spruce himself up and court some well-to-do woman who won't see through him."

Matt helped her down from the buggy. "You look all tuckered out. First we see Doc Brown then the captain. You can stay at the hotel until you feel like coming out to the ranch." A poignant light darkened his blue eyes. "Just don't make it too long."

Sarah's heart gave a little skip. "I won't. Right now all I want is food and a bed." She looked down at her filthy hands and dress. "Mercy, the captain won't want me dirtying up his nice hotel. I must look a sight."

Matt cupped her face in his hands. "If we live to be a hundred, you will never be more beautiful to me than you are right now," he said huskily.

"Dirt and all?"

"Dirt and all." A teasing look crept into his face. "A little dirt never hurt a rancher's wife."

Long after Matthew headed back to the ranch, Sarah treasured his words and hugged to herself the joy in store for her as mistress of the Diamond S.

❧

It took Sarah two days to get over her stiffness and soreness enough to leave the Yosemite Hotel. She chafed at the delay but was amazed to discover God had a reason for her to be there: her friend Abby. Along with clean clothing, Abby provided information that sent Sarah's spirits sky-high.

"When we discovered you were missing, I got the girls together," Abby said. Tears sparkled in her dark eyes. "Some of us don't know God very well, but we figured He'd listen since we were praying for you."

Sarah took Abby's hands in hers. "Your prayers were answered. If it hadn't been for God, I wouldn't be alive. Anytime you want to know Him better, all you have to do is tell Him so." Desire for her friend to experience the love and caring of their heavenly Father spilled out. "Abby, He is the only One who can save you, and you will never have a better friend. When Jesus is in your heart, it doesn't matter if others persecute you. Once you are His, nothing can harm you unless He allows it."

Longing filled Abby's sweet face. "It sounds wonderful." She sniffled. "When I found out you were missing, I thought I'd go crazy, but it's like you're at peace no matter what. Sarah, what must I do to get what you have?"

"Paul tells the Romans in chapter 10: 'If thou shalt confess with thy mouth the Lord Jesus, and shalt believe in thine heart that God hath raised him from the dead, thou shalt be saved.'"

"It sounds awfully simple."

Sarah's heart throbbed with gladness. "The way of salvation is a free gift and so simple even a child can understand. Do you want to accept Him?"

Abby nodded. A few heartbeats later a new name was written in the Book of Life.

When Sarah got back to the ranch and told Matt and Seth the good news, she added, "I didn't dream God would bring good from Tice and Gus coming out here after me. Or from Red Fallon waylaying me." She blinked back tears of joy. "If they hadn't, Abby wouldn't have accepted the Lord, at least not right now."

"Another good thing came out of it," Matt told her when they mounted Chase and Pandora and rode out together later that day. At the foot of the promontory they both loved, Matt halted Chase and took Sarah's hand. "Sarah, when will you marry me?"

She cocked her head to one side and pretended to consider. "I believe the proper length for an engagement is a year—"

"Are you really going to make me wait that long when it feels like I've been waiting for you my whole life?" Mischief danced in his eyes. "If you'd come sooner, I wouldn't have been tricked into thinking Lydia Hensley was pure gold, not just iron pyrite—*fool's gold*."

Sarah threw caution to the winds. "Senor Mateo, if you'll give Pandora and me a head start to the big oak tree and still beat us back to the ranch, I'll marry you whenever you choose!" She touched her heels to the chestnut gelding's smooth sides, and laughter floated back over her shoulder.

Matt erupted into a shout of glee worthy of an Indian on the warpath. He waited until the fleeing pair reached the oak tree then sent Chase into a full gallop. Despite Pandora's best efforts, Chase caught and passed him just before they reached the corral. Matt reined in, leaped from the saddle, caught Sarah as she slid down from the gelding, and announced to the crowd of staring, openmouthed cowboys nearby, "Don't make any plans for Christmas. We're gonna have a wedding, and you no-good, lazy cowpunchers are all invited!"

Matt threw his hat in the air and let out another war whoop, echoed by the grinning outfit. He whipped around toward Curly and pounded his shoulder. "Saddle up. I need you to ride into Madera and send a telegram to Dori. This is one Christmas on the Diamond S my sister had better not miss!"

Once upon a time, Sarah Joy Anderson had stood for the final fitting of a wedding gown she hated. Her fingers had itched to tear it off and throw it in the dressmaker's smug face. Instead she had closed her eyes and wondered what it would be like to walk up the aisle of the church in Madera and find Matthew Sterling waiting for her.

Months later Matt had unwittingly described Sarah's dream: *"Someday you're going to walk up the aisle of our Madera church on Seth's arm, all gussied up in a fluffy white dress and ready to become Mrs. Matthew Sterling."*

On Christmas Day the dream became reality. Sarah wore no fancy, pearl-beaded gown but Matt's grandmother's carefully preserved wedding dress. No veil with orange blossoms decked Sarah's hair but a gorgeous lace mantilla Solita provided. No gawkers marred the occasion. Instead a host of smiling well-wishers crowded the church. They included a lovely, dark-haired girl in an elegant blue velvet cloak. She had arrived on the westbound train and been enveloped in a joyous bear hug from her bridegroom brother.

"Ready?" Seth grinned. "You don't want to keep Matt waiting."

Sarah nudged him. "Just remember, your turn's coming." She sent a pointed glance toward Dori Sterling, seated in the front row with Solita.

Seth retaliated by whispering, "Naw. She's too Bostonish, and I'm just a poor, lonesome cowpoke." He smirked. "Get a move on, will you, before Matt changes his mind."

Sarah placed a lace-mitted hand on Seth's arm. The wonder and love in Matthew Sterling's face showed Seth's warning was foolishness. The Sierra Nevada would crumble to dust before the boss of the Diamond S would go back on Sarah Joy Anderson.

Thank You, God, for bringing us here, even though it was by long and tortuous paths. Thank You most of all for the gift of Your Son, whose birthday we celebrate this day. No matter how rough the trails ahead of us may be, we can ride them together because Jesus goes before us.

Fortified by the prayer, secure in God's and Matt's love, Sarah squeezed Seth's arm and started up the aisle. Each step brought her closer to the man in the faded photograph now pinned beneath her wedding dress—Matthew Sterling, who had lassoed her heart.

ROMANCE RIDES THE RIVER

Dedication

For Susan K. Marlow, research expert and editor extraordinaire.

A Note from the Author

Thank you for reading *Romance Rides the River*. Life on the Diamond S Ranch near Madera, California, in the 1880s fascinated me so much when I wrote *Romance Rides the Range* that I didn't want to leave. I also wanted to get better acquainted with Seth and Dori, who clamored to step back on the stage—in this case, stagecoach. *Romance Rides the River* was born.

As a tweenager, my favorite reading place was an enormous willow tree outside our home near a small logging town. Two sturdy branches crossed close to the trunk and made a seat. There I read Zane Grey's exciting book *The Border Legion*. A red bandana with the corners tied on top lay beside me. It held a comb, toothbrush, and extra socks. Should I be kidnapped like the heroine in my book, I was prepared with the same things Joan Randle had in her saddlebags when she was abducted.

Reading those exciting westerns and traveling through the western states with my family fostered dreams of someday writing books of my own, especially westerns. *Frontiers* and *Frontier Brides* [Barbour Publishing] are two of my best-selling collections.

I hope that seeing God at work in Seth's and Dori's lives reminded you how much He cares for us, especially in times of trouble. It did me!

Colleen

Chapter 1

June 1880
San Joaquin Valley, California

I'm not going to school in Madera any longer."

Dolores Sterling's personal Declaration of Independence hit the spacious kitchen of the white stucco, Spanish-style ranch house on the Diamond S cattle ranch like a burst of gunfire.

Solita, the diminutive Mexican housekeeper, dropped the tortilla she had been tossing. Dori's brother, Matt, straightened from lounging in the doorway. Storm signals flashed in his bright blue eyes, eyes the same color as his sister's. He parked his hands on his hips and glared down at her. Four inches taller than Dori's five-foot-seven height, Matt's high-heeled cowboy boots allowed him to tower even farther over her.

"You what?"

Dori gave Matt her most charming smile. "I'm going to Boston for a three-year term." She clenched her hands behind her back and tossed her head until her black curls danced. "I already wrote to the school. They are holding a place for me. All you have to do is to send the money."

Matt snorted. "I do, do I? What if I refuse?"

"Then you'll cause me to break my word. I told them I was coming." Dori ignored Solita's gasp. "It's a matter of honor, Matt."

"What's honorable about going behind my back and promising such an outlandish thing?" he raged.

If Dori hadn't known how much her brother—who had taken their father's place after he died—doted on her, she'd have been intimidated. She mumbled, "Sorry, but I figured you'd say I'm too young. I'm not. I'll be sixteen years old in a few months. You need to start treating me like a young lady, not a little girl."

Matt exploded with laughter. "You, a young lady?" He pointed at her worn riding skirt and vest. "How do you think you will stack up against those Boston blue bloods?"

Dori proudly raised her head. "I'd rather have good, red, western blood than all the blue blood in America," she retorted. "Besides, I can become just as much a lady as any sissy East Coast girl." She ignored the cynical little voice inside that challenged, *oh yeah?* and rushed on. "This is where I'm going." She held out a worn magazine advertisement extolling the virtues of Brookside Finishing School for Young Ladies in Boston, Massachusetts.

Matthew said nothing.

Dori turned to Solita. "*You* think I should go, don't you, Solita?"

The housekeeper, who had become Matt and Dori's substitute mother after the death of Rebecca Sterling many years before, waited until Matt finished reading the advertisement. Then she quietly said, "Senor Mateo, I think that Senora Sterling would be glad for her daughter to attend such a school."

"Gracias, gracias, Solita." Dori grabbed the housekeeper. She whirled her into a mad dance, blew Matt a kiss, and dashed out of the kitchen. With Solita on her side, Matt would never refuse to let her go—or would he? Not quite certain, Dori paused just outside the doorway. She knew eavesdropping was wrong, but her whole future hung in the balance.

"Our casa will seem empty, but you must release the senorita," Solita said. "She is unhappy here, like a little bird wanting to try her wings and fly. Your *mamá* and *papá* would have allowed it, had they lived. Since they are no longer with us, you must decide what is best for her, not what is best for you." She sighed. "And for me."

Dori sneaked away, knowing she had won.

☙

Once Matt reluctantly consented, the next few weeks flew by in a maze of preparations. Matt paid the exorbitant fee required by Miss Genevieve Brookings, owner and headmistress of the Brookside School. He imported a dressmaker from Fresno. If Dori was going back east, she would go in style with the proper clothing.

Unfortunately, Dori's idea of "proper clothing" did not coincide with Miss Mix's. When the prim dressmaker produced a pair of corsets, Dori rebelled. "I don't wear corsets. My brother thinks it's unhealthy for young girls to be forced into instruments of torture for the sake of fashion."

Miss Mix gasped. "You discuss ladies' undergarments with your *brother?*"

Dori reveled in the woman's horror. "Of course," she said innocently. "He's so much older than I that he helped dress me when I was a little girl."

Disapproval oozed out between the pins in Miss Mix's pinched mouth for the remainder of the dressmaking sessions, and she reminded Dori that "Pride goeth before a fall."

Dori came off triumphant by correctly quoting Proverbs 16:18: " 'Pride goeth before *destruction*, and an haughty spirit before a fall.' " When Dori's trunks were packed and ready for the long train trip, they contained both lovely and practical clothing: hats, gowns, shoes, etc.—but nary a hated corset.

☙

Dori enjoyed the train ride back east with Matt, despite being cooped up in a small space. When she grew weary of sitting in the plush seats, she strolled through the cars, wondering. Where were her fellow passengers headed? Dori smiled to herself. Surely no one else was going to the Brookside School. The knowledge made her feel superior. So did dreaming about what Madera would think of her when she finished her schooling. *I'll come home a young woman,* she realized. *The cowboys on the Diamond S will gape—but my girlhood will be left behind. Will becoming a lady mean giving up the freedom I've always enjoyed?*

Like a summer squall that attacks the unwary without warning, a new and unwelcome thought plagued Dori. She had shrugged off Matt and Solita's warnings that some of the young ladies at Brookside might look down on her. Who cared? She could hold her own against any snobbish girl. *But what if I meet and fall in love with an easterner? Someone who considers everything west of Chicago uncivilized? Could I give up my home for him?* Dori sniffed. *Lord, it was fine for Ruth in the Bible to promise she'd follow her mother-in-law wherever Naomi led, but I'm no Ruth.*

Dori squirmed in her seat. How foolish to be concerned over what might lie ahead. A scripture Solita often quoted when Dori or Matt worried about what might happen came to mind. *"Take therefore no thought for the morrow: for the morrow shall take thought for the things of itself. Sufficient unto the day is the evil thereof."*

It was enough for now that each day brought new sights—the wonder of America. Dori had never been farther from Madera than Fresno, and a visit to San Francisco several years earlier. She shivered. The tall buildings huddled together for protection against the Pacific Ocean on one side and San Francisco Bay on the other had seemed to close in on her. Dori had never seen so much water, not even when the rivers around Madera flooded. She'd sighed with relief when she and Matt left the city behind.

Dori found Chicago even more crowded and stifling than San Francisco. Changing trains swept away her feelings of superiority. Big and bustling, with people rushing to and fro in and out of the station's doors, Dori felt dwarfed by its immensity. She stayed close to Matt until her personal needs could no longer be denied. A smiling agent directed her to the proper place.

"Don't be too long," Matt warned. "Our train was late so we only have a short layover here."

"All right." Heart pounding, Dori took careful note of the way to the facility so she would know how to get back to Matt. She had no trouble reaching the room marked LADIES and hurriedly took care of her needs. She washed her hands at one of the gleaming sinks and started back toward Matt, but was caught up in a horde of people rushing in the opposite direction. All of them appeared to know exactly where they were going. Feeling like she'd been trapped in a stampede, Dori became hopelessly disoriented. She couldn't see over the tall hats many of the gentlemen wore. Was this how a salmon felt while trying to swim upstream? For the first time in her life, Dori panicked. Where was Matt? What should she do? What if they missed their train?

She swallowed hard. *Please, God, help me find my brother.*

It was the first prayer Dori had uttered in weeks, except for asking God to make Matt let her attend Brookside School. Fear threatened to suffocate her. What if God didn't answer? The crowd of pushing, shoving people swept her along. Caught in their midst, Dori screamed at the top of her lungs, "Matt! Where are you?"

Her cry for help was lost in the clamor. A train whistle shrieked a warning, summoning passengers to get on board or be left behind. The multitude reached the outside doors, Dori still in their midst. If she couldn't free herself, she would be carried onto the train with Matt left behind. Or—Dori blanched—forced onto the wrong train.

Terror changed her to a wildcat. Elbows out, Dori rammed into those around her. "Get out of my way!" she shouted. Muttered curses from those she struck rang in her ears, but she cleared a passage and fought her way to the side. She clung to a doorpost while the uncaring crowd rushed on.

The wheels of the train began to move. Dori screamed for her brother again. A heavy hand fell on her shoulder. Tears streaming, she looked up. "Matt! Thank God." Dori sagged in his arms.

Matt snatched her up and raced toward the already-moving eastbound train.

"Hurry," the conductor cried from his position at the bottom of the steps.

With a mighty leap Matt reached the bottom step and lunged up to safety. The conductor followed and raised the steps behind him.

All Dori could do was cling to her brother and cry.

⋇

The *clackety-clack* of the incoming train's wheels dwindled into silence. Brakes screeched. The engine shuddered, gasped, and died—as if glad to have reached its destination. It had been a long, hard run from Madera, California, to Boston, Massachusetts: three thousand miles of mountains and canyons, cities and small settlements, and always that monotonous *clackety-clack* of gigantic wheels carrying Dolores Sterling away from everything she knew.

"Well, we're here." Matt stepped into the aisle and stretched. "Need a hand?"

Dori shook her head, not trusting herself to speak. What she could see of Boston through the train's dirty windows depressed her. The drizzle from the weeping skies added to her misery. So did the tall buildings closing in on each side of the street and threatening to smother her.

Dori shuddered and pulled her traveling cloak closer around her trembling body. She clutched her reticule and followed Matt up the aisle and onto the station platform. Once inside the horse-drawn carriage that rumbled and swayed over the cobblestone street, she huddled in the corner of the musty-smelling vehicle, closed her eyes, and gulped back homesickness. *I can't look back.* Yet she couldn't help reliving the frightening incident in the Chicago train station.

A hard jolt flung Dori against Matt. She opened her eyes. She was no longer lost and terrified in the Chicago station. Or on the train, badly shaken and unable to tell Matt what had happened and how frightened she'd been. She was in Boston with a single, unanswerable question drumming in her brain: *Why did I plead, beg, and insist on coming east to school instead of staying home on the Diamond S where I belong?*

Chapter 2

The creaking carriage stopped in front of an ivy-covered building that jutted three stories into the scowling sky. Dori stared at the fancy sign identifying it as the BROOKSIDE FINISHING SCHOOL FOR YOUNG LADIES. Several smaller attached buildings trailed away from the main structure like the tail of a kite. This gloomy place couldn't be the academy Dori had seen advertised. Enticed by glowing descriptions of sunlight sifting through huge trees and dappling the manicured lawn, she'd dreamed about drinking lemonade there. Or—better yet—beating a bevy of well-dressed young ladies at croquet. Now the only sign of life in the sodden front yard was a pair of long, skinny legs beneath a black umbrella.

Matt paid the driver and held out his hand to assist Dori.

"Step lively, miss," the driver advised. "Looks like it's going to pour."

Stepping lively was the last thing Dori wanted to do, but Matt helped her out of the carriage and hurried her along a cobblestone walk. Before he could lift the heavy knocker, the massive doors swung open. A cadaverous-looking individual with an expression as mournful as his night-black clothing bowed. "Come in, sir, miss. I'm Scraggs. May I take your coats?"

Dori stared. This caricature of a man who looked like he'd stepped out of a Charles Dickens novel must be a butler. How Curly and Bud and Slim would howl if they could see her now. A ripple of laughter escaped.

Matt sent her a disapproving glance but Scraggs didn't even blink. He efficiently hung their wet garments on a nearby rack and said in a voice as colorless as his long face, "This way, please. Miss Brookings is in her office."

He even talks like a Dickens character, Dori thought. *If he ever smiles, I'll wager his face would crack.* She followed Matt and Scraggs down the hall that appeared longer than the main street in Madera. Their footsteps sounded loud on the marble floor and echoed from the high ceiling and cream-colored walls adorned with a frieze of smirking cupids. How different from the Diamond S ranch house and its colorful Spanish-style decor. No wonder Scraggs looked like he never smiled. Who *could* smile in this morgue watched over by those awful cupids?

When they reached a door marked OFFICE, Scraggs tapped.

"Enter."

The chill in the word sent shivers down Dori's spine.

Scraggs swung the door open and announced, "Mr. Sterling. Miss Sterling." He waited for Matt and Dori to go in, then stepped out and closed the door behind him.

Dori's heart fell like a rock with her first glimpse of Miss Genevieve Brookings, owner and headmistress of the Brookside School. Worse, Dori's besetting sin flared. Solita had warned her since childhood about the danger of relying on first impressions, but Dori continued to make them. Now, inwardly rebelling about her intolerable situation, she curtseyed when presented, then sank into a hard chair. She looked at the skeleton-thin, pale-faced headmistress with flaming red hair seated behind a huge desk and decided she detested her. Especially when the middle-aged woman in stark black silk turned to Matt, who occupied the chair next to Dori.

"*Dear* Mr. Sterling," Miss Brookings gushed, "we are *so* pleased that you chose our school for your charming sister. I am sure she will be a credit to Brookside. We cater to only the finest young ladies."

Dori's lip curled. *She should be called Babbling Brook. She runs on and on like the creeks in the Sierra Nevada.* Dori bit her lip to keep from disgracing herself by laughing.

"We *do* have a slight problem." Miss Brookings's thin hands twisted a white handkerchief. "I, however, am sure it can be worked out to everyone's satisfaction. As you know, we limit our enrollment to twenty young ladies. When we accepted Dolores, we didn't realize Gretchen van Dyke would be returning this year. She is the only child of one of our wealthiest merchants and has been with us since she was twelve. Unfortunately, the poor girl fell ill last spring and was forced to leave school. I'm happy to say she has now regained her health and is eager to return."

She bared her teeth in a travesty of a smile. "I apologize for not informing you of this earlier. By the time we realized Gretchen was returning to school, you were already on your way." She spread her hands in a helpless gesture. "We can't afford to offend dear Mr. van Dyke, now can we?"

Joy exploded in Dori like fireworks on the Fourth of July. Bless Gretchen, the merchant's daughter. Dori tingled with anticipation until she could barely sit still. Her heart raced. She felt her mouth widen into a delighted grin. Thanks to "dear Mr. van Dyke's only child," Dori Sterling could go home without losing face.

Yippee-ki-ay!

She clapped one hand over her mouth, fearing she had spoken aloud.

Matt stared at Miss Brookings. His words fell like ice pellets into the silence. "Madam, we paid your fee in good faith. This van Dyke girl will not be taking my sister's place." He stood, as if to end the conversation. "Now if you will excuse me, I have a train to catch."

Dori felt her heart break from disappointment. In a matter of seconds, she had plunged from the heights of happiness to the depths of despair. She stood, tried twice to speak, and at last got a few words out. "M–Matt," she stammered, "if the other girl really wants to come back, I. . ."

Her brother's jaw set in a way that boded no good for Miss Brookings, who had sprung from her chair and come around from behind the desk. "You are staying, Dori, or I'll see that the authorities hear of this." He took Dori's arm. "Walk me to the door."

Miss Brookings's pale eyes filled with alarm. *So she's human, after all,* Dori thought. *Or maybe afraid of what Matt might do. A lot of good that will do me. The Babbling Brook will hate me for sure if Matt makes her let me stay.*

"Please, Mr. Sterling, you misunderstand me." Miss Brookings's crumpled handkerchief fell to the carpet. "I am making an exception to accommodate your sister. Dear Gretchen is just your age, Dolores. You'll be in the same grade. But"—she shook her head—"you'll have to work hard to keep up with her. Gretchen is our finest student." She paused, then added, "I just know that you two will become bosom friends."

Dori ducked her head to hide a grin. Had the prim and proper headmistress really said *bosom* in front of Matt? Become friends with the van Dyke girl? Dori would sooner get bucked off a wild mustang. The Babbling Brook rushed on.

"The only thing is, she will have a roommate instead of occupying the private room you requested. Miss van Dyke has always occupied that particular room and—"

"And now it will be necessary for her to be assigned elsewhere," Matt cut in.

Miss Brookings looked as appalled as Dori felt. "But, *dear* Mr. Sterling, Mr. van Dyke is our strongest financial supporter."

Matt's eyes flashed. "I don't care if he is Governor John Davis Long. I paid for a private room for Dolores, and I expect her to have it." He glared at the distraught woman. "And it had better not be some cobbled-up makeshift."

"I am sure it shall be as you say." But the venomous look she gave Dori when Matt turned toward the door warned the reluctant new addition to Brookside Finishing School for Young Ladies: Dori already had an enemy.

Chapter 3

Hope for delivery from Dori's troubles fell to the marble floor when she took Matt's arm and traversed the long hall to the forbidding front doors. Ignoring Scraggs, who hovered nearby like an unwelcome wraith, Matt hugged her.

He looked troubled. "If the scene with Miss Brookings has made you feel unwelcome, there's still time to change your mind. There must be other schools, although it may be too late to get you in this term."

Matt's offer shone like a rainbow after rain. Dori hid her face against his shoulder. Every beat of her heart urged her to go home—but it was too late. She had teased to come. Matt had paid an exorbitant price for her tuition. With Miss Brookings so upset, Dori knew not one penny of the fee would be refunded.

The Sterling pride that had built the Diamond S from a small spread into one of the largest cattle ranches in the San Joaquin Valley meant Dori must stay if it killed her—*and it may,* she silently added.

Dori straightened her shoulders and summoned every ounce of the acting ability she had developed over the years to get her own way. *I must give a performance worthy of Sarah Bernhardt. A performance so convincing Matt will go home believing I'm exactly where I want to be. And I must do it without lying.* She took a deep breath, mustered a smile, and looked into her brother's face.

"Don't be silly," she said, hoping the tears that welled behind her eyes would produce a sparkle but not fall and betray her. "When have you ever known me to cut and run when there was rough water? Besides," she quickly added, "I intend to hold my own against 'dear Mr. van Dyke's daughter.'"

The relief in Matt's laugh showed Dori how well she was succeeding in her role of delighted student. He hugged her and dropped a kiss on her forehead. His blue eyes so like hers darkened. "Besides, you outrank Miss Gretchen van Dyke."

"I do?" Dori gaped at him.

"Yes, my dear sister," Matt quietly told her. "She has a wealthy merchant for a father, but you are a child of the King of heaven and earth."

Scraggs coughed.

Dori freed herself and whirled toward him. Was that actually approval she saw in his faded eyes?

135

The butler cleared his throat. "Ahem. If I may be so bold, sir, I'll be happy to look after Miss Sterling as much as my duties allow."

Remorse swept through Dori. She had unjustly categorized the butler as dour and without feelings. Now she saw kindness in his worn face—kindness that melted a bit of the ice surrounding her heart at the thought of Matt leaving without her.

Matt must have read her thoughts. He thanked Scraggs, shook his hand, then pulled Dori to him and whispered in her ear, "Remember what God told Samuel: 'The Lord seeth not as man seeth; for man looketh on the outward appearance, but the Lord looketh on the heart.' Who knows? Maybe even Miss Brookings has hidden depths." With a grin and a final hug, he stepped out into the rain, leaving Dori and the butler alone in the great hall.

"I'll have someone show you to your room," Scraggs said. "You will find a list of rules posted on the door. You need to memorize them."

A look of understanding crossed between them, making Dori feel she wasn't entirely friendless in this strange, new world.

The maid Scraggs summoned, who looked to be about Dori's age, smiled and announced, "I'm Janey." She took Dori to a corner back bedroom on the second floor. Although smaller than Dori's room at home, it was still spacious and attractively furnished. The single bed wore a damask spread that matched the draperies at two large windows. A study desk, two lamps, an ornately carved wall mirror, a comfortable-looking chair, a chest of drawers holding a porcelain bowl and water-filled pitcher, and a large wardrobe completed the ensemble.

Janey wrinkled her freckled, upturned nose. Mischief flashed in her eyes. "Miss Gretchen's going to throw a catfit when she finds out you have this room. It's the best in the school." She made a face. "Don't pay that one any mind. She's just used to having her own way." Janey began lifting gowns from Dori's trunk and hanging them in the wardrobe. "Ooh, how pretty." When she finished, she said, "You'd better change your clothes for dinner, miss." A bell chimed. "That's the first bell. The second means hurry." She gave Dori a friendly grin and vanished into the hall.

Dinner? Oh yes, eastern folk called *dinner* "lunch" and *supper* "dinner." Dori removed her traveling clothes, sponged her face and neck, and slipped into her finest gown. The rich, white silk was the epitome of elegance yet gave Dori the freedom of movement she insisted on. Miss Mix had boasted, "It's the very latest fashion. Wear it the first night, so you can make a lasting impression," she advised. "In it, you can hold your own against the finest there."

Dori caught up a gorgeous shawl Solita had made for her in Mexico's national colors: scarlet, emerald, and white. Before leaving her room, Dori paused to read the posted rules. "Ugh. There are enough rules here to choke the biggest work horse on the Diamond S." She grimaced. "God only gave the Ten Commandments. If Brookside listed all these in their advertisements, no one would ever enroll."

Among other things, Brookside young ladies were forbidden to eat in their rooms, walk beyond the school property unless accompanied by a teacher, run in the halls, or be out of their rooms after lights out. They were warned that talking, laughing, note writing, conversation by signs, eating, and leaving of seats were forbidden during study and recitation hours. Loud talking and romping were prohibited. For every perfect lesson scholars received four good marks. Two entire failures in answering or general imperfect answers incurred a forfeit mark, whatever that was.

And the young ladies must never, ever be late for meals.

"I might as well be in jail," Dori muttered. She quickly read the final rule: "The Bible is the great rule of duty for both teachers and scholars. Truth and virtue, Christian kindness and courtesy, will be the governing principle of conduct to all the members of this school."

Dori raised a disbelieving eyebrow. "Teachers and scholars? I wonder if the Babbling Brook ever reads her own rules."

A second bell sent Dori scrambling to the wall mirror for a last reassuring glance, in spite of Janey's warning that it meant hurry. The white gown and brilliant shawl set off Dori's dark curls and blue eyes to perfection. She blew the looking-glass girl a satisfied smile, sailed out her door, and lightly tripped down the stairs. She followed the sound of voices and stopped in the doorway of the large dining room. Light from two chandeliers sparkled on gleaming silver and dishes. The aroma of good food lured. Suddenly hungry and fully prepared to dazzle the Boston blue bloods with the dress Miss Mix had predicted would "make a lasting impression," Dori stepped inside.

Chapter 4

Dori entered the dining room and stopped short.

She had wanted to show the girls at Brookside Finishing School for Young Ladies that living in the West didn't mean being a barbarian. Instead, she wished she could sink through the floor.

She was the only girl in the room wearing a fancy gown.

The others wore long-sleeved gray dresses with voluminous white pinafores, identical to the school uniforms hanging in Dori's wardrobe. And the girls were staring at her with open mouths and scornful eyes.

In the pool of silence that followed Dori's grand entrance, Miss Mix's warning flashed into her mind. Pride *did* go before destruction, and mighty was the fall of Dori's haughty spirit.

"Miss Sterling, you are late," Miss Brookings snapped from her place at the head table. Triumph dripped from every word. "If you hadn't wasted time decking yourself out as if you were going to a fancy dress ball"—she cast a disparaging look at Dori's shawl—"or a costume ball, you wouldn't be tardy."

Titters ran through the room.

Humiliated but undefeated, Dori refused to take the Babbling Brook's belittling comment meekly. She quelled the roomful of giggling girls with a lightning glance, turned to the headmistress, and put on her most injured expression. "Why, Miss Brookings, I took for granted that since this is Boston, proper etiquette required me to dress for dinner. When in Rome, do as the Romans do, right?"

The headmistress's face reddened. "This is not Rome. Our young ladies only wear such garments on special occasions." She pointed to an empty chair at a nearby table where seven girls sat staring. "Take your place."

Inwardly seething, Dori obeyed. She bowed her head while Miss Brookings mumbled a boring blessing. What good was it to win the first skirmish? Dozens of hard battles lay ahead, and what chance did she have of winning the war? A quick survey of the girls around her in their regulation uniforms left Dori unimpressed. Not one looked like she had enough spunk to say boo to a goose.

After introducing themselves, the girls ignored Dori until one smirking brunette spoke up. "You're the girl who stole Gretchen van Dyke's room, aren't you?"

Dori felt hot color spring to her cheeks. "I have the room my brother paid for."

"Gretchen won't like it," Harriet sneered. "Neither will her father."

Dori resisted the temptation to blurt out that Gretchen and her father could go hang. Instead, she daintily raised one shoulder and met Harriet's unfriendly gaze head-on. "The room is mine now." She smiled sweetly. "Perhaps Miss van Dyke can room with you. If you like, I'll speak to Miss Brookings about it."

Harriet choked, gulped water from her crystal goblet, and retorted, "We'll see about that." Her eyes smoldered.

Appetite gone, Dori choked down what was put before her, but only for the sake of appearance. She'd eat dirt before letting this pack of snobs see how upset she was. When Miss Brookings dismissed them, Dori fled as if pursued by ravening wolves.

Back in the coveted room, the ivy-covered academy walls that had looked so picturesque in the advertisement closed in on Dori. She slowly removed the white dress, its charm besmirched by the unpleasant Miss Brookings and her flock of simpering sheep. She hung it at the back of the wardrobe and donned the drab uniform. It changed her from a cattle rancher's sister into one of the sheep. Dori shuddered. She, a sheep? Never—unless it were a black sheep.

Footsteps followed by low voices sounded outside Dori's door. Ears made keen from the need to be alert while riding the range, she tiptoed to the door and opened it a crack. The hall was dimly lit, but Dori recognized the girl who had questioned her at the table, huddled in a circle with two other girls.

"Just who is this Dolores Sterling, anyway?" Harriet challenged.

"She's no lady in spite of her fancy clothes and airs," a second girl said.

"That's right," the third agreed. "Look how tan she is. Ladies are known by how white their skin is." A quickly stifled giggle sounded.

"She looks Mexican to me. Besides, Dolores is a Spanish name, isn't it?" Harriet's tone was so spiteful it set Dori afire with anger. "So what is *she* doing at Brookside? My parents didn't send me here to hobnob with foreigners. And," she added, "whatever are the van Dykes going to say?"

Dori threw caution to the winds and flung the door wide open. "The van Dykes can go hang." Hands on her hips, a cauldron of hot words trembled just behind her tongue, threatening to burst out and scorch her adversaries. "I am not—" A daring thought halted her denial. She scornfully raised her head. There wasn't a drop of Spanish blood in her, but why not capitalize on her name and her ink-black hair?

"My name is Dolores Sterling. I am not a foreigner. However, you may call me the *Spanish senorita*—and the last thing I intend to do is to hobnob, as you so inelegantly put it, with either you or the van Dykes." Ignoring the collective gasp that followed her bold announcement, Dori turned on her heel and marched back into her room. She slammed the door with a resounding thud, rejoicing over the shocked faces she'd left staring at her, but also feeling guilty.

I didn't say I was Spanish, God, she said, salving her conscience. *Only that they could call me senorita. Besides, what if I were Spanish? Solita and my Mexican friends are worth far more than this bunch of East Coast ninnies. What am I doing here, anyway?*

In the days that followed, Dori asked herself the same question over and over. She hated the regimentation and ached for wide open spaces. She despised the gray dresses and white pinafores Miss Brookings's "young ladies" were forced to wear. "Life is worse than the stories Captain Perry Mace used to tell about the discipline of military life," she often told herself.

Too proud to admit defeat and go home like a frightened calf bawling for its mother, Dori decided to seek revenge. One look at Miss Used-to-Having-Her-Own-Way van Dyke, on whom Miss Brookings openly fawned, and Dori determined to oust "dear Gretchen" from first place in the academic standings. Thanks to an excellent teacher in Madera and Matt's insistence that his sister always do her best, Dori was well prepared to carry out her plan.

The first marking period established a running competition between the girls. Dori edged Gretchen into second place in every class except deportment.

"Why should I be penalized for breaking rules that make no sense?" Dori complained to Scraggs. "Why am I forbidden to climb out my window and down the ivy on starlit nights? I hate being cooped up, and I'm not hurting anyone." She scowled. "Janey overheard Gretchen—the sneak—report me. Tale bearing is far worse than what I do."

Scraggs looked sympathetic. "It is to you. . .or to me," he whispered, "but what we think doesn't count. Gossip has it that Miss Gretchen is Miss Brookings's pet student. She hasn't forgiven you for being in 'her' room, you know. I hear things." His smile made Dori wonder why she had ever considered him gloomy.

Scraggs glanced around the hall as if fearful of being overheard. "Mr. van Dyke's coffers are very well filled, you know." He patted Dori's shoulder. "Don't fret about it. I understand your. . .uh. . .pranks are winning admiration from some of the other young ladies." His posture remained as rigid as ever, but a telltale gleam in his pale eyes betrayed his approval. "Of course, Misses Brookings and van Dyke can't have that."

Dori felt a bit better until she was called on the carpet again the next day.

The Babbling Brook wore her wrinkled-prune face. "Why must you be so impertinent?" she demanded. "Miss Allison says you openly challenged her authority."

Dori's lips tightened. "Anyone who states that 'the wild West is filled with uncouth persons and is not a fit place to live' needs challenging. Besides, I only quoted Exodus 20:16: 'Thou shalt not bear false witness against thy neighbour.' I could have said that westerners are at least polite enough to keep quiet about people and places they have never seen and know absolutely nothing about."

The woman's face turned purple. "What do you mean?"

Dori clenched her hands into fists. "Yesterday Miss Allison said I was fortunate to have escaped the Indian massacres by coming here. I had to set her straight. It's been years since any California Indians went on the warpath."

The headmistress made a strangling sound and waved toward the door. "You may go, but if you feel the need to correct an instructor from now on, do it privately and respectfully."

"I *was* respectful." Resentment shot through Dori. "I thought Brookside Finishing School for Young Ladies wanted its students to know the truth, not lies. It says so right in our list of rules. 'The Bible is the great rule of duty for both teachers and scholars. Truth and virtue, Christian kindness and courtesy will be the governing principle of conduct to all the members of this school.' Am I wrong? Or don't the teachers practice what the rule preaches?"

"Go!" Miss Brookings thundered.

Dori flounced out—and received another failing mark in deportment.

Chapter 5

An unexpected holiday offered Dori temporary respite from her troubles. Filled with anticipation instead of dread, she bounded out of bed on the Friday set aside to honor the settling of Boston: September 17, 1880, the city's 250th birthday celebration.

Dori had written to Matt as little as possible, for fear he would know how miserable she was. How could she tell him her only real friends were the butler and a maid?

"Scraggs doesn't dare show he likes me for fear of losing his position. Janey works so hard she seldom has time for fun," Dori lamented. "Well, now at least I'll have something interesting to write about. It's too bad Matt can't be here. He'd like it, I know." A pang went through her, but she shook off regret and determined to make the most of the holiday.

Dori had never seen such a spectacle. Chaperoned by teachers and forced to remain with the other girls, she stared open-mouthed as 14,500 people marched four and a half miles, amidst a multitude of decorations. The march took three and a half hours. Several of the Brookside young ladies grew tired and went back to the school, but Dori couldn't bear to miss anything. Fortunately, one of the teachers displayed equal enthusiasm, and Miss Brookings allowed Dori to remain in her charge.

That evening sixteen floats and a thousand torchbearers paraded, illuminating the streets of the city. Dori fell asleep with a happy heart for the first time since she had arrived in Boston. The next day she wrote to Matt and Solita:

I saw Mayor Frederick O. Prince. He had requested citizens to close their stores and places of business in honor of the anniversary. At a gathering at the Old South Meeting House, he stated, "The sea has been converted into land; the hills have been leveled—the valleys filled up, the sites of the Indian wigwams are now those of the palaces of our merchant princes." I suppose the van Dykes occupy one of those palaces.

It made me sad for the Indians who once lived here. . . .

By the grace of God and sheer willpower, Dori stayed in school. As time passed, she noticed that her independent attitude was winning grudging respect. Her teachers seldom challenged her. Some of her more daring classmates showed signs of having backbone and standing up to queen bee Gretchen van Dyke. A few tentatively offered friendship. Dori suspected this enraged Miss Brookings, but she also knew Matt continued to send generous contributions to offset his sister's shenanigans. Why worry? Nothing she did hurt anyone or anything—except her deportment mark.

Dori got a great deal of secret amusement from observing how Gretchen ignored her. Gretchen and her hangers-on swept by the "Spanish senorita" as if Dori didn't exist. But after she bested Gretchen for still another marking period, Gretchen accosted her in the upper hall, backed up by Harriet and a few other girls.

"I've had as much as I am going to take from you, Dolores Sterling," she spat out. Her pale eyebrows arched over her washed-out blue eyes until she resembled an angry cat with its back up. "You think you're so smart. Well, you aren't. The only way you could ever get better marks than I is by cheating."

The unfair accusation left Dori speechless, but only for a moment. Rage started at her toes and engulfed her body. She clenched her fists and took a menacing step closer to her accuser. "I have never cheated in my whole life, Miss van Dyke. I don't have to cheat to be first in my studies with you as competition." She stopped for breath then added, "Stop your whining."

Gretchen fell back, face paper white. "Miss Brookings will hear about your impertinence."

"I'm sure she will." Dori spun on one heel, pushed open the door to her room, and whirled back toward the group of cowering young ladies. "Just be sure when you run bleating to Miss Brookings that you tell her who started this. If you don't, I will." She shriveled the other girls with a lightning glance. "There must be a least *one* person here who won't lie for you." She entered her room and slammed the door behind her.

To Dori's amazement, Miss Brookings said nothing about the confrontation. Had Gretchen's followers convinced her it wouldn't be wise to report it? Perhaps. But the ill-concealed enmity in Gretchen's face showed she was lying in wait like a cougar stalking a fawn, ready to strike when the opportunity arose.

In late November, Dori made the hardest decision of her life, so startling she felt it necessary to justify it to Matt, to herself, and to God.

"If I go home for the holidays or for summer vacations, I will never come back. I won't be able to tear myself away from home," she told the Lord. "The only way to finish what I started is to stay put."

She agonized over what to say in her letter, but finally settled on writing:

Once I return home, I won't be back, so I should see everything I can while I'm here. There will be other girls staying as well. Scraggs says it isn't so bad.

The teachers who remain during school breaks get up excursions for those of us who don't go home. Not just in Boston, but to other cities, as well— perhaps Philadelphia or New York. Maybe even to Washington. I know you will be disappointed. So am I, but the best thing is for me to stay.

Love to everyone,
Dori

Dori was forced to copy her letter three times. If Matt saw a tear-splotched edition, he would order her home posthaste.

Dori remained adamant in her decision, in spite of Matt's continued protests. She dug in her heels and made it through two seemingly endless years, hating the freezing winters and longing for Madera's mild climate.

Propped up in bed one late fall day in 1882, she mused, "I can last one more school year. After spring term, I'll leave Boston to Miss Brookings and the van Dykes and their ilk." A familiar feeling of jealousy that had been nagging her for months dimmed her expectations for going home. Dori sighed. "I don't feel I've changed, but things won't be the same on the Diamond S."

She punched her pillows into a more comfortable position. "It's bad enough that for the past two years Matt's letters have been filled with praise for that. . .that Seth Anderson. Matt acts like the dumb cowhand is a long-lost brother and not simply hired help." She blew out a breath. "I suppose it's because Matt saved his life." Dori slid out of bed and crossed to the window. "Worse, now Matt's crazy about Seth's sister. According to his letters, Sarah is one in a million and 'a paragon of virtue.' "

Dori viciously dug the toe of her slipper into the carpet. "I want Matt to myself when I get home, not dancing attendance on some girl who sounds too good to be true." She raised her gaze to the ceiling. "Of course I'm sorry for what Sarah's stepfather put her through, God, but what if she's after Matt because he owns the largest spread in the valley? What if she breaks his heart the way Lydia Hensley did?"

Dori chilled. Had she made a terrible mistake by staying in Boston so long? Had Matt turned to the Andersons for the companionship he and Dori used to share?

She knelt beside the window and bowed her head. "I need to know what to do, God. Should I chuck school and go home?" The idea caught fire until she was ready to pack her clothes and take the first train west. "Lord, if I were home, I could halt any schemes Seth and Sarah Anderson may have to worm themselves into Matt's life and the Diamond S."

Chapter 6

Seth Anderson stamped into the living room of the Diamond S ranch house. "Here's the mail, Boss. Curly just got back from Madera." He tossed the bundle to Matt, who was sprawled in a comfortable chair, staring at Seth's sister, Sarah. Light from the blazing logs in the fireplace turned her hair to glistening gold and brought the colors of the gorgeous Mexican wall tapestries alive.

Seth hunkered down in front of the huge rock fireplace and grinned. *Looks like one of these days I'm gonna have me a brother-in-law.* He glanced at their beloved housekeeper, who gave him a knowing smile. *I bet Solita thinks the same thing.*

"Thanks, Seth." Matt riffled through the mail and looked disappointed. "Nothing from Dori." He frowned. "Another letter from the Brookside head-mistress though. Wonder what my dear sister has been up to this time? And how much it's going to cost me to keep her in school."

Seth set his lips in a straight line and fought the irritation any mention of Dolores Sterling always generated. The girl had left for some high-falutin' school back east two years earlier—shortly before Matt saved Seth's life and brought him to the ranch. In Seth's opinion, Matt's sister was a spoiled brat and one of the few things that kept life on the Diamond S from being near perfect.

He sent a fleeting look at the large picture that adorned the mantel of the hacienda-style ranch house. How could such an innocent-looking girl be so devilish and cause a grand fellow like Matt endless trouble?

Seth's heart swelled with indignation. Dori seldom wrote and refused to come home from her precious school for vacations and holidays. Yet the picture of the feminine replica of dark-haired Matt held a certain fascination. "Sure not like what happened with Matt and Sarah," Seth muttered under cover of poking the fireplace logs until they crackled and blazed.

His annoyance vanished. He had "innocently" supplied Matt and Sarah photographs of each other in a clumsy attempt at matchmaking. The photographs had done their work well. Attraction sprang up between his sister and his boss before they ever met. Seth grinned. The chance of him doing likewise and falling in love with Dori's picture was the most ridiculous thing he could imagine.

Matt slapped his leg and howled with mirth.

It stopped Seth's woolgathering. "What's so funny?"

"Dori." Matt whooped again. "She's done it this time. I know I should be furious, but it's just too—" He broke into gales of laughter. "Listen to this." He wiped away tears and began to read. " 'Dear Mr. Sterling, it gives me no pleasure to be the bearer of bad news yet again, but something must be done about your sister. I realize how important it is to you for Dolores to remain at Brookside, and I have bent over backward to accommodate you.' " Matt stopped reading and snorted. "Hogwash. Any bending over backward is because of my money."

❧

Seth silently agreed but kept his own counsel. He didn't dare look at Sarah for fear she'd discern what he was thinking. She'd warned Seth never to let Matt know how he felt about Dolores. "In many ways," she reminded him on many occasions, "Matt looks at you as a replacement for his dead brother, Robbie. He would be heartbroken to know your feelings about his sister are less than charitable."

Seth ducked his head and stared at the floor, torn between loyalty to his boss and the unholy desire to give Dori Sterling the tongue-lashing he felt she richly deserved.

"Go on, Senor Mateo," Solita urged, hands clasped tightly.

❧

" 'Mr. Sterling, I regret to inform you that Dolores's recent behavior is unacceptable and brings dishonor to the name of my fine establishment. It pains me to relate such an unseemly matter, but I feel I must. One of my young ladies, Gretchen van Dyke, has shown true Christian charity regarding the change of rooms. Your sister, however, continues to spitefully plague and belittle dear Gretchen and undermine her leadership among the other girls.' "

Seth chuckled. The headmistress sounded like someone out of a dime novel, with her fine airs and pompous "regrets" about criticizing Dori. It looked to Seth like Dori and Gretchen were cut from the same cloth and deserved each other. But he kept his opinion to himself.

Matt raised a skeptical eyebrow. "I'll eat my Stetson if Gretchen van Dyke ever showed Christian charity, especially to Dori." He continued reading. " 'I have been patient, but your sister's latest indignity toward Gretchen cannot be brushed aside. Dear Gretchen found a little black cat mewing outside in the rain. Too kind to leave it there, she begged to be allowed to keep it, even though pets are normally forbidden. I didn't have the heart to say no, so I reluctantly agreed. I also explained to the other girls that kindness to animals is akin to biblical teachings about treating with compassion those less fortunate.'

" 'Dolores had the audacity to remind me of my reprimand when she fed a stray dog, which of course, is not the same thing at all.' "

❧

Seth felt an unexpected twinge of pity for Dori. It didn't lessen his annoyance with her for treating Matt shabbily, but anyone who fed a stray dog couldn't be all bad. "What a hypocrite Miss Brookings is," he burst out. "No wonder Dori plays tricks."

"She certainly did this time. It looks like Dori sneaked into 'dear Gretchen's' room, swiped the cat, and"—Matt chortled— "wait till you hear what happened next: 'Several of the girls and teachers were gathered in the drawing room for a musicale. Gretchen was at the piano. The door opened. A ghastly-looking beast darted in, closely followed by Dolores.'

" 'Some of the girls screamed. Then your sister said, "What is that?" She pointed to the creature, and a look of horror crossed her face. She frightened everyone with her next words. "Oh Miss Brookings, I do hope it isn't a hydrophobic skunk. We have them out west. Sometimes skunks go mad. If they bite people, the people also go mad...and die." ' "

❧

This was too much for Seth. He rolled on the floor and cackled. Blessed with a vivid imagination, he could picture the scene: Miss Brookings, an assembly of people, and an unrepentant Dori. The others joined in, but at last Matt controlled himself and went on. " 'Dear Gretchen swooned, striking her head on the piano. The other girls leaped onto the furniture.'

" 'Fortunately, Scraggs heard the commotion and came to the rescue. He bravely picked up the beast and discovered it was dear Gretchen's cat. Someone had painted a white stripe down its back. All evidence pointed to Dolores as the instigator of this cruel deception.'

" 'She confessed immediately and showed not the slightest remorse for her actions. Needless to say, Dolores is confined to her room except for meals and classes.' "

❧

Matt tossed the letter into the fire. "What does Miss Brookings expect me to do about this?" He sighed. "I suppose another bank draft will help the woman simmer down. It always does." He looked shamefaced. "I can't wait to tell the hands—and Brett, too. My foreman is as guilty of spoiling Dori as I am, and this is too good to keep to ourselves. They'll all get a chuckle over it."

Solita leaned forward, face earnest. "It is like Senorita Dolores to play tricks, especially on those who are unkind to her."

"If you remember, she wanted to go," Matt said. "Nothing is keeping her there."

Solita shook her head. "Her pride, Senor Mateo."

"Maybe I should relieve Miss Brookings of her burden and bring Dori home."

"No!"

Seth couldn't believe he'd blurted it out. What business was it of his what the boss did with his rebellious sister?

Before he could answer, Sarah spoke for the first time. "I agree with Seth. Evidently Dori has determined to finish her course. She must be allowed to do so."

Solita nodded. "Sí. This year will pass, and Dolores will come home to our casa." Her deep brown eyes glistened. "We shall laugh and sing and give thanks to Dios."

The depths of love reflected in Solita's face stirred Seth. Why couldn't Dori see what she was doing to those who loved her? She was eighteen now, the same age Sarah had been when she fled St. Louis to avoid being sold in marriage to a riverboat gambler. Far too old to be playing childish tricks.

The girls were so different. Both had spunk, but Sarah's faith in God kept her in check. Everything Seth knew about Dori indicated she was a raging, out-of-control river. According to the hands, she ruled the ranch with a rod of charm.

She won't rule me. I'll keep as far away from her as possible, Seth decided. He sobered. Once the bothersome girl came home, nothing on the Diamond S would ever be the same.

Chapter 7

Three thousand miles from Madera, trouble blew in from across the Atlantic. It started when the Babbling Brook, more atwitter than usual, announced, "I have the most wonderful news." For once color tinted her pale face, and a sparkle glimmered in her eyes. "Stancel Worthington III is coming to Brookside from London. Dear Stancel is my very own nephew, but he has always been more like my son. He will teach dancing."

A pleased smile crept over her face at the murmur of interest among the girls. It broadened when Gretchen van Dyke trilled, "Oh Miss Brookings, how exciting!"

Dori's lip curled. How could anyone get excited over one of the Babbling Brook's relatives, especially one named Stancel Worthington III? *Wonder if anyone ever calls him Mr. Third,* she thought. *He is probably as stuffy as his name.*

Stuffy didn't begin to describe the new dancing master. The day he arrived, Dori had just checked the upper hall to make sure she was alone, then taken a glorious slide down the banister rail. She crashed into Stancel at full speed. If the huge front doors had been open, she would have knocked him out of them.

He lurched back, yet all he said when she landed in a heap on the marble floor was, "Upon my word, what have we here?"

Dori gawked at the man struggling to regain his footing. For once, she didn't speak. She dared not. One hand flew to her open mouth to keep from laughing. She knew she looked ridiculous sprawled on the floor, but not nearly as absurd as Miss Brookings's newly arrived nephew.

Tall and meticulously dressed in the latest men's fashion, "dear Stancel" could have hung a lantern on his aristocratic, hooked nose. Neatly combed black hair—each strand in place—peeked out from beneath a bowler hat. He seemed at a loss but quickly regained his composure and offered Dori a flabby, pasty hand. "I say, miss, that was quite a—"

"Sorry," Dori interrupted, scrambling to her feet. She ignored his outstretched hand and fled back up the stairs two at a time. Once in her room, she threw herself on the bed and released her bottled-up laughter. "Judged against the men and boys back home, he makes a mighty poor showing." She wiped away tears of amusement. Then a new thought suffocated her laughter. "This. . .this. . .insipid Englishman is my dancing teacher?" Dori groaned.

The thought of Mr. Worthington's pale hand taking hers in a dance was repugnant.

Dori had dreaded the class, but Stancel's presence made it pure torment. Give her a good, old-fashioned barn dance any day, not the mincing steps and low curtseys Mr. Worthington insisted the girls learn. She avoided him as much as possible and secretly rejoiced when he paid Gretchen marked attentions, to the obvious delight of Miss Brookings.

Alas for Dori! Her indifference evidently pricked Stancel's pride. He began ignoring Gretchen and choosing Dori for a partner. Stumbling and stepping on his feet did no good. The more she attempted to escape the dancing master's unwelcome attentions, the more persistent he grew. In addition, what little civility existed between Dori and "dear Gretchen" suffered a total collapse.

Things came to a head in early December, a few days after Matt summoned his sister home for his and Sarah's wedding. He wrote:

> When that scoundrel Red Fallon conspired with Sarah's stepfather and kidnapped her, I knew she might be lost to me forever. I vowed then and there that if God would help me find and save her, I'd marry Sarah as soon as she'd set a date.

It wasn't a surprise, but Dori still felt she'd been hit by a train. She'd long since given up the idea of rushing home to save Matt from the Andersons. But in spite of sympathy for Sarah, the thought that never again would Matt be all hers—as he had been since their father, mother, and Robbie died—hurt intolerably.

She looked out the window into a cheerless day, her spirits at their lowest ebb. "Maybe it won't be so hard coming back to school in January after all," she whispered. "Sarah might not want me at the ranch, even though her own precious brother, Seth, is more than welcome."

Torn by emotion, she was in no mood for a confrontation with Gretchen van Dyke. When the fiery-eyed girl burst into Dori's room and slammed the door behind her, Dori demanded, "Don't you have manners enough to knock?"

Gretchen's face mottled. "I know what you are up to."

Dori had never seen Gretchen so distraught. "Anything I may be up to doesn't concern you."

"Indeed it does." Gretchen raved. "Stancel Worthington is mine, do you hear?"

"Lower your voice or half of Boston will hear you," Dori retorted. "I have no interest whatsoever in your property, if that's what he is."

"Rubbish! Miss Brookings told me Stancel is determined to turn the Spanish senorita into a lady, and marry her. Miss Brookings is outraged—and so am I," she sputtered.

Dori sprang to her feet. She clenched her hands until the nails bit into her palms. "Not half as outraged as I am. You think I'd marry that English codfish? Never!"

Before Gretchen could answer, someone knocked at the door. "Miss Dolores?"

"Come in, Janey."

The maid opened the door and stepped inside. Every freckle stood out on her frightened face. "Miss Brookings says you are to come to her office immediately."

"Thank you, Janey." Dori waited until the girl scuttled away, then rounded on Gretchen. "Now get out of my room or you'll be sorry."

Gretchen smirked. "You're the one who is going to be sorry. Miss Brookings will surely put you in your place once and for all." She flounced out.

Now what? Dori wondered. She had kept out of Miss Brookings's way since the cat incident, and only a short time remained until she would go home for the wedding. How ironic for fate to ambush her just after she had schooled herself to come back for the spring term.

Miss Brookings sat behind her desk; her nephew lounged in a chair beside her. One look told Dori that the headmistress was loaded for bear and ready to fire.

"Of all the shameless hussies, you are the worst, Dolores Sterling. Coquetting with dear Stancel, leading him on, and brazenly attempting to weasel your way into society by underhanded means. Let me tell you this, young woman. Stancel will marry you only over my dead body."

"I say. It's not very cricket for you to disapprove before I have declared my intentions," Stancel protested.

Dori's heart slammed against her chest. She glared at her accuser and discharged both barrels of her fury. "What makes you think I would even consider being courted by a skim-milk specimen like Stancel?" she blazed. "God willing, if or when I marry, it will be to someone who is pure cream, not a whey-faced sissy like your nephew."

"Get out," the headmistress demanded. "Pack your clothes. You will leave immediately. Go—and never darken the door of Brookside Finishing School for Young Ladies again."

"You couldn't pay me to stay after this," Dori said scornfully. "I can't wait to tell my brother how I have been insulted. As for you"—she rounded on Stancel, who was gaping like a fish out of water—"if you were in Madera, the Diamond S hands would make quick work of you." Dori sailed out the open door, leaving stone-cold silence behind her. But before she turned a corner, she heard Stancel say, "Jove, but she's magnificent. It makes a man want to—"

Dori neither heard nor cared what Stancel Worthington III wanted to do.

151

All she wanted to do was to shake the dust of Brookside Finishing School for Young Ladies from her shoes and take the first train west.

Dori's outrage and humiliation sustained her through her final hours in Boston. If it hadn't been for Janey, Dori's clothing would have reached Madera in sad condition.

"Let me help you," the little maid pleaded when Dori began tossing dresses helter-skelter into her trunks. Her eyes twinkled as she pointed to a stack of uniforms. "You'll not be wanting these, I suspect."

Dori glared at the garments that represented the mountain of indignities she had suffered for two years. "Keep the pinafores if you like, but tear up those ugly gray dresses and use them to scrub the floors." Dori thought for a moment. She would soon be gone, but why not fire a parting shot? One that would echo through the halls and ensure she would not soon be forgotten. Her heart raced with anticipation. "I have a better idea," she gleefully told Janey.

The maid cocked her head. "What are you up to, miss?"

"Deliver the dresses to Gretchen van Dyke when I'm gone." Dori seized writing materials, quickly scribbled a note, and read it aloud. "What do you think of this? 'Gretchen, the Bible says to do good to them that hate you. And to pray for them which despitefully use you and persecute you. You can have *my room* and my castoff uniforms. You can also have Stancel, if you aren't too proud to take a man I don't want any more than I want these secondhand uniforms. The Spanish senorita.'"

&

Janey went into a fit of giggles. "Miss Gretchen will have an attack of the vapors," she predicted. "But oh, what a perfect way for you to have the last word."

Dori exploded with delight and felt suddenly lighthearted. Miss Brookings's untrue accusations still rankled, but knowing she had again bested "dear Gretchen" had released some of Dori's anger and humiliation.

The girls barely finished packing before a tap came at the door. "The carriage is here to take you to the station, Miss Dolores," Scraggs called. "And the men to carry your trunks down."

A rush of thankfulness for the butler's surreptitious friendship filled Dori. She flung the door open and threw her arms around his stiff, unbending frame. "I'm going to miss you," she told him. "You and Janey."

He coughed and smiled down at her, correct as ever but with warmth in his eyes. "And I, you, Miss Dori. I fear there will be no more incidents to liven up this rather staid place." His droll observation sent the two girls into peals of laughter, but he quickly shushed them. Then he led the way downstairs and into a day as gray and gloomy as the one on which Dori had arrived.

Her final glimpse of the prison of her own making was of Scraggs and Janey waving to her from outside the forbidding doors.

Chapter 8

*C*lackety-clack. *Clackety-clack.* Each turn of the westbound train's wheels took Dori farther away from the scene of her disgrace and closer to the Diamond S. Exhilaration over getting in the final lick at Gretchen van Dyke kept her spirits high. When the train reached the outskirts of Boston, Dori studied the last of the tall buildings that had threatened to squeeze the life out of her.

"Good riddance to bad rubbish," she exulted. Yet niggling unease set in. Every incident had consequences. Was being expelled when she was innocent retribution for all the times she'd been guilty? Because of Matt's forbearance, she'd never paid a high price for her previous escapades.

Dori scooted down in her seat. "What is Matt going to say about this fiasco?" she whispered. "He will be furious with Stancel, but he's bound to be disappointed in me. He spent all that money, and now I won't even graduate." Shame scorched her, and her thoughts rushed on. *If I hadn't broken rules and made Miss Brookings hate me, she wouldn't have accused me of trying to ensnare her pompous nephew.*

Righteous indignation temporarily killed Dori's self-chastisement. No red-blooded American girl would want milk-and-water Stancel Worthington III, at least none she knew. Too bad he didn't come out west and meet some real men. Curly, Bud, Slim—even Red Fallon, rotten as he was—made "dear Stancel" look sick. And if what Matt said about Seth Anderson were true, the young cowboy would cast a mighty tall shadow over the insufferable Englishman. Anger gave way to mirth. Dori could just imagine Stancel's reaction to being compared with a bunch of cowboys, let alone kidnapper and scourge of the range Red Fallon.

An outrageous plan gripped her unrepentant mind. "Why don't I get even with Miss Brookings by inviting her precious nephew to visit the ranch? Boy, would he get his comeuppance." She snickered and felt excitement mount. "The Diamond S outfit would laugh his high-and-mightiness off the range." Dori sighed and reluctantly dismissed the idea. Stancel's parting words— "I say, but she's magnificent. It makes a man want to. . ."—had sent warning chills up and down her spine. The farther she stayed away from Stancel Worthington III, the better.

As the train chugged its way west, depression set in. The thought of having to tell Matt hung over Dori and troubled her conscience. "Just like the sword of Damocles," she muttered.

"Pardon me, miss, do you need something?"

She turned from the window and gazed into the face peering down at her. "No. I was just mumbling to myself."

"You said something about a sword?" the conductor asked.

She nodded. "Yes, the sword of Damocles."

An interested gleam crept into his gray eyes. "Begging your pardon, but what might that be?"

"A story from my history book. Damocles was a member of the court of Dionysius II, who ruled in Sicily before the birth of Christ. The Roman orator Cicero said Damocles was a flatterer, forever talking about Dionysius's happiness and good fortune. To teach him a lesson, Dionysius gave a great feast. He dangled a sword over Damocles' head. It was suspended by a single hair."

The conductor's eyebrows shot up. "Did it ever fall?"

"History or legend doesn't say." Dori burned with anger. "But it just fell on me."

The conductor patted her gloved hand. "It can't be that bad."

Dori gulped. "It's worse. I just got fired, I mean expelled, from Brookside Finishing School for Young Ladies. It wasn't even my fault."

A wise expression creased the conductor's face. "Oh, that place. Rumor has it the headmistress is a tartar. I reckon you aren't the first and won't be the last to cross swords with her." He smiled. "Cheer up, miss, and look out there." He pointed to the window. "My old mother always said things didn't seem so bad when the sun was shining. The rain's letting up now, so 'twon't surprise me if we see a rainbow." He touched his cap and moved down the aisle.

Dori took heart from the conductor's comments. . .and from the glorious rainbow that split the sky. "Thank You, God," she whispered. She watched until creeping dusk swallowed the last shimmering remnants of the rainbow before stirring herself to go to the dining car for a long-delayed supper.

Whenever the conductor could spare a moment from his duties, he hovered over Dori like a mama cat over her kittens. He expressed indignation when she told him of Stancel's intentions and Miss Brookings's allegations. He also chortled about Dori's final message to "dear Gretchen." Although he looked nothing like Scraggs, Dori appreciated the same kindly concern the butler had shown her.

Before they reached Chicago, Dori confessed her previous experience in the train station. Fear surged up inside her and dried her mouth. "I'm just afraid it might happen again," she confided to the conductor. "It was all so confusing with people pushing and shoving me. This time I don't have Matt to rescue me."

"Don't you be fretting, miss. I'll see to it that you don't get left behind," her new friend promised. He kept his word, both in Chicago and at the other stops along the way. But after they reached Denver and were well into the snow-clogged mountains, an anxious look replaced his usual caring expression. "When did you say your brother's wedding was to take place?"

Dori felt wings of apprehension brush against her nerves. "On Christmas Day. Why?"

He shook his head. "It doesn't look good. We just got word that avalanches ahead are causing delays." Worry lines creased his forehead. "We may have to turn back."

"We can't go back," Dori protested, appalled by the idea. "If I'm not there for Matt's wedding, he will never forgive me." *Even though you know in your heart it's the last place you want to be,* a little voice mocked.

"Surely they will postpone it. They know you're coming, don't they?"

Dori clasped her gloved hands. "Yes, but not which train I'm on. I was in such a hurry when I left Boston, I forgot to send a telegram."

"That's actually good," the conductor comforted. "If they don't know you're on this particular train, they won't be concerned about you." He scratched his head. "The only thing is, wouldn't the headmistress inform them?"

Hope died. "Probably. Although"—Dori brightened—"under the uh. . . unusual circumstances, the Babbling Brook may have decided to keep mum. She couldn't very well tell my brother I was sent home for refusing 'dear Stancel's' unwelcome advances."

The conductor chuckled. But he wasn't chuckling a few miles up the track. The screaming of brakes followed by a rumble and a roar brought Dori out of a sound sleep. Dazed and only half awake, she landed in the aisle amidst screams from other similarly afflicted passengers. She scrambled up, rubbed an aching elbow, and grabbed the arm of the porter, who was helping people to their feet. "What's happening?"

"Avalanche." His mouth set in a grim line. "Thank God we were traveling up instead of down. If we'd hit that pile of snow at full speed, we'd all be goners." He freed himself from Dori's frantic clutch and hurried on to assist others.

Dori's heart sank. How long would it take to get tracks cleared so they could go on? She pressed her nose to the window but saw nothing except swirling white. It made her feel even colder than during the last two winters in Boston. The door of the car burst open. A blast of freezing air rushed in. Dori shivered and huddled deeper into the blue velvet cloak she had purchased shortly after reaching Boston and discovering how miserable their winters could be. Yet in spite of its warm lining and the glowing fire in the box at the end of the car, she still felt chilly.

It seemed like hours before the conductor appeared. When he did, Dori

155

could see in his concerned face the news was not good.

"A huge mass of snow came down on the tracks," he told the passengers. A murmur arose, but he raised his hand. "Help is on the way, but we don't know how long it will take for them to get here and dig us out."

"Then take us back to Denver," a high-pitched, hysterical voice ordered. Others joined in, muttering complaints against the railroad, the weather, and the conductor.

Dori felt like jumping up and ordering them to be quiet, but decided prudence was more desirable than defending her new friend.

He blew out a great breath. "I'm sorry to say it won't be possible to go back. There's also been an avalanche between here and Denver."

"You mean we're trapped! We're all going to die! Why did I ever leave home?" the speaker shouted above the clamor that arose. Dori remained silent while the conductor attempted to calm the passengers' fears, but her heart echoed the frantic cry: *Why did I ever leave home?*

"Well, Lord," she prayed under cover of the furor. "There's no use crying over spilt milk, even though the cowcatcher is evidently stuck against a mountain of snow." She shivered again and sent the beleaguered conductor what she hoped was a comforting smile. How anyone could blame him for an act of God was beyond her.

"If you'll give me a shovel, I'll help dig," she told him. He just laughed and shook his head before going on to the next car.

The train remained snowbound all night. Unable to fall asleep again, Dori had ample time to consider her precarious position. She might miss the wedding, but unless help came, she and others could lose their lives. The conductor had reported that a work train was being sent to them from the next station, but how long would it take to get there? What if other avalanches came? They could be buried alive.

Dori's fear of being confined in small spaces rose to haunt her. She paced the aisle when it was clear, silently asking God to deliver them. She also reached a decision. *Even if I reach Madera in time for the wedding, I won't let anyone at the Diamond S know I've been expelled. There will be time enough when Matt and Sarah return from their San Francisco honeymoon for them to learn I won't be going back.*

Dori groaned. Although she vowed not to spoil Matt's special day, the secret hanging over her was almost more than she could bear. She refused to consider what she'd do if Sarah disliked her and didn't want her on the ranch. Right now, surviving the avalanche was the most important thing in Dori's world.

Late the next morning, the beaming conductor appeared, "Good news, folks. The work train is here, and it looks like we will be on our way in a few hours." Loud cheers resounded through the train.

Most of the passengers let out whoops of joy. But a few well-dressed men continued to complain. They threatened to write to the railroad company, their congressmen, and even President Chester A. Arthur about the "inexcusable inconvenience and suffering" caused by the delay.

Dori had had enough. She leaped to her feet and faced the grumblers, feeling hot blood rush to her face. Scorn dripped from her unruly tongue. "I didn't hear any of you offering to lend a hand."

"Did you?" a portly man who looked like he'd never done a day's hard work barked.

"She sure did." A wide grin spread over the conductor's seamed face. "As soon as this spunky young lady knew about our predicament, she volunteered to help dig us out if I'd give her a shovel."

Laughter echoed throughout the car. The man who had challenged Dori subsided, and peace was restored.

Once the train was free to go on its way, there were no more delays. After what felt like an eternity, the *clackety-clack* of the great wheels slowed and stopped at the Madera station.

The prodigal sister had come home.

Chapter 9

R ide 'em, cowboy." Curly's stentorian yell, accompanied by raucous laughter from Bud and Slim, who were perched next to him on the top rail of the Diamond S corral, made Seth Anderson grin. He leaned forward in the saddle, tightened his legs against the pinto mare's sides, and waited for the next buck. The mare obliged, but after a few half-hearted pitches she stopped short, turned her head, and surveyed her rider as if to say she'd had enough.

"Easiest horse I ever broke," Seth mumbled. "Open the gate," he called to the heckling trio. "I'll give her a good run and see what kind of ginger she has."

Curly whooped and sprang to obey. Seth and the mare raced out of the corral and down the road toward Madera as if pursued by a grizzly bear. Wind whistled in his ears and he bent over the horse's neck. "Go, Splotches. I'll eat my Stetson if Dori Sterling isn't crazy about you. Matt couldn't have found a better Christmas present for her."

He laughed. "You're a far cry from the nags Dori's probably been forced to straddle in Boston. Riding sidesaddle, bound up tight in a fancy riding habit, and plodding along at some fool ladylike trot? She may as well have been riding a rocking chair." The freedom of the range surged through Seth and aroused his pity for Dori. It must have been frustrating for a girl used to the wide-open spaces to be so constrained. "Say, Splotches, if she isn't thrilled with you, I'll keep you myself. You're the prettiest little pinto in the country, and you move right along."

The mare's ears pricked up. She stretched into a ground-covering gallop. Seth let her run, feeling wild and free, the way he had ever since coming to the ranch. At last he reined Splotches in beneath a huge oak tree. "Time to take a breather." He slid from the saddle and patted the mare's neck. She rewarded him by rubbing her nose against Seth's shoulder. Would Dori appreciate the pinto? He hoped so for Matt's sake.

He stroked Splotches's mane. "No matter. She'll be heading back to Boston after the wedding, and I'll ride you." He chuckled. "Just so Copper doesn't get jealous." Seth's happiness faded. His faithful sorrel gelding, companion and friend for many years, had stepped in a gopher hole a few weeks earlier and pulled a ligament.

"My fault," Seth grumbled. "I should have been paying attention instead of thinking about Dori coming home." The swelling on Copper's leg had been reduced with hot packs, and Matt said the horse would be fine, but Seth's guilt remained. Now he raised his head, removed his wide hat, and gazed into the blue December sky. He watched a hawk circle in the clear air before confessing, "Lord, I have an even bigger problem. I've been judging Matt's sister by the trouble she's caused him." Seth heaved a great sigh. "Even if Dori turns out to be as wayward and heedless as Matt says she is, I need to respect her because she's Your child." Seth scratched his head. "I reckon the best way to do that is to just keep out of her way." He paused and allowed the silence to fill him. "Thanks for listening, God."

Seth got to his feet and stretched. Talking with his Trailmate always made him feel better. Besides, it should be easy enough to avoid Dori for the short time she would be home without his avoidance becoming obvious.

What about when she comes home permanently? a little voice taunted. Seth shrugged. Summer was a long way off. Anything could happen before then. He swung into the saddle and turned Splotches toward home, but the sound of hoofbeats stopped him. Seth looked back and stared at the rider. When freckle-faced Johnny Foster raced a horse like that it usually meant bad news.

"Trouble, Johnny?" Seth called.

"Yeah." The boy pulled his horse to a stop. "Evan Moore said to get this telegram to Matt right away. Evan told me what it says. Miss Dori is on her way home, but that ain't all." He gasped for breath. "Evan got word the train is stuck in the mountains somewhere this side of Denver. Avalanches are blocking the tracks. The message said the railroad don't know how long it will be till they can get a work train and crew there and dig the passenger train out."

Seth's heart turned to ice. "Give me the telegram. My horse is fresher than yours."

"Okay, Seth." Johnny handed it over. "I sure hope those folks, 'specially Miss Dori, get rescued real quick. It'd be awful if she has to miss Matt and Sarah's wedding." He turned his horse and headed back to Madera.

Missing the wedding is nothing compared with what could happen, Seth thought grimly. *Being trapped in a snowbound train for who knows how long could claim lives.* He flinched. He'd seen snow storms cripple St. Louis. What would it be like in the Colorado mountains?

Seth goaded Splotches into a run and spoke from a heart filled with fear. "God, there's nothing any of us here can do for those stranded passengers and the crew. Please deliver them." A scripture learned in childhood crept into Seth's mind. Moses, reminding his people of God's goodness to Jacob, said: *"He found him in a desert land, and in the waste howling wilderness. . .he kept him as the apple of his eye."*

"Lord, be with everyone on that train and those sent to rescue them," Seth prayed. "Keep them as You kept Jacob. They are also in a howling wilderness and desperately need You." He paused and whispered, "In Jesus' name, amen."

The time between leaving Johnny and reaching the Diamond S felt like an eternity. When Seth and Splotches thundered up to the corral, Seth leaped to the ground, threw the mare's reins to one of the vaqueros and ordered, "Take care of her, will you?" Then he sprinted toward the ranch house. He didn't stop to knock, but burst into the hall and raced to the sitting room where Matt, Sarah, and Solita were gathered. "Telegram. Evan sent Johnny with it."

Apprehension sprang up in Matt's eyes, and he bounded to his feet. "Now what?" He snatched the telegram, ripped it open, and read aloud,

DOLORES ON WAY HOME *STOP* LETTER FOLLOWS *STOP* GENEVIEVE BROOKINGS.

Matt's shoulders sagged in obvious relief. "So what? Dori evidently decided to surprise us by coming earlier than planned. It's just like her."

Hatred for what he must do filled Seth. "There's bad news, Matt. The train Dori is on is snowbound west of Denver. It can't move until help gets there to dig it out."

Matt stared at him. "Dear God, no!"

Sarah echoed his prayer, but Solita put both hands over her head and wailed, "Dios be merciful to our senorita and the others."

Matt staggered to a chair and dropped into it. His shoulders shook as if he had palsy. "I don't know how Dori will stand it. Confinement in small spaces terrifies her. It always has." He groaned. "How can she stand being shut up inside a cramped railroad car with no way to escape?"

Sympathy for both Matt and his sister emboldened Seth. "God will be with her." His voice rang loud in the great room. "He has promised never to leave or forsake us."

"Yes," Sarah agreed. "He is our rock and our strong salvation." She knelt beside Matt and held her hands out to Seth and Solita. "We need to pray."

If Seth lived to be a hundred, he would never forget what followed. One by one, they stormed heaven on behalf of Dori and the others held in a prison of snow hundreds of miles away. The fear Seth had seen in the others' faces and felt in the air itself gradually lessened. Peace and the assurance all would be well tiptoed into Seth's heart. He raised his head. "I can't help but believe they'll be all right."

Solita and Sarah smiled. Matt gripped Seth's hand until it hurt and brokenly said, "I hope so. Now all we can do is to wait—and continue to pray."

Hours passed. Night fell. The four huddled close to the fireplace and each other. No one suggested going to bed. Seth had passed the word about Dori's predicament on to Brett Owen, and the foreman had promised to tell the hands. No good-natured banter or voices raised in cowboy songs sounded from the bunkhouse. Seth shuddered. The usually rollicking Diamond S felt like it was already in mourning. Still, he clung to the comfort that had come to him during the prayers—and continued to pray.

The dark hours passed. Dawn came. As soon as it was light enough to ride, Matt and Seth headed for Madera. They hung around Moore's General Store and Post Office until they received word that the work train had reached the passenger train and the railroad expected to have the tracks cleared in a few hours.

The bald storekeeper-postmaster's eyes twinkled. A wide grin spread across his round face. "Looks like that sister of yours will be here for the wedding, after all."

"Thank God!" Matt exclaimed, but Seth saw in Matt's eyes that the heart-felt cry of gratitude was for a lot more than Dori not missing the wedding.

❧

The time between receiving the gladsome news and the train's arrival gave Seth the opportunity to reflect. Like it or not, his life was bound up with Dori's. Any dislike on his part was a breach of loyalty to Matt. Despite all that had happened, Seth still had misgivings about Dori and didn't want to be present when she came. But when Matt made it clear that his heart was set on Seth going to the station with him, Seth agreed.

The train pulled in. Passengers streamed off. Where was Dori? Seth's mind spun. Had Miss Brookings's telegram been wrong? Had Dori missed the train she was supposedly on? Had all of his, Matt's, Sarah's, and Solita's distress been for nothing? Seth caught sight of Matt's set jaw and clenched his hands. If that dratted girl had once again caused her brother to suffer, Seth would—

"Dori!" Matt deserted Seth and hurtled toward the train, leaving Seth to gape at the young woman daintily holding her long skirts up enough to step down from the train. The black-and-white picture on the mantel at the Diamond S had often caused Seth to wonder how such an innocent-looking girl could be so troublesome. Now that picture came alive in glorious color—and Seth wondered again. Curly dark hair peeped from beneath a stylish bonnet and framed a lovely face. Dori's sapphire velvet cloak was no bluer than her tear-filled eyes. She was one of the prettiest fillies Seth had ever seen. As pretty as his sister, Sarah, with her red-gold hair, or dark-haired, dark-eyed Abby Sheridan, who worked at the Yosemite Hotel.

Seth shook his head to clear his thoughts. Could this glorious creature whose head reached her tall brother's shoulder be the bothersome girl who had caused Matt so much worry? The girl Seth considered childish and inconsiderate? Seth's ability to size up those he met with a single lightning glance now served him well. With all her shortcomings, Dori was devoted to Matt. It showed in her eyes, in the way she flung herself into his arms, and her joyous cry, "Oh Matt, I've missed you so much!"

Yet in spite of her obviously sincere greeting, Seth's keen gaze caught a shadow in Dori's eyes that betrayed her. All was not well. Something was disturbing the long-awaited visitor. Was Matt in for even more trouble?

Chapter 10

Dori slid from Matt's bear hug and caught at her bonnet. The strings had come untied, and the hat threatened to slip off her head. "Don't squeeze me to death!" She threw her arms around Matt again. The bonnet slipped farther down her back. Dori didn't care. She'd missed Matt terribly. Seeing him after all this time intensified her love. He was so big and brown and strong that Dori never wanted to let him go.

Two years' worth of tears that she'd only permitted to escape in the worst circumstances threatened to gush. She shook her head to keep them from falling. The movement dislodged her bonnet; it fell to the muddy street.

Before Dori could free herself and retrieve it, a deep, rich voice spoke from behind her. "I believe this is yours."

"Dori, this is Seth Anderson," Matt said. "Seth, my sister, Dolores." The pride in his voice was so undeserved it made Dori squirm. She loosened herself from Matt's arms and turned toward the tall cowboy holding her hat in one hand and trying to remove a thick coating of dust with the other.

Dori gulped. *This* was Seth Anderson? The tenderfoot she'd convinced herself might be harboring a devious plan to hoodwink her brother? If those lake-blue eyes were to be believed, he was not the villain she'd pictured.

Seth bowed, doffed his Stetson, and held out her bonnet. "Sorry I couldn't do a better job, Miss Sterling." A ray of sunshine rested on his bare head and changed his hair to molten gold, shot through with gleams of red.

The memory of Stancel gaping like a fish intruded on Dori's mind and left her speechless. Horrors! That must be how she looked now. *Don't stand here like a ninny,* she ordered herself. *It must be the sun that makes him look like the statue of a Greek god in my history book.*

Dori knew better. The light in Seth's face silently shouted it came from within. Unless looks were mighty deceiving, he was everything Matt had said and more.

An unfamiliar feeling stirred within Dori, as if her spirit rushed out to Seth's. The thought left her shaken. She tried to toss off a bright greeting but no words came.

"Cat got your tongue?" Matt teased. "Or is Sleeping Beauty waiting for a prince to come and awaken her with a kiss?" He chuckled. "What do you think, Seth?"

163

If the gibe bothered Seth, he didn't show it by the flicker of an eyelash. "I think Sarah will never forgive us if we don't get Miss Sterling home. She can't wait to meet her almost-new sister." Before Matt could reply, the cowboy strode toward the pile of luggage clearly marked with Dori's name. He stopped short and shoved his Stetson back on his head. "Looks like Evan will have to send most of this stuff out in a wagon. It won't fit in the carriage."

As soon as Seth was out of earshot, Dori rounded on Matt. "How could you embarrass me like that?"

Matt donned a look of innocent surprise—the same look he always wore after besting her. He raised his palms. "What did I say?" He looked at Seth, then back at Dori. "Hey, what did you do, bring everything you owned?"

Dismay replaced Dori's exasperation. Would she have to confess then and there that she'd been expelled? "Never you mind," she evaded. "After all, it *is* Christmas, with a wedding to boot. Let's go home. We mustn't keep Sarah—and Solita—waiting." She took the bull by the horns and boldly marched over to Seth. "I apologize for my brother," she said with what little dignity she could muster. "His sense of humor is—"

"Don't fret yourself, Miss Sterling. Brothers are like that. Just ask Sarah." An unreadable expression lurked in Seth's eyes.

Dori felt a river of hot blood stream into her face, and she silently climbed into the waiting carriage. Seth obviously hadn't given a second thought to the comment that had caused her so much mortification. His response had been perfectly courteous, but Dori felt like a child who had been patted on the head and told to go play.

Torn between chagrin and resentment, Dori remained silent most of the way to the Diamond S, despite Matt's attempts to include her in the conversation. *What difference does it make what Seth thinks?* she asked herself. *He's just another cowhand on my brother's ranch.* Yet her innate honesty forced her to admit it did make a difference—a huge difference, and one she couldn't explain.

It seemed to Dori's disturbed mind as if they would never reach the ranch. By the time they pulled in, the western sky was a study in reds and purples. Dori caught her breath. No Boston sunset could compare with this. She climbed from the carriage and gazed at the sprawling, hacienda-style ranch house, its white stucco walls rosy from the kiss of the setting sun. Light streamed from every window and from the open front door, welcoming Dori home. Two women waited on the wide front porch. One hurried to the top of the steps and met Dori's headlong rush with open arms.

"Querida. Dios be praised. You are home." Solita folded Dori into a tight embrace.

The familiar endearment changed Dori into a small girl, safe and secure in Solita's arms. Worn and weary from life in Boston followed by the fearsome experience of being trapped in the blizzard, she laid her head on the diminutive housekeeper's shoulder and let her tears fall.

Solita patted her shoulder and crooned, "Don't cry, little one. You are home and safe. Now you must meet Senorita Sarah, who has waited for your coming."

"Welcome home, sister," a musical voice said.

Dori freed herself from Solita's embrace and turned. A smiling replica of Seth stood with both hands outstretched. The shy appeal in the young woman's wistful blue eyes showed the same anxiety Dori had felt about meeting Sarah. All Dori's preconceived notions vanished. Unless badly mistaken, she'd been as wrong about Sarah as about Seth.

Dori managed a shaky laugh and clasped Sarah's hands. "I'm so glad to meet you." It was true. The identical feeling she'd experienced when meeting Seth flowed through her. *What is it about the Andersons that calls to something deep inside me?* Dori wondered. *The goodness that Matt raved about?* She sighed. She was just too tired to figure it out.

The evening passed in a blur. Dori's mental turnaround concerning Seth and Sarah had left her feeling bewildered. Yet certainty that her brother was in no danger from either of them filled Dori with relief. She sank into her soft bed and murmured, "Thank You, God, for bringing me safely home." She burrowed farther down under the covers. "Please don't let anyone find out until after the honeymoon that I won't be going back to Boston." A few moments later, she fell into the soundest sleep she'd known since she left the Diamond S. Except for the Andersons' presence, it seemed like nothing had changed, after all.

The few days before Christmas fled like shadows before the rising sun. On Christmas morning Dori awoke to the shrill whinny of a horse. She ran to her window and looked outside. Curly, Bud, and Slim were standing by the prettiest pinto mare Dori had ever seen. Seth was in the saddle, patting the horse's neck. Curly's voice floated up to Dori.

"You are one lucky cuss, Seth. Miss Dori's gonna hug your neck when she sees Splotches."

Bud and Slim guffawed.

Dori felt herself turn scarlet. What did Curly mean? Had Seth Anderson bought her a horse? She thrilled to the idea even while knowing it was impossible and watched Seth slide to the ground. How would he answer Curly?

Seth just laughed. "Naw. It's her brother who's gonna get hugged. I just broke the mare." Splotches nosed him. "Hope she likes you, girl. If she doesn't, she's a mighty poor judge of horseflesh."

Like the pinto? Dori already loved her. She scrambled into her old riding clothes and pelted down the stairs and out to the corral, where Matt had joined the others. "Is she for me?" she burst out.

Matt raised one eyebrow. "What makes you think that? Do you deserve her?"

Dori's joy fled. She shifted uneasily but didn't flinch from Matt's probing gaze. Honesty forced her to admit, "No, but I love Splotches."

The cowboys went into spasms of laughter.

Matt took the reins from Seth and held them out to Dori. "Good enough. Merry Christmas, sister."

Excitement filled Dori. "A brand-new horse!" She threw her arms around Matt, then around the mare's neck. Splotches whickered and stamped one foot. Dori took the reins and swung into the saddle. "Thank you. She's gorgeous."

"She's also gentle. Seth broke her for you," Bud put in.

"Thank you, Seth."

Slim added before Seth could reply. "Aw, 'twasn't nothin'. Seth said Splotches was the easiest horse he ever broke. Say, ain't you gonna try her out?"

"You bet I am." Dori touched the pinto's sides with her boot heels and called over her shoulder, "I hope I can still ride western."

Splotches took off like a startled jackrabbit, followed by Curly's bellow, "Can she still ride? I'll tell the world she can." A chorus of approving cowboy yells warmed Dori through and through.

She didn't head for home until the sun was high in the sky and her growling stomach clamored for the breakfast she had skipped. "Fine thing, running off on Christmas morning," she told her new horse. "But it was worth it." She reached the ranch and burst into the kitchen. "I'm starving."

Solita stopped tossing tortillas and smiled at Sarah, who was seated at the table with a cup of delicious-smelling Mexican cocoa that made Dori's mouth water. "You haven't changed."

Sarah laughed. "I don't wonder that you're hungry. You've been gone for hours."

"I lost track of time."

"I don't blame you. When I'm on a horse, I forget everything else. Riding gives me a sense of freedom." She stood. "Speaking of freedom, I'll still be a free woman tomorrow if I don't hustle. If you'll excuse me, I have to do some packing. After all, I'm marrying the most wonderful man in the world just a few hours from now."

If Dori hadn't already been won over by Sarah's integrity, the bride-to-be's expression would have settled all doubts. "Is there anything I can do to help you?"

"Feed that mountain lion raging inside you," Sarah advised. Her eyes twinkled. "One other thing. I like your riding outfit, but you might want to change for the wedding." A trill of laughter floated back as she ran out of the kitchen.

Dori had barely finished eating when Matt burst in. "Where's my girl— I mean, my other girl?" he wanted to know.

"Getting ready to become your wife," Dori told him.

"Yes." A poignant light came into his blue eyes. "Little sister, this is the happiest day of my life. I just pray that one day you will feel the way I do right now. Sarah completes my life."

As I once did.

Dori felt a twinge of regret for days that were gone forever, but it soon passed. No one in her right mind could be jealous of Sarah. Even in the few days Dori had been home she'd observed the way Matt and Sarah fit together like two blades on a fine pair of scissors. They would have a good life.

Dori swallowed hard. Would Matt's prayer for her be answered? Would she one day be readying herself to marry someone who would make her life complete? Someone as fine as her brother—someone she considered the most wonderful man in the world?

Dori wasn't the only one thinking about a life companion. While Seth waited to walk Sarah down the aisle of the Madera church, a pang of envy knocked at his heart's door. *God, do You have a girl like Sarah picked out for me?* He put aside the thought. Christmas and the wedding were making him soft. If God had someone in mind, He wasn't telling. . .and wouldn't until the time was right.

Seth grinned to himself and told Sarah, "You don't want to keep Matt waiting."

She nudged him and sent a pointed glance toward Dori, seated in the front row with Solita. "Just remember: Your turn's coming."

Seth felt his pulse quicken. He took revenge by whispering, "Naw. She's too Bostonish for a poor, lonesome cowpoke," and tried to ignore his poor, lonesome cowpoke's heartbeat that had changed from a slow walk to a full gallop.

Chapter 11

For the next few days, Dori reveled in her freedom. Despite Solita's protests, she rode Splotches when and where she chose. She teased Brett Owen until the foreman told her she was wilder than an unbroken mustang. Dori just laughed, pulled his Stetson down over his eyes, and danced away. Yet beneath her enjoyment, the guilty secret she carried stabbed at her conscience. Matt and Sarah would be home from their San Francisco honeymoon soon. What would they say when they learned Dori wasn't going back to Boston?

☙

The morning of their scheduled return, Dori followed the tantalizing tang of good food down the staircase and through the open hall door into the sunny Diamond S kitchen. "What smells so good? I'm starved." She plunked down at the table.

"Huevos rancheros." Solita set a plateful of steaming fried eggs with chili sauce in front of Dori and added warm tortillas. Her white teeth gleamed in a broad smile. "The Brookside Finishing School for Young Ladies did not serve such food, no?"

Dori grinned. "Hardly. It was mush, mush, mush for breakfast. If I never see another bowl of porridge it will be too soon." She lifted a forkful of the mixture, blew on it to cool it down, and put it in her mouth. "Mmm. Better than I remember."

Solita beamed. "In a few months, you will be here in our casa for good. I promise you will never have to eat mush again."

The huevos rancheros suddenly lost all their taste. Before nightfall, Dori would have to confess she was already home for good. A letter from Miss Brookings lay on the desk in Matt's office. Dori's fingers itched to burn it before he and Sarah came, but knew she couldn't. She was already in enough trouble.

Dori sighed. She hated to spoil her brother's homecoming, but she just had to tell him before he saw the letter. She couldn't afford to have Matt read the Babbling Brook's recital of the events leading to her dismissal before he heard Dori's side of the story.

"I thought you were starving."

Solita's reminder yanked Dori back into the present. "I'm waiting for it to cool." She glanced at the counters laden with flour, sugar, spices, and a dozen large bowls and baking pans. "Are you planning to feed an army instead of Matt and Sarah, or are you going to open a bakery?"

Solita shook her head and her dark eyes glistened. "There must be pies and cakes and cookies for the shivaree. Senor Mateo and Senora Sarah escaped being troubled on their wedding night by staying at the Yosemite Hotel." She rolled her expressive eyes. "Even the most daring vaqueros would not dare holler and beat on pans outside the hotel until invited in for treats." She shrugged. "Tonight they will come here so we must be prepared."

Dori's heart sank. Shivarees were always fun, but being invaded by a horde of well-wishers on this particular night meant she would have no chance to confess. It was more than she could stand. She looked into Solita's kindly face and blurted out, "Solita, I'm in terrible trouble."

The housekeeper stared at her. "Senorita, how can this be? Dios be praised. He brought you safely home to us."

Dori drew in a great breath. "He did, Solita, but I'm not going back to school."

An icy voice spoke from the doorway leading into the great hall. "Begging your pardon, Miss Sterling, but you are going back. Haven't you caused your brother enough trouble without kicking up a fuss and refusing to finish the course you insisted on taking?"

Dori spun out of her chair so quickly it crashed to the floor. Her unflinching gaze bored into Seth's blazing blue eyes. She tried twice before she could hurl words at the glowering cowboy "This is a private conversation, Mr. Eavesdropper. It doesn't concern you in the least."

"That's what you think," Seth shot back. "Sarah is my sister. She has a right to be happy. Anything that disturbs Matt affects her." He shook a finger in Dori's face. "Nothing is going to spoil their lives, get that? You're going to be on that train the day after tomorrow as scheduled." He paused and added, "You're going if I have to tie you on Splotches and wait at the station until I see the train leave."

Seth's words *spoil their lives* did what no amount or ranting or raving could do. Dori threw herself into Solita's arms and wailed, "I can't go back. I've been expelled."

An ominous silence pervaded the kitchen, broken only by Solita's gasp and Dori's hard breathing. Then Seth demanded, "What did you do this time?"

The scorn in his voice helped Dori gather her wits. "Nothing." She jerked free from Solita's embrace and glared at Seth. "I didn't do anything. How would you like being called a shameless hussy and accused of coquetting with the headmistress's nephew in a brazen attempt to weasel your way into society?" Memory heightened Dori's fury.

"What would you do if you were insulted and humiliated? An insufferable

Englishman named Stancel Worthington III announced that he was going to civilize and marry me. His aunt said it would be over her dead body."

Seth's lips twitched. "Never having been a young lady, I can't really say. I'd sure be put out at being called names, but. . ." To Dori's amazement Seth threw his head back and roared. "If I were a girl—a young lady—and anyone with the moniker 'Stancel Worthington III' tried to lasso me, I'd tell him adios in a hurry."

The blood that had been furiously rushing through Dori's veins slowed, and she simmered down. "I did, but not before giving it to the Babbling Brook and 'dear Stancel' with both barrels." She felt her lips tilt in a grin.

"So she kicked you out of her precious school."

"Yes." Dori drooped. "She told me to never darken the door of her ladies' academy again. I skedaddled out of there as quick as I could." Dori spread her hands wide and she choked back tears. "I don't want to spoil Matt and Sarah's life, but I can't go back. Miss Brookings was so furious that all the gold in California during the gold rush can't buy my way back into the school."

"Matt doesn't know." The quiet finality of Seth's comment sent misery flooding through Dori.

"No. I couldn't say anything before the wedding and ruin the happiest day of his life."

Solita stood as if frozen. Seth took a deep breath, expelled it in a long sigh, and advised, "Don't tell Matt and Sarah today. Tomorrow will be time enough."

It suddenly seemed tremendously important for Dori to know what Seth was thinking. She took a step nearer and implored, "You don't believe I was wrong, do you?"

His face went blank, as if he'd pulled down a shade and turned an OPEN sign to CLOSED. "Not this time, Miss Sterling." He stalked out, leaving Dori smarting from his subtle references to her past behavior.

She crossed to the table and sank back in a chair. "Well, just when I thought Mr. Know-It-All was beginning to thaw, he closes up like an oyster. Doesn't he like girls, or is it just me?" The thought hurt.

Solita's round brown eyes opened wide. "Senor Seth likes senoritas, but not as much as they like him."

"I'll bet they do," Dori muttered.

"Sí. He could court many of them if he had time." She smiled and looked wise. "Especially Senorita Sheridan."

An unreasonable pang of jealousy flowed through Dori. "You mean Sarah's friend Abby, from the Yosemite Hotel?" *Why should you care?* a little voice whispered. *He is nothing to you.* Why then, did she hold her breath and wait for the reply?

Solita nodded. "When she comes to visit, her dark eyes look at Seth, and she blushes."

Dori clenched her hands under the table. "What does he do?"

Solita reached for a large bowl and measured flour into it. "Senor Seth teases her, the same as Curly, Bud, and Slim do. They are all glad when she comes."

That explains it, Dori thought. *No wonder Seth has no use for me. Abby is probably the perfect little lady who would never dream of doing the things I do.* Much as Dori wanted to deny it, ever since she'd met Seth at the station, she'd hoped to find favor with the tall cowboy. Brief encounters during the last few days had whetted her desire to get to know him better, but in vain. Until today, anywhere she was he usually wasn't.

The imp of mischief that lurked on Dori's shoulder, poised and ready to take off, sprang to life. She would make Seth Anderson like her. She would show him that she was more than an irresponsible nuisance.

How? Seth's curt "not this time" clearly showed his sympathy for her present plight wasn't enough to tip the scales in her favor. *If only I could do something worthwhile, something noble and selfless and grown-up. I can start by giving up this morning's ride and help Solita with the baking. It isn't much, and Seth probably won't even notice, but maybe I can think of something else while I work.*

"It feels good to be in the kitchen," Dori told Solita while they chattered away and filled the kitchen with rows and rows of baked goods. "Finishing schools don't train young ladies to cook. Just to be young ladies." She bit into a warm cookie and mumbled, "I suppose you and Sarah spend a lot of time here."

"Sí." Solita deftly trimmed excess pie crust off an apple pie and cut designs in the top with a sharp knife. "We also teach the Mexican children to speak English." A ripple of laughter set her shoulders shaking. "The senoras, too."

A tingle started at Dori's toes and moved upward. Such a worthwhile undertaking might make Seth sit up and take notice. "Do you think I can help?"

The skepticism on Solita's face wasn't very flattering. Neither were her raised eyebrows, but she only said, "We shall see." She rolled out another pie crust. "If you begin, you must come each time and not disappoint the students."

"I will." *If it kills me.* Dori felt a twinge for what would mean lost riding time. Was such a commitment really worth it, just to impress Seth? She smiled to herself. Right now, she wanted his approval so much she would do just about anything to get it. Besides, working with Solita and Sarah would give her time to get better acquainted with her new sister-in-law—and through her, learn what made Seth Anderson tick.

Dori and Solita had barely finished the baking and gotten supper underway when a laughing Matt and Sarah arrived. As Dori feared, there was no time for confessions. At supper, the newlyweds bubbled over with tales of

San Francisco: the trip across San Francisco Bay, with icy waves attacking the ferry. The multitude of tall buildings. The salty smell from the seemingly endless Pacific Ocean. The hustle and bustle of carriages and horse-drawn carts. The steep hills and cable cars. The Chinese theater.

"Showing Sarah the wonders of San Francisco was like seeing it through new eyes," Matt told them with a sly look at his bride.

Sarah's eyes shone with love. "It was exciting and interesting, but I was glad to shake the dust of San Francisco off my shoes and come home. I don't like cities. Madera is big enough for me."

It was the perfect opening for Dori's not-so-gladsome news, but her throat dried, and her tongue cleaved to the roof of her mouth. Now was not the time to confess she had shaken the dust of Boston off her shoes. Yet she had never felt more miserable and alone than during the shivaree.

Even Solita's unspoken sympathy couldn't lift Dori's spirits. Standing to one side while the others made merry, Dori thought of her conductor friend on the journey home, and of the story she had told him. The sword of Damocles had fallen on her in Boston, but Dori suspected the real damage was yet to come.

The jovial crowd finally left. All was quiet. Seth had said good night and gone out, leaving Matt, Sarah, and Dori alone in the great room. He banked the fire and told his bride, "Go on up. I'll just have a quick look at the mail and be right with you."

Dori froze with one foot on the bottom stair. "No! I mean, why tonight? Surely there's nothing that can't wait until morning."

"I agree." Sarah linked her arm in her husband's, but Matt's gaze never left Dori. It made her feel like a butterfly on a pin. Why did he have to know her so well?

"You seem mighty concerned." He cocked an eyebrow. "What have you been up to now?"

Every resolution to wait fled. Dori sank to the bottom stair, buried her face in her hands, and said, "I've been dismissed."

"Dismissed? Dismissed from what?" Matt demanded.

Dori licked her dry lips. "Expelled. Kicked out. I can't go back to Brookside—ever."

Chapter 12

Hot tears burned behind Dori's aching eyelids. She kept her head down, unable to face Matt, Sarah, and the accumulation of sins that had led to her being banished from Brookside. *Forgive me, God, and please let Matt and Sarah forgive me.* Her heart added what her mind refused to ask: *Seth, too.*

Matt's voice sliced into the quiet room like a sharp knife. "You had better explain yourself, Dolores."

Dori flinched. Matt only called her by her full name when she was in trouble. She raised her head and looked into his set face. "It. . .it wasn't my fault, Matt." The skeptical look in his eyes hurt her even more than the disappointment she saw. "You know I don't lie."

She got up from the bottom stair and clasped her hands behind her back. "I did a lot of things that should have gotten me expelled, but this time, I wasn't to blame. If Miss Brookings's nephew hadn't come from England, I'd still be at school. He was trouble from the minute I almost knocked him out the front door and—"

"Up to your old tricks, I see."

"Not this time. He just happened to be in the way." Dori quickly related her trials and tribulations with Stancel Worthington III. "He was impossible. If you ever met him, you'd know what I mean."

"Spare me the lurid details."

"I can't." Dori told how she was called on the carpet, insulted by the headmistress, and ordered to leave Brookside posthaste. She ended with, "Even if I *could* go back, would you want me to after being called hussy and brazen? I'll bet Miss Brookings didn't put *that* in the letter on your desk."

A muscle twitched in Matt's cheek. "Why don't we see?" He grabbed the letter, opened it, and read aloud. "'Mr. Sterling, your sister Dolores is no longer welcome at my school. I have been patient and long-suffering in order to abide by your wishes and keep her here. She, however, has been a disturbing element ever since she arrived. She should have been sent home long ago. In any event, her latest transgression cannot be overlooked.'

"'Dolores set her cap for my dear nephew Stancel the moment he arrived. In order to attract his attention, she slid down the banister rail—which is strictly prohibited—and boldly pursued him at every opportunity. Stancel clearly showed his preference for Gretchen van Dyke, but Dolores wove an evil spell around him. She so enmeshed him in her wiles that Stancel actually considered civilizing, then marrying her.' "

❧

A muffled snicker from Sarah, who had kept silent all through Matt and Dori's conversation, halted Matt's reading. Dori gaped at her. Sarah had both hands over her mouth. Her face was redder than the last embers in the fireplace. "Sorry," she apologized, tears streaming. "It's just that no one in real life says 'wove an evil spell,' or 'enmeshed him in her wiles.' Dori, your headmistress must have been reading dime novels on the sly."

Dori sent Sarah a look of approval. She turned to Matt and caught a flicker of his bride's contagious amusement cross his face before he said, "Let's have the rest of it. 'I do believe Dolores actually thought Stancel's temporary aberration would gain her an entrance into a level of society she could achieve in no other way. When she discovered I would not stand for it, Dolores called dear Stancel all kinds of barnyard names that plainly showed her lack of breeding.'

" 'Now that this unspeakable troublemaker is out of the way, Stancel will naturally seek someone eminently more suitable than the uncivilized sister of a keeper of gentleman cows.' "

❧

Matt paused. The flicker of amusement grew into a blaze. A chuckle escaped. "Gentleman cows? I wonder where she got that. 'As you know, Mr. Sterling, there is no monetary refund for those who do not complete their schooling, unless there is serious illness. I commend Dolores back into your keeping, and may God have mercy on your soul.' "

❧

Matt threw the letter aside and looked at Sarah, then Dori. His lips broadened into a grin. "You notice I am no longer 'dear Mr. Sterling.' " A belly laugh followed. "So it's hail-and-farewell to Brookside Finishing School for Young Ladies."

Dori ran across the room and threw her arms around him. Was this how Christian, the hero in *The Pilgrim's Progress*, felt when the heavy burdens he carried on his journey from the City of Destruction to the Celestial City finally dropped away? Dori wanted to skip, leap, and shout. If Matt could laugh like this, surely she wasn't in too much hot water. His arms closed around her. Dori sighed with relief. Let Miss Brookings and her pompous nephew go hang. Miss Dori Sterling was home, safe, and forgiven.

Dori's joy was short-lived. All too soon, Matt removed her clinging arms from around his waist and dropped his hands on her shoulders. Every trace of amusement had vanished. "I can't condone Miss Brookings's behavior," he said quietly, "but neither are you blameless. You've been taught since

174

childhood that actions have consequences. There's always a day of reckoning."

Dori shivered in spite of the warm room. "What are you going to do with me?"

"I don't know yet. Drastic circumstances call for drastic measures."

Dori's heart plummeted to her toes. This was not good.

Sarah's soft voice brought the dialogue to a standstill. "It's late, and I'm sure we're all tired, Matt. Suppose you and Dori continue this conversation tomorrow."

Dori could have hugged her. The journey from confession through hilarity to facing an unknown future had taken its toll. Her energy was at such a low ebb she wondered if she could make it up the stairs to her room. "Good night, Sarah. Good night, Matt." She grasped the rail of the staircase and began to climb, too tired to worry over what tomorrow might bring.

❧

After a restless, nightmare-filled night, Dori slept long past the usual rising hour for the Diamond S. When she came downstairs, she found Solita and Sarah at the kitchen table, steaming cups of coffee before them.

"Did you sleep well?" Sarah asked. Concern shadowed her voice.

"No. Do you know what Matt is going to do?"

Sarah shook her head. "I'm not sure he knows. We didn't discuss it last night."

Dori stared out the window into a sunny day. The sound of stamping hooves and a whinny from the corral chirked her up a bit. "Where's Matt?"

"Right here." He stepped into the kitchen. "How about a second cup of coffee, Solita?"

How can he look so rested and free from worry? Dori resentfully wondered. "So what's the verdict?" She hated herself for sounding flippant but couldn't stand one minute more of not knowing what lay in store for her.

"Do you want Solita and me to leave?" Sarah asked.

"Please stay," Dori said. "You can be the jury when Judge Sterling pronounces sentence on the accused. Maybe you will plead for mercy on my behalf."

"That attitude won't help you," Matt stated. He accepted the coffee from Solita, waited until she sat down again, then seated himself in a chair beside Sarah. "You're eighteen years old. Too old to think you can rule the roost, act as you please without regard for others, and not be held accountable."

Dori wilted. This was worse than she'd expected, especially when Matt's reception of Miss Brookings's letter had brought hope for a lesser scolding.

"First of all, you are going to finish your last term of schooling. Just because you aren't going back to Brookside doesn't mean you can run wild on the ranch."

Stunned, Dori clenched her fingers until the nails bit into the palms of her hands. "I can't go back to school in Madera. I'm older than everyone there. They'll ask why I didn't stay in Boston." The thought of being humiliated lent Dori the courage to continue. "Please, Matt, don't make me do that. I'll never live down being kicked out of Brookside."

"You've lived down other things," Matt reminded her.

"Not like this." Dori shook her head until her black curls flew every which way. "It will be the ruination of me. Besides, only you three and Seth know why I'm not going back. Can't we keep it that way?"

Matt drummed his fingers on the table. "You do have a point, but. . ."

Sarah placed one hand over her husband's. A glow filled her eyes. "Matt, I never had a chance for advanced schooling. Would you—could you hire a tutor to come to the ranch and teach both Dori and me? I feel so ignorant compared with you."

"Ignorant? You're the smartest person I know," Matt argued. "There's nothing you can't do, even teach the Mexicans to speak English."

"Pooh, Solita does most of the teaching," Sarah scoffed. "Besides, I don't mean ignorant about living, just about books and things."

Humbled by Sarah's frank admission of her shortcomings, Dori did likewise. "I know I don't deserve it, but having a tutor and studying with Sarah would be wonderful." She inwardly groaned at the thought of being cooped up doing lessons when Splotches and the entire great outdoors beckoned her. But it was better than having to tuck her tail between her legs and go back to school in Madera.

"The tutor will see to it that I make up what I'll be missing at Brookside," Dori added. *And it will not include ballroom dancing,* she silently vowed, wise enough to hold her tongue. She was already skating on the thinnest of ice.

Matt's brows drew together in a straight line. "So where am I to get a tutor? Any teacher worth his salt will already be teaching this time of year."

"Pray for one." Dori clapped her hand over her mouth. Had she really said that?

Matt looked astonished. So did Sarah and Solita.

"I'm serious," Dori told them, surprised to discover it was true. "Doesn't the Bible tell us that if we ask, we shall receive?" Laughter bubbled out. "And if we seek, we shall find? Well, you need to seek a tutor."

Matt tilted back in his chair and clasped his hands behind his head. "It never ceases to amaze me how you can quote scripture when it's to your benefit, sister dear. I have to admit, though, it's a good idea." He stretched. "Now if this discussion is over, I have work to do." He stood, leaned down and kissed Sarah, and strode out.

"Dios will surely help Senor Mateo find the right person," Solita observed. She smiled at Dori. "I will make your breakfast now."

"Can I help?"

"No. You sit and talk with Senora Sarah." The housekeeper disappeared into the pantry.

The postponement of Dori's day of reckoning released her mischievous spirit. While Solita was out of the kitchen, Dori whispered to Sarah, "I wonder what kind of tutor God will send?"

Sarah laughed and patted her hand. "Who knows? God has such a sense of humor He will probably surprise us. Maybe even shock us."

"I just hope the tutor has a sense of humor," Dori flashed back. "If he's anything like 'dear Stancel,' we're sunk."

For several days, it appeared there were no unemployed tutors anywhere near Madera. Dori conscientiously made it a matter of prayer, but when time went by with no success, despair set in. If no tutor could be found, she was doomed to return to school in Madera. She intensified her prayers.

Two full weeks after her return to the Diamond S, the tutor arrived. When the sound of buggy wheels halted in front of the wide front porch, Dori and Sarah rushed out. Sarah giggled. She pinched Dori's arm and said, "I told you God might shock us. Now we'll see if He has."

Matt helped someone from the buggy. "Sarah, Dori, meet Miss Katie O'Riley, your new tutor."

"I'm actually for bein' a teacher and a governess," Katie said.

Dori's jaw dropped. Her new "tutor" had the reddest hair, the greenest eyes, and the most freckles on her tip-tilted nose that Dori had ever seen. She looked to be only a few years older than Dori and her accent was pure, lilting Irish when she said, "So you're for bein' Mrs. Sarah and Miss Dolores. Mercy me, but you're two fine colleens." A trill of laughter set Katie's eyes asparkle. And as Dori's grandmother used to say, "It warmed the very cockles of a body's heart."

Thank You, God, Dori breathed—and stepped forward to welcome Katie O'Riley.

Chapter 13

"Whoa, Copper."

Late one Saturday afternoon, Seth Anderson reined in his sorrel gelding just outside the corral and wearily slid from the saddle. He'd been riding the range, looking for a small bunch of cattle that were either lost, strayed, or stolen—most likely stolen—without success. He glanced toward the ranch house. An assortment of riderless horses and a couple of buggies littered the front yard.

Seth scowled. His earlier predictions about life on the Diamond S never being the same once Dori Sterling turned up had been fulfilled. The coming of Katie O'Riley had added to the problem. With two attractive, unmarried females on hand, single and widowed men for miles around flocked to the ranch like honeybees to a clover field.

Seth snorted. "A bunch of lovesick pups, as far as I'm concerned. I've never seen so many duded-up visitors or smelled so much hair tonic. I can't tell yet how Katie feels about all this masculine attention, but anyone who isn't blind can see that Dori glories in it. She holds court as if every male age eighteen and over is her private property."

Seth unsaddled Copper and continued to grumble while he rubbed the sorrel down. "You're the best listener on the ranch," he said. Copper whinnied and nudged his soft nose against Seth's shoulder as if to agree. His master went on with his complaints.

"Curly, Bud, Slim, and most of the outfit are just as bad. In all my born days I never heard such a passel of excuses for laying off work. Curly's had more bellyaches lately than in all the time I've been here. Bud can't ride 'cause his 'rheumatics'—whatever that is—are acting up."

Seth groomed Copper until he shone brighter than his name. "Slim takes the cake. I heard him tell Brett this morning that he reckoned he was just 'too tuckered out to chase rustlers or cow-type critters today.' Matt's gotta do something and do it pronto, or we may as well kiss the rest of the herd good-bye."

Disgusted and discouraged, Seth turned Copper loose in the pasture, got himself slicked up, and went to find Sarah. Maybe she could do something with Dori. To his amazement, he got little sympathy.

"Dori is still young, even though she's eighteen," Sarah told him over coffee

178

in the kitchen. "Of course she has the bit in her teeth. She's been penned up at school for two years. Although she won't admit it, I suspect she hated every minute there but was too proud to come home. Don't let her get under your skin, Seth. She'll settle down." Sarah smiled at him. "Katie is good for her. Even in the short time she's been with us, she's been rubbing off on Dori."

A merry laugh floated through the open hall door and into the kitchen. "From what I can see, it's the other way around," Seth growled. "Sounds like Dori has Katie wrapped around her little finger."

Sarah shook her head. "Don't you believe it. Our Irish colleen is full of fun, but she's a strict disciplinarian in the classroom. If Dori or I don't have our lessons prepared to her satisfaction, she looks at us with those big emerald eyes and says, 'You'll be for doin' this over—as many times as it takes for it to be done right and proper.'"

Sarah's imitation of the new teacher brought a grin to Seth's face. "I'm glad to see there's someone on this ranch who Dori can't push around. I would have thought she'd pitch a fit at having to be taught."

"I'm sure she'd like to, but the alternative is spending spring term at school in Madera." His sister raised one eyebrow and smirked. "By the way, I'd say there are two someone's here on the ranch who Dori can't push around." Before Seth could answer, Sarah changed the subject. "Matt says there's going to be a barn raising soon, followed by a barn dance. Are you taking anyone?"

Feeling he had been bested concerning Dori, Seth was in no mood for frolicking. "Probably not."

"How about Abby?" Mischief lurked in Sarah's blue eyes.

Seth stood and glared down at her. "As Katie would say, 'Don't you be for matchmaking.' It beats all that when folks get married, all they can think of is getting everyone else hitched up."

"So do you plan on spending your life in single blessedness?" Sarah teased.

"Better single blessedness than double cursedness," Seth retorted. He got up and stalked toward the kitchen door, pursued by his sister's mocking laughter. A moment later, her soft voice halted him.

"I'm sorry, Seth. Matt and I are so happy. I want you to be, too." Her voice trembled.

Repentant for acting so cussed, Seth spun around. "I know. It's just that I won't marry until God sends the right girl and lets me know she is the right one. Stepping into double harness any other way is asking for a heap of trouble."

Sarah flew to his side and hugged him. "Maybe He has already sent the right one."

Seth blinked. Why should her remark set a vision of a dark-haired young woman in a velvet cloak as blue as her eyes dancing in his mind? His heartbeat quickened. "What do you mean?"

Sarah looked innocent. "You've paid attention to Abby, and she's a good Christian girl. You like her, don't you?"

Seth felt his muscles relax. "Sure. She's pretty and fun." He bent a stern gaze on Sarah. "Just don't get ideas in that head of yours. Save the room for 'book larnin,' as Curly calls it." He tweaked the red-gold braid wrapped around Sarah's head. But she had the last word.

"Why don't you invite Dori to the barn raising and the dance?"

With a mumbled protest against females, matchmaking sisters in particular, Seth fled. But the suggestion Sarah had planted in his mind took root. Half the countryside would be on hand to help replace the barn on the Rocking R that had caught fire and burned to the ground a few weeks earlier. Seth would be the envy of Madera if he took Dori to the raising.

How ridiculous to even consider such an idea. "Escorting a young lady in order to show off is not fit behavior, God," he prayed. "Help me stay true to Your teachings and 'do unto others.' I sure wouldn't want anyone to show up at a barn raising with me just to make other folks sit up and take notice." Yet a feeling of regret nagged at him. If Dori were as innocent and good as she appeared, what a wife she would make. Seth sighed. Since she wasn't, he would continue to keep his distance and not subject himself to her charm.

Fate and Matt Sterling tossed Seth's carefully laid plans to the four winds. After Dori sneaked away from her studies for the second time and took off on Splotches, Matt sought out Seth. "Ride with me, will you?"

"Sure." Seth laid aside the currycomb with which he'd been grooming Copper. The grim expression in his boss's eyes warned of trouble.

Matt lost no time in confirming Seth's suspicions. Once Copper and Matt's buckskin, Chase, swung into an easy canter, Matt abruptly said, "You know what 'fightin' wages' are, don't you?"

What on earth? The feeling that rough water lay ahead made Seth wary. "Of course. Extra pay for hands who fight rustlers and other dangers."

"I have a proposition for you. I'd hoped Dori would settle down. She hasn't." Matt spit the words out like bullets. "It's bad enough having a herd of lovesick boys and men, including a couple bad eggs from town, hanging around all the time. What's worse is that Dori believes she can ride as well as she did two years ago. She can't, and she's pushing Splotches too hard and too fast. I caught her trying to jump a fence the other day after I told her not to. The pinto hesitated long enough to break her stride, then nicked the top rail and took a nasty fall. Dori sailed over Splotches' head. If it had been hardpan ground instead of pastureland, they could both have been badly hurt."

A brooding look crept into Matt's eyes. "What worries me most is that Dori is bound and determined to ride every horse on the ranch, even the mustangs that haven't been broken."

Pity for his boss and friend shot through Seth, but he remained silent.

After a long moment, Matt continued. "This is no way to start married life. I need to be with Sarah, not keeping track of my sister twenty-four hours of the day. Seth, if you'll take over for me, I'll up your pay to fightin' wages."

Had the sky opened and sent a thunderbolt down on Seth, he couldn't have been more shocked. "Me ride herd on Dori? Excuse me, Boss, but you must be out of your mind. Rustlers are one thing. Your sister is a heap worse."

"I know it's a lot to ask, but I'm desperate," Matt confessed. "In addition to disrupting my schedule and driving me to the point where I'm about ready to fire the entire outfit, Dori is rapidly becoming the talk of Madera because she likes being popular and doesn't care who knows it." He sighed. "I'd hoped her narrow escape from being trapped on the train home from Boston would curb her high spirits. Or that making her study would help. Katie O'Riley is doing her best, but she can't compete with this." He waved across the flat land that rolled away to the foothills, with the snow-capped Sierra Nevada in the distance.

Unwilling sympathy caused Seth to say, "I can understand that." He found himself repeating what Sarah had said. "After all, Dori has been cooped up and away from all this for a long time."

"I know, but she needs to learn self-control. That's where you come in."

Another ripple of shock went through Seth. He'd rather wrestle ornery cattle than be responsible for the wild girl. Besides, in spite of his scorn, he secretly admitted a powerful attraction hid deep inside him. It would be downright dangerous for him to spend the time in Dori's company that would be necessary should he agree to Matt's outlandish proposition. "I—"

Matt cut him off. "Wait until you hear what I have in mind. Before Dori went to Boston, she was a fine rider. Like I said, the trouble is, she thinks she's as good as ever. On the surface she is. However, two years of occasional sidesaddle rides on Boston trotting paths have undermined her ability. She needs to restore the range skills you and I know are necessary to live here. This land is beautiful; it can also be harsh and unforgiving. Varmints both two- and four-legged roam the range. Splotches is a great horse, but she's still young and relatively untried."

A poignant light came into Matt's troubled eyes. "Sarah and I would both feel better with Dori in your care. Take her out riding every day except Sunday. On school days, make it in the afternoon. Be sure Dori carries either a Colt .45 or a Winchester .73 carbine when she rides, and see to it that she can shoot as straight as a man. Teach her trick riding and roping, anything to hold her interest. If I know my dear sister—and I do—she will be on her mettle and determined to conquer whatever task you give her. Keep her at it, and wear her out until she's too tired to think up mischief."

Seth snorted. "Is that all?" Dislike for the idea warred with loyalty to Matt and the knowledge someone needed to take the high-spirited girl in hand.

Matt's keen eyes bored into him. Seth had the feeling the boss could read his mind. "It won't be easy," Matt warned. "I'd say it will pretty near be a full-time job. So what do you say?"

Seth didn't answer until they reached his favorite spot on the ranch, a place he had learned to love. The promontory that overlooked the ranch offered both privacy and beauty. The entire valley spread out below them, dotted with dark clumps of the vineyards and orchards that had sprung up north of the San Joaquin River. Diamond S cattle roamed the rolling rangeland that lay closer to their lookout.

Seth slid from Copper and let the reins hang to the ground. Matt swung from his saddle and did likewise. Unless something spooked them, the horses were trained to stand, so the men were in no danger of being left afoot. After a long silence, Matt quietly said, "Well?"

Seth squared his shoulders. How could he turn Matt down? He owed him more than he could ever repay. "I will do it on two conditions. First and most important, if I take charge of training Dori, I must be allowed to handle her in my own way. That means no matter what I do, you, Sarah, Brett, or anyone else can't interfere. If it's a problem, the deal's off." He took a deep breath and held it, torn between wishing Matt would argue and secretly hoping he wouldn't.

Matt's strong hand shot out and grabbed Seth's. "Agreed."

Seth's breath came out in a loud *whoosh*. "Second, no fightin' wages. My thirty dollars a month and keep are plenty."

"Doesn't seem right to me," Matt objected. "You'll be taking on a bigger job than any of the other hands."

Seth didn't give an inch. "Those are my terms. Think about it. If it ever got back to Dori that I was being paid for looking after her, she'd blow the whole thing sky-high."

Matt's heartfelt chortle signaled his relief. "You've got that right. When do you want to start?" He looked shamefaced. "Who should tell her? You or me?"

Seth ignored the tingling sensation of stepping from light into the dark unknown and nonchalantly said, "Might as well be me. If I'm going to boss her, she needs to know it right away. Just one thing. I have a feeling I'm not Dori's favorite person on the Diamond S. What if she turns me down flat?"

The grim expression that had disappeared with Seth's acceptance of the scheme returned. It boded no good for a wayward sister. "She won't. I promise you that." Matt leaped to Chase's saddle. "Let's go home. I can't wait to see Dori's face when she learns what we have in store for her."

Seth didn't reply. But on the long ride back to the ranch, he wondered. *Lord, what am I getting myself into? I'm going to need Your help and need it bad.*

Chapter 14

I t was the best of times, it was the worst of times, it was the age of wisdom, it was the age of foolishness.' "

Dori flung the worn copy of *A Tale of Two Cities* to her desk in the Diamond S schoolroom and cast a longing glance out the window. A hint of frost glistened in the sunlight, and the whinny of horses in the corral was enough to drive her to distraction. "Studying about the French Revolution on a day like this is foolish," she grumbled. "Charles Dickens was wrong. Not being able to ride until afternoon is the 'worst of times.' " She slumped in her seat and silently dared her teacher or Sarah to challenge her.

Katie O'Riley's emerald eyes darkened. Her usually laughter-filled voice turned to ice. "You're for knowing nothing about the worst of times," she retorted.

Dori felt ashamed of her outburst but felt compelled to defend herself. "It was the worst of times when I was in Boston. You can't imagine how bad—"

"Can't imagine?" Katie cut her off midsentence. She placed her hands on her hips, elbows akimbo, and tossed her red head. Every freckle stood out on her pink and white skin. "It's you who can't be for imagining what real hardship is. Hundreds of thousands of men, women, and children died from hunger during the Irish Potato Famine in the 1840s. Mother and Da nearly starved to death. For years they hoarded money to purchase passage to America, though 'twas sorely needed for food."

Dori's insides twisted at the pain in Katie's face. Her own face burned. How could she have been so insensitive? Whenever Katie was at repose, her usually merry face revealed a sadness that should have warned Dori that life had not always been easy for the Irish colleen. Yet caught up with herself, Dori hadn't known or cared about Katie's story.

Her teacher wasn't finished. Her eyes blazed and words poured out like water over a broken dam. "Conditions on the journey in those times were so unspeakable that the ships were called 'coffin boats.' If it hadn't been for the mercy of our heavenly Father, Mother and Da would have been among the hundreds who died at sea. Even when they reached the 'Promised Land,' as America was said to be, their troubles weren't over. Irish 'micks' weren't welcome.

"I was born in a New York City tenement. Da worked on the docks.

Mother took in washing. We were mocked and despised." Katie's lips trembled. "The hard work finished what the famine and terrible journey began. Mother and Da went home to heaven a few years back."

Sarah, who had remained quiet during Katie's story, gasped. "How did you live?"

Katie proudly raised her head. "Irishwomen aren't for giving up. I hired myself out to a wealthy woman who was more interested in society doings than in her children. But I wanted more than being a nursemaid all my life. The master of the house had a great library. When he saw I hungered to learn, he told me to help myself to his books."

Enthralled by the story, Dori burst out, "How did you end up here?"

Some of the tension left Katie's pretty face. "The Father in heaven was surely looking out for me," she reverently said. "The master had business connections everywhere. A little over a year ago, a man from Fresno wrote asking if the master knew anyone capable of handling his three motherless daughters. I'd always wanted to see the West and agreed." She sighed. "All was for going well until the flood."

Dori straightened. The threat of winter flooding was a fact of life. This year, the Fancher, Red, and Big Dry creeks had surged into Fresno. Despite the townspeople's best efforts, the flood could not be controlled. It swept through town, tearing down hastily-constructed levees and leaving the streets under so much water folks had to be rescued by boat.

"Were you caught in the flood?" Dori breathlessly asked Katie.

She shook her curly red head. "No. But the worst-hit building was the schoolhouse. A foot-deep layer of mud covered the first floor. It will take weeks to repair. The master decided this was a good time to send his daughters to a school for young ladies in San Francisco for spring term."

"I hope they have better luck there than I did in Boston."

Katie's eyes twinkled for the first time since the conversation had taken a disastrous turn. "At least they are too young to interest an English dancing master," she teased. Dori groaned, but the next moment Katie grew serious.

"The master asked to wed me, but I had no love for him, nor he for me. He was just for being kind." A look of awe crossed her expressive face. "I prayed to our Father in heaven, and a few days later, the master came in with news. He'd heard that a Mr. Matthew Sterling was looking for a teacher. Your brother came to Fresno and fetched me here." She added in a choky-sounding voice, "It's been like I found a home." Bright tears fell.

Dori couldn't speak, but Sarah quickly slipped her arm around Katie and said, "This is your home, Katie, for as long as you want to stay." Mischief filled her blue eyes. "I'm just not sure how long that will be. If my eyes don't deceive me, a certain young cowpuncher will have something to say about that."

Katie turned scarlet, but Dori's heart leaped to her throat. She stared at the two. Did Sarah mean. . .surely she couldn't think. . .was the young cowpuncher Seth? Just a little shorter than Matt, and not quite as broad-shouldered, Seth's crown of hair glowed as brightly as his sister's. It contrasted nicely with his richly tanned face and made his eyes look bluer than ever. Astride Copper, the cowboy was attractive enough to capture any girl's attention.

Confusion fell on Dori like a saddle blanket on Splotches. According to Solita, Seth had been keeping company with Abby Sheridan. Had he transferred his affections to Katie? Well, why not? Any man who won the Irish maiden's heart would be blessed.

Jealousy as green as Katie's plaid dress sped through Dori and battled with disgust for feeling that way. After what Katie had gone through, she deserved happiness. Unbidden, a prayer winged its way upward. *Please, just don't let it be with Seth. There are plenty of other single men to choose from.* A little voice inside mocked, *Then why don't you take one of them?*

Heat rushed to Dori's face. That was not a question she wanted to answer.

Reprieve came in the form of a knock on the schoolroom door and the sound of chattering. "Are you ladies finished in there?" Matt called. "The children are here for their lesson, and I need to see Dori."

Katie pulled away from Sarah. "Just a minute, please." She quickly crossed to Dori, who stood frozen. "Will you be for forgiving me for losing my temper?"

Dori shook her head. "You're the one who needs to forgive. I didn't know." She impulsively held out her hand. "Friends again?"

"Of course." Katie looked surprised. "Irish temper is like the wind. It comes without warning then is gone, *poof*." She pressed Dori's hand and grinned. "Better run along and see what your brother wants."

"Wonder what I've done now?" Dori whispered. She stepped outside and blinked in the sunlight. Matt and Seth stood nearby, arms crossed and gazes fixed on her.

"Seth has something to say to you," Matt said. "I'll leave you to him, but before I go, you need to know I approve of everything he's going to tell you." He walked away, leaving Dori speechless and staring after him.

Dori's mouth fell open. What was Seth going to say to her that had her brother's approval? It didn't—it couldn't mean Seth had received permission from Matt to court her. *Don't be stupid,* she told herself, *There's Abby and Katie. . .* Dori's thoughts trailed off, but her traitorous heart taunted, *What else could it be?*

The tall cowboy doffed his Stetson. "If I may have your attention, Miss Sterling?"

The hint of sarcasm in his voice shattered the cocoon of silence that surrounded Dori. "Yes?" Her heart thumped.

"From now on, we'll be spending afternoons together," Seth told her.

"Together?"

"Yes." Seth raised one eyebrow. "I'll be in charge at all times. You'll do what I say, when I say it, and how."

Dori blinked. This didn't sound like a suitor eager to please. Rebellion rose, although Seth's masterful attitude intrigued her. "What if I don't?"

His measuring gaze never left her face. "Then the deal's off. Either I'm the boss, or Matt can get someone else to train you."

"Train me?" Her voice rose a full octave from its usual pitch. Did this...this oaf think he was going to train her to be his wife? She'd had enough of that with Stancel. "Train me for what?"

He looked surprised. "For fitting you with the skills you need to survive. Matt promised that you wouldn't turn me down."

If Dori hadn't been so angry she would have laughed in his face. Seth was even more insufferable than Stancel had been. As for Matt, she couldn't wait to tell him a thing or two.

"Matt wants me to turn you into the rider you used to be before going east." Anticipation sparkled in Seth eyes. "Roping, too, and trick riding, as well as shooting."

Thud! Dori's hopes of being courted crashed to the hard ground. She took a deep breath. Seth must never know what she had thought. *The best of times, the worst of times,* she thought bitterly. Another phrase from the story came to mind. *"The spring of hope, it was the winter of despair."* She had sprung from hope to despair in less time than it took to spring into a saddle.

Dori opened her mouth to blast Seth, to tell him he was the last person on the ranch she wanted to teach her anything. She paused. No. There was a better way. She would go along with his and Matt's scheme. She would learn everything he could teach her, then flaunt it by showing Seth she was as good or better than any hand on the range, including him.

Glee over her decision erased some of Dori's frustration. Long hours together would give her the opportunity to crack the wall of indifference she sensed in Seth when she was around. "So when do we start?"

"After dinner. I'll see that Splotches is saddled and ready."

Dori gritted her teeth at his nonchalance. She wanted to tell him she was perfectly capable of saddling her own horse but refrained. A small smile tilted her lips upward. She'd fooled Matt with her acting ability in Boston years ago. Surely she could hoodwink the brash cowboy who thought he could teach her skills she had possessed since childhood.

For the first few rides, Dori donned the docile attitude of a novice at the feet of a learned sage. But her fierce resolve to get the best of Seth leaped like wildfire a short time later. Tired of keeping the pace Seth and Copper set, she leaned forward in the saddle and urged Splotches into a full gallop over uneven ground, even though she knew better. "Can't that nag of yours keep up?" she shouted back to Seth.

The pound of hooves sang in Dori's ears, followed by Seth's, "Stop!" He pulled even with her and snatched the reins. Both horses came to a screeching halt.

Dori scorched with rage. "How dare you interfere."

"How dare you risk your horse by running her here?" Seth bellowed. Dori had never seen him so angry. "I didn't train Splotches just to have an idiot girl injure her by showing off. All it takes is one gopher hole to break a leg, not to mention what could happen to you."

Stung by feeling guilty and knowing that he was right, Dori still wouldn't give in. "As if you'd care. You're more concerned over Splotches getting hurt than you are about me. Fine teacher you are."

A curious expression crossed Seth's face. "If you get hurt, it's your own fault. Splotches has no say in whether she stays whole—and alive. Let's go home."

They rode in silence for a good mile before Dori blurted out, "Are you going to tell Matt?"

"That depends on you," Seth said with a look that boded no good for her. The twitch of a muscle in his cheek betrayed his wrath. "One more stunt like that, and I'm through. I agreed to ride herd on you to help Matt out, but if you're going to continue being a blasted nuisance, the deal is off."

Dori felt like she was bleeding inside from Seth's condemnation. Today's escapade had surely killed all hopes of her ever gaining Seth's respect—respect she suddenly realized she had craved from the time she returned to the Diamond S. Now all was lost because of her stubborn determination to have her own way.

Chapter 15

*Z*ing.

Dori's lasso sang through the air from her position atop her pinto mare. It captured the target stump for the fifth time in a row.

"Good job." Seth called from Copper's back. Ever since he'd read the riot act to her about racing Splotches, Dori had settled down and worked hard to master the tasks he gave her. Seth frowned. Working hard didn't hide the biding-my-time expression she sometimes still wore. Sure as the sun came up in the east, sooner or later Dori would rebel again.

Seth shook his head and watched Dori coil her lasso for another throw. He'd known taking charge of her would be tougher than chasing rustlers. What he hadn't counted on, but was forced to admit, was his growing admiration for the plucky girl.

You also didn't count on falling in love with her.

Seth set his jaw. Ha! That's just what he was *not* going to do. So what if his heart beat faster when she came running out to go riding? Or the softness in her manner at times indicated she might not be indifferent to him? No way would he consider anyone with her attitude as a possible life companion.

"You're my Trailmate, God," Seth mumbled for the dozenth time. "The woman I marry has to put You first in her life. Dori's aim in life seems to be having good times and her own way. Once she sets her mind, she's as immovable as El Capitan." Seth grinned. Miss Dolores Sterling would not appreciate being likened to the thirty-six-hundred-foot granite mass reaching for the sky in the Yosemite Valley, but the comparison was accurate.

Her voice interrupted Seth's soliloquy. "I'm tired of roping, Seth. Can we do something else? Practice jumping, maybe?"

"Only if you ride Copper. Splotches isn't trained enough yet to be safe jumping."

"Pooh." Dori patted her pinto's neck and looked rebellious. "Just because she balked and tossed me off doesn't mean she isn't ready. I simply wasn't prepared for her to stop." She grinned. "You didn't mean it, did you Splotches?"

The mare whinnied as if in agreement but it didn't change Seth's mind. "Either ride Copper, or no jumping," he ordered.

Dori's deep sigh sounded like it came from her boots. "Well, all right. Copper is a good horse, too."

Fighting words. *"A good horse?* Are you blind? Copper's the best and most dependable horse on the Diamond S except for Matt's buckskin, Chase."

Dori bristled. Red flags waved in her cheeks. "He is not. I'll show you." She kicked Splotches with her boot heels and galloped away, straight for the narrow draw where she'd been thrown the day before.

"Stop." Seth leaped into Copper's saddle and took off after her.

"Never!" the flying figure called. "Faster, Splotches."

The mare responded with a burst of speed that sent chills through Seth. Had Dori regained enough of her riding skills to handle the mare? Seth shook out his coiled lariat. "Run, Copper." The sorrel sprang forward. Heart in his throat, Seth swung his lariat in a wide circle over his head.

Splotches reached the narrow gap in the earth and faltered just enough to break her stride. But when Dori called, "Go," the pinto sailed into the air and made it to the other side. She slid to a stop and Dori jumped from the saddle. "I told you she could do it."

Copper cleared the draw. Seth didn't miss a twirl of his lariat. The triumph in Dori's eyes triggered anger so strong that he flung the lasso. The rope fell over Dori and tightened before Seth realized what he was doing. It was as natural as roping a stubborn little calf but not nearly as pleasurable. Copper came to a standstill, and Seth slid from the saddle. Three long strides brought him face-to-face with the impossible girl.

Dori struggled against the lasso. "Let me go," she shouted, "or do you plan to hog-tie me on Splotches and take me back to the ranch?"

Seth saw fear in Dori's eyes in spite of her reckless words. Good. He had tried reasoning with her. It hadn't worked. Neither had threatening to stop the lessons and tell Matt why. Seth freed her, coiled his lariat, and hung it on the saddle horn. With one giant stride, he grabbed Dori by the shoulders, shook her until her hat sailed off, and said through gritted teeth, "For once in your life you're going to get what's coming to you, Dori Sterling."

"Let me go!" she screamed.

"Not until you've learned your lesson." Heedless of the consequences, Seth dropped to one knee, turned the struggling girl over the other, and whacked the back of her riding skirt—not hard enough to hurt her, but until dust flew.

"You—you. . ." Dori tore herself free and bounded to her feet. "I thought you were a Christian and a gentleman. You're no better than Red Fallon."

Seth's temporary insanity fled. He felt sick. What had he done? "I reckon you're right. I'll pack my gear and be off the ranch before night falls." He mounted Copper and looked down at her. "One thing, Miss Sterling. There's no excuse for my smacking you, but folks are treated the way they deserve to be treated. You may want to take a look at yourself before condemning me. Let's go, Copper." The sorrel leaped forward, leaving Dori alone with Splotches.

Dori watched until horse and rider were out of sight, then sank to the ground. She buried her face in her hands, feeling again the humiliation of being spanked like a naughty child. Yet Seth's words overshadowed all else.

"I'll pack my gear and be off the ranch before night falls. . . . Folks are treated the way they deserve to be treated. You may want to take a look at yourself before condemning me."

"Dear God, what have I done? Worse, what is Matt going to say?"

The thought cut through Dori's misery and brought her to her feet. Matt must never know. It would break his heart to learn that the cowboy he loved and trusted had laid hands on Dori, even though she deserved it.

"I'm the only one who can make sure Matt doesn't find out," Dori muttered. She ran to Splotches, mounted, and prodded the mare into a gallop in the direction Seth had taken. Wind burned her face, but she didn't care. She must overtake Seth before he reached the Diamond S. It would be just like him to feel he must confess what had happened when he told Matt he was leaving—and his going would devastate Sarah.

What about you? the wind mocked.

Dori shook off the thought and bent low over Splotches's neck, urging her forward with every muscle in her body and praying that Seth wasn't too far ahead to be caught. She rounded a bend. Relief nearly unseated her. Copper stood beneath a huge oak tree just ahead. Seth leaned against the mighty trunk, head bowed and shoulders slumped.

Dori raced toward them and reined in the pinto. Seth looked up. The suffering in his face went straight to Dori's heart. She slid to the ground. "Don't go." She reached out and clutched his hands.

Seth's mouth fell open. "You want me to stay? After what I did? Why?"

Not willing to confess what lay in her tumultuous heart, Dori stammered, "Because I. . .you. . .what difference does it make?" The shadow didn't leave his eyes so she added, "It was as much my fault as yours. I'm sorry."

Seth gripped her hands until they ached. "I'm the one who's sorry. I hope Matt will forgive me."

"He won't ever know," Dori flashed. "Didn't you tell me when you started 'riding herd' on me that it would be without interference from anyone? That works two ways."

The radiance in Seth's face when he freed her hands set a candle glowing in Dori's heart. It sparked an idea to convince Seth she was sincere. Could she do it? She must. Heart thundering, Dori gathered her nerve and said, "There's one condition."

A wary look crept back into Seth's eyes. "Which is. . . ?"

She took a deep breath. "Will you escort me to the barn raising?"

Dull red surged into Seth's tanned cheeks. "I can't."

Dori fell back. Embarrassment flowed through her like a river when Seth added, "Any man would be proud to escort you, but I've already invited Abby."

"I see. Have fun." Fighting tears of disappointment and anger at herself for making the preposterous suggestion, Dori climbed back on Splotches. "We'd best go home. It looks like rain."

"I'm sorry," Seth said, while swinging into Copper's saddle. "I had no idea you would ever consider going with me."

Pride forced Dori to raise her chin. "I wouldn't have if it had been any day but today." *Oh yeah?* her conscience jabbed. She turned Splotches, praying to make it home without betraying her further humiliation.

They rode silently until they reached one of the streams that fed the Fresno River. The stream was swollen and churning from recent rains. "Now what?" Dori asked.

Seth cast a glance toward the darkening sky, then up and down the stream. "We're a long way from home. If we go back the way we came, it will be pitch black before we get there. We should be all right crossing here. It's the only really good place for miles. Change horses with me."

Dori silently obeyed, and Seth adjusted both sets of stirrups.

"I'll go first. Come on, Splotches, show your stuff." Seth gave Dori a tight-lipped smile and nudged Splotches down the steep bank. Dori watched the pinto gingerly step forward, then begin to swim. Splotches appeared nervous, but Seth kept a firm hand on the reins. Dori could see he was talking to the horse, although the roar of the stream drowned out his words. They scrambled out of the water, up the opposite bank, and Seth beckoned to Dori.

"Our turn, Copper," Dori told the sorrel. He snorted and stepped into the flooded stream. All went well until they were halfway across. A floating tree, several branches still intact, barreled down the stream and blocked their way. Copper swerved to avoid the obstacle. The current caught him broadside. He staggered and regained his balance but had already been swept past the bank where Seth and Splotches waited.

Terror filled Dori, but she hung on for dear life. "You can do it, Copper," she encouraged, sticking in the saddle like a burr.

The sorrel tried again and again, but he could not outswim the tree. Tossed by the current, it stayed between horse, rider, and the opposite bank. Dori didn't dare try to turn back. The bank was too steep to climb even if they could make it.

They rounded a sharp bend. A short distance ahead, another stream gushed white water into the one where she and Copper were trapped, changing it into a river. Unless they could get out before they reached that point, it meant certain death. Only God could save them now. "Please, God, help us," Dori cried.

Copper stumbled, bringing a fresh spurt of fear, but Dori whispered, "God, I know Your promises are sure. 'When thou passest through the waters, I will be with thee; and through the rivers, they shall not overflow thee.'" A mighty bellow from the opposite shore where Seth and Splotches were racing alongside the bank of the stream caught her attention.

"Let go of the reins. Raise your hands over your head. Take your feet out of the stirrups." Horse and rider plunged into the water.

Dori's throat dried. Following Seth's orders meant she could be swept out of the saddle.

"Trust me, Dori!"

She obeyed and swayed in the saddle. Only the pressure of her thighs against Copper's heaving sides kept her upright.

The next instant a rope dropped over her raised arms and tightened. A mighty yank threw Dori out of the saddle and into the river. She desperately tried to keep her head up—and prayed for Seth. Just when she felt she couldn't make it, Seth and Splotches hauled her out of the flood. She lay on the bank, numb from cold and whispering, "Thank You, God."

Seth's voice roused her. "We have to find shelter." He sounded so grim it roused Dori from her misery. She sat up. Splotches stood with head down. Seth looked as if he'd lost his best friend.

Dori glanced back at the flooded stream—and understood. "Copper?"

Seth's expression and the slump of his shoulders cut into Dori's heart like sharp knives. She'd never heard such agony in anyone's voice than when Seth said, "He's gone."

Dori's tears gushed, but Seth helped her up.

"We have to get going. Can you walk? Splotches is tuckered out."

"Yes." It was all Dori could get out past the boulder-sized lump in her throat. She silently trudged after Seth and the pinto, away from the river that had taken Copper. Water sloshed in her boots. A keen wind cut through her clothing. She didn't complain. What was her discomfort compared with Seth's loss of the horse he loved?

What felt like a lifetime later, Seth led Splotches and Dori down a rocky ravine and stopped in front of a large clump of bushes. He parted them and grunted. "Good. We're on the right track."

Dori stared at the opening in the rock wall. Her hands went clammy, and she felt faint. Memories rushed over her: tall buildings in San Francisco and Boston threatening to squeeze the life out of her. The crowd of people in the Chicago train depot, pressing her in on all sides. Being trapped in the train car, knowing an avalanche could bury her alive.

Dori's fear and horror culminated in a wail. She put her hands over her face, backed away, and pleaded, "A cave? Please, Seth, don't make me go into a cave."

Chapter 16

Pity for the shivering girl who stumbled away from the large hole in the rock wall filled Seth. Two agonized voices rang in his ears: Dori's plea, *"Please, Seth, don't make me go into a cave."* and Matt's concern when he learned his sister was trapped in the snowbound railway car: *"Confinement in small spaces terrifies Dori. It always has."*

Now her face shone pale as death in the growing dusk. Naked fear darkened her eyes until they looked midnight black. Seth ached for what he had to do but set his jaw and quietly said, "I'm sorry, Dori. We have no choice. This is the only shelter for miles around." His voice roughened, and pain flooded through him. "Copper's gone. Even if he were here, we couldn't get back to the ranch tonight. It's getting dark, and Splotches is in no condition to travel. Neither are we."

"Y–you d–don't understand," Dori spit out between chattering teeth. "If my life d–depended on it, I c–couldn't g–go in the c–cave."

Seth steeled himself against her appeal. "You can, and you will." He hated the role he'd been forced to play but knew he must not weaken. "The cave is large enough for all three of us. I'll have a fire blazing in no time so we can dry our clothes." When Dori just stared at him, he took a deep breath and snapped, "I thought you were a thoroughbred, Miss Sterling. Stop acting like a baby and get in the cave. If you don't, I'll pack you in."

She was obviously too tired and cold to defy him. "Please, Seth. Don't make me go in there."

It was all Seth could do to resist her appeal, but in such dire circumstances, he dared not show it. "I will do whatever's necessary," he said. "Matt put me in charge of you on my terms. Now get in that cave, and get in there now."

For a moment, he thought she would refuse; then with a look that cut him to the heart, she stepped into the cave and hovered as close as she could to one side of the entrance. "I hate you for this, Seth Anderson."

"I know." Seth herded Splotches inside. "Stand next to her until I get a fire going," he told Dori. "You can get some body heat from her."

Dori silently nudged the pinto between her and the dark rock wall at the back of the cave, keeping her own position as near the entrance as possible.

Seth quickly gathered dry oak leaves and pine needles blown into the floor of the cave. He stacked them into a tepee-shaped pile, then strode outside and brought in great armfuls of downed pine branches. Moments later, a roaring fire just inside the entrance banished the chill.

Dori needed no invitation to step close to the blaze. Steam rose from her sodden clothing, and she huddled in the welcome warmth, slowly turning as if on a spit. Seth rejoiced to see some of the fear leave her face and a bit of color return. Heedless of his own discomfort, he unsaddled Splotches and removed the saddle blanket, which had miraculously stayed fairly dry except near the edges.

"Hold one side," Seth told Dori. "As soon as it's dry, you have to get out of your wet clothes. Give yourself a good rubdown with the blanket, and wrap up in it. You can't stay in those wet clothes overnight." Seth held his breath, wondering what to do if she refused, which she probably would. He gave an audible sigh of relief when she nodded instead of arguing.

"Good girl. Things could be a lot worse. We're safe, and we'll soon be dry. But I'm afraid there'll be no supper. It's too dark to hunt, and fishing in that swollen creek is out of the question."

His remark earned him a small smile from Dori.

"I'm not very musical," Seth added. "My stepsister Ellianna is the one with a singing voice. But being here reminds me of an old hymn." He began singing:

"Rock of ages, cleft for me,
Let me hide myself in Thee;
Let the water and the blood,
From Thy wounded side which flowed,
Be of sin the double cure,
Save from wrath and make me pure."

For a long moment, Dori didn't respond. Then she said, "Thank you. We really are hiding in a rock, aren't we?" Her face gleamed in the firelight, and her fingers clenched and unclenched.

Seth's heart soared. Dori had opened the door for him to speak a word for his Master. "Yes, but Jesus, the Rock of ages, is truly our shelter. We never need be afraid, no matter how bad the storm." *Lord, let her know how true this is,* he silently prayed. To his disappointment Dori only said, "I think the blanket is dry enough now. If you don't mind, I'll step into my dressing room and change." She took the warm blanket, squared her shoulders, and walked around behind Splotches.

Seth knew from the tilt of her head that leaving the bright fire for the darkness at the back of the cave was one of the hardest things Dori had ever done, but she didn't falter. When she said in a determined, but shaky voice, "Keep singing, will you?" he had never admired her more. He bellowed until the echoes rang from the rock ceiling and walls, "Rock of ages, cleft for me, / Let me hide myself in Thee."

He also prayed with all his might that the night would hold no further terrors for Dori; then he stripped branches from the pine limbs to make a bed for her near the fire.

⁊ঌ

Long after Dori lay asleep, wrapped in the saddle blanket like an Egyptian mummy, Seth kept watch. The firelight played on her exposed face. "So young and defenseless, in spite of all her bravado," he murmured. Had she really meant it when she said she hated him? After they reached the Diamond S, how would she feel? Would she remember God's goodness in helping Seth's lasso fly strong and true? Would she appreciate the dreaded cave where they had found shelter? Would she consider the things Seth had told her? Or would she only remember the humiliation he had seen in her face when she asked him to take her to the barn raising and he refused? And the way he had laid hands on her in a moment he would always regret?

Seth sighed. His head drooped. How could he have let the iron grip on his emotions loosen? Fear for Dori's safety when he saw Splotches leap the draw was no excuse. No matter what the provocation, he should have been able to control himself.

All through the long, dark hours, Seth kept the fire going and relived the day's events. Pain for losing Copper settled to a dull ache. No more would they fly over the range or stop to rest on the promontory that overlooked the valley. There would be other horses, but none would ever replace the sorrel gelding Seth's father had given him what seemed like a lifetime ago.

Just before dawn, fatigue replaced sadness and self-recrimination. Seth fell into an uneasy sleep. The nicker of a horse awakened him. His pulse quickened and he sat upright. "Copper?"

"No. It's only Splotches," a soft voice said. "I'm so sorry about Copper."

Seth's spurt of hope died. He rubbed sleep from his eyes and sprang to his feet. Dori, fully dressed and holding the saddle blanket, stood watching him. Sympathy shone in her blue eyes. Seth couldn't read her expression other than knowing it wasn't hatred. "Let's go home. I'm starved," she said.

In spite of his misery over losing Copper, Seth rejoiced. Except for tangled hair and a dirty face, Dori looked none the worse for her dunking in the creek. He couldn't say the same for himself. It seemed they had been away from the ranch for a week instead of less than a day. "All you can think of is your stomach," he teased. "What about the worry we've caused our folks?"

Dori's grin showed the unplanned night in the cave had dampened but not drowned her high spirits. "Why should they worry? They know you'll take care of me." Leaving Seth gasping, she demanded, "Well, are you coming? Or do I have to ride Splotches home and send someone back to get you?"

Lord, if I live to be older than the Sierras I will never understand Dori Sterling, Seth silently confessed. *In less than a day, I've seen her change her mood more times than a day in March. One thing for certain: Whoever marries her will never be bored.*

Once outside the cave, Seth saddled the pinto. After the trio climbed out of the ravine, he made Dori ride while he walked beside her. He shuddered, thinking of the distance they had to cover before reaching the ranch. Even if Matt and the hands were out searching for them, Seth and Dori were far afield from where they had planned to ride. It would hamper the search party.

Shortly after the sun climbed over the top of a nearby hill, a shrill whistle split the morning air. Then another. A bunch of riders rode into sight, with Matt and Curly in front and Bud leading a saddled horse.

"How did they find us?" Dori cried

"I don't know, but I'm mighty glad they did," Seth replied. He snatched off his Stetson and waved. *"Yippee-ki-ay!"*

Answering yells came back from the rescue party, and a few minutes later, they surrounded Seth and Dori. "Are you all right?" Matt asked.

"We're fine, especially now that you've come." Dori smiled. "We spent the night in a cave, and—"

"A cave?" Matt's jaw dropped, and he shot Seth a quick glance.

Dori's smile wobbled. "It was a very nice cave, as caves go, if you like that sort of thing." The next moment her eyes filled with tears. "If Seth hadn't been there yesterday I'd have died." Bright drops spilled from her eyes, and her face twisted. "Oh Matt, the river took Copper."

Matt's mouth dropped open; then he reared back in the saddle and laughed. "Well, it may have taken him, but it gave him back. Copper was standing outside the corral this morning, wet and tired, but not hurt. That's how we found you—by following his tracks."

Could a man burst with happiness? Seth's, "Thank God!" mingled with Dori's delighted cry. Their gazes met. Locked. Dori's expression after all the hours of worry and fear made Seth's eyes sting. His joy at knowing Copper was safe and waiting reflected in the girl's eyes like twin bonfires. No matter what might come, he would carry that look in his heart and cherish it.

Seth's joy continued until they reached the ranch. The stable hands had already cared for Copper, but Seth patted his horse and whispered to him before cleaning up and heading to Solita's kitchen for a much-needed meal. His good mood, however, died when Katie O'Riley joined them for a cup of coffee and brought up the last subject Seth wanted discussed.

"Miss Dori, what's a barn raising?" she innocently asked. "Curly asked if I'd go with him, but I don't for the life of me know what 'tis." She shook her curly red head and chuckled. "How can a barn get raised up? For sure not like Lazarus in the Bible."

Seth avoided looking at Dori but couldn't ignore the ice in her voice when she said, "When a neighbor's barn burns or falls down, folks for miles around gather early in the morning to raise—build—a new one. The womenfolk bring food enough to feed a regiment, and there's a square dance at the end of the day when the building is done."

Seth couldn't help stealing a look at Dori. His heart sank and he lost his appetite. The tilt of her pretty chin boded no good for one Seth Anderson.

"Curly will be a wonderful escort and you will have a lot of fun, Katie." She paused and sent Seth a disdainful glance. "So will Seth. He's taking Abby, you know."

"The pretty young lady who works at the Yosemite Hotel?" Katie's green eyes sparkled. "She's a fine colleen, I'm for thinking."

Dori shoved back from the table. "She is. Any man would be proud to take her." She left the room with her head high.

Katie looked stricken. "Did I say something wrong?"

Seth forced a smile and stood, leaving half his breakfast uneaten. "No, Katie. Miss Dolores is just tired." But he winced as he went out. Dori had parroted the very words he'd used when turning down her invitation to the barn raising. Seth sighed. Hang it all, he'd only invited Abby because she'd taken for granted that he'd escort her. This was what came of paying attention to only one girl at a time. Would Dori ever forgive him for refusing the invitation it had obviously cost her dearly to make—an invitation Seth suspected would never be repeated?

Chapter 17

Dori slowly trudged up the staircase on feet that felt heavier than lead. Exhaustion and disappointment washed through her like the waves of the swollen stream that had threatened to overwhelm her.

"Don't be a ninny," she ordered herself. "You should be glad Curly invited Katie to the barn raising. You don't want him, so why feel betrayed? Curly, Bud, Slim, and a dozen others have practically camped on your doorstep ever since you came home. You've laughed at them. It's natural for them to be attracted to Katie."

Katie? a little voice mocked. *This has nothing to do with her or with the cowboys. You're jealous of Abby Sheridan because Seth Anderson is paying attention to her and taking her to the barn dance.*

"That's stupid!" Dori exclaimed as she burst through her bedroom doorway.

Solita looked up from turning down the covers on Dori's bed. Her round, brown face showed surprise at Dori's outburst. "What is stupid, *querida*?"

Solita was not the person Dori wanted to face right then. The housekeeper's dark, knowing gaze saw far too much. Keeping secrets from Solita was like trying to keep the sun from rising.

"I'm just mumbling," Dori quickly said, then blurted out the last thing she wanted to discuss. "Did you know that Curly invited Katie to the barn raising?"

Solita's wide, white smile deepened the laugh crinkles around her eyes. "Sí. Senor Curly admires our Senorita Katie. She returns his regard."

The news jolted Dori. "She does? How do you know?"

"Is your head so far up in the clouds that you cannot see what is happening under your very nose? Unless my eyes deceive me, Senorita Katie will be Senora Prescott *muy pronto*." Solita plumped the pillows and patted Dori on the shoulder. "Now you must rest." She smiled and went out, closing the door behind her.

Dori doubted she could stay awake long enough to don night clothes and tumble into her soft, welcoming bed. "It sure is different from the pine branches in the cave," she muttered. The thought roused her from the stupor into which her tired body was sinking. A multitude of memories pounded her weary brain. Scene after scene replayed, clarified by hindsight and accusing her in no uncertain terms. "If I hadn't defied Seth by jumping Splotches over

198

the draw, I wouldn't have been humiliated, almost drowned, and forced to spend the night in a cave," she whispered.

An all-too-familiar rush of fear made her tremble, followed by the memory of Seth's voice when he said, *"Jesus, the Rock of ages, is truly our shelter. We never need be afraid, no matter how bad the storm."*

The words stilled the tumult in Dori's soul like no amount of reasoning or berating herself had ever been able to do. She remembered how safe she'd felt, wrapped in the saddle blanket and knowing nothing could harm her while Seth kept watch. How vulnerable he had looked when she awakened to find him sleeping. Dark shadows beneath his eyes attested to the strain he had been through while hauling her out of the raging stream. The shadow of a beard as red-gold as Seth's hair showed on his usually clean-shaven face. Dori's first impression slipped into her mind: *everything Matt had said and more.*

Now a lump rose to her throat. Why did life have to be so hard? Why couldn't Seth love her, instead of Abby?

Dori cried herself to sleep.

☙

The day of the barn raising came all too soon for Dori. Much to Bud and Slim's delight, she had accepted their gallant invitation to "*es*-cort" her, but she dreaded the event. Even the new, yellow-sprigged gown that made her hair look darker and her eyes bluer, failed to comfort her. "Lord, I'm going to need Your help," Dori impetuously prayed. "I can't beg off going. Even if I fooled everyone else, Solita would know why." She made a face at herself in the mirror and raised her chin. "If You'll help me make it through the day, I'll—"

"Come on, Dori, time's a-wasting," Matt sang out from the bottom of the staircase before Dori figured out what to promise God in return for His help. She wrapped herself in a cape against the early morning chill and lightly ran downstairs. Too bad she couldn't trip and twist an ankle.

☙

Busy with women's work at the barn raising, Dori longed to be out riding Splotches. "Will this day never end?" she muttered to herself. Barn raising was a hard, hungry job and required a multitude of meals. Dori helped serve the horde of workers midmorning sandwiches, cake, and lemonade; a hearty dinner; more sandwiches, cake, and lemonade in the midafternoon; and a full supper. In between, she listened to Sarah, Abby, Katie, and a bevy of other women and girls chatter, and assisted in washing a mountain of dishes. When she had a few moments to rest, she stepped outside and watched the barn going up under the magic of many willing hands.

By the time the kitchen chores ended and Dori threw out the final pan of dishwater, she never wanted to attend another barn raising. How could Katie, in her favorite green-checked gown, and Abby, radiant in pink, be so excited about the barn dance to follow? All Dori wanted to do was to crawl in a hole and pull it in after her.

She sighed. "Sterlings don't quit," she admonished herself. "Now get out there and be the belle of the ball." She grinned in spite of herself.

The first discordant notes of fiddles tuning up jangled in her ears. The three musicians swung into a lively hoedown. "Grab your partners, ladies and gents," the caller commanded. "Line up for the Virginia reel."

Bud reached Dori a few steps ahead of Slim and led her to the head of the line. Matt grabbed Sarah. Curly and Katie came next, then Seth and Abby. A dozen other laughing couples took their places, men in a long line with their partners facing them.

"Swing your partner.

"Do-si-do.

"Allemande left.

"Grand right and left."

Dori's feet responded to the calls. Her reluctance gave way to enjoyment. When she encountered Seth and he swung her in time to the music and asked if she were having fun, she could honestly answer, "Yes."

"Feel like riding tomorrow?" he wanted to know.

"Of course." Dori's heart sang. Seth might be Abby's "*es*-cort," but the look in his eyes gave rise to a faint hope. The lively young woman had obviously set her cap for Seth, but he didn't appear to be roped and hog-tied yet.

❧

March gave way to April, April to May, then early June and time to drive the cattle to the high country, turn them loose, and let them graze until the fall roundup. Dori was wild to go. "Sarah's never seen the high country," she pleaded when Matt, Seth, and Solita violently opposed their going along. "It's been years since I've been there. You won't mind roughing it for a couple of weeks, will you Sarah?"

Sarah's eyes glistened, but she sighed and said, "No, but if Matt thinks we shouldn't go, it's all right with me."

"It's not all right with *me*." Dori crossed her arms and glared at her brother. "Brett says we'll be just fine and no trouble at all. Curly, Bud, and Slim can look after us."

"And who will be looking after the cattle?" Matt inquired in a deceptively mild tone.

"All of us." Dori smirked. "Sarah is a good rider. Seth says I have the makings of a great cowhand. I can ride and rope and shoot. Please, Matt, take us." She clasped her hands around his arm and met his gaze straight on.

Matt raised his hands in defeat. "Ganging up on me, are you?" He appealed to Katie, who sat nearby. "I suppose you want to go, too?"

"Me?" She gasped, eyes enormous. "Mercy, I never thought I'd be for doing such a thing. May I?"

Mischief glinted in Matt's eyes. "Why not? I won't have to tell Curly to look after you. Seems he's taken over that job on his own."

Katie turned red as a poppy. "Begging your pardon, sir, but you're for being a bit of a spalpeen." She rose and shook out her skirts.

"And what might that be?"

"An Irish rascal, as you well know." She fled in the burst of laughter at Matt's expense. He turned to Solita.

"How about you?"

The housekeeper stared at him as if he had gone loco. "No, Senor Mateo. I will stay here and run the ranch while you are away."

Matt grunted. "Probably do a better job than Brett or me." He stood and stretched. "All right. We'll leave as soon as we can get ready."

Dori could hardly wait. She pestered Solita, who was in charge of making lists to ensure enough provisions were purchased, until the housekeeper staged a Mexican mutiny. "Out of my kitchen or there will be no trip."

Dori hugged her. "Sorry. It's just that I'm so excited. I love the high country."

Solita rolled her eyes. "I know." She chuckled. "Does it also have something to do with the fact a certain Senor Anderson is going?"

"Whatever do you mean?" Dori challenged. Not willing to hear the answer, she spun out of the kitchen and up to her room in order to hide her hot cheeks. "Not that it does any good." She sighed. "Solita has eyes like an eagle. She doesn't miss a thing."

It didn't take eagle eyes for Dori to see the stranger who descended on the Diamond S one afternoon a few days before the time set for departure to the high county. She was pulling on her boots by her open window and watching the activity at the corral. Curly, Bud, and Slim sat perched on the top fence of the corral observing Seth break a colt and jeering good-naturedly. A rig from the Madera livery pulled up.

Dori leaned forward. A stranger climbed out. The driver set two valises on the ground, nodded to the trio on the fence, and headed back for town.

Who on earth...?

Dori felt hot blood flood her face. She blinked and looked at the stranger again. Her hand flew to her mouth to stifle a cry. No one on earth could be stranger than the person standing in her yard. The scarecrow-like man was clothed in someone's cockeyed idea of western apparel: A purple-and-white-striped satin shirt. Kelly green pants. Fringed chaps. Spanking new high-heeled boots—and the widest Stetson ever seen in California. Twin pistols in a low-slung holster belt completed Stancel Worthington III's outfit. A mail-order cowboy, if Dori had ever seen one.

After a moment's hesitation, Stancel approached the fence and the staring cowboys, who were obviously struck dumb by the apparition. "I say. Where might I find Dolores Sterling?"

Curly, always the trio's spokesman, was evidently the first to recover his wits. "Miss Sterling may be out riding."

Dori suspected Curly bit his tongue to keep from adding, "Not that it's any of your business" and blessed him for his evasion. Curly knew perfectly well where she was—he'd waved to her just a few minutes earlier.

The answer obviously didn't faze "dear Stancel."

"I am Stancel Worthington III, of England and Boston," he announced in a haughty voice that made Dori long for one of her cowboys to flatten him. "I'm taking advantage of the summer break at the Brookside Finishing School for Young Ladies in Boston. I have come to tame Dolores, marry her, and take her back to civilization."

He produced a handkerchief and delicately held it to his nose. "My good man, please be so kind as to show me to my accommodations—as far away from this dreadful odor as possible."

Chapter 18

The colt Seth had been breaking gave a final snort of independence, ended his fight against the inevitable, and stood quivering in the corral.

"Good boy." Seth patted the horse's neck, slapped him on the rump, and sent him flying. An explosion of mirth whipped Seth around. Curly, Bud, and Slim were draped over the fence howling and holding their sides. A stranger stood outside the fence glowering at the trio. Seth's jaw dropped in disbelief. The colors of the man's clothing far outshone even the outfits the guitar-strumming vaqueros wore on fiesta days.

Seth gave a low whistle.

Bud recovered enough to gasp, "The things a feller sees when he don't have a gun."

Seth joined in the laughter that followed. "Who's the tinhorn?" he inquired, his gaze never leaving the man outside the fence.

Curly sprang down from his perch, wiped tears of mirth from his eyes, and donned his most innocent expression. "Show some respect, Brother Anderson. This here gent says he's come all the way from England and Boston to marry up with Miss Dori. 'Course he has to tame her first, like she was a colt. Then he aims to take her back to civ'li-za-shun."

"His moniker's Stan-sell Worthington," Bud helpfully put in.

"The Third," Slim solemnly added. "Don't fergit the Third. Hey Seth, d'yu s'pose the First and Second will be moseyin' along soon?"

The devilry in the cowboys' eyes and their outrageous drawls were contagious. Ever ready for fun, Seth decided to join in the byplay. He knew all about the arrogant Mr. Stancel Worthington III, who had caused Dori to get expelled from the fancy Boston school. Seth's blood boiled just thinking about it, even though it had brought her home where she belonged.

"If Dori's going to marry this long-nosed Englishman, I'm a ring-tailed raccoon," he muttered. A lightning glance toward the hacienda showed Dori watching through the open window of her upstairs room. Seth's heart leaped. What an opportunity to get even with Worthington on her behalf.

Seth grabbed the top fence rail, vaulted over it, and landed with a resounding thud. He wiped sweaty fingers on his vest and shook his hair down over his forehead. He stretched his mouth into a wide grin and crossed his eyes.

Reaching Worthington in one long stride, he grabbed the visitor's hand.

"Welcome to this yere Diamond S," Seth said in a nasal twang that set the cowboys off into another paroxysm. He yanked Stancel's flaccid hand up and down as if priming a stubborn pump. "You done got yere just in time. I shore need help breakin' this colt. These lazy, no-count hands"—he sent a warning glance at the three compadres—"ain't worth a plugged nickel when it comes to breakin' horses." Seth tightened his grip. "Say, Mr. Third, how about *you* givin' it a go? I done got most of the ginger out of the ornery beast."

Stancel jerked his hand free. "My name is *Mr. Worthington*." Icicles dripped from his words.

"Sorry." Seth dug the toe of his boot in the dust as if abashed, then looked up and confided, "You gotta make 'lowances fer Slim. He's done been tossed off broncs and lit on his noggin so much he ain't alwuz quite right. Shall I round up the colt fer you?"

The ridiculously garbed man's pale gaze impaled him like a tomahawk in the hands of an expert. If looks could kill, Seth Anderson would be dead and buried on the spot. "I didn't travel thousands of miles into this godforsaken country to break horses or converse with a bunch of ruffians. I insist that you take me to my accommodations." His voice was muffled by the handkerchief he still held to his nose.

He spun on one high-heeled boot, tripped on an uneven spot in the ground, and sprawled full length just outside the dusty corral. Obviously stunned, he lay there blinking—until Dori Sterling exploded through the ranch house door. Her clear voice rang in the air.

"Just what are you doing on the Diamond S, *Mr. Worthington?*"

Seth's lips twitched. He started forward to help the man up, but Stancel rudely shoved Seth's extended hand aside in an obvious attempt to gather the remnants of his dignity. "You know why I came," he told Dori in a condescending voice. It stilled the laughter and brought Bud and Slim off the fence to align themselves next to Seth and Curly. "A Worthington always gets what he wants." Stancel cast a disparaging glance at the four cowboys, then back at Dori. "You should thank whatever gods there may be that I've come to save you from marrying one of these louts."

Dori's magnificent eyes shot blue sparks. "I'd marry any of my cowboys before I'd marry you," she blazed. "Where are those English manners you boast of having? Not one of these gentlemen would arrive on a girl's doorstep and tell a group of complete strangers he has come to marry her." She paused and took a deep breath.

"*Yippee-ki-ay,*" Curly chortled, but Dori wasn't through.

"Western hospitality demands that we allow you to stay for a time, but I'm warning you: Watch your step. I don't know anything about how girls and young women in England are treated, but out here, folks hold them in high regard. Westerners get riled up real easy by anyone who persists in making a nuisance of himself." She flounced away, then sent a conspiratorial look back at Seth. "Show our visitor to the bunkhouse, will you, Seth? He can eat at the house, but I'm hoping the boys will teach him some things he needs to know."

"Yes, Miss Sterling." Seth picked up Worthington's valises and smothered a grin. As soon as he could get Curly, Bud, and Slim to one side, he'd put a bug in their ears and ask them to enlist the rest of the hands in a campaign guaranteed to send Stancel Worthington III packing. Aided and abetted by Dori, who had wordlessly made it clear she was throwing Stancel to the wolves, the boys would topple Stancel from his high horse in short order.

Dori had always laughed when Solita reminded her that Dolores meant "sorrows" or "sorrowful." But the day Stancel Worthington III arrived on the Diamond S was the beginning of misery. The insufferable man dogged her steps, either blind to Dori's contempt or convinced he could show her how far superior he was to any westerner. He seemed bent on impressing the "laughing hyenas" who jeered at him from the corral fence and in the bunkhouse. Ignoring advice about riding alone, the day following his arrival, Stancel took off by himself. An hour later, he dashed into the yard and up to the porch where the womenfolk were sitting with Matt and Seth.

"Rustlers. Out there." Stancel waved back over his shoulder.

"How do you know they were rustlers and not our hands?" Dori demanded.

"My dear woman, uncouth as they are, surely your employees wouldn't shoot at me." Stancel triumphantly exhibited a hole in his oversize hat.

Galvanized into action, a dozen men, including Matt and Seth, galloped off in pursuit of the cattle thieves, leaving Dori to stew over being left behind when she itched to be part of the chase. "It isn't fair," she blurted out. "I can ride and rope and shoot, and I own half the cattle."

Stancel looked horrified. "No lady hunts outlaws."

Dori rounded on him. "Will you get it through your thick head that I am not a lady? I never have been and never will be. Why don't you go back to Boston and marry Gretchen van Dyke?"

Stancel gave her what was as close to a leer as Dori could ever imagine him showing. "I. . .ah. . .Miss van Dyke does not possess one of the qualities I admire in you."

His remark stunned Dori, but she said in an imitation of Gretchen's simper, "And which quality, pray tell, is that?"

Stancel checked both ways, as if to make sure he wouldn't be overheard. His long face reddened. "A bit of fire. A man wants more than a pretty face."

Dori fled—and stayed in her room until she heard the pound of hooves in the yard hours later. She rushed downstairs and outside, ignoring Stancel, who rose from a chair on the porch. Fear in her heart, she counted the riders. *Six. Seven. Eight. Nine.* Terror gripped her throat until she could barely breathe. "Where are the others?" she finally asked Matt. "Curly and Bud and"—her voice broke—"and Seth?"

Matt leaped down from his horse and caught her when she swayed. "They'll be along soon. Right now they're busy taking a couple of two-bit rustlers to Sheriff Meade and the Madera jail." He snorted. "The rustlers didn't put up much of a fight." Matt's forehead puckered. "I thought one might be Red Fallon. No such luck. In spite of rumors, it appears he's long gone from the valley. Good riddance." Matt went up the steps and plumped Dori into a chair.

"Thank God our hands are safe," Dori whispered.

Just then an unwelcome voice grated on her nerves. "I say, I'm a bit of a hero, right-o?" Stancel beamed at the assembled crowd.

"You? A hero?" The men's faces reflected Dori's incredulous exclamation.

Stancel puffed up until he looked like an overstuffed owl. "It's jolly well true. If I hadn't risked life and limb and been shot at, you wouldn't have known about the blighters, much less been able to catch them."

It was the last straw. For the second time that day, Dori fled, only this time it was amid shouts of glee that rang to the heavens at Stancel's taking credit for the arrest. Sick of the houseguest who showed every sign of staying until, as Matt put it, "The last dog is hung," Dori hatched a devious plan. A discussion at supper solidified it. As usual, Stancel took center stage. After Matt asked the blessing, Stancel said, "A family custom?" He helped himself generously to roast beef so tender it cut like butter and mounded mashed potatoes on his plate.

Dori opened her mouth to reply, but Matt beat her to it.

"In this house we give thanks to God for what He provides."

"How quaint. Commendable, of course, if one believes there is a God." Stancel stroked his chin with a bony finger. "I personally find it hard to swallow."

Matt laid down his fork and said, "God not only exists, He created and rules the world and all that is in it. He loved us so much that He sent His Son, Jesus Christ, to die on the cross so all who believe on Him might have eternal life. You appear to be a learned man, Mr. Worthington. Surely you have read John 3:16 in the Bible."

Stancel gave a dismissive wave. "Oh yes. Something Jesus Christ supposedly said. If Jesus really lived, He appears to have been a pretty good chap. Perhaps even a great teacher, but the Son of God? Surely you don't believe that."

Matt's voice rang. "I do. We all do. You are sadly mistaken. Jesus was not just a good man or a great teacher. He was either insane to claim divinity, the greatest liar who ever lived, or who He said He was—the Son of God. The subject is closed. There will be no more such talk in this house."

Stancel blinked and subsided, but Dori inwardly raged. Stancel had shown his true colors and removed any second thoughts she had about carrying out her brilliant plan.

Chapter 19

When Stancel spouted off about God at the supper table, Seth longed to shake the Englishman until he rattled. A quick look at Dori showed that for once they agreed. It also showed she was up to no good. Mutiny darkened her eyes and warned she'd hatched a plan designed to penetrate even Worthington's thick hide. Seth silently cheered. Stancel the Third needed straightening out.

Dori's voice yanked Seth from his musings. "I have something in mind that may interest you, Mr. Worthington. Do stay for a while after supper."

Seth noticed she avoided looking at the others around the table. No wonder. The sudden change from her frigid treatment of their self-invited guest to warm and friendly had caught even Seth off guard. Dori's barely concealed excitement verified his suspicions. He'd bet his bottom dollar it had to do with the upcoming cattle drive. Seth inwardly groaned. Stancel's purple-and-white satin shirt and fancy green pants were enough to stampede the herd.

When supper was over and everyone gathered in front of the sitting room fireplace, Dori fired her opening gun. Seth noted she directed her remarks to their guest.

"In a few days, we're going to drive a great many of our cattle to the high country," she said. Anticipation sparkled in her eyes. "Can you imagine the joy of sleeping out under the stars, breathing mountain air, and eating food prepared in a chuck wagon, Mr. Worthington?"

Seth grinned. Dori had scrupulously omitted mention of dust, ornery cows, possible storms, rattlesnakes, and the like. He stifled a laugh when she tossed out what was undoubtedly the clincher.

"Sarah and Katie and I are all going, but if you think it's too much for you, we'll understand. You're welcome to remain at the ranch."

The animation in Stancel's face told Seth all the wild horses in California wouldn't keep Worthington from the high-country trip.

He confirmed this by saying with more spirit than Seth had seen him show, except after he'd been shot at by rustlers, "How ripping. When do we go?"

The conversation turned to planning but Seth scarcely heard it. For better or for worse, Stancel Worthington III would be on the cattle drive. And if Dori carried out whatever outrageous plan she obviously had in mind, it would be for the worse.

That night, Dori lay in bed, looking out her window at the stars. Her conscience jabbed. How fair was it to expose a greenhorn to the hardships of the trail?

"With so many real men along, nothing much can go wrong, God," she whispered. "The trip might even change Stancel's life. He made it plain at supper that he doesn't know You or Your Son. How can he not respond to the wonders of Your creation: the elk and pronghorn antelope, the rushing streams and pine-scented air? If they don't convince him there is Someone behind it all, Stancel will surely be affected by the deep faith Matt, Sarah, Seth, and even Katie display in everyday life."

She squirmed and sighed. "I have to admit, Lord, it won't be from watching me. I'm not much of a witness for You."

"You could be."

But Dori was too involved thinking of what tomorrow might bring to heed the quietly spoken message to her heart.

In spite of Stancel buzzing around Dori like a persistent mosquito, plus annoying the outfit with ridiculous suggestions, the cattle drive went well. Perfect weather prevailed, with mornings as crisp as Cookie's bacon and stentorian call, "Come an' git it before I throw it out." Sunny afternoons and glorious star-studded nights followed.

"I'm more alive than I ever was in Boston," Dori told Seth the afternoon they reached the high country and turned the cattle loose. "I haven't forgiven Miss Brookings, but I'm so glad to be home that her accusations don't bother me as much." Dori's laughter trilled. "Still, revenge is sweet. If only Genevieve could see 'dear Stancel' now." She pointed to the disheveled man, unkempt from life on the trail. "She would clasp her hands in horror and pray for her nephew to be delivered from the savage West. . .and from me."

"He sure is a sorry sight," Seth observed.

Dori smirked. "You ain't seen nothin' yet."

Suspicion flickered in Seth's eyes. "What's that supposed to mean?"

"Wait and see."

That night around the campfire Matt announced, "We'll head back to the Diamond S tomorrow."

In spite of Stancel's presence, Dori didn't want the trip to end. "Matt, can we go home by way of the logging camp? I haven't been there since I was a little girl, but I remember how lumber from the sawmill boomed down that sixty-mile flume to Madera." She added, "It's sure to interest Sarah and Katie and Mr. Worthington. Seth, too, if he hasn't been there."

"I've seen it," Seth agreed. "It's a sight to behold."

"Wouldn't you like to see it, Stancel?" Dori held her breath waiting for his answer.

Obviously saddlesore and weary of the woods, Stancel hesitated, then said, "Perhaps I should, since this is my only chance. Once we're married and living in Boston we won't return to California."

Any chance of Dori abandoning her latest and most diabolical plan vanished. She felt hot and cold by turns but finally broke the stunned silence. "It is your only chance to see the flume, Mr. Worthington."

A murmur rippled through the circle around the fire, but Matt quickly said, "I doubt the hands want to visit a lumber camp. They'll want to get back to the ranch."

A chorus of approval confirmed Matt's statement, but Curly looked at Katie and drawled, "I don't mind stayin'. Without the bawlin' critters, we can make good time on the way home. Say, Boss, why don't you send Cookie and the chuck wagon back? I'm a pretty fair camp cook. Besides, Mr. Worthington can help me."

Dori's hand flew to her mouth. Leave it to Curly to come up with such an idea.

Stancel only tucked his chin into his neck and declined. "I'm afraid I wouldn't be much good at such demeaning chores."

Curly put his hands on his hips and glared, but Katie piped up.

"I've never cooked out in the open, Curly, but if you'll be for teaching me, I'll be glad to help." Her offer raised an outcry from the cowboys.

"Aw, Boss, if I'd know Miss Katie was gonna be assistant cook an' bottle washer, I'da volunteered to stay," Bud protested.

"Me, too," Slim growled.

Curly smirked. "Too late, pards. See you back at the ranch."

His disgruntled friends marched off, leaving Dori filled with glee.

It didn't last. The departure of the outfit left her vulnerable to Stancel's unwelcome wooing. When not busy with the cattle, Curly, Bud, and Slim had foiled the easterner's attempts to get Dori away from the crowd. Now it took all Dori's cunning to avoid being alone with him. Matt and Sarah were still in the honeymoon stage and often wandered off together. Curly appeared unwilling to let Katie out of his sight. That left Seth to protect Dori. Instead, he infuriated her by standing aside and acting amused at her predicament.

One afternoon, Stancel followed Dori to a shady glade where she'd gone to hide from him. Taking her by surprise, he pinned her arms and attempted to kiss her. Dori jerked free and slapped his face with a resounding crack. Tears of rage stung her eyes.

Stancel shrugged. "Why fight the inevitable? Remember, Worthingtons always get what they want."

Dori raced back to camp, vowing to show him up so badly he'd tuck his tail between his legs and slink back to Boston.

A full moon and a crackling campfire on the night the travelers reached

Sugar Pine Logging Camp and the flume gave Dori the perfect opportunity. She encouraged Matt to relate some of the local legends. She then added, "Of all the escapades concerning the Sierra Nevada area, the most thrilling is 'riding the flume.' Daring men jump into crude, sixteen-foot boats called 'hog troughs' or 'hog boats.' They are lowered into the gushing water as it cascades from the mountains down to the valley."

"Yes, and it's both dangerous and foolhardy," Matt snapped.

Dori didn't give an inch. "I admire anyone brave enough to ride the flume." The growing interest in Stancel's face showed how well her scheme was working. "I'd ride a hog boat myself except that Matt would skin me alive."

"You've got that right, little sister. Remember what happened to H. J. Ramsdell?" Matt didn't wait for her answer. "The *New York Tribune* reporter, two millionaires, and a drunken carpenter rode a flume back in 1875. Ramsdell climbed to the top of the trestlework to see the huge logs roar down the flume. He later wrote, 'It was like the rushing of a herd of buffalo.'"

"What happened?" a wide-eyed Sarah asked.

Dori said nothing. She'd heard the story since childhood. Now she secretly gloated. Stancel's enthralled attention showed that tomorrow would repay everything she'd suffered at his hands.

"The two-hundred-pound Ramsdell thought if the millionaires could afford to risk their lives, so could he. Only one of the fifty mill hands and loggers standing around agreed to go with them. An experienced flume shooter warned, 'You can't stop, or lessen your speed. Sit still, shut your eyes, say your prayers, take all the water that comes. . .and wait for eternity.'

"The hog trough was lowered into the flume. The carpenter jumped into the front and Ramsdell into the stern, with a millionaire in the middle. The second millionaire leaped into a boat behind them. When the terrified reporter finally opened his eyes, they were streaking down the mountainside. The trestle was seventy feet high in some places. Lying down, Ramsdell could see only the flume stretching for miles ahead. He thought he would suffocate from the wind. The hog trough hit an obstruction. The drunk carpenter was thrown into the flume and had to be dragged back inside.

"The second boat crashed into the first. Another man was hurled into the water. Splintered boats and bodies slid the rest of the way to the bottom of the flume."

"I say, old chap, it sounds like jolly good fun," Stancel exclaimed, eyes gleaming.

"Are you a raving lunatic? Those men fell fifteen miles in thirty-five minutes. They were more dead than alive when they reached a place where they could get off." He stood. "Enough of such stories, folks. Time to hit the sack. Tomorrow comes early."

Dori stayed to stare into the fire after the others left, then started to get up.

A firm grip on her shoulder pressed her back down. *How dare Stancel touch me.* She whirled and froze. "You."

"Yes, me," Seth spit out. "I'd like to wring your pretty neck. Pranks like putting a wet rope under Worthington's tarp and making him think it was a snake is one thing. Goading someone into a situation where he can be injured or killed is a different story. Wasn't slapping Stancel when he tried to kiss you enough punishment?"

Dori scrambled to her feet. Embarrassment surged through her. "You saw?"

"I did." Seth crossed his arms and his face looked like a thundercloud in the dim light. "I despise Worthington's attitude, but he's still a human being, created in the image of the God he doesn't believe exists. What if Stancel dies while showing off for you, trying to prove he can do everything westerners do? Is 'getting even' worth knowing someone may be hurled into eternity without God?"

Dori saw in Seth's clear eyes what her conscience had been trying to tell her. Sickness rose from the pit of her stomach. Sickness and the knowledge she had demeaned herself in Seth's eyes. How could she have allowed the desire for revenge to carry her to such unspeakable lengths? She grabbed Seth's arm, fear washing away everything but the need to undo what she had wrought. "You don't think Stancel really means to ride the flume, do you?"

"I believe he will do anything to impress you."

Horrified, Dori cried, "We have to stop him."

Seth's strong hand covered hers, but he sounded defeated. "I only hope we can."

Chapter 20

I only hope we can."

The concern in Seth's voice about Stancel riding the flume haunted Dori and robbed her of sleep. What if they couldn't stop him? Dori took a long, quivering breath. What had she done? She knew from past experience that once Stancel set his mind, his stubbornness made the most uncooperative mule on the ranch look tractable as a lamb.

Dori planned to approach Stancel first thing in the morning, but she couldn't get him alone. Sugar Pine Camp buzzed with activity, and for the first time since Stancel arrived at the ranch, he appeared to be avoiding her.

"If I say anything in front of the others, he will ride the flume just to save face," Dori reasoned. "He didn't actually say he was going to do it. Surely when he sees the hog troughs, he will back down."

That's what you think, her conscience jeered. *What if Matt has to tell Miss Brookings her nephew drowned while trying to show he has more courage than the experienced loggers and mill hands who are smart enough not to jeopardize their lives?*

The thought sickened Dori but steeled her determination. She must stop Stancel at all costs, even if it meant groveling. She hated doing so but had no choice. If that didn't work, she would ask Matt to start them back to the ranch immediately. Muleheaded as Stancel was, he wouldn't defy his host.

Dori caught up with Stancel at the top of the flume a few minutes before the rest of the Diamond S party arrived. He stood with a group of loggers who were obviously dumbstruck with his garish outfit. Gaze fixed on a hog boat tied at the head of the flume, Stancel's expression made Dori's flesh creep. She forced a laugh through a throat dried with fear.

"It's quite a sight, isn't it?" She pitched her voice so only he could hear and pointed to the rushing water encased in a V-shaped trough that zigzagged down the hillside "You can see why it takes a fool to attempt riding the flume. I apologize for what I said last night. I don't really admire men who do stupid things. I was just spouting off."

"Reah-ly." Stancel turned from staring at the flume and looked down his long nose at her. "Nevertheless, I intend to go. It will be the thrill of a lifetime."

Dori froze. "Your lifetime may be mighty short if you insist on riding the flume."

He ignored her.

She raced back to her brother who, along with the rest of the party, had caught up with them. "Stancel is determined to ride the flume," she cried. "Stop him, Matt."

Matt leaped from Chase's back and strode toward the Englishman. "Get this and get it straight, Worthington. No one in his right mind, especially a foolhardy easterner, is going to ride the flume while I'm around."

A rumble of agreement rose from the loggers.

"Rubbish. You have no right to tell me what I can and cannot do."

Cold chills rushed up and down Dori's spine at the sneer in Stancel's voice.

Matt's eyes flashed in the way that warned of trouble ahead for anyone who crossed him. "*You are not riding the flume.* Seth, Curly, bring your lassoes. We'll hog-tie this fool until he gets some sense in his head."

Worthington shrugged but only said, "That won't be necessary."

A sigh of relief went through the crowd. It changed to disbelief then cursing when before anyone could stop him, Stancel freed the boat and leaped into it. "Worthingtons always get what they want," he called.

To Dori's horror, Stancel's legs tangled. His face changed from triumph to terror. He pitched forward in the hog trough and sprawled on his belly, head facing downstream. No sound came from his tightly clamped lips, but the appeal for help in his fear-filled eyes threatened to tear Dori's heart up by the roots.

In a twinkling, Seth raced alongside the flume and dug his boot heels into the needle-covered ground.

"God, give him strength!" Dori cried.

From his precarious position on the bank above the flume, Seth stretched out a long arm. Stancel caught Seth's wrist in a death grip and leaped to safety—but his sudden movement threw Seth off balance and into the hog trough. Before he could right himself, the boat hit an obstruction. Splinters flew. The impact hurled Seth into the flume, ten feet ahead of the boat.

"Oh Lord, forgive me." Sobbing and crying out to God to save Seth from the results of her willfulness, Dori staggered down the incline, clutching at branches and small trees. Realization hit like an avalanche: If Seth died, life would cease to have meaning for her. Her boots slipped on the needle-covered ground. She wildly tried to save herself—and failed.

The next instant, Matt's powerful grip bit into her shoulder. She stumbled and fell to her knees, hitting one on a rock. Scarcely aware of the pain, Dori's gaze riveted on the flume where Seth was fighting for his life. *Please, God, don't let Seth die. I am so sorry. Save him and I promise. . .* She could not continue.

"Stay where you are," Matt ordered before sprinting after Seth, who had been unable to launch himself back into the hog trough. Dori strained her eyes to follow Seth's progress. Her heart beat with joy when she saw that, several yards ahead, the flume leveled out slightly. The clutching water wasn't quite so swift. Matt's giant strides had taken him parallel with the boat. With a mighty bound, he managed to hurl himself into the hog trough.

A split second later, fresh horror stopped Dori's breathing. Just ahead, the flume took a sharp, downward turn. Seth's only hope was to get back into the boat before it reached that point, but he obviously was fighting a losing battle. Would the two men Dori loved more than life itself perish because of her petty desire for revenge?

ã

When Seth hit the icy flow he knew that every ounce of stamina built up by hard work and clean living couldn't save him unless he got into the hog trough. No one could survive the battering he was receiving from the rushing water, but his attempts to reach the boat were futile.

"God, unless You intervene, I'm a goner," he cried through chattering teeth, but his words were lost in the churning water. Then a Bible promise learned in childhood brought hope to his weary mind. *"When thou passest through the waters, I will be with thee; and through the rivers, they shall not overflow thee."*

With a final burst of energy Seth grabbed the sides of the flume in a death hold, hoping he could hang on long enough for the boat to reach him. A strange calm settled over him, a sense that he was not alone. He clutched the sides of the flume. The hog trough was almost within reach, but the greedy current was too strong. Fingers numb with cold, his grip loosened. He flung his arms forward in a last attempt—and missed. This, then, was the end. *Please, God, take care of Sarah. And Dori.*

A heartbeat later, strong hands clamped on Seth's wrists like bands of iron and yanked him into the hog trough. Yet the danger was not past. Above the ever-increasing roar of untamed water, Matt bellowed in Seth's ear, "Hang on and pray."

In the twinkling of an eye, the two men in their splintered boat plunged headlong into the ever-increasing torrent.

ã

Heartsick and trembling, Dori watched the men vanish around the bend. The sound of weeping told her she was not alone. Sarah and Katie, white-faced and clinging to one another, had reached her. Curly tore past, slipping and sliding in his downward rush beside the flume.

Sarah's fingers bit into Dori's arm. "What's happening?" she cried.

"I don't know." Dori licked her parched lips. "All we can do is wait. Curly will come back and. . ." She couldn't continue.

"I can't bear to wait." Sarah cried. She dropped to the ground and covered her face with her hands. "We have to do something to help."

Katie knelt beside Sarah and gathered her in her arms. "I'm for thinking the best way we can help is to pray, then decide what we should do."

"Do?" Dori asked, too numb to understand.

The Irish colleen nodded. "For sure. Should we wait here, hoping Matt and Seth will escape harm and return? Start back to the ranch?" She shook her head. "We'll know better when Curly returns. Now, let's pray."

Dori caught the black look Katie sent toward the bedraggled man who had silently joined them. "Mr. Worthington, if you don't care to pray, then begone with you."

Stancel stared for a moment, then stumbled a short distance away and sat down under a tree, leaving the three women to petition heaven on behalf of Matt and Seth.

Pain washed through Dori. *Surely they will manage to get out of the flume and come back,* her heart insisted. *Although this escapade has probably killed any chance of Seth's ever caring for me.* She pushed the thought aside. Now was no time to think of herself. Dori also tried to banish visions of the splintered hog boat and rushing water, but to no avail. As Katie said, all they could do was to wait.

Several hours later, Curly returned with a battered and bruised Seth Anderson, both riding unfamiliar horses. "The boss is down below with a wrenched ankle. He's gonna be fine, but it hurts too much for him to ride," Curly reported. "The man who lent us these horses is taking Matt to Madera so Doc Brown can give him a once-over."

"Thank God!" Sarah threw herself into her brother's arms, tears streaming.

Dori swallowed the lump of relief that sprang to her throat and turned away to hide her desire to hug Seth like Sarah was doing. Stancel's voice stopped her in her tracks. He looked more than ever like a scarecrow in his torn clothes when he shuffled over to Seth and held out an earth-stained paw.

"Much obliged, old chap. Ripping of you to lend a hand. Puts me in your debt, and all that." He cleared his throat. "I was a bit distracted there for a bit, but I could have extricated myself shortly. Of course, you couldn't know." He shrugged.

Dori wanted to hit the obtuse man. Instead, she fixed her gaze on Seth. A white line formed around his lips. He ignored Stancel's outstretched hand, clenched his fists, and stuck his face close to the braggart's. Then he let loose with both barrels.

"You just don't savvy, do you, Worthington? You deserve the licking of your life. I'd love to give it to you, but I am not going to do it. If you don't start using whatever brains God gave you, there's a lot worse ahead for you." Seth paused. "You think you could have saved your own worthless hide? Never on this green earth. You're right about one thing. You're in my debt. But you owe a far greater debt to Someone else."

A poignant light crept into Seth's eyes, a light that made Dori feel more ashamed than she had ever been in all her years of careless living.

"I risked my life to save yours, Mr. Stancel Worthington III. Jesus Christ, the Son of God, did a lot more than that. He died on a cross to save your soul. If you're any kind of man, you'd best get your nose out of the air and start admitting who's really in control. Otherwise, you're no better than the braying donkeys on the Diamond S."

Dori wanted to applaud, but Curly had the last word.

"A-men," he drawled. He clapped Stancel on the shoulder so hard the Englishman staggered. "Cheer up, old chap. If the good Lord could save a miserable cowboy sinner like me—which He did—then I reckon He can save an ornery critter like you." Curly freed his hand and scratched his head. "I'll tell the world, though, it's gonna take some doin', even for Somebody as big as God."

Chapter 21

Stancel Worthington III was strangely silent on the long trip home. He kept to himself for much of the way, riding apart from the others in the party and only speaking when spoken to. For the first time in Dori's acquaintance, she saw uncertainty in his eyes. Had what she privately called "Seth's Sugar Pine Sermon" pricked Stancel's vanity and begun to make a difference in his life? She fervently hoped so.

"How could it not make a difference?" Dori asked herself a dozen times while riding through the forests and back down to the Diamond S. "If I live to be an old woman, I'll never forget Seth's blazing face and the words that poured out of him." A boulder-sized lump of regret rose to her throat.

"Lord, Stancel is guilty of not believing in You. I've been guilty of taking Your Son's sacrifice lightly, even though I knew better. In Your eyes, I must be guiltier than Stancel, the scoffer."

The voice of truth that had so often risen to condemn her and been drowned out by her refusal to heed it would not be silenced.

You've flitted through life seeking pleasure like a butterfly searching for nectar. Matt and Solita's attempts to rein you in have been in vain. You've been sullen and angry with Matt without just cause. You've whined and complained and done everything but stomp your feet because your brother is making you finish your schooling: a far lighter punishment than you deserve for your behavior at Brookside.

Dori squirmed. The indignity of being made to do lessons like an unruly child still rankled. "Young ladies shouldn't be forced to study if they don't want to," she sputtered in self-defense.

The voice continued. *Young lady? Sarah and Katie and Abby are young ladies. You're nothing but a spoiled child who is determined to have her own way, no matter what the consequences are. What happened to your grandiose plan to impress Seth by helping Sarah and Solita teach the Mexican women and children to speak English? You ran at every opportunity and left the teaching to Sarah, Solita, and now Katie.*

Dori drooped in the saddle and allowed Splotches to fall behind the band of travelers. Everything the little voice said was true.

Have you forgotten so soon how God saved you from the river?

The forest around Dori faded. Memory replaced the oaks and pines with a deadly, rushing stream. She shuddered in spite of the warm day. But for the grace of God, she would be dead. How had she repaid Him? By hanging on to the desire for revenge and putting Stancel, then Seth and Matt, in terrible danger.

Never before had Dori so felt the enormity of her offenses. The crushing knowledge caused her to plead, "God, forgive me. Jesus, please be my Trail-mate and Guide, as You are Matt's and Sarah's and Seth's. . ." Words failed her. Reining in Splotches, she slid to the ground and fell to her knees beneath the widespread arms of a huge oak tree. Scalding tears fell.

"Jesus, you told Peter to forgive seventy times seven. You forgave him even though he denied You three times. I've never denied You in words, but through my actions. I'm so sorry. Please, help me to start over and be what You want me to be."

Dori stayed under the tree for a long time, searching her soul for any hidden wrongdoing. When she finally remounted Splotches, an indescribable peace filled her heart. She patted the pinto's neck and whispered, "I feel pounds lighter. And clean. Clean and forgiven. Now I have to find Stancel and apologize." Dread of having to humble herself before the prim and proper Englishman filled her, but a scene from the past came to mind.

"Solita, I don't feel like saying my prayers."

"Perhaps it is because you have anger in your heart at Senor Mateo for not taking you with him to Madera."

"I don't see why I couldn't go."

"Senor Mateo had an important meeting. He had no time to watch out for you."

"Why does that make me not want to pray?"

"It is always so, querida. Prayer is our gift to God. The Bible says that before we bring gifts to Him, we must first make things right with others."

Alone on the hillside, Dori smiled. She could still remember running barefoot down the stairs and flinging herself into Matt's forgiving arms. "I sure won't fling myself into Stancel's arms, but I'll try to make amends," she told Splotches. "I humiliated him publicly, so I need to apologize the same way." She clucked to her horse and started down the long trail to find the others.

That evening around a blazing campfire, Dori waited until conversation dwindled. Then she took a deep breath, held, and released it. "Stancel, you wouldn't know it from my actions, but I became a Christian when I was a little girl. Sadly, it didn't keep me from wanting revenge for"—she faltered—"for what happened in Boston. I deliberately brought up the subject of riding the flume. Deep down, I figured you wouldn't really do it when you saw what it was like. I wanted you to back down so I could show you up in front of everyone and crow over you."

Dori curled her fingers into the palms of her hands so tightly the nails bit. "This afternoon I asked God to forgive me. I know He did. I hope to forgive myself when that awful incident stops haunting me. I need one more thing. Will you forgive me?" Dori's pulse drummed in her ears, but she never took her gaze off Stancel.

After what seemed like an eternity of shocked silence, he mumbled, "That's awfully big of you, my dear." Stancel waved a dismissive hand. "Think no more about it." He cleared his throat and gave his own offhand apology. "I may have been a bit to blame as well." Then he awkwardly got up and said, "May I speak to you privately?"

Dori's heart sank. *Oh dear, is he going to propose again?* She rose to her feet and slowly followed Stancel out of hearing distance at the far edge of the firelit circle, dismayed by what must be the final showdown between them.

Stancel cleared his throat again. "Since the matter of the flume ride is settled, it's time for you to stop this nonsense about not marrying me. We need to get on with our plans. We'll have a jolly time in Boston and go back to England often. Not, of course, until you have instruction in proper etiquette concerning castles, riding after the hounds, and all that. When you're properly trained, I will present you at court, but only after I know you are ready and won't disgrace me."

Had Stancel learned nothing during his time in the West? Dori fought the urge to laugh in his face, breathed a prayer for help, and replied, "I can't marry you. Not now. Not ever."

Stancel peered at her through the flickering light. His voice turned cold. "It's because I'm not a Christian, isn't it? If you were my wife, I might someday put aside my beliefs and become one."

Dori knew she must sound a death knell to that line of thought. "You must never become a Christian for such a reason, Stancel. Besides, it wouldn't make any difference. I don't love you. I never have. It's as simple as that."

His colorless gaze sharpened. "I say. Is there someone else?"

Dori felt herself tingle from the toes of her dusty boots to the top of her curly dark head. "You have no right to ask such a question."

"I have *every* right," he stubbornly persisted. His mouth pursed so tightly the words came out like buckshot. "Dolores, I have done you the honor of laying my heart and hand at your feet, but you continue to trifle with me. I demand to know: Do you fancy yourself in love with some blighter out here?" He grabbed her wrists. "That's it, isn't it? Who is he? One of the cowboys? Young Anderson, perhaps?"

His jeering laughter grated on Dori's nerves. She jerked free. Only one answer would get through his thick hide. "Yes," she snapped, "but you're not to say a word to anyone, you hear?"

Stancel's mouth fell open. "Surely you can't believe I will disclose your folly in choosing a California ruffian when you might become a *Worthington*." He tucked his chin into his neck and added in the condescending tone Dori hated, "My dear girl, the day will come when you will look back to this moment. You will realize what you gave up and regret it for the rest of your life."

His arrogance loosened Dori's unruly tongue. "Don't hold your breath waiting," she muttered before she could stop herself. Then she turned and headed back to the campfire. "Well, Lord, I did it again. Will I ever learn to control my temper? On the other hand, being a Christian doesn't mean I have to stand for Stancel Worthington III's insults."

"My Son took the worst kind of abuse and didn't open His mouth in reproach."

Dori swung around and returned to where Stancel still stood in the shadows. His long arms were crossed over his chest, and a bitter look covered his face. "Mr. Worthington, once again I apologize. The Bible says all things work together for good. Perhaps this will convince you that I could never be the kind of wife you want." Pity overrode contempt and softened her voice. "Go back to Boston. Marry Gretchen and be happy." Dori summoned all the courage she possessed. "I wish you well and hope you'll remember what Seth told you at the flume." She held out her hand.

Stancel looked at Dori's hand as if it were a poisonous snake. "I shall certainly consider your suggestion—the one about Gretchen, that is." He stalked off.

Dori sighed. She'd done what she could. Now it appeared the travelers would have to put up with a fit of the sulks by the rejected suitor for the remainder of his stay.

Her prediction proved accurate. Stancel remained unapproachable during the time it took him to sufficiently recover from the cattle drive and announce that the sooner he got back to Boston the better.

On the day he left, Dori wavered between bidding him good-bye at the ranch and going to town when Matt drove him in. Still hoping for some kind of reconciliation, she decided to go.

I may as well have stayed home, she thought when the visitor refused to respond to Matt's and her efforts to rouse him on the way to Madera. Stancel gave no sign of compromising his dignity other than stiffly saying, "Thank you for your hospitality, such as it was."

Dori's heart sank. Did she dare say anything that might help the seeds of Christianity Stancel had witnessed during his stay stir his parched heart and grow? Or would speaking out do more harm than good?

Matt evidently held no such reservations. Just before Stancel stepped onto the eastbound train, Matt grasped his hand and said, "We realize this hasn't been a happy vacation for you. I hope you will overlook our brand of humor and remember what Seth told you about God and Jesus."

For a moment, Dori feared there would be no relenting. Then an unexplainable look stole into Worthington's eyes, and he gruffly said, "Tell Anderson I will think about it." He swung up the steps of the train without looking back.

Dori wanted to applaud. "Godspeed," she called to her troublesome swain, meaning it with all her heart. The train whistle sounded. Dori watched Stancel Worthington III chug out of her life, torn between tears, laughter, relief, and the desire that he would one day find salvation.

Chapter 22

Two weeks later, Dori halted Splotches under a giant oak tree on a knoll above the Diamond S and slid from the saddle. Matt had ordered her to stay within sight of the ranch house when riding alone, due to rumors about unsavory-looking strangers being seen on the range. Now she sank to the ground. If she didn't let out her pent-up feelings she'd burst.

"I don't understand, Lord," she said in the direct approach that made God her Trailmate, as well as her Savior. "I've repented, groveled, and apologized. I've studied until my head ached to make up for ducking out on my lessons earlier. Unless I'm sadly mistaken, I did well on my final examinations. I've helped teach the Mexican women and children, been nice to Abby when she comes to visit, and done everything Matt tells me. Yet things are worse with Seth than ever."

Splotches nickered and nudged Dori's shoulder with her nose.

"What do you know?" she asked. "You're only a horse. Sorry, girl. If I didn't have God and you to talk to, I'd be sunk. I told Solita if my life were a storybook, Seth would recognize I've turned over a new leaf—now that Stancel's gone. We'd have a grand reconciliation scene, and the book would end with us living happily ever after."

She groaned. "Know what she said?" Dori mimicked the housekeeper's voice. " 'Life isn't a storybook. This is only the end of a chapter. Dios will show you what comes next. Trust Him and wait. He knows what is best for you and Senor Seth.' "

Dori sprang to her feet. "Lord, I don't want to wait. Seth is as polite as can be but the biding-my-time look in those blue eyes is driving me crazy. Why can't he see I'm sincere?"

The autumn leaves do not change color overnight, but gradually. Seth needs time to be shown that you are not the same Dolores Sterling.

All the fight went out of Dori. Her voice of conscience was right, as usual. But what would it take to convince the man she loved that she had truly changed?

A horrid thought came. "Abby is hot on Seth's trail. He's also mighty friendly with Katie. If she's in love with Curly, like Solita says, why was she whispering with Seth on the porch the other evening? What if God knows

I'm not the best mate for Seth?"

Splotches had no answer beyond another whinny, and the little voice that sometimes plagued and at other times comforted Dori remained silent.

She swung into the saddle and turned toward home, so lost in misery that even the western sky flaunting red, orange, and purple banners failed to raise her spirits. Seeing Seth talking with Katie by the corral didn't help. He appeared to be pleading with her, but as Dori drew closer, she saw Katie shake her head and heard her say,

"Faith and mercy, has that spalpeen Curly been for getting your help to argue his cause? 'Twill do him no good." Laughter rippled. "We'll wed when I say the word, and not one minute sooner."

Dori's despair over Seth changed to joy. *One down, one to go,* she exulted. *With Katie marrying Curly, that just leaves Abby for competition.* She grinned and called, "Grand evening, isn't it?" then dismounted and led Splotches into the corral. Her heart thundered while she removed the saddle, rubbed Splotches down, turned the mare loose in the pasture, and headed for the house. Thankfully, she reached the privacy of her room without encountering anyone.

She sat down by her window and stared into the growing night. Katie had disappeared, but Seth still stood by the corral, face turned in the direction of the house. Dori's hands flew to her burning face. How could she face him— or anyone—blushing like tonight's sunset? Surely they'd see the love she'd tried so hard to hide.

Sterling pride won out over Dori's dismay. She changed from her riding clothes into a red-checked gingham dress with a white collar and cuffs and ran downstairs. The family was gathered in the sitting room as usual, along with Seth, Curly, and Solita. Conversation stopped when Dori entered. She chose a chair where her face would be in shadow and asked, "Am I interrupting something?"

"Not at all," Matt said. "In fact, we were talking about you."

Dori sat up straight. "What did I do now? I thought I'd been pretty good lately." She hated the quaver in her voice. Was Matt, as well as Seth, questioning her sincerity?

Matt's laughter boomed. "I'll let Katie tell you."

Dori took heart. It didn't sound like she was in trouble. "Katie?"

Her teacher's eyes sparkled. "You've been for studying so hard recently that you've passed your final examinations with highest honors. Congratulations."

Dori sagged with relief, but Katie wasn't finished.

"Being here has been a blessing, one I'll be for remembering long after I'm gone."

Curly raised one eyebrow, and his eyes twinkled. "I don't think you'll be for movin' on any time soon," he drawled.

Katie turned rosy red and sent a quick look at Seth, who said, "That's for sure," and smiled at Dori.

She felt the telltale blush she hated crawl into her cheeks. Best to get away before she betrayed her feelings. She yawned. "Excuse me, folks. I think I'll turn in." She stood up and started for the staircase, but Seth's voice stopped her.

"Now that you're finished with your studies, maybe we'll have time to ride again."

Dori gulped. "I thought my lessons were over."

"Really? I may still have a few things to teach you."

The twinkle in Seth's eyes made Dori feel she'd stepped onto shaky ground. Drat. He'd always been able to see right through her. Had he caught the relief in her face that Katie wasn't a candidate for his affections? She gathered her wits and raised her head.

"Why, of course." Dori forced herself to slowly walk upstairs when she longed to run. She wanted to ride with Seth. Yet doing so meant giving herself away, and refusing would bring down a storm of questions on her hapless head. Before falling asleep, she pounded at the gates of heaven, asking for a reprieve.

❧

If Dori had ever questioned whether God had a sense of humor, she'd have tossed the notion to the four winds the very next day. A buggy pulled up to the ranch house. Abby Sheridan stepped down.

"Howdy, everyone. I have a few days off." Abby's pretty face shone with excitement. "I'm taking the stage trip up to Big Tree Station. Anyone want to go along?"

"Where's Big Tree Station?" Sarah wanted to know.

"In the Yosemite Valley," Matt told her. "You stay overnight and the trip is quite an experience." He grinned. "Remember when we went, Dori? You couldn't believe that a tree could be big enough for a stagecoach to drive through."

"It was, though." Dori added, "I also remember the endless forests and canyons and snow-capped mountains. You'll love them, Sarah. Guess what: Even former president Ulysses S. Grant took the trip."

Sarah's eyes glowed. "It sounds like just this side of heaven."

Abby clapped her hands and giggled. "What's good enough for a president is good enough for me." She paused and dramatically added, "Besides, we may be held up."

"Held up? Does that happen often?" A little worry line creased Sarah's forehead.

"It's nothing to worry about," Abby reassured her. "Holdups are so commonplace that the tourists almost hope they will happen. The robbers are usually real gentlemen. They hold up the stage, relieve passengers of their valuables, politely thank them, and ride away without harming anyone." Abby beamed. "We'll outsmart them. We'll leave our valuables at home and enjoy being held up without losing our possessions."

Sarah laughed so hard she had to hold her sides. "It sounds wonderful and really quite safe. What do you think, Matt? Can you get away?"

He shook his head. "I wish I could, but I have to attend a cattleman's meeting." His face brightened. "Seth can take my place, and you can chaperone, Sarah. How does that sound?" He grinned at Dori. "The trip will be a reward for your hard work."

"Thanks." Dori kept to herself the fact she saw the trip as twofold. She could gauge Seth's reaction to Abby. There also might be a chance to show Seth she wasn't the same spoiled girl she used to be.

On the appointed morning, Seth, Sarah, Dori, and Abby met at Captain Mace's Yosemite Hotel just before six o'clock. At the last minute, Katie had decided to stay at the ranch. She didn't say why, but Dori suspected it was because Curly wasn't going.

Dori shrugged and vowed to shelve her worries and enjoy what lay ahead. The day loomed bright and beautiful; the stagecoach sat ready and waiting. Dori shivered as much from excitement as from the chilly morning. She thought of Stancel Worthington III and laughed. What would he think of the open-sided stagecoach with its canopy top, horsehair-filled seats, and great wheels? He'd surely look down his nose at the other two passengers: rough-dressed ranchers who said they'd be getting off at Fresno Flats. And he'd jeer at Charley, the grizzled, loquacious driver who had Seth riding next to him.

Dori couldn't have cared less. Nothing could spoil the day. She reviewed their itinerary. Arrive and change horses at Adobe Ranch, nine miles east of Madera. Go through Dustin's Station. Stop for dinner at Coarsegold. Travel through Potter's Ridge, Fresno Flats, and Burford's Station. Reach Big Tree Station in the late afternoon.

"I can hardly wait to stay at the Wawona Hotel," Abby said when they were underway. "I heard all about it from a woman who took the trip." Peals of mirth brought an answering smile to Dori's face.

"You won't believe this. First she raved about the hotel, which is a large, two-story building with a lobby, sitting room, dining room, office, twenty-five guest rooms, lots of flowers, and wonderful food. Then she sighed and said, 'Now if it were only in San Francisco instead of way up here in the wilderness, it would be perfect.' "

"Sounds like. . .uh. . .someone Dori knows," Sarah teased.

"Enough of that, Mrs. Sterling. Pay attention to the trip."

"I am." Sarah's eyes reflected the wonder Dori felt in spite of having to keep her balance in the swaying stagecoach. A bull elk meandered across the dusty road, and Charley warned, "Be keerful of animules up here. You gotta watch out if'n you sleep on the ground floor at the *ho*tel. Don't leave yore winders open. Coyotes 'round here have been known to sneak up an' snatch at a body's bedroll."

Seth chuckled. "Come on, Charley. That only happens in the woods, not in the hotel." He seemed more carefree than he had for weeks.

"I'm just joshin'. Yu'll be perfectly safe at Big Tree Station."

By the time they reached Coarsegold, Dori couldn't wait to get out of the jouncing stagecoach. The trip so far had surpassed expectations but she secretly wondered how much of her would be left by the time they reached Big Tree Station. Once on solid ground, Dori clicked her teeth. "Lead me to the food. At least no robbers yet."

No robbers. Something worse. When the travelers returned to the stage after dinner they discovered a new passenger.

Red Fallon was perched beside the driver.

Chapter 23

Stunned, Seth Anderson stared at the gaunt man on the high seat beside Charley.

"Red Fallon!" Sarah cried.

Red doffed his worn sombrero. "Yes ma'am. Howdy, Anderson."

Red's reply freed Seth from paralysis. Although the cowhand's formerly unkempt red hair and beard were now neatly trimmed, there was no mistaking Red's steel gray eyes.

Hatred Seth thought he had conquered rose like bile. He launched himself at the man who had nearly killed him and had kidnapped Sarah. Seth's powerful left arm grabbed Red by the vest and yanked him from the seat. He clenched his teeth and drew back his right arm to deliver a blow Red would never forget.

Red made no effort to free himself. "Go ahead. I got it comin'."

The words stopped Seth in his tracks. "Either you come up with a good reason for being in Coarsegold, or I'll beat the living daylights out of you."

Red's face showed no trace of fear. "I'd do the same in yore place. You want my story short an' sweet?"

"As short and sweet as you can make it." Seth tightened his hold.

"After Matt an' Sheriff Meade fired me off the range, nobody else'd hire me. I always had a hankerin' to see San Francisco, so I ended up there. I got mugged and nearly beaten to death." A strange expression crept into Red's craggy face. "You'll find this hard to swaller, but it's the best thing that ever happened to me."

Seth loosened his hold and reeled back. "Are you serious?" The question cracked like a Colt .45. Was this another of Red's lies?

"Dead serious, which I woulda been if a kid, 'bout the age you were when you came west, hadn't stumbled over me in an alley back of a rescue mission." Red's steely eyes softened. "The folks there practiced what they called 'soup, soap, and salvation.' Hanged if they didn't clean me up, feed me, and tell me about a feller named Jesus."

Red heaved a great sigh. "They said Jesus died on a cross so even the worst sinners could be forgiven if they believed in Him. I thought He must be loco. Why would anyone want to die for a bunch of ornery skunks? But watchin' and listenin' to the kid and the folks who ran the mission finally got it through my thick head. God loved me, no matter how bad I'd been—and I didn't have to be like that no more."

Seth clamped his mouth shut. Low exclamations from the three young women and a loud, "Well, if that don't beat all" from Charley showed their reaction to the amazing story. Seth's skepticism remained, in spite of the light in Red's eyes. Yet God did send Jesus to save sinners. In His eyes, Red was no worse than any other unbeliever. But was Red sincere?

"Ah-huh. And you just happened to be catching the Madera-Big Tree Station stage the same day we were on it." Seth accused.

The light in Red's face increased. "Mebbe it's for a reason."

The words of an old hymn flashed across Seth's churning mind:

God moves in a mysterious way
His wonders to perform;
He plants his footsteps in the sea
And rides upon the storm.

What if Red was right? What if God had arranged for the cowhand to be in this place at this time? Seth wracked his brain, trying to figure out why. All he could come up with was that if Red had really accepted Christ, then Seth, Matt, and Sarah need never fear him again. And Seth could finally be freed from lingering anger.

Lord, I thought I turned my hatred over to You long ago. I hadn't. One sight of Red showed that. So what do I do now? Seth silently prayed.

"Wait."

The admonition pushed into his brain and lodged there. Yes, he would wait. In the meantime, "I still want to know why you're here," he told Red.

Some of the tension left Red's face. He started to hold out his hand, then evidently thought better of it. "Not by chance. The folks at the mission got word the hotel in Yosemite was lookin' for trail guides to show tourists around. I figgered if I made good there, I'd have the nerve to someday go back to Madera and show folks I'd changed. Trouble was, I needed a horse." A trace of the old Red showed when he added, "After askin' Jesus to ride along with me, I couldn't up and steal one."

Seth laughed in spite of himself, but Charley's snort nearly drowned him out. "Not hardly. So what'd you do?"

Red's face turned somber. "The mission folks gave me train fare to Madera, but I got off at Merced, knowin' there wouldn't be no welcomin' party in Madera. I bought a sorry excuse for a horse and made out all right till last night. The ornery critter broke his hobbles and took off for parts unknown. I had to hoof it on in to Coarsegold today." He sagged back against the stagecoach.

The gray look in Red's hollow-cheeked face lent credibility to his story, but Seth still had qualms. Could a hawk really become a dove? He glanced around the circle of faces. Sarah and Abby looked convinced. Dori did not. Doubt lurked in her deep blue eyes, the same doubt Seth harbored. Again the word *wait* beat into his brain. Time alone would establish Red's credibility.

Charley's unshaven face crinkled into annoyance. "That's a mighty purty story, if it be true. I ain't a-sayin' one way or t'other, but we got no more time fer tales, tall or otherwise. Get in the coach, folks. We gotta move out if we're gonna get to Big Tree Station when we're due."

Red swung back up beside Charley. Seth was profoundly grateful. He helped the women to their seats and climbed on. The two Fresno Flats-bound ranchers, who had remained inside the eating place until Charley bellowed, "All aboard," joined them.

"Do you think Red's telling the truth?" Sarah whispered, low enough so that the ranchers couldn't hear.

"I don't know." Seth stared at Red's back. "All we can do is to wait and see."

The ride from Coarsegold to Potter's Ridge proved jolting, but just before they reached Fresno Flats, the stagecoach lurched, shuddered, and stopped.

Charley climbed off the high seat and began to inspect the wheels. He swallowed what Seth suspected was a colorful oath not fit for ladies and said, "Sorry. Thet last big rut wuz a humdinger." He scratched his grizzled head with a bony finger and spat a stream of tobacco juice alongside the road. "The axle 'pears to be all right, but we cain't take chances. 'Tain't far to Fresno Flats an' a blacksmith. It's likely we c'n make it by goin' slow 'n' easy. I don't take this coach on no dang'rous mountain roads 'nless it's fit to drive."

One of the ranchers climbed out of the coach. "I'm going to walk on into town," he told Charley. "I'll tell the blacksmith you're on your way." The second rancher joined him, but Red and the Diamond S party elected to stay with the coach. "Too dusty for me," Sarah commented, and the others agreed.

By the time the coach limped into Fresno Flats and was examined and pronounced fit by the blacksmith, Charley looked disgusted enough to spit nails instead of tobacco juice. "Get a mosey on," he barked to his remaining passengers. "We got no more time to waste." Seconds later, he prodded his team into a bone-wrenching trot that threatened to shake members of the Diamond S party to pieces. They grimly clutched one another and held on.

≈

Throughout Seth's conversation with Red, Dori had listened with all her might, trying to sort truth from fabrication. Did Seth buy Fallon's far-fetched story? Yet if it were a pack of lies, why had Red come back to a place that offered nothing but trouble for him? Had he ever even been in San Francisco? Had he really heard about Jesus and repented of the horrible life he'd led? Or was Red up to some new and devious scheme?

229

Dori decided to approach the knotty question the way she tackled hard school lessons. First, identify the problem. Next, weigh the evidence. Finally, come to a conclusion. *The problem? Whether Red is telling the truth. If not, why is he here? His changed appearance seems to bear out what he says. On the other hand, cutting his hair, trimming his beard, and pretending to get religion would be a surefire way to convince people he's changed. But if it's all a bluff, how could he know Seth, Sarah, Abby, and I would be on the stage today?* Dori shook her head. Based on the facts as she knew them, it was impossible to reach a conclusion.

The coach rounded a bend. Three armed, masked horsemen blocked the road.

Charley pulled the team to a sudden halt that threw his passengers forward in their seats. "What th—"

"Everyone down, and nobody reach for a gun," the man in front ordered. "Hand over your jewelry and money, and no one will get hurt."

"Sorry, boys," Seth called to the bandits after helping the girls down. "We're plumb out of valuables today." He grinned. "We heard how the stage gets held up so the ladies left their jewelry home. I've got a few dollars. Charley and Red may have a few more."

"Think we're gonna settle for chicken feed?" the man snarled. "Since you ain't got any valuables, we'll take one of your ladies. From the looks of them, someone will pay dear to get any one of them back." He guffawed, and his two followers joined in.

Dori glanced at Sarah and Abby. Their paper-white faces convinced her that these were no "gentlemen" robbers. Sarah's expression cut Dori to the heart. Sarah had been through one kidnapping. She must not be forced to endure another.

"You skunks! My brother will have you hunted down for this." Too late, Dori realized her uncontrollable tongue had once again gotten her into deep water.

"Who's your brother?" the bandit growled.

Dori considered refusing to tell him. A quick look at Sarah changed her mind. She must save Sarah at all costs—which meant the bandit must not find out she was Matt's wife. Dori raised her head and looked straight into the slits of the kerchief that covered the outlaw's face. "Matthew Sterling."

"Hey fellers, we got us a good one." The bandit leader vaulted off his horse and forced Dori to mount. "Move, and one of my boys will put a bullet in you."

With a cry of rage, Seth lunged toward them. A second bandit spurred his horse and smashed the butt of his gun onto Seth's head. Seth dropped senseless to the ground. Sarah and Abby screamed. Dori could only pray that Seth was still alive.

"Driver, get word to the Diamond S to expect a ransom note," the leader said. "Tell Sterling if he wants to see this mouthy sister of his again, he'd better pay." He grabbed for the reins of Dori's horse. The horse reared. The bandit dropped the reins and tried to get out of the way, to no avail. The horse's shoulder sent him sprawling. His gun went off, then flew out of his hand.

The trouble the other two bandits were having with their horses showed Dori that the shot had spooked the animals. If only she could reach the gun. She flung herself out of the saddle, but her foot caught in the stirrup of her frightened horse. Dori fell, striking her head and shoulder. Pain ripped through her, but she jerked her foot free and crawled toward the gun.

Before she reached it, Dori saw Red Fallon jump from the driver's seat and leap toward her. He swung onto the horse and snatched Dori up by the back of her blouse. He threw her across the saddle and sent the horse into a full gallop. Dori's last thought before surrendering to pain was, *So Red was lying after all.* Then, merciful blackness.

Chapter 24

Seth Anderson groaned. Where was he? Why was water splashing on his face? Was he back in the river trying to save Dori?

A strong hand gripped his shoulder and shook him. "Wake up, young feller."

"Charley?" Seth's head throbbed with the granddaddy of all headaches but he managed to open his eyes. Sarah and Abby bent over him, their tears dripping onto his face. He brushed them away. "What are you doing? Trying to drown me?"

"Thank God, you're alive." Sarah buried her face on his shoulder. Seth saw relief in Abby's frightened face, but he couldn't collect his thoughts enough to figure out what was happening. He gently put Sarah aside and struggled to sit up.

The movement left him dizzy. He shook his head to clear it. Big mistake. His brain pounded like hammers on an anvil.

"Lemme have a look-see at yore noggin," Charley said. "That jasper gave you a mighty sharp rap."

"I'm all right." Seth jerked away when Charley touched the back of his head. "Ow!"

Charley grunted. "Not so you'd notice. You got a lump the size of a duck egg back there. Not much blood though." He handed Seth a canteen. "Drink. Then we'll get you in the coach. We gotta go back to Fresno Flats and get the law after the bandits and Fallon. Good thing it ain't far."

Seth's memory kicked in: Red Fallon; the bandits; the holdup; the ruffian throwing Dori on a horse—

Alarm attacked with the venom of a rattlesnake. "Where's Dori?" Seth peered up the dusty road that stretched empty and menacing ahead of them.

Sarah burst into tears. "Gone."

Seth felt like he'd been kicked in the gut. "The bandits took her?"

Charley shook his head. "Naw. A gun went off, an' their horses spooked. Yore friend Fallon got away with the girl. 'Pears to me that in spite of all his fancy talkin' 'bout gettin' religion, he wuz in on the holdup. Or mebbe he decided to pick up a ransom for himself."

Seth's world turned black. Red's story had almost convinced him of the wild cowhand's change of heart. *Lies, all lies.*

"Get in the coach, Seth," Sarah pleaded.

The horror in her eyes showed she was reliving the ordeal of being kidnapped by Red. Seth stood, but tottered and almost fell. "We can't wait for the sheriff. I'm going after Dori right now."

"No, you ain't," Charley barked. "You cain't ride one of my team—it takes two horses to haul us back to town."

Seth clenched his hands into fists and fought a fresh wave of dizziness. "I'll walk."

"No!" Sarah protested. "You're hurt worse than you think. What good will you be to Dori if you take off after her and end up passing out by the road?"

"Yore sister's right," Charley chimed in. "Shut up and get back in the coach, or I'll put another lump on yore head and throw you in."

Convinced more by the way his head spun than by Charley's threat, Seth obeyed. The short ride back to town would steady him. Charley turned the team and goaded them into a dead run. Seth leaned back against the seat and gritted his teeth at every jar of the stagecoach. The rough ride did, however, help restore his senses.

"Sarah, Abby, I'll leave you at the flats and ride with the sheriff and his posse." Seth took his sister's hands in his. "We're going to get them. All of them. When we do, God have mercy on their souls. The law won't and neither will I."

Sarah gave a broken cry. "If only Matt were here. What will he say when he learns we've lost his sister?"

Seth cringed. His brain told him he could have done nothing to prevent Dori's kidnapping, but his promise to Matt to take care of her flayed him. When Dori had needed him most, he'd been sprawled senseless in the road—and Red Fallon had ridden away with the girl Seth loved. If the law didn't punish Red, he would.

Seth slumped in the seat and lashed himself with regrets. *Why did I refuse to tell Dori how I feel, even after she recommitted her life to You, Lord, and the barrier between us was shattered? Now I may never have the chance. What will happen if the bandits catch up with her and Red?* Seth bit his lip until blood came. Even if Matt paid a ransom and Dori's captors released her, would she come home unharmed?

"Trust Me."

"A lot easier to say than to do," Seth mumbled, but he clung to the words every inch of the way back to Fresno Flats. Charley drove like a madman, yet it felt like a lifetime before they reached town and found the sheriff.

The lawman hastily scared up a posse as rugged looking as he was, including the two ranchers who had been in the Madera-Big Tree Station stage.

"Don't worry," one said. "We'll get that pretty little gal back." The other nodded.

Seth felt warmed by their concern. "Thanks. I'm going to marry her if she'll have me." He felt himself redden when they guffawed, but the sheriff interrupted.

"You gonna be able to keep up, what with that bump on your head?" His keen gaze bored into Seth. "If not, stay here with the women and let us do the trailin'."

Fire ran through Seth's veins. "I can keep up. Besides, a couple of their nags are carrying double."

"That will slow them down some. Mount up, men, and let's ride. We've got fresh horses, and they don't."

It didn't take long to ride back to the scene of the holdup. Seth seethed with impatience when the sheriff insisted on stopping to examine the site. Every minute Dori was in the hands of the bandits, Red, or both, felt like a year.

"Nothing here to show what happened 'cept for some roiled up ground and a few drops of blood," the sheriff announced.

"That's where I fell," Seth told him. "Begging your pardon, Sheriff, but can we get going?"

"Shore." He swung into the saddle and led the dozen grim-faced men who formed the posse back on their pursuit. The riders remained silent for the most part, but Seth occasionally heard mutters of "catchin' the low-down thieves an' makin' short work of them," and "holdups are bad enough; abductin' innocent gals sticks in my craw."

Seth silently agreed, straining his eyes for a glimpse of the hunted men.

Time limped by. The posse didn't catch up with either the bandits or Red and Dori. Seth's hopes dwindled to a mere flicker. Despair left him feeling sick. A splitting headache made it hard to trust God. Never in his life had Seth found it so difficult, not even when Red kidnapped Sarah. Seth had been laid up at the ranch and spared from knowing she was missing until after Matt rescued her. Now fear returned with a hundred armed companions. What if they didn't find Dori before darkness fell? *Lord, how can I live through a night, wondering what may be happening to her?*

A comforting thought came to mind. "I trained Dori well," he murmured. "If she has an opportunity to escape, she can survive." He slitted his eyes, trying to recall every detail of what had happened before he'd been struck. The bandits had flourished pistols. Had there been rifles and lariats on the horses' saddles?

"Seems like I saw both," Seth mumbled, "but I'm so used to seeing fully outfitted horses, I didn't pay any attention." His pulse quickened. "I probably would have noticed if they hadn't been there. Maybe it's wishful thinking, but it seems like outlaws would be well equipped." Seth felt his lips curl into a smile, the first since the holdup. "If Dori gets her hands on a lasso or a rifle, she can sure use it." The thought helped lift his mood.

By the time the posse reached a fork in the road, the sun sat high in the sky. A careful examination of horse tracks in the dust showed that two horses had continued on the main road; one had veered off to the left. "Looks like the bandits haven't come up with Fallon and Miss Sterling," the sheriff said. "Here's where we split up. Half of you go after the bandits." He eyed Seth. "Anderson, you and the rest come with me."

About an hour later, Seth's sharp eyes noticed something odd. He leaned over from the saddle and stared at the tracks in the trail. "Hey Sheriff, come here, will you?"

"What is it?"

"Look." Seth pointed to the ground. Excitement mounted. "It doesn't make sense, but the tracks are turning back toward the main road to Fresno Flats."

The others crowded next to him. "You shore got good eyes, son." The sheriff scratched his forehead and looked puzzled. "It ain't what I was expectin'. What's Fallon up to, anyway?"

"The girl might be hurt from being thrown, worse than Fallon knew when he rode off with her," someone said. "Maybe he's taking her back to Fresno Flats to find a doctor. Having a dead girl on your hands is a heap more serious than kidnapping."

"Shut up, you fool," the sheriff roared with a quick glance toward Seth. "We ain't seen no blood, have we?"

Seth felt his own blood turn to ice. The pity in the lawman's eyes showed that, despite his protest, the unwelcome suggestion might be true.

"I'll wager Fallon decided to take the girl back and turn himself in," one of the ranchers put in. "He might reckon the law will go easier on him. Anderson, how do you figure it?"

All Seth could get out of his constricted throat was, "I don't."

"Well, we ain't gonna find out standin' here flappin' our gums," the sheriff growled. "Let's get going."

Seth's bones ached with weariness before the posse rounded a bend and reached the main road back to Fresno Flats. The sheriff reined in his horse.

"What th—"

Seth gave a loud cry. He kicked his horse into a gallop, heart thundering in time with the racing animal's hoofbeats and the pounding of the posse's horses behind him. He pulled his mount to a halt beside something that lay under a tree, trussed up like a roped calf: Red Fallon.

But where was Dori?

Chapter 25

The staccato beat of hooves brought Dori back to consciousness. Why was she face down in the saddle of a galloping horse? She struggled to remember, and it all came back. The holdup; the bandits; Seth being felled by a cruel blow; a gunshot; Red Fallon yanking her onto a horse.

Dori twisted her head, gazed up at Red, and opened her mouth to scream. A rough hand silenced her.

"Shhh. The bandits'll hear you. Promise not to yell if I take my hand away?" Dori nodded. One bandit at a time was more than enough.

Red removed his hand.

"Don't you mean the other bandits?" Dori spit out in a low voice.

"I ain't one of 'em." He reined in the horse. "Let's get you in a more comfort'ble position." He stepped down from the horse and set her upright.

Too confused to attempt an escape, Dori gasped. "You kidnap me, and now you're concerned about my comfort?"

Back in the saddle with Dori in front of him Red mumbled, "It ain't that way."

"Are you going to hold me for ransom?"

Red glanced over his shoulder and sent the horse into a run. "Naw."

What scheme lay beneath Red's battered sombrero? "You won't get away with this."

"Sit still and keep quiet," Red ordered. "We'll be in a heap of trouble if those three galoots catch us. I'm tryin' to save you."

If anyone had told Dori that she'd ever choose Red Fallon over a gang of outlaws, she'd have laughed herself silly. What had changed her mind—his so-called repentance? His assurance he was trying to save her? His changed appearance? No. Satan himself could appear as an angel of light. She didn't know if she believed Red. His actions during the holdup gave lie to his claim.

"Lord, what has calmed me enough to keep from kicking, screaming, and taking my chances with the bandits?" she whispered. The answer came like a lightning bolt. Red had shown her no disrespect. The grasp on her blouse when he heaved her onto the horse had not been unkind. He'd clapped his hand over her mouth only to silence her. He'd shown consideration by changing her position to make riding easier.

When they reached a fork in the road, Red turned into the lesser traveled path. "The bandits should be too busy tryin' to outrun the law to come after us, but we can't take chances. Soon as it's safe, we'll get back on the main road." An hour later he cocked his head to one side. "Hear that?"

Dori's ears perked up. "Rushing water." Her lagging spirits lifted. A mountain stream meant relief for her parched throat and dust-covered hands and face.

When they reached the brook, Red helped Dori off the horse. Stiff and sore, she threw herself down on the bank and drank water so icy her teeth chattered. She splashed her hot face, shivered, then splashed again.

"Are you hungry?" Red reached in the saddlebags and hauled out a chunk of hardtack.

Dori grimaced. "I had a big dinner."

"Good." Red unsaddled the horse and tossed the saddle blanket to Dori. "Rest a spell till it's safe to get back on the road. You c'n use the saddle for a pillow." He didn't wait for a reply, but watered the horse and tied him to a nearby manzanita bush. Only then did he fling himself down beside the stream and drink.

Dori kept a wary eye on Red while spreading her blanket on the ground. She hadn't expected him to care for a horse before himself. Maybe he really had changed. She dropped to the blanket and propped herself up against the saddle, determined not to close her eyes, but her weary body refused to cooperate.

A call roused her from deep sleep, "Wake up, Dori. We c'n go back to Fresno Flats now."

Dori opened her eyes and blinked.

"Sorry to wake you, but we need to get movin'." Red's gaunt face split into a grin. "You slept most an hour, plenty of time for the bandits to get ahead of us."

She sprang to her feet. "You're taking me to Fresno Flats?"

Red's grin faded. "You gotta learn to trust folks, even when it's tougher than hardtack. I hadta get you outta there while I could. Charley was tryin' to control the team, and young Anderson was bad hurt or dead."

"Don't say that. Seth can't be dead."

"Yore in love with him, ain't you?"

She couldn't answer.

"He might not be so bad off as that," Red mumbled. "It takes a heap of hurtin' to keep fellers like him down."

Dori suspected Red was trying to comfort her, but she appreciated it. "You're really trying to save me from the bandits?"

"Yeah. Even if yore brother paid a ransom, you'd still be in danger. I've knowed a lotta bad men." Pain and regret darkened his eyes. "I was one till God got hold of me."

"Why didn't you just head back to Fresno Flats with me?" Dori challenged.

Red sighed. "First off, I needed to get you away. Then I started thinkin'. If I took you back right off, who'd believe I was tryin' to save you? I figgered I had to make you b'lieve me. Do you?"

The story sounded plausible, but more than likely, Red had abducted her in hopes of collecting a ransom and then had second thoughts. What better way to guarantee escaping punishment than to play on her sympathies? "I don't know."

"Most folks won't." He sounded more resigned than fearful.

Pity battled with reason. Red's life might hang on whether she believed him and could convince Seth and Matt that Red had finally tried to do something good.

By the time he saddled up and they reached the road back to Fresno Flats, Dori's head and shoulder ached. Distrust swooped down like a bird of prey. *My thinking's too muddled to separate truth from fiction,* she reflected. *All I want to do is to escape, but the only thing that may work means throwing aside modesty.* So be it. Face aflame and hoping Red would assume the obvious reason for her request, she asked in a small voice, "Can we stop here? I need to. . ."

Red fell for her ploy. He swung out of the saddle and helped her down, then walked a little way up the road. "Lots of tracks. A posse, I reckon."

She ran to the horse, uncoiled the lariat, formed a wide loop, and swung it. *Zing.* The lasso dropped over Red's head and shoulders. Dori jerked the rope so hard it tightened. Red sprawled to the ground. Before he could recover his senses, she hog-tied him and sprang to the horse's back. Then she headed for Fresno Flats, haunted by the look in Red's eyes that made her feel as if she had unjustly slapped a child.

❧

Seth had ridden like a crazed man along the trail, praying to find Dori. He rounded a bend. A trussed-up man lay by the side of the road.

With a cry of rage, Seth yanked his horse to a standstill and dismounted. "Red Fallon?" he bellowed, jerking the bound man to his feet. "Did the bandits do this? Have they got Dori?"

Red grunted. "She should be in Fresno Flats by now. She roped and tied me before I could get her back to town."

"Bully for Dori. She may have roped you, but you can't expect me to believe you were bringing her back after kidnapping her."

Red's reply was lost in a rumble from the posse.

"I'm fer hangin' him here and now," one of the men called.

The sheriff leaped from his horse. "There'll be no necktie parties today. It's up to a judge and jury to take care of that. First, we go see if he's lyin' about the girl." He glared at the vengeful man. "Two of you will have to ride double. Fallon gets roped to the saddle." The man grumbled but climbed on behind another posse member.

Seth freed Red, forced him to mount, and tied his hands to the pommel. "Try to run and you won't get far," he warned.

Red gave him an inscrutable look. "I ain't runnin' no more. No one's gonna swaller it, but I took Dori to save her from the skunks who bashed yore head."

Seth's nerves twanged. "Save it for a jury." *I won't believe Dori's safe until she's in my arms,* he vowed. *When she is, I won't let her go until she says she'll marry me.* His heart thumped with anticipation.

Yet Red's apparent sincerity troubled Seth. Red's past weighed against him, but what if he was telling the truth? Hangings sickened Seth. Executing an innocent man was unthinkable. *Lord, You're the only one who knows the truth. It's all up to You.*

Leaving Fallon's fate in God's hands, Seth lost himself in dreams of his own future. He let out a yell and sent his horse into a full gallop. When he reached Fresno Flats, a crowd stood in front of the sheriff's office. Seth saw Dori, Sarah, and Abby elbow their way through the crowd and race toward him, but he had eyes only for Dori. He hurtled from the saddle and scooped her up in his arms. The look in her eyes shouted all Seth needed to know. He bent his head and kissed her upturned face.

Dori drew back, cheeks scarlet.

Seth laughed and kissed her again. "Get used to it, sweetheart. I don't aim to stop until you promise to marry me."

The roguish look Seth knew so well stole into her eyes. "You can stop right now."

Seth's jaw dropped. "You mean it?"

"I'm calling your bluff." Dori hugged Seth so tightly it left him breathless. "It took long enough for me to get you, and I don't aim to let you go."

The crowd cheered but fell silent when the *clip-clop* of horses' hooves sounded and Red and the posse halted before the sheriff's office.

Even the thrill of holding Dori close couldn't dispel the feeling of doom that clutched Seth. He had left Red's fate in God's hands, but did God need some human help? "Dori, do you believe Red was trying to rescue you?"

"I don't know," she faltered. "My head says he's guilty, even though he was respectful. My heart says he may not be."

"Same here. If you press charges, it will take a miracle to save Red."

He felt Dori tense, then she whispered, "God specializes in miracles, but I can't accuse someone who may be innocent and expect Him to save Red. What if God has put the truth in our hearts for a reason?"

Inspiration struck Seth. "We can find out by sending a telegram to the San Francisco mission. If Red truly accepted Jesus as his Trailmate, it will be safe to believe he didn't kidnap you—but there's still a chance he's in with the bandits."

Dori's face turned pearly white. She clasped her hands against Seth's vest. Hope shone in her clear blue eyes. "I hope not. I really want to believe Red."

Her words rocked Seth on his boot heels. "So do I, Dori." Amazed to discover he meant it, Seth felt the last of his bitterness die.

"Rest of the posse's comin'," Charley announced. "They got the dirty skunks who held up my stage." An angry murmur rippled through the crowd. But Seth clenched suddenly sweaty hands. The time for truth had come.

He whipped toward Red and marveled. How could a man whose future hung on the word of holdup men and kidnappers appear so untroubled?

"Peace I leave with you, my peace I give unto you: not as the world giveth. . . . Let not your heart be troubled, neither let it be afraid."

Seth needed no confirmation from the mission workers. Sinful as Red had been, he was now cleansed, forgiven, and obviously secure in the assurance that whatever happened, God was in control.

"You, there," the sheriff roared at the outlaw leader when the band of men stopped their horses. "Is this fellow one of your gang?" His meaty hand pointed toward Red.

Seth held his breath, but Red's expression didn't change.

The bandit's face twisted in disgust. He spat into the dusty street. "Not on yore tintype. We're choosey about who we ride with."

Seth's breath came out in a loud *whoosh. Thank You, God.*

The sheriff wheeled. "Well, Miss Sterling? Are you pressin' charges?"

"No." Her voice rang. "I believe Red tried to save me."

"So do I," Seth said. The poignant light in Red's eyes sank into Seth's soul, but the sheriff scowled.

"I ain't sayin' what I think, but it don't matter now. Untie Fallon and let him go. Just one thing, mister. Don't come back to Fresno Flats, or I'll run you in for disturbin' the peace—my peace of mind."

Several days later, Seth and Dori rode to the promontory that overlooked the ranch. Seated on a big rock, Seth put his arm around her and spoke from a full heart. "God is so good. He rescued us from flood and outlaws, saved Red, freed me from hatred, and gave me you." He paused. "Dori, do you look forward to our riding through life together as much as I do?"

"Yes, but there's one thing. . . ."

A cold wind of disappointment blew through Seth in spite of the warm evening. *Lord, I thought everything that separated us was in the past. I guess I was wrong.* "What is it?" he finally asked.

Dori had never looked more bewitching. Her laugh trilled out. "I can't wait to ride through life with you, Seth Anderson—but not on a log flume or in a raging river."

Seth roared. His long-ago prediction was right on target: Being married to Dori would be many things. But if they lived to be a hundred, it would never be boring.

ROMANCE AT RAINBOW'S END

Dedication

For Susan K. Marlow—the story continues. . .

A Note from the Author

Dear Readers,

History really does repeat itself. When I finished writing *Romance Rides the Range*, book one of my western series, I was planted (in spirit) on the Diamond S Ranch near Madera, California, in the 1880s. I couldn't bear to say good-bye and move on.

The same thing happened with book two, *Romance Rides the River*. Tangled, unexplored trails in the beautiful San Joaquin Valley and surrounding countryside lured me. Characters, old and new, grabbed me and clamored for a place in the sun. *Romance at Rainbow's End* is my response to my true-to-life "book friends" who refused to be silent.

This title—like *Romance Rides the Range* and *Romance Rides the River*—recognizes God's unfailing love for *all* of His children, particularly for the "mavericks" who stray from His presence. May it serve as a reminder that we are branded with the name Jesus Christ and are called to round up others and establish His ownership.

God bless you all,
Colleen

Chapter 1

March 1885
St. Louis, Missouri

Angry voices drifted up to the loft of the shack the Stoddard family called home. They yanked eleven-year-old Ellianna out of a sound sleep. She shifted on the rustling corn-husk mattress and buried her head in her thin pillow. Hands clenched, she lay rigid, wanting to scream at Pa and Agatha to stop fighting.

A cold, skinny hand touched her hair. "Ellie? Are you awake?"

She opened her eyes. Timmy stood beside her, shivering in his thin nightdress. His frightened eyes looked enormous in the dim light that filtered through unpatched holes in the attic roof.

"Who can sleep in this racket?" She scooted over. "Crawl in before you freeze."

Timmy scrambled under the blanket and snuggled close. "Make them stop, Ellie."

"I can't." A pang went through her. Years of neglect and lack of love had toughened her, but her little brother shouldn't have to live with the likes of Gus and Agatha. *It's bad enough for me,* her heart protested, *but Timmy's only eight.*

A loud crash from below brought her bolt upright. Timmy's fingers dug into her arm. "What's that, Ellie?"

"Probably a chair turning over." She loosened his death grip. "Stay here. I'll find out." She slid to the floor, crept over to the opening at the top of the rickety ladder, and peered down. Agatha was shaking her fist in Pa's face.

Ellie sneered. When Pa had married Agatha two years earlier, the woman had been all smiles. "My name means 'kind and good,'" she'd gushed. "I just know we are all going to be a wonderful, happy family."

Ellie felt like throwing up. A few weeks after the honeymoon, *kind* and *good* gave way to screaming and stinging blows for the two youngest Stoddards. Agatha didn't dare hit Ian or Peter. At twelve and fourteen they were already nearly as tall as their father. Instead, Agatha made up lies about them that earned beatings from Gus. A few months ago, the boys had disappeared. Agatha pretended to be sorry, but Ellie overheard her mutter, "Good riddance."

Now Ellie held her breath and watched an ugly scowl cover her stepmother's face. "I've put up with your brats long enough," Agatha shrilled. "It's time for them to go."

Pa's black eyes narrowed to slits. "*Go*? You already drove Ian and Peter away."

Agatha snorted. "Gus Stoddard, you are such a hypocrite! If you cared one whit about your family, you wouldn't have left them to shift for themselves all those months while you were out West, trying to make your stepdaughter marry a gambler to pay your debts. If neighbors hadn't lent a hand, they'd have starved."

"And you've never let me forget it!" Gus spit out, his face an angry red. "Lay off me. It's none of your business how I handle my kids!"

Her raucous laugh brought him a step nearer, but she wasn't through. "It is my business. I got taken in with your butter-wouldn't-melt-in-your-mouth ways, just like your other two wives. They up and died on you, but I've no intention of dying. I've had enough of living in this shack with two worthless brats. You're going to get rid of them, stop drinking, get a job, and be respectable."

Not likely. Ellie covered her mouth to keep back a laugh that turned into a silent sob. Childish voices, taunting and cruel, pounded in her brain: *"You ain't nothing, Ellianna Stoddard. Neither's your Pa. Trash, that's what you are—and you ain't never gonna be nothin' else."*

Ellie cringed. Resentment toward her father, who had made her the target of jeering schoolmates, swelled until she found it hard to breathe. Then Agatha's voice sliced into her consciousness, cold and hard as an ice-covered rock:

"I mean it, Gus. Either ship Timmy and Ellie out West to that rich rancher Sarah married, or send them to the orphanage. I don't care which." She paused, then hissed, "Listen, and listen good. I want those kids out of here!"

Stunned by Agatha's viciousness, Ellie staggered back to bed. She found Timmy scrunched under the covers with his hands over his ears.

"What's happening, Ellie?" His voice trembled.

"Shhh. Go to sleep. I'm here." Yet after he fell asleep and silence reigned below, Ellie lay wide awake, glad for the warmth of her brother's frail body. What would tomorrow bring? And the day after that?

It can't be any worse than the past. Ellie sighed. *I've never been more to Pa than just another mouth to feed. And since Sarah left, someone to do for him.* Her bitter thoughts rushed on. The only kindness she had ever known was when Gus married Virginia Anderson, a wonderful Christian woman. Virginia conscientiously cared for Ellie and her three brothers, along with her own teenagers, Seth and Sarah.

A lone tear slid from beneath Ellie's tightly closed eyelid, followed by rebellion. Two months after Virginia died, Sarah had slipped away in the night.

Seth had already fled Gus's wrath. Their leaving made eight-year-old Ellie the woman of the house.

"It's not fair," she whispered, too low to disturb Timmy. "I did everything I could to please Pa and the boys. All I got were slaps and complaints when the food burned."

Powerless to stop the raging memories, Ellie thought of how she'd lived in fear when Gus was drinking or lost at gambling. The older boys took off, but she and Timmy hid. During the past three years of drudgery, she'd tried to remember what her stepmother had taught her about Jesus. Was there really such a Person? She sadly shook her head. No man of her acquaintance bore any resemblance to the kindly, loving Christ Virginia had described.

Shortly after Sarah fled, Pa had announced he and Tice Edwards were going to California to fetch her home. Ellie's poor, tired heart bounced. She and Sarah hadn't gotten along very well, but maybe things would be different now. If Sarah and Tice got married like Pa said, would they let her live with them? Or at least help out so Ellie didn't have to work so hard?

A second tear crawled out. Pa came home without Tice, blaming the gambler's death on Sarah's stubbornness and sourly saying she was going to marry a rancher. Now his threat was, "If you younguns don't behave, I'll ship you off to California and let the mountain lions eat you."

It struck terror into the already cowed children. Ellie continued to do as she was told, seldom spoke, and silently bore the shame of being Gus Stoddard's daughter. Although longing to learn, she secretly felt relieved when Pa ordered her to stay home and tend the house and Timmy. It meant temporary freedom from tormenting schoolmates who delighted in mocking her, leaving scars so deep she felt they would never heal.

What they said was true. She was nothing. Pa was nothing. And nothing would ever change. She'd go on day after endless day cooking, scrubbing, and mending. When she was a little older, she'd be sent out as a laundress as Sarah had been. Ellie sighed. Was Sarah happy now that she was married? Or had a mountain lion eaten her?

One day, Pa had come in from the few days' work he did at a time on the St. Louis docks, just enough to keep the family from starving, and dropped into a chair. "Tomorrow you slick this place up, you hear? Ellie, make the best supper you can. Tim, help her." A self-conscious smirk crawled across his face, and he dropped into a rickety chair. "We're havin' comp'ny."

Company? Ellie didn't dare ask, but Timmy had no such qualms. "Who?"

Gus scowled. "Mrs. Batdorf, that's who. You're to mind your manners. She's a widow-lady I met at church."

"Church?" Ellie blinked. Pa hadn't gone to church since he'd married Virginia Anderson.

"Sure." Gus guffawed. "Best place there is to find good, hard-working wives."

Ellie sniffed, then brightened. Would Mrs. Batdorf be as nice as Virginia had been, even when the children didn't mind her?

"Do we have to call her Ma?" Timmy persisted.

Gus slapped him, then leaned back until the tired chair screeched in protest. "You'll treat her with respect, or I'll send you to Seth and Sarah."

"To California? Where the mountain lions are?" Timmy wailed. "I don't wanna go, Pa. Please don't make us go!"

The chair came forward with a crash. "You'll do what I tell you, hear? Don't you forget: mountain lions have powerful big teeth and are mighty fierce."

Timmy cried himself to sleep that night. . .and a cold, hard knot that chilled Ellie through and through began to form in her breast.

❧

The morning after Agatha's ultimatum dawned gray and cheerless. Breakfast was a disaster. The biscuits Ellie had learned to make light and fluffy didn't rise. Pa fired one at the wall. "Seems like a man should be able to have decent food around here."

Ellie didn't bother to tell him they had what he provided, but Agatha did. "Baking powder's probably too old. Time to change it—and other things."

Timmy's big brown eyes, so unlike Ellie's crystal blue ones, opened wide. "What's gonna change?" he asked.

Gus hesitated, then pulled a soiled sheet of paper from his pocket. Ellie noticed how he refused to look at them when he said, "I'm sending this telegram to Seth and Sarah this morning." He smoothed out the crumpled page and read:

REMARRIED *STOP* PETER AND IAN ON OWN *STOP* ELLIE AND TIMMY ARRIVE MADERA 23 *STOP*.

Even though she'd known it was coming, the words hit Ellie like a runaway freight train. She stared at Pa, who still avoided her gaze; at Agatha, swelled with triumph; and last of all, at her little brother's peaked, terrified face. Bile rose in her throat. She shoved back her chair, snatched Timmy by the hand, and dragged him away from the man who had betrayed his children.

"Git back over here," Gus ordered.

They had no choice but to obey. Ellie tightened her hold on her brother and returned to the table, vowing to protect Timmy as best she could. She sent Agatha a look of loathing and asked, "When do we go?"

Gus cleared his throat. "Today. If they don't want you, there'll be no time for them to say so."

Fear spurted. What if Seth and Sarah didn't want them? It was no secret Ellie and Timmy had given Sarah plenty of grief. She still remembered snatching up Sarah's hand one time and biting it. She winced.

But Ellie couldn't think of that right now. She pushed her terror aside and dropped to her knees beside Timmy, who was sobbing uncontrollably. "God is going to pay you back for this," she told the two adults towering above her.

Agatha put on an aggrieved look. "Why, Ellianna! How can you speak so to me and to the father who loves you and knows best? Surely the stepmother I'm always hearing about must have taught you that children are to obey their parents in all things. The Bible says so."

Criticism of Virginia, who had tried to be a good mother in spite of Ellie's rebellion, overcame her fear. If she didn't speak out, she'd burst. She leaped to her feet. "How dare you quote the Bible to me? *You're* making Pa send us away. I heard you shrieking at him last night." Her voice became a perfect imitation of Agatha's:

" 'I've had enough of living in this shack with two worthless brats. You're going to get rid of them, stop drinking, get a job, and be respectable.' "

"You ungrateful girl! What if I did?" Agatha thrust her mottled face close to Ellie's. "No one wants the likes of you around. They never will. If Sarah takes you in, which she may not, it will be from pity and duty, not love."

Ellie's tongue cleaved to the roof of her mouth, and her heart felt like lead. What if Agatha was right? She felt Timmy tug at her worn, calico gown. Tears streaked his dirty face.

"Won't they want us, Ellie?"

"Don't be foolish. Of course they will," she soothed. But the question hammered at her brain until she thought it would burst.

❧

A few hours later, Ellie and Timmy stood beside the train that would carry them to California. Timmy screamed again that he didn't want to go, but Gus shook the daylights out of him, turned without so much as a *Godspeed*, and walked away.

In that moment, the meekness behind which Ellie had always masked her feelings for her father turned to hatred. She put a comforting arm around her brother and led him up the train steps. The conductor took them to their seats, and Timmy snuggled down next to her, crying as if his heart would break. "Don't worry, Timmy. I'll take care of you. So will Seth and Sarah. They live on a big ranch, remember? It will be lots of fun. Why, I'll bet they'll even have a pony you can ride."

"You won't let a mountain lion get me?" Timmy quavered.

"No." Feeling years older than she actually was, Ellie gently laid his head in her lap and stared out the train window. But she didn't see the scenery through which they were traveling. What would California be like? Would Sarah and Seth—and that rancher fellow, what was his name? Matt?—be sorry that she and Timmy had come? A lifetime of misery swept through her. *Jesus, if You are really like Stepmama said, please. . .*

She couldn't continue, but a small, comforting thought came: *No matter what lay ahead, she and Timmy were free from Gus and Agatha.*

Chapter 2

Spring 1892
San Francisco

The *rat-a-tat-tat* of knuckles against the ornate door of Joshua Stanhope's study at Bayview Christian Church yanked him from his concentration. He flung down his fountain pen and muttered something more annoyed than elegant. *Of all the rotten luck!*

After struggling all morning with Sunday's sermon, his train of thought had finally gotten on track. Why did he have to be derailed just when he was finally forging full steam ahead? The knocking came again. Louder, and not to be ignored.

Josh heaved a sigh. "Come in."

The door swung open. "Hey Reverend, who do you know in Madera?" a laughing voice demanded.

Josh stared at his mirror image. Same six-foot height. Same lean build. Same gray eyes and short blond hair, except every hair on Edward's head was in place. Josh grimaced, knowing his own locks must bear evidence of his running his fingers through them while trying to solve knotty problems.

"Well?" Edward persisted.

"No one. And don't call me Reverend."

Edward donned an innocent expression that didn't fool Josh one bit. "You *are* a minister, remember?" He smirked. "Besides, doesn't the Bible tell us to respect our elders? This means that since you're five minutes older than I am, you're the big brother."

Josh winced. He loved his twin more than life itself but wished Edward wouldn't take things so lightly. "Why the sudden interest in Madera?"

Edward handed him a letter. "Your secretary gave it to me when I told him I had to see you on a matter of life or death."

"Life or death?" Josh raised a skeptical eyebrow. "You look pretty healthy to me."

Edward slumped into the massive chair across from his brother. "Beryl will kill me if I'm late for lunch. That fiancée of mine is a stickler for being on time, so I dropped by to see if I could get a loan. Believe it or not, Dad's playing the heavy-handed father. He wouldn't give me an advance, and Mother's

250

off at some do-gooder meeting." He scowled. "Why'd Grandpa have to tie up the principal of what he left us until we're thirty? I could use the cash now, not three years from now."

Josh gritted his teeth. "I manage all right."

Edward hooted. "*You* have a fat salary. Even if you didn't, don't forget John the Baptist. Preachers aren't supposed to have a lot of money. So. . .I'm here to relieve you of some of yours."

Josh knew he shouldn't encourage Edward by laughing, but he couldn't help it. Indolent, always out for a good time, Edward Stanhope possessed a sunny personality few could resist. "Why can't you take life seriously?"

"Moi?" Edward's eyes twinkled. "No thanks."

A familiar ache attacked Josh's breastbone. *Why, Lord? I'm giving my life to serving You, but I can't show my own brother how much he needs You.*

Edward stood and stretched like a lazy cat. "Aren't you going to open your letter? On the other hand, why bother? It's probably someone asking for money. Hey, while we're on the subject, how about that loan?"

A strange reluctance to open the letter in Edward's presence caused Josh to reach for his pocketbook and hand Edward a few crumpled bills.

"Thanks, old man. You'll get it back the first of next month. *Au revoir.*" He sent Josh a brilliant smile and hurried out the door, closing it behind him.

The young minister dropped his head into his hands. Most encounters with Edward left him feeling frustrated and helpless to change his twin's carefree ways. Five minutes in their birth order had made him the elder brother, but Josh's relationship with the Lord cast him in a brother's keeper role he often felt inadequate to play.

"It's not that Edward doesn't believe in You," Josh prayed. "He does, but it isn't enough to make a real difference in his life." He sighed. "Once Edward marries Beryl Westfield, there's even less chance of him ever having a real relationship with You."

An image of the haughty, dark-haired woman flickered into Josh's mind. Five years older than the twins and a self-proclaimed infidel, Beryl had unsuccessfully pursued Josh before turning her charms on Edward. Josh tolerated her for his brother's sake but considered her a threat to his and Edward's close relationship.

Feeling like Atlas forever trying to hold up the sky, Josh slid to his knees, one hand resting on his highly polished desk. "Lord, how many times have I given Edward over to You, then snatched him back? Help me remember that You love him even more than I do and are in control." After a long time, he raised himself with one hand, feeling a measure of peace. The forgotten letter rustled, reminding him it needed to be read. Josh sat down again and opened it. His gray gaze riveted on the scrawled first line: *You may not remember me, but you saved my life nine years ago.*

Who on earth. . . ? Josh quickly looked at the bottom of the page. The signature sent shock ripples through him—*Red Fallon*. The letter fell to the desk from nerveless fingers. Remember! How could he forget?

Josh closed his eyes. In a heartbeat, he was eighteen again, hurrying through a dark alley on one of San Francisco's meanest streets—a place he'd been strictly forbidden to go. He could see the expensively furnished drawing room in the Stanhope Nob Hill mansion and his mother's face a few hours earlier. . . .

Jewels sparkled on Mother's hands, and she held them up in shocked protest. "No son of mine is going to be part of some so-called rescue mission! It doesn't matter that your uncle runs it. It isn't fitting. No gentleman would be caught dead down there with a bunch of criminals and the scum of the earth! That's what you'll be if you try to follow in Marvin's footsteps—dead."

Josh didn't argue. He just waited until the mansion lay silent and sneaked out. Guilt dogged every step of the way to the mission, but something greater than the "honour thy father and mother" commandment he'd learned as a child compelled him to continue. He reached his destination without mishap and decided to enter through the door behind the mission. If a Stanhope servant had seen Josh slip out and reported him, Mother would already have sent a carriage to "rescue" him.

He held his breath and groped his way down the dark alley. A short way from the mission door, he stumbled and nearly fell. His hands shot down to regain his balance—and encountered rough material.

Horrified at the contact, Josh forced himself not to run. "God, help me!" he whispered. Strength beyond description surged through him. He gritted his teeth, picked up the inert body that lay at his feet, and stumbled his way to the mission door. He gave it a hard kick and cried, "Uncle Marvin! Help!"

The door swung out and back. A tall man pulled Josh inside. He slammed and bolted the door, then relieved Josh of his burden. He laid the lifeless body on a nearby cot and bent over to examine it. "What are you doing here, Joshua?"

The stiffening in Josh's knees gave way. He sank into a chair. "I don't know. I just felt I had to come." He peered at the man on the cot. Dark stains matted the red hair, and dried blood nearly covered the craggy face. "Is he"—Josh choked—"is he dead?"

"Almost. Son, if you hadn't found him when you did, this man—whoever he is—would be a goner." Marvin shook his head. "He still may not make it. . . ."

Josh wiped a hand across his eyes and erased the scene from his past. It did not erase the hard beating of his heart. Or the memory of what followed that terrible night at the mission. God had once again been merciful to a sinner: a wild cowboy who had been beaten almost to death. Josh thought of how he'd sneaked away from home as often as he could without being detected. He'd hated deceiving his parents but had recognized much more than obedience to his parents hung on what was happening at the mission.

Now he bowed his head. Gratitude raced through him. "Lord, 'soup, soap, and salvation' healed Red Fallon's body, mind, and soul." A lump rose to Josh's throat. That fateful night had also irrevocably changed his own life. Watching God work through Uncle Marvin as he cared for Red Fallon had set a blaze burning in Josh's soul that had never died.

He picked up the letter again. Except for a few sporadic notes from Red over the years, they'd lost touch. Why was he writing now? The further Josh read, the more he marveled. Red wrote:

It took a heap of time for folks here in Madera—especially Abby Sheridan, the prettiest little filly in the valley—to believe I'd really changed. They finally did. So did Abby. Now we're married with a couple of little cowpunchers.

I been tryin to tell others about Jesus. There's a lot of cowhands just like me who oughta grab hold of Him. A few are willin to listen. I guess they figger if God could forgive the likes of me after all the bad I did, He could save most anybody.

The minister here's leavin in a few months. I hear tell you're some punkins at that big city church, but it don't cost nothin to ask: Will you come to Madera? We need you. Bad.

Josh stared at the final words until they blurred, then looked around the tastefully decorated study and out the window that overlooked San Francisco Bay. Lazy, white waves ruffled the shore. A horse-drawn carriage rumbled over the cobblestone street. The mournful cry of a ferryboat in the distance slowly dwindled into silence.

Josh took in a long breath, held it, then slowly released it. He'd come a long way since that night in the alley. Not just blocks away from the mission, but to Bayview Christian. High atop a hill with an incomparable view, the church was one of the most imposing and respected in the city. Filling the pulpit meant the height of San Francisco success for any minister, especially one as young as Josh.

Why then should Red's letter fill him with emotions he couldn't understand? What had a plea from a rescued cowboy who was *"tryin to tell others about Jesus"* and needed help *"bad"* to do with Joshua Stanhope?

Chapter 3

Dozens of sparkling prisms hanging from a large chandelier reflected off Letitia Stanhope's diamond necklace and set rainbows dancing around the large dining room. Correct in the formal attire his mother insisted on for dinner, Joshua forked his Lady Baltimore cake into infinitesimal pieces and ignored the table conversation.

Edward's mocking voice interrupted Josh's woolgathering. "So, Reverend, what did your letter from Madera want? Money, I'll wager."

For once, Josh didn't tell his brother not to call him *Reverend*. Instead, the first words that came to mind popped out, "Not money. Me." The next instant, he wished he could crawl under the table—anything to get away from the accusing faces turned toward him.

"What?" Edward's eyebrows shot up.

Mother gasped and dropped her silver fork to the damask table covering. A red tide rose from her lace collar to her carefully coiffed blond hair. She opened her mouth to speak, but Charles forestalled her. Josh caught his father's significant glance at Maria, the maid who helped serve and now stood frozen beside his chair.

"We will discuss it later." The finality in his announcement offered Josh a temporary reprieve but didn't erase his regret. Why had he blurted out the last thing he should have said? His mother's expression warned of an impending storm. Josh dreaded the session that would surely be as relentless as the gale-force waves that sometimes beat against the rocky shore of San Francisco Bay.

If only he could get away for a few moments to collect his wits before the family left the dining room! Josh glanced around the table, looking for a way to escape. His gaze stopped at his crystal water goblet. He raised it to his lips, then jerked his arm. Water cascaded down the front of his waistcoat and dripped onto the table. He snatched his linen napkin and began mopping up. "Sorry."

"Of all the awkward—let Maria do that and go change your clothes," Mother ordered. "Don't dawdle. We'll wait for you in the library."

"Yes, Mother." Josh stood. But before leaving the room, he saw Edward's eyes narrow. Josh sighed. Fooling his mother was one thing. Putting anything over on his twin was almost impossible. Well, at least the diversion had given him a few moments alone before facing his family.

Josh changed into dry clothes and knelt beside his heirloom bed. "Lord, why am I feeling so defensive? It's not like I'm going to Madera."

"Oh?"

The unspoken word left Josh gasping. He tried to laugh off his reaction but failed miserably. "Surely You don't mean for me to leave San Francisco," he prayed, trying to ignore his rapidly beating heart. "Not when everything is going so well at Bayview Christian." Yet doubt niggled. What if God meant just that? Josh shook his head, remembering the tempest that had followed his decision to go into the ministry nine years earlier. A tempest so strong it almost tore his family apart.

Josh's mind flashed back to the day he'd chosen God's path instead of the path his parents—especially his mother—had selected. His heart thundered, just as it had on that long-ago day. He'd honored his father and mother since childhood, but he *could* not, *would* not deny his Master's call—even if it meant alienation from his family. After rescuing Red Fallon, the call had grown from a spark to a living flame, fueled by stories from the Bible of those who left all to follow God. . .most of all, Joshua's challenge to the Israelites: *"Choose you this day whom ye will serve. . . : but as for me and my house, we will serve the Lord."*

Josh had thrilled to the words that had extinguished any lingering doubts. Then he'd girded himself for battle and shattered the silence of the quiet library with his announcement.

"Mother, Dad, I don't want to disappoint you, but I'm not going to be a 'doctor, lawyer, merchant, or chief,' as the old saying goes." His parents and Edward sat like statues. Only the crackle of the fire broke the stillness. Josh licked his dry lips and added, "God is calling me to be a minister."

Josh recalled the bitter scene that followed, but warmed at the memory of how Edward had defended him.

"Don't get upset, Mother," he'd said. "The last I heard, the ministry was still a respectable profession." Edward flashed the winning smile that seldom failed to get him what he wanted. "Think how proud you'll be when the *San Francisco Chronicle* reports, 'Reverend Joshua Stanhope, son of Charles and Letitia Stanhope, continues to fill the pews of First Church, or Bayview Christian, or one of the other leading churches with his powerful preaching and persuasive personality.'"

Mother hadn't been convinced. "But what will our friends think?"

"Letitia, our friends will be happy for us or kind enough to mind their own business," Father had said. "I'm proud that one of our sons is choosing to follow his heart."

Mother immediately ruffled her feathers on Edward's behalf. "Don't be so judgmental, Charles. Edward's music is just as important as Joshua wanting to preach."

"Hardly." Edward stood and stretched. "It might be different if I thought God wanted me to do something important with my music."

"You may find out if you take the time to listen," Josh told him. "Remember what happened to the man in the Bible who buried his talent?"

"Of course I remember. God called him a wicked and slothful servant." Edward grinned and clasped his hands behind his head. "I won't forget what our Sunday school teacher said when I asked her to explain *slothful*." He pursed his lips and raised his voice to a high treble. "'A sloth is one of the ugliest animals ever created and by far the laziest.'"

The corners of Mother's mouth turned down. "You aren't slothful. You just haven't decided what you want to do with your life. It's probably best, considering what Joshua is planning."

Edward shrugged. "Let him go ahead and become a preacher. If he doesn't like it, he can always be something else." Mischief danced in his eyes. "Maybe someday Josh can convert me."

Josh recoiled, as he always did when his brother treated eternal issues lightly. "Only God can do that."

"I know."

But after the family meeting ended, Edward had gone to his brother's room. "Sorry for being flippant, old man. The truth is, we're so much alike, I'm afraid if I ever get serious about religion, God might want more of me than I can give." He strode off, leaving Josh speechless and praying for his unpredictable twin.

Josh's thoughts returned to the present. Still on his knees, he sought out his heavenly Father. "Lord, give me a quiet spirit and the right words when I go downstairs. The idea of my going to Madera will send my family into turmoil. Mother found it nearly impossible to swallow when I became a minister. If You call me to preach to cowboys and ranchers, she'll feel it's beyond the pale."

A scripture that had sustained Josh in his revolt nine years earlier rushed into his mind: "*Then said Jesus unto his disciples, If any man will come after me, let him deny himself, and take up his cross, and follow me.*"

Did "taking up his cross and following" mean losing Mother and possibly Edward? Dad might not agree with his son's decision, but he would never forsake him. Neither would God. Taking a deep breath, Josh got to his feet and slowly went downstairs.

Mother's first words showed she was primed for battle. "What did you mean about someone in Madera wanting you? Who is this person? How dare he approach you?" She broke her staccato questions to add, "I presume it's a he. Or is some brazen girl or woman attempting to lure you to that godforsaken place?"

Josh quelled the desire to laugh. "Not a girl or woman. A man I once helped."

Mother pounced. "Helped? Who? How? When? Where? Why do I know nothing of this?" She sniffed. "Really, Joshua, sometimes you are so quixotic. Helping a person doesn't give him a claim on you. Why can't you be more like Edward?"

Josh winced. If only Mother would accept him as he was. "Why are you getting upset over something that may never happen? The letter simply asks if I'd be willing to come to Madera. The pastor of the church is leaving, and—"

"Go to Madera?" Mother shrilled. "Leave San Francisco and Bayview Christian? Is this person a lunatic?"

Josh's hopes of making her understand died aborning. "No." What would she think if he repeated parts of Red's letter, words that had indelibly etched themselves into his brain: *Will you come to Madera? We need you. Bad.*

How Mother and Edward would jeer! The minister of the most prestigious church in San Francisco summoned to a cow town by an illiterate ne'er-do-well? It was almost more than even Josh could comprehend, yet a flutter of anticipation stirred inside him. What if God was using Red Fallon to carry out His purposes in Madera—and in Josh's life?

The family meeting continued amid protests from his mother that cut Josh to the heart. She ended with a final thrust. "We had this discussion nine years ago, Joshua. I gave in to your whims. I admit things have turned out better than I ever expected. However, if you even consider this outrageous proposition, there will be consequences." She swept out of the library.

When Josh closed his bedroom door for the night, he couldn't shut out the feeling that he stood at a crossroads. For the second time that day, he knelt beside his bed. "Father, my heart feels heavy enough to crush my chest. Please give me peace." He waited. Instead of peace, conviction came. He owed it to God to take Red's plea seriously.

"Lord, I need to know if this is Your will. It means bucking Mother, but I'll contact Red and see if the church board wants me to come preach. If they do, I'll arrange for a leave of absence and go to Madera. . .then leave the future in Your hands."

Once in bed, Josh stared out his open window at the starless sky until his vision blurred. He fell asleep with Red's words echoing in his heart.

"We need you. Bad."

How long had it been since anyone at Bayview Christian had spoken those words?

Chapter 4

June 1892
Madera, California

Ellie halted her paint mare beneath a huge oak tree on the wide promontory overlooking the Diamond S Ranch. She slid from the saddle and dropped the reins. Trained to being ground tied, Calico nosed Ellie's shoulder then found a sparse patch of grass and began to graze. Ellie walked to the large boulder where she had spent many happy hours and sat down. Her heart swelled. She never tired of the view. She never would. Not if she lived on the ranch seventy years instead of the seven she'd already been there.

She flung off her sombrero and ran a hand through her hair. Thank goodness it had finally grown long enough to turn under at the nape of her neck! Ellie remembered sobbing when she recovered enough from pneumonia to comprehend she'd been shorn like a lamb.

"Young lady, you don't realize how sick you've been. Sick and out of your head a lot of the time," Doc Brown had told her. "Any doctor worth his salt orders long, heavy hair to be cut in severe cases of pneumonia."

His explanation didn't console Ellie for losing her dark tresses. "I don't see how cutting a person's hair can help."

"Well, it does," he said. "High fever and the hair's weight sap a patient's energy." Doc's voice softened. "We were doing everything we could to save your life, Ellie."

Now she whispered, "Thank You, Lord, for sparing me. I'm just happy to be alive." She turned her attention to her surroundings. Could any spot on earth be lovelier? The rocky outcropping high above the Sterling ranch offered a bird's-eye view of rangeland, vineyards, orchards, and the San Joaquin River. Nothing disturbed Ellie's solitude except an eagle circling in the sky and the bawling of cattle far below. She laughed and tried to pick out Timmy from among the riders tending the herd. "Oops. He's Tim, not Timmy now," she told Calico. No wonder. At fifteen, her brother topped her five-foot-six inches by half a foot.

Ellie flung her arms to the sky, heart bursting with joy. "Thank You, God!" she cried, feeling as free as the eagle above her. She'd never dreamed she

258

could be this happy. She reveled in the moment, wishing she could hug it to her heart and keep it there forever. But when a cloud drifted across the sun and cast a shadow over the smiling land, she stared unseeingly into the valley.

"Seven years, Lord. So much has happened! And much more to come." She drew her knees to her chest and laughed. "Including the fiesta." Excitement spurted through her. Needing someone with whom to share her excitement, Ellie glanced at Calico. Long experience had shown the mare to be a safe confidante.

"Folks from Madera and the neighboring ranches will come this afternoon for games and races and a barbecue supper."

Calico stopped grazing and looked mildly interested. Ellie continued.

"It's so hard to believe all the hustle and bustle at the ranch is for me! It's Solita's doing, you know." She pictured the Sterlings' diminutive Mexican housekeeper. Solita had planted her hands on her apron-covered hips in the spotless ranch house kitchen and announced in a voice that brooked no opposition, "Senorita Ellie will only have one eighteenth birthday. We will make una gran fiesta for her, Senor Mateo."

Ellie chuckled. Matt Sterling might own the Diamond S, but Solita ruled him and everyone else with a kind but unyielding hand.

Drifting shadows reminded Ellie she wasn't accomplishing the purpose for which she'd ducked out on the fiesta preparations and ridden to the promontory. A sigh started at her toes and crawled up. Where should she begin her journey from the past? At the St. Louis station when her father put her and Timmy on the westbound train and turned away without a backward glance?

"No!" Ellie shivered in spite of the warm day. She wrapped her arms more tightly around herself. Reliving that moment brought back feelings better left buried. Only then could she hold back the bitterness toward Gus Stoddard that lingered after all these years. "I'll start with when we arrived in Madera. . . ."

Heart beating double time, eleven-year-old Ellie took Timmy by the hand and slowly stepped down from the train, hating to leave the frail security it had afforded on the long journey west. *What if Sarah and Seth don't want us?*

A welcoming voice called, "Where are Ellie and Timmy?" The next moment, Ellie was in Sarah's arms, with Seth lifting Timmy off his feet and swinging him around in a circle.

"Thought you'd never get here, old man," Seth said.

"Where are the mountain lions?"

Ellie caught the fearful glance Timmy sent around the station.

Seth looked puzzled. "Up in the mountains where they belong. What made you think we have mountain lions in Madera?"

Timmy bit his lip. Ellie suspected it was to hide its trembling. "Pa said if we didn't mind, he'd send us out here and we'd get eaten up by mountain lions."

"I told him I wouldn't let it happen," Ellie put in.

"We won't either," Sarah promised. "You may never even see a mountain lion. Now, get in the buggy so we can go home. It's ten miles, and it looks like rain. We got more than our fair share this past February, and it looks like a few more drops might be headed this way." She laughed. "I like a sprinkle now and again, but it's nicer being inside looking out than outside when it pours!"

The tight knot in Ellie's chest loosened. It didn't sound like Sarah and Seth were angry with Pa for sending her and Timmy. She climbed into the buggy. Sarah took her hand, and Ellie gradually relaxed against her stepsister's shoulder. Soon the *pitter-patter* of raindrops on the top of the buggy lulled her to sleep.

A gentle shake awakened Ellie. How different from Gus's usual bellow: *"Git up, girl. There's work to be done!"*

Ellie slowly opened her eyes. She blinked. The sun had come out over a distant hill. Its rays mingled with the light rain and produced the most beautiful rainbow Ellie had ever seen. It arched the sky, and one end rested on a hacienda-style ranch house. Yet the rainbow shone no more dazzling than the love in Sarah's face. Both shouted *home*.

Sarah put an arm around each of the children and softly said, "Welcome to the Diamond S. We sometimes call it Rainbow's End. We don't believe in leprechauns, and we don't have pots of gold, but we have far greater treasure here: happiness."

"And no mountain lions?" Timmy prodded, with a big-eyed glance at the corral filled with horses and cowboys.

Seth's blue eyes twinkled. "No mountain lions, but I'm as hungry as one. How about you, buckaroo?"

Timmy nodded and hitched his too-big pants farther up onto his stomach. His thin face lit up with anticipation. But Ellie continued to watch the rainbow until its glorious colors faded and disappeared before following Seth and Sarah into her new home. . . .

Other memories crowded in on Ellie and demanded her attention, so many she could scarcely contain them. After all the turbulent years with Pa, she and Timmy had found a home that long-ago day. A home and seven years filled with love.

Faces trooped through Ellie's mind like soldiers on parade: Matt, Sarah, and their two boys, Caleb and Gideon. Seth, Dori, and their adorable twin girls, Susannah and Samantha. Curly and Katie Prescott, with their children Riley and Kathleen. A bevy of laughing Mexican children who called Ellie Senorita and giggled when they saw her.

Vaqueros and vineyard workers. People at church in Madera.

Last of all, Solita's smiling face gladdened Ellie's heart. A lump parked in the girl's throat. Solita, *little sun*, healer of bruises and bringer of sunshine to all. How many tears had been shed on the housekeeper's apron? How many times had the wise woman offered comfort without ever speaking a word? The touch of her work-worn hand on Ellie's head soothed away childish hurts like salve on a wound.

Calico nudged Ellie, as if reminding her they needed to head back to the ranch. But Ellie could not go without another prayer of thanks for one of the most important days of her life. Heart overflowing, she slipped from the rock and knelt.

"Lord, thank You so much that Gus allowed Matt and Sarah to adopt Tim and me. Matt never told us how he knew I hated being a Stoddard. Perhaps he guessed." She thought of the seemingly endless time she and Timmy had waited for Matt's return from St. Louis. Before he left, he had told the family, "I don't trust doing this by mail. I'm going to sew Gus Stoddard up so tight that if he ever decides to renege on his bargain, he won't have a legal leg to stand on."

Ellie never asked, but she suspected Matt had paid Gus for her and Timmy. The important thing was they'd been set free. Tears gushed. The first time Matt introduced her as Ellie Sterling, she'd nearly burst with pride. She still did. As the adopted children of one of the richest ranchers in the valley, she and Timmy could "walk tall," as Matt said, and hold their heads high.

Calico shoved her nose against Ellie's shoulder, obviously wanting attention. Ellie patted the mare's neck and obliged. "That's just what I'm going to do when I sing in church tomorrow," she told her faithful horse. "Hold my head high, even though I'm scared out of my wits." Calico whinnied and tossed her mane. "I just hope I don't faint and disgrace the family." Ellie grimaced. "Now where did that horrid thought come from? I've sung in church before." She grimaced. "Just not when a new preacher will be here. Maybe I should tell Matt to get someone else."

God gave me a voice and expects me to use it. Am I going to let the minister of some fancy church keep me from glorifying God with my talent?

Ellie felt a wave of shame crawl up from the bandana around her neck. "No, but I'd better practice." She snatched up her sombrero, jammed it onto her head, and swung into the saddle. A quick touch of her heels to Calico's sides sent the two of them on their way. Ellie opened her mouth and sang the song she had made her own, each note crystal clear:

"When peace, like a river, attendeth my way,
When sorrows like sea billows roll;
Whatever my lot, Thou hast taught me to say,
It is well, it is well with my soul."

It is well, echoed back from the wooded hills.
*With my soul. . .*The echo came again, and Ellie's voice soared in triumph. "It is well, it is well with my soul!"

Filled with the joy of living, Ellie sang the second and third verses then poured her heart into the final stanza:

"And Lord, haste the day when the faith shall be sight,
The clouds be rolled back as a scroll;
The trump shall resound, and the Lord shall descend,
Even so, it is well with my soul."

The final note shimmered in the still air. Ellie leaned forward and called in Calico's ear, "Run!" The mare leaped forward. Ellie bent low, exulting in the feel of wind whipping against her face. A glance at the sky showed she had stayed far too long on the promontory. If she didn't get home and into the lovely yellow dress and white mantilla Sarah had bought her, the fiesta would start without the guest of honor!

Ellie reached the ranch house, skidded to a stop by the corral, and dismounted. Then she tossed Calico's reins to one of the hands lounging against the rail. "Take care of her, will you, please?"

He doffed his Stetson and gave her a wide grin. "Sí, senorita."

A small tornado in a cowboy suit raced toward her. "Hey Aunt Ellie," Caleb shouted, "where've you been? Folks are comin', and everybody's ready but you. Even Uncle Tim." He pointed toward a group of men standing nearby.

"Oh dear! If Tim's ready, then I really am late!" Ellie started toward the house at a dead run, then glanced back at the sturdy boy trying to keep up with her. "Thanks, partner." She started to whip around but her momentum carried her forward. She lurched for a few more steps and tried to ignore the muffled laughter she suspected was incited by the spectacle she was providing.

Tim confirmed her suspicions by hollering, "Hey Ellie, looks like you have two left feet. Don't ask me to square dance with you!"

She ground her teeth, wanting to throttle her brother. Wasn't it humiliating enough to stagger like a newborn calf or a rowdy cowboy on a Saturday night spree? The last thing she needed was for Tim to call more attention to her plight!

Ellie made a final desperate effort to regain her footing. Just when she thought she'd make it, disaster struck again. One foot slipped. She lost her balance and pitched forward. Her arms flailed but could not stop her from falling. A heartbeat later, she crashed smack-dab into a large, immovable object. Ellie hit so hard she reeled backward.

Strong arms closed around her.

Furious at her clumsiness and even more with Tim, Ellie jerked free. She looked up.

And up.

A stranger towered over her. A stranger wearing a broad grin, whose gray eyes were alight with amusement.

Chapter 5

Ellie gaped at the man looming over her. Her hands clenched. How dare he look as if he was ready to join in the raucous laughter coming from behind her? She reared back to escape the stranger's amused gaze—and ran head-on into Caleb.

He clutched at her and let out a warning yelp, but it was too late. *Thud.* They landed on the hard ground in an ignominious heap.

"Ow! Get off, Aunt Ellie. You're breaking me!"

Embarrassment gave way to concern. Ellie rolled over and sat up. "I am so sorry," she told her nephew. "Are you hurt?"

"Naw." Caleb scrambled to his feet. He frowned and flexed his arm. "Uh, not bad."

"Let me look." She rolled up his plaid sleeve and inspected his elbow, but after a quick glance, Caleb squirmed and protested.

"Let me go, Ellie. I ain't bleeding. Solita says if you're hurt much, you bleed." He tugged his shirtsleeve back down and grinned at her.

Relief flowed through her. "Thank goodness you're all right."

Caleb gave her a gap toothed grin and announced with childish candor, "You better get cleaned up. You're a mess." He brushed dust off his shirt and trotted away, leaving her sitting on the ground.

Caleb's comment on Ellie's appearance brought a fresh surge of humiliation, interrupted by a deep voice from which all trace of merriment had fled.

"May I help you?"

Viewed from her lowly position, the tall stranger who blocked the summer sky took on mountainous proportions. The words *you've done quite enough* trembled on Ellie's tongue. She bit them back. The man was in no way to blame for her mowing down Caleb. Ellie wordlessly took the hand he offered, noting its strength in spite of her agitation. "Th–thank you," she stammered.

When she managed to get back on her feet, Tim's laughter-choked voice tightened her lips into a straight line. Ellie freed her hand and whirled, intending to get even with her brother if it was the last thing she did. He forestalled her—and made matters worse.

"You probably haven't been properly introduced, even though I see you've already run into our visiting minister." Mischief danced in Tim's brown eyes. "Reverend Stanhope, meet my sister, Ellie Sterling."

Minister? Reverend? Ellie shut her eyes, wishing the hard-packed earth would open and swallow her.

The stranger laughed. "Make that Pastor. Better yet, Joshua or Josh. I'm not much on formality." A puzzled expression crept into his gray eyes. "Are you the Miss Sterling who will be singing in church tomorrow?"

Ellie couldn't have answered if her life depended on it.

Not so Tim. "Yup." He smirked. "We're all mighty proud of our Ellie's singing."

Why must he babble like the brooks that tumbled down the mountainside to the rivers below? Ellie wondered, wishing her brother were in China or Timbuktu—anywhere far enough from the Diamond S to keep him from adding to her misery.

"Then we'll be in for a treat," Josh said. "What will you be singing, Miss Sterling?"

Her tongue cleaved to the roof of her mouth.

"Call her Ellie," Tim urged, "although folks around here call her the Sierra Songbird."

Ellie had never been more embarrassed. Why did Tim have to brag on her? Now she'd be more nervous than ever, singing in front of the visiting minister. Josh's understanding look helped. His expression plainly showed he knew all about younger brothers. It helped to restore a tiny bit of her dignity.

"I'll settle for 'Miss Ellie,' if that's all right with her," Joshua said.

"Sure it is." Tim patted Ellie's shoulder. "Caleb's right. You're a mess. Get a move on if you're gonna put on some fancy duds before the fiesta starts."

Ellie shot Tim a fiery glance, turned her back on him, and summoned a smile for Josh. "If you'll excuse me, I'll do just that. Oh, I plan to sing 'It Is Well with My Soul.'" She started to pass Josh, but his deep voice stopped her.

"Although that's one of my favorite hymns, would you mind saving it?"

Humiliation engulfed her. "You don't want me to sing tomorrow?"

"Oh no! I'm looking forward to hearing you," he quickly assured. "It's just that a different song will fit my sermon better. Do you know 'The Ninety and Nine'?"

"Sure she does," Tim blared. He began to sing. "'There were ninety and nine. . .'"

A twinkle leaped into Josh's eyes before he said, "Begging your pardon, Tim, but I think we'd best let your sister sing tomorrow."

Tim stuck his nose in the air. "Well! Some folks don't recognize good music when they hear it. I'll save my singing for the horses and cattle. They don't seem to mind when I bed them down for the night." His cheerful grin spoiled his false indignation.

Ellie felt her face scorch. Was there no end to Tim's shenanigans? "I know the song and will be glad to sing it." She climbed the steps to the veranda, snatching at the reins of her temper. A minute more, and she'd be screeching at Tim. But her rage weakened when he said, "Wait till you hear her, Josh. Ellie can beat a western meadowlark all hollow when it comes to singing." Pride rang in every word.

Josh's quick "I'll bet she can" sent tingles through Ellie. She raced inside, through the great hall, and up the broad staircase to her room.

Heedless of her dusty riding skirt and the need to bathe and change clothes, Ellie dropped to her bed. She idly fingered the rich tapestry of the hand-woven Mexican spread: red, emerald green, and white—the national colors of Mexico. Matching draperies hung at the large casement windows set deep into the thick adobe walls.

Ellie only covered the windows while dressing. She loved watching the moon and stars from her bed on nice nights and the rain sluicing down the windowpanes in stormy weather. She thrilled to jagged lightning bolts and even the boom of thunder.

"Well, Lord, I feel like I just came through a thunderstorm," she said. "My nerves are twanging like the strings of my guitar when it's out of tune." She paused. "Joshua Stanhope sure is polite. Outside of Matt and Seth, he seems to be the nicest man I've ever met. I can hardly wait to hear him preach tomorrow." Ellie screwed up her face. "Wish I could say the same for wanting to sing. At least I won't have to face him during my solo. I do not need a reminder of how we met." She felt a reluctant smile curve her lips. "Lord, I know it will be well with my soul, but I'm going to need Your help to settle the rest of me down."

For the first time since she'd crashed into Josh, Ellie had wits enough to remember more than how tall Josh was and the way he'd looked at her. At first, laughter had lurked in his eyes, as if held back by sheer willpower. She'd seen it replaced with compassion. And after Tim prattled on about her singing, genuine interest and admiration flickered in the gray depths. Now Ellie pictured his short, well-brushed light hair and his honest countenance.

"It's like goodness shines through him," she whispered. "Is it because he's a minister?" She shook her head. No. She'd met many ministers—godly men who gave their lives to the service of the Master. Yet never had she seen one whose presence affected her so deeply as Joshua Stanhope had done during their brief encounter. She'd always been too practical to believe in love at first sight, but now she wondered. . . .

A knock brought Ellie out of her reflections. "Are you about ready?" a woman's voice demanded. "May I come in?"

"Of course." Ellie clambered off the bed and opened the door. Sarah stepped inside, lovely in a light blue, tiered fiesta dress that matched her eyes. "Sorry, but I had a little accident and—"

"And landed at a certain handsome stranger's feet," Sarah finished with a trill of laughter.

"You heard?" Ellie's heart sank.

"Everyone heard, thanks to that rascally Tim." Mischief sparkled in Sarah's eyes, and she cocked her head to one side. "Just remember. God brings good from everything that affects His children."

Ellie grunted. "I made a fool of myself in front of a visiting minister, Sarah!"

Sarah donned an innocent expression. She cocked her head to one side and placed her hands on her hips the way Solita did when about to deliver a lecture. She even sounded like Solita when she said, "Land sakes, child. Every single girl, young woman, and eligible widow in Madera will be doing somersaults up and down Main Street to attract Joshua Stanhope's attention if he becomes our minister. Especially Amy Talbot. You have to admit, Ellie, you have a running start." Sarah giggled but didn't look at all repentant. "Sorry. You probably don't care for the word *running* right now."

Ellie laughed in spite of herself, but annoyance swept through her at thought of the petite and predatory Amy, with her oh-so-perfect blond curls and fluttering eyelashes.

"You're right. *Running* isn't my favorite word at the moment. As for Amy being a minister's wife. . ."

"My sentiments exactly." Sarah's eyes twinkled. "So how about getting you into your fiesta dress so you can do something to help prevent such a catastrophe?"

Ellie felt as if she'd been struck. She sank back down on her bed. "I can't. I'm no more fit to be a minister's wife than Amy is."

"Why not?" Sarah sounded genuinely astonished. "You aren't still holding on to the past, are you?" She sat down next to Ellie. Sympathy filled her face.

Ellie twisted her hands. How could she confess that the little girl who cowered before Gus Stoddard still lurked inside, coloring her attitude toward love and marriage? It wasn't right to open old wounds by reminding Sarah that she'd once felt unworthy to marry Matt. The subject had remained closed ever since they talked about it years earlier, at the time of Ellie and Tim's adoption. Yet in spite of all the love that surrounded Ellie, childhood scars had not completely healed over. She hadn't realized how raw they still were until Sarah teased her.

Don't be a ninny, Ellie told herself. *Joshua Stanhope would never fall in love with me. Even if he did, marrying me would be asking for trouble. Minister's wives have to be beyond reproach, not related to the likes of Gus Stoddard. Josh would find himself out of a job and eventually begin to hate me.*

Sarah clasped Ellie's hands in hers. Warm tears cascaded. "Ellie, honey, you are my sister. You are also Matt's and my beloved daughter, but much more. The apostle Paul tells us that when we accept Christ, old things are passed away. All things become new, including us." She dropped Ellie's hands and gathered her into a close embrace. "You are a Sterling, Ellie, not a Stoddard. Don't look back." She gave a shaky laugh. "Remember what happened to Lot's wife. You don't want your partners at the fiesta lugging around a pillar of salt, do you?"

"No." Ellie hugged Sarah, warmed by the fragile feeling that just maybe things would be all right, after all. "Thank you."

Tim's bellow from beneath the window broke into the tender moment. "Hey Ellie, are you coming or not?"

Caleb's shrill, "Yeah, Aunt Ellie. Where are you?"

Sarah wiped away her tears. "So much for private conversations on your birthday." She ran to the window. "Hold your horses, you two. It's Ellie's birthday. She'll come when she's ready." She turned from the window, hurried to the large wardrobe, and took out Ellie's fiesta dress. Each tier of the sunshiny yellow skirt and modest, ruffled neckline wore bands of white lace that matched the mantilla Sarah laid on the bed. "Are you going to be all right?"

For now trembled on Ellie's lips but she quickly substituted, "Yes." She summoned a smile. "Better get down there before they send out a search party."

"Yes ma'am!" Sarah saluted. But before leaving the room, she looked straight into Ellie's eyes. "Remember what Matt tells us. 'Walk tall and hold your head high.' You have every right: You are God's child—and ours." The door closed behind her, leaving Ellie feeling as if she'd been sitting in the sunlight for a very long time. She hurried through a sponge bath and slipped into the lovely gown. Her fingers shook as she stepped to the mirror and pinned the mantilla on her dark brown hair.

Pleased with the reflection that stared back at her, Ellie muttered, "First impressions may be lasting, but here's hoping the way I look now will erase Joshua Stanhope's memory of me sprawled at his feet." She snatched up a stiff, white lace fan, swept out of her bedroom, down the staircase, and into the swirl of the fiesta.

Chapter 6

Buggies and buckboards. Carriages and cowboys. Would they never stop arriving? Ellie stood on the veranda, tingling with excitement. Half the countryside must have come to honor her on her birthday. The sound of jingling spurs whipped her around. She stared at Tim. "What are you doing in those clothes?"

Tim smirked. "You like, *mi hermana*?" He smoothed down the short, black jacket lavishly embroidered in silver and ran his hands down the tight, black pants bound at the waist by a scarlet sash. "*Soy un gran caballero.*"

Ellie fixed her fascinated gaze on the widest Mexican sombrero she'd ever seen. "There's enough silver braid and conchas on that hat to give you a headache. What are you going to do? Fight a cow or do the Mexican hat dance?"

Tim put on a wise look and stroked his fake mustache. Ellie suspected one of the horses in the corral had a bald spot. "I might." He glanced over his sister's shoulder and into the yard. His voice dropped to a whisper. "Hey, take a gander at Red Fallon over there with our new minister. Red looks prouder than a mama cow with a new calf."

Ellie surveyed the tall cowboy whose red hair showed streaks of silver. "He does, but Joshua Stanhope isn't our minister yet."

"He will be if *she* has anything to say about it," Tim drawled. He nodded toward a pink-clad girl and her father approaching Red and the minister. She wore an unmistakable where-have-you-been-all-my-life expression. "Amy Talbot has her daddy wrapped around her little finger, and Luther's chairman of the church board. C'mon. We'll go rescue Josh."

"We? I don't think so." Ellie put her fan up to smother a giggle and watched Josh free his arm from the white hand Amy had laid on it. "Besides, he looks perfectly capable of taking care of himself."

"He's probably used to women on his trail," Tim agreed. "But Amy's after anyone wearing pants. She even flirts with me."

"You should feel honored," Ellie teased. Satisfaction at being able to get even with her brother erupted into another giggle. "After all, she's an older woman, and—"

Tim snorted. "Yeah. Just like you. You're pretty near an old maid, you know!" He settled the gigantic sombrero more fully and marched down the veranda steps, spurs clanking. A few long strides took him to the foursome they'd been discussing. Tim said something to Josh and glanced in Ellie's direction. The minister promptly left the others and headed toward the veranda.

Ellie's breath caught when she observed Amy's pout and the scowl on Luther Talbot's face. If Joshua Stanhope wanted to become minister of Christ the Way Church in Madera, walking away from the Talbots was not a good way to secure the position. Josh reached the bottom step. The desire to warn and protect him caused Ellie to say in a low voice, "The Talbots don't look happy about your leaving them."

Mischief shone in Josh's gray eyes, but all he said was, "They don't, do they?" Then he added, "Your brother suggested I go over the order of service with you for tomorrow. No one should object to that, should they?"

The feeling of being in cahoots with him against a common enemy made laughter bubble up past Ellie's ruffles. "They shouldn't." The words *it doesn't mean they won't* hung unspoken in the air.

"I know I'm a stranger, but would you consider allowing me to escort you for at least part of the fiesta?" Josh looked back at the Talbots. "Perhaps you can alert me to any...uh...pitfalls that lie ahead, should I be accepted as your minister."

Ellie's spirits rose, lighter than the balloons decorating the yard. Brighter than the dozens of luminaries to be lit at dusk. Not trusting herself to speak, she smiled and nodded. She felt a blush begin at the modest neckline of her gown. As it worked its way up, Ellie took refuge behind her fan. She held it so only her eyes showed, praying they wouldn't give away the unexpected feelings churning inside her.

Josh didn't seem to notice her confusion. "Shall we go over the service so we can join the fiesta?"

Ellie sternly bade her unruly heart to be still. She might never see Josh again after tomorrow. So why should she feel he might be the long-awaited stranger she'd yearned for each time she saw Matt and Sarah's happiness? Or the way Seth and Dori shared understanding glances? Or the teasing between Curly and Katie?

The notion left her breathless. But as the fiesta continued, her sense of wonder increased: bittersweet and haunting, like a persistent cloud dimming the sunshine of Ellie's day. Amy Talbot's obvious but futile attempts to pry Josh away from Ellie's side didn't help. Or the bevy of girls and young women who flocked around them, waiting to be introduced and expressing delight at Josh's coming.

When Josh turned away to greet a newcomer, Tim sidled up to his sister. "I gotta hand it to you, Ellie." Admiration filled his voice. "Our new minister's a goner. You've got him roped, tied, and liking it."

"What?" Ellie croaked, feeling the telltale red creeping into her face again. "Josh is just being polite."

"Horse feathers!" was Tim's inelegant reply. "Just watch your step. Amy's wearing her hunting expression and loaded for bear. And she isn't the only one."

Ellie couldn't help laughing, but Tim's remark made her recall Sarah's prediction: "*Every single girl, young woman, and eligible widow in Madera will be doing somersaults up and down Main Street to attract Joshua Stanhope. . . . You have to admit, Ellie, you have a running start.*" Ellie bit her lip. She must not let the young minister's marked attentions go to her head.

Event followed event. Josh remained at Ellie's side, except when participating in the games and races. If his broad smile was an accurate indication, he was having the time of his life. He joined in the three-legged race with Tim, so awkward they thumped to the ground after only a few steps and earned the good-natured jeers of the onlookers. At Tim's insistence, Josh accepted the loan of a Diamond S gelding and entered the horse race. He rode well but was no match for his range-trained opponents. He came in last.

A little later, a score of men and boys lined up for a foot race. Josh sprang forward at the starting gun, widened the gap between him and his competitors, and outdistanced them all. He accepted the blue ribbon but said, "Put the cash prize in the collection plate tomorrow. The church needs it more than I do." It earned him a loud cheer of approval from the merrymakers.

When Josh returned to Ellie, his mouth twitched. "Did I redeem myself?"

"Of course. Where'd you learn to run like that?"

"I was talking about the three-legged race, not the foot race." The twitch grew more pronounced.

Ellie felt her mouth fall open. She tried three times before she could speak. "You—you—are you saying you fell down on purpose?" she stuttered.

A mysterious light came into his eyes. "Shhh! Don't tell Tim, but I thought if folks saw me sprawled on the ground, maybe they'd forget your spill."

Ellie's heart lurched. What kind of person was Josh? They'd just met, yet he'd cared enough about her feelings to turn attention from her clumsiness to his. "You redeemed yourself. Thank you." Ellie could say no more.

A fiesta highlight was the piñata hung on a tree branch. One by one, Matt and Sarah blindfolded the children and gave them a long pole. Each had three chances to strike and break the burro-shaped container and set the children scrambling when candy and toys showered down. Yet child after child struck and missed, or only rocked the piñata.

At last the time came for Curly and Katie's children to try. They looked wide-eyed up at the piñata. Riley's lip quivered. "It's too high."

"We're too little," Kathleen said. Tears sprang to her Irish blue eyes.

Ellie wanted to cry, too. Why hadn't they hung a piñata on a lower branch to give the smaller children a chance? Evidently this one was stronger than most. Neither of the Prescotts would be able to break it if the bigger kids hadn't succeeded.

Quick as a flash, Josh demanded, "Where are those poles? No blindfolds for us. We'll show you how to break a piñata." He scooped Riley up in one arm and Kathleen with the other. Then he snatched a pole from Tim and said, "Kids, put your hands above mine. Everyone else stand back."

The crowd fell silent and edged away.

"Ready. Set. Swing!"

Crack. The pole smashed into the piñata. It burst and spilled its contents onto the ground below. A great shout went up from the crowd. The children surged forward. Tim restrained the others while Josh lowered the Prescotts. "Riley and Kathleen get a head start," Tim said. "They broke the piñata."

Moments later, happy laughter rang across the yard—but none happier than Ellie's. If Josh hadn't already redeemed himself, his caring actions with the disappointed little ones would have done the trick. Needing time to sort out her turbulent feelings, Ellie slipped away to her room. She crossed to the window and stood so she could remain unobserved but view the throng stretching from yard to corral and beyond.

A parade of children—led by Caleb and his brother Gideon—crowded close to Josh, holding up their treasures for him to see. Their delighted shouts curved Ellie's lips in a sympathetic smile. She thought of Jesus. He, too, had gathered the children around Him. He had ordered His disciples not to turn them away, as Luther Talbot was vainly attempting to do with the children below. What a wonderful, godly father Josh would make!

Ellie left the window and removed her lace mantilla. Lovely as it was, she longed for the cool evening breeze to waft through her hair. Besides, this was no time to think about Joshua Stanhope's qualifications for fatherhood. Not with the fiesta reaching its height. Not when the spicy aroma of barbecued beef drifted up to tantalize and remind her of the long plank tables resting on sawhorses and laden with food. Not when several fiddlers and the best square dance caller in Madera county waited to step into the limelight and provide joy for young and old alike.

Ellie felt her face flame with anticipation. She loved square dancing and never lacked for partners, especially freckle-faced Johnny Foster, who used to deliver telegrams to the Diamond S. For the past year or two, his worshipful gaze followed Ellie whenever she encountered him.

She washed her hands, cooled her sun-warmed face, and whispered, "Will Joshua dance with me? Or does he refrain from dancing because of his calling?"

There was but one way to find out. With a last, reassuring glance in the mirror, Ellie left her bedroom. At the top of the staircase, she checked to make sure she was alone. Then she bundled her skirts around her, slid down the banister rail, and hurried back to the fiesta—and Joshua Stanhope.

Chapter 7

Joshua watched Ellie Sterling vanish inside the heavy front door of the Diamond S ranch house. A pang went through him, as if with her going he'd lost something precious. He scoffed at the idea. In his years as minister of Bayview Christian he'd been flattered and fawned on, praised and put upon. He'd been pursued by marriage-minded maidens who made it clear they considered him the answer to their own and their scheming mothers' prayers. Yet his heart had kept its steady rhythm in spite of their wiles—and in spite of his mother forever producing suitable candidates for his affections.

Josh smothered a grin. Avoiding the little traps set for him had grown to be a game. He'd secretly enjoyed foiling the elaborate plans laid to ambush him. The last thing he wanted—then or now—was some female hot on his trail. Josh pictured Beryl Westfield's lips curled with scorn. After Edward finished flitting from woman to woman and asked the dark-haired woman to marry him, Beryl had delighted in goading Josh. Disgusted with her prodding, Josh once asked, "Whatever happened to modest maidens who allowed the men to do the pursuing?"

Beryl had hooted. "That idea went out with hoopskirts, Josh. Women have as much right as men to go after what they want."

A small hand slipped beneath Josh's arm and brought him back to the present. He looked down into Amy Talbot's upturned face. The avid gleam he'd learned meant another hound on his trail sparkled in the girl's eyes. Josh choked back annoyance. Good thing the tiny blond couldn't read his mind. Red Fallon had already stated how much influence she had with her father—and that Luther ran the church board as if the other members had been hired to do his bidding.

"Reverend Stanhope, will you lead the Virginia Reel with me?" Her confident expression showed she believed her invitation was the same as accepted.

Josh inwardly sighed and freed himself. "Thank you, Miss Talbot, but I don't dance."

A pout replaced her smile. "Oh, but you must," she gushed. "Why, everyone in Madera dances." She batted her golden eyelashes at him and moved closer. The scent of heavy perfume assailed Josh's nostrils. "If you don't know how, I'll teach you."

"Thank you for your kindness, but I must decline. I really don't care to learn."

A loud *harrumph* sounded from behind them. Josh turned on his heel, expecting to see a scowling Luther Talbot. Instead, the tall, gaunt man wore what Josh figured was as near a look of approval as he could muster.

Luther harrumphed again. "Commendable, Reverend Stanhope. Very commendable. Run along now, Amy. I want to speak with the reverend about tomorrow's sermon." He gave a glance of disapproval toward the merry crowd choosing partners for the square dancing. "We'll just step off a ways to where we can hear ourselves think."

Dismay shot through Josh. Good grief, was this officious-acting man going to tell him what to preach and how?

Luther hooked a bony finger in his vest. "What text are you using?"

Josh didn't like Luther's waiting-to-pass-judgment look. "Matthew 18. The lost sheep."

"Hmmm." Luther's nostrils quivered as if warding off a bad smell. "Not wise. Not wise at all. This is primarily cattle country, you know." He sniffed. "Although a few. . .uh. . .sheepherders do come to church."

A lesser man would have quailed at the scornful look that accompanied the criticism, but Josh kept his voice steady, although apprehension stirred within him. "That's why I chose the story," he said. He almost added *sir*, but discarded it. If he were to become pastor of Christ the Way Church, he didn't intend to kowtow to a local dictator. Josh had dealt with them before. The only way to handle such men was to show strength.

Luther Talbot's eyebrows threatened to shoot off the top of his head. "I beg your pardon?"

First round. Stanhope, 1. Talbot, 0. The irreverent thought exploded into a hearty laugh. "The story shows God's boundless love for those who have wandered away. Red says the church will be packed tomorrow. Cowboys will be riding in from the ranches to 'check out the city preacher.' Maybe even a few extra sheepherders." Josh's heart bumped against his chest wall. "I pray some of them will be touched enough to want to return."

Luther snorted. "The only reason they'll come to church is because Dunlap's saloon is closed on Sunday."

Josh fought a wave of hostility for the self-righteous man but contented himself with saying, "Thank God for that." No sense antagonizing the chairman any sooner than absolutely necessary.

Luther shrugged. "What we want in a minister is someone who will tend to the flock, not spend time consorting with range riffraff."

Rage licked at Josh's veins. Was this how Jesus had felt when He cleared the temple of money changers? The young minister set his jaw, longing to shake the hypocrite who dared dictate to him. Josh clenched his teeth. If this was a sample of what he'd have to endure in Madera, the best thing would be to preach in the morning as promised, then catch the first train back to San Francisco.

"*We need you. Bad.*"

Memory of Red's cry for help echoed in Josh's ears, followed by a vision of Ellie Sterling's crystal-blue eyes looking up at him. He felt his anger die. With it went uncertainty about the future. His heart leaped like an antelope. He would not turn tail and run. If given the chance, he'd accept the challenge of pastoring Christ the Way Church—and trust in the Lord for the wisdom to handle the battles that surely lay ahead.

In the meantime, Luther was waiting for him to respond.

Josh looked straight into his opponent's unfriendly eyes. "Jesus tells us in Luke 5:32 that He came not to call the righteous, but sinners to repentance."

A heavy hand fell on Josh's shoulder. "A good thing for me," Red's voice boomed. "I wouldn't be here now 'cept for that."

Luther gave an unpleasant laugh. "That may be, but it's the righteous who fill the offering plates with money to pay the preacher." Head held high, Luther turned on his heel and marched off.

Second round. Talbot, 1. Stanhope, 0.

"Well, of all the...," Red sputtered. "Don't pay that old windbag any mind. Luther thinks God can't get along without his help, which I say's more like meddlin'." A crooked grin appeared. "Talbot ain't righteous, and he sure don't do much plate fillin'. Makes a big show of how much he puts in, but I happen to know it's nothing compared with what a lot of folks give. Some that can't really spare it."

"How do you know that?" Josh inquired.

Red guffawed. "Word gets 'round when there's only a few hundred people in town. Hey, looks like folks are gettin' tuckered. Maybe we can talk Miss Ellie into singin' for us."

Alas for Red's hopes and Josh's fervent wish for the girl who had so impressed him to favor them with a song. When approached, she said, "I'll save my voice for church. Besides, Tim's going to do the Mexican hat dance." Her eyes twinkled. "Perhaps you gentlemen would like to join him?"

"Not me," Red said. "I'll leave that to the reverend."

Josh shook his head. "Sorry. There are some here who'd think it was undignified for a minister." He cast a pointed glance at Luther Talbot, who stood nearby, arms crossed and wearing a disapproving look.

A look of understanding crept into Ellie's lovely eyes. How changeable they were! Josh had seen them flash with indignation, soften with concern for Caleb, and surreptitiously observe him.

A burst of music from the Spanish guitars that had replaced the fiddling filled the air. Josh experienced a multitude of sensations. Had he been unconsciously looking for a mate all the years he avoided entrapment? Had God led him to Madera to find love as well as to preach the gospel? A Bible verse Josh had used while performing weddings sang in his mind: *"For this cause shall a man leave father and mother, and shall cleave to his wife."*

Joy became despair. If Ellie proved to be the wife Josh now realized he'd longed for, it meant further estrangement from his family. The fact she was the daughter of the richest rancher in the San Joaquin Valley wouldn't make her worthy of a Stanhope in the eyes of San Francisco society.

Who cares? Josh fiercely asked himself. *I will not allow Mother or Edward to decide whom I shall marry, only God.*

Relief at having chosen his pathway for better or for worse made Josh feel pounds lighter. He smiled at Ellie. "I can hardly wait to see Tim."

Her eyes darkened. "I just hope he doesn't make a fool of himself. He's only persisting in this because I teased him earlier."

"I wouldn't worry about it." Josh chortled. "I suspect your brother can do anything he sets his mind to."

"I guess we'll find out."

Ellie's concern proved groundless. Tim threw his silver-laden sombrero on the ground, nodded to the musicians, and began his dance. He stomped. He minced with fingers outstretched like a haughty senorita. He circled and leaped. Then amid wild applause and ear-splitting whistles, Tim snatched up the sombrero and swept it to the ground with a low bow. The performance was the funniest thing Josh had seen in years, and it signaled the end of the fiesta.

When the final shouts of, "See you at church tomorrow!" floated back from the multitude of guests, Josh climbed into the backseat of the Fallons' carriage and put his arms around David and Jonathan.

"What hymns would you like tomorrow?" Abby asked. "I'm the organist." By the time they finished their discussion, the boys had fallen asleep. Red and Abby talked in low tones. It gave Josh a chance to relive the hours since Red had met him at the train station and taken him to the Yosemite Hotel.

"It's a ten-mile ride out to the Diamond S. You may wanta change clothes," Red had advised. "A fiesta's no place for city duds." The suggestion proved wise. Once they reached the ranch, Josh had wondered if they'd ever get the dust brushed off.

The day's highlights paraded through Josh's mind, always ending with thoughts of Ellie. Did the little Sierra Songbird really have a voice to rival the western meadowlark? Or did Tim's love for his sister color the boy's judgment? Josh yawned. It had been a long day. Tomorrow would tell...and in all probability settle his future concerning Madera and Christ the Way Church.

Chapter 8

Even though most of Madera lay quiet and sleeping when Josh returned from the fiesta, he decided to visit the church. His first glimpse of the brown wood building sheltered by trees and topped with a steeple filled him with awe. Light from a full moon and countless stars streamed down like a heavenly benediction. Modest and unassuming, Christ the Way Church could never compete with Bayview Christian. Yet something about it drew Josh.

He stepped inside. Moonlight streamed through the clear glass panes. It lit some of the wooden pews and left others in shadow. He walked up the center aisle and knelt before the altar. Peace fell over him like a mantle.

After a long time, Josh rose and silently slipped out into the glorious night. A sense of Someone walking beside him grew as he began his walk back to the Yosemite Hotel. "Why does this cow town church cry out to me?" he whispered. No answer came, but the Presence remained. The faith that had led Josh to test God by coming to Madera became knowledge: This was where he belonged.

The next morning, Josh awakened to the chime of church bells summoning the faithful to worship. He sprang from bed and peered out the open window. No fog or shining bay greeted him, only smiling skies and a dusty street leading to Christ the Way Church. Josh filled his lungs with morning air. "Thank You, Lord, for bringing me to this place. Help me speak words of truth and of You."

After a hearty breakfast in the hotel's pleasant dining room, Josh escaped Captain Perry Mace, the talkative proprietor, and hurried to the church. To his delight, the church had lost none of its charm in daylight. The sensation of being inexorably drawn to it intensified, and the sound of music lured him inside. Dark-haired Abby Fallon sat at a small organ. She smiled, continued softly playing, and said, "Good morning. Did you sleep well?"

"Thank you, yes. I'll just put my Bible on the pulpit and get back outside."

Abby's eyes twinkled. "Good idea. Folks will want to see you."

Josh grimaced. "I know. Preacher on trial and all that." To his amazement, Abby didn't argue. It gave him food for thought.

Josh stepped outside and watched an assortment of conveyances roll up and disgorge their passengers. He saw townspeople, singly and in groups, hurrying up Main Street. Riders hitched their horses to a nearby rail and tried to rid their boots of clinging yellow dust. A battery of eyes turned toward Josh: friendly and welcoming except for the four men who stood with Luther Talbot, all wearing wait-and-see expressions. Josh targeted them as the church board. Luther looked like he'd been drinking vinegar. Had he already expressed doubts about the visiting minister?

"Morning, Josh." A cheerful voice sang out.

He turned to see a grinning Tim Sterling helping Ellie out of a buggy. She looked absolutely fetching in a simple, light blue gown and matching hat. Josh searched for something to say to keep from betraying his excitement at seeing her again. "Good morning to you both. Nice clothes, Tim. Not as flashy as what you wore for the fiesta though."

Tim twitched the string tie adorning his plaid shirt. "Naw. I gave them back to Juan." He cocked his head and blurted out, "How come you're wearing a suit?"

"Tim!" Ellie protested. "That's rude." Color stained her smooth cheeks.

"Why?" her brother wanted to know. "Matt said city preachers mostly wear fancy robes and turn their collars backward."

Josh couldn't stifle his amusement. "Not this preacher. Besides, I may be a country preacher pretty soon."

Tim's enthusiastic "*Yippee-ki-ay*" turned heads and made Josh cringe. But the light in Ellie's eyes and her barely audible "I hope so" helped restore his equilibrium enough to change the subject.

"I forgot to ask Red how the church got its name. It's certainly unusual."

"A real jim-dandy," Tim announced. "Matt and Dori's folks helped build the church. Folks didn't know what to call it, but William Sterling said flat out it was Christ's church and should be named for Him. It's been Christ the Way ever since."

"A good name and a good story," Josh approved.

The church bell pealed a warning note. Tim looked worried. "You better get a move on, Josh. Luther Talbot looks sour enough to curdle milk. C'mon, Ellie." He hurried her up the steps and inside with Josh at their heels.

This is it, Lord, Josh prayed. He took his place on the raised platform. Luther settled into a chair beside him. Josh surveyed the packed church. Sunlight streamed through the clear glass windows. It reflected on steel-rimmed spectacles and Sheriff Meade's badge and sent rainbows dancing around the room. It touched worn hymnbooks and the faces of a congregation far different from Bayview Christian. Clothing ranged from spotless but unfashionable to brand-spanking-new. Captain Perry Mace removed his ever-present top hat and gave Josh an encouraging smile.

Josh's gaze landed on Caleb Sterling. Face still damp from a recent scrubbing, cowlick slicked down, the small boy gave Josh a gap-toothed grin.

It changed the course of the service.

Lord, everyone here needs to hear of Your great love, but none more than the children. Give me the courage to do what I feel I must.

Luther stepped forward, exuding importance. He cleared his throat. "Most of you know that as chairman of the church board, I've been in charge of the services since our former minister moved on to new pastures."

Josh fought the insane desire to howl. *New pastures.* Bad choice of words. After today's sermon, Luther would be more careful how he used that phrase!

Luther continued. "Reverend Joshua Stanhope is here with us today. I ask for him your kind attention. But first we will sing 'Bringing in the Sheaves.'" He added, "Our Lord told us the harvest is white but the workers are few. This has never been more true than now." Luther droned on and on, louder and more emphatic, until Josh wondered if there would be time for a second sermon.

Luther didn't stop expounding until Tim gave a loud cough and muttered, "Sorry." The chairman nodded at Abby and said, "Let's stand for the opening song."

Josh didn't dare look at Tim. He concentrated on the hymn. Bayview Christian never sang it, but "Bringing in the Sheaves" had been one of Uncle Marvin's favorite songs at the rescue mission. It brought back memories. The down-and-outers had sung it as fervently as this congregation, now on the last line of the refrain: "We shall come rejoicing, bringing in the sheaves."

God, grant that the harvest may be great, Josh prayed.

The song ended. Luther offered a long prayer before directing the congregation to be seated. He returned to his chair and Josh relaxed. Having Luther behind him was a blessing, considering what "Reverend Joshua Stanhope" was going to do.

Blood pounding in his ears until it threatened to deafen him, Josh walked to the front of the platform but didn't step behind the pulpit. "I'm glad to be here with you." He took a deep breath. "Will the children please come forward?"

Eyebrows rose. A gasp from Luther echoed through the church. It did not deter Josh. In all the time he'd been preaching, he'd never been more sure of himself.

At first, no one moved. Josh saw Caleb look at Matt for permission before heading toward the front of the church. Gideon followed; then a whole flock of children surged forward. Josh seated himself on the shallow steps leading up to the platform and motioned for the children to join him. "I have a story for you. Your mothers and fathers are welcome to listen, too."

Luther's chair tipped over with a bang. "Really, Reverend, I must protest."

Josh turned. "Please be seated, Mr. Talbot." Their gazes clashed and held. Then to Josh's relief, Luther gave a loud *harrumph* and resumed his place.

Third round. Stanhope, 1. Talbot, 0.

Josh swallowed a chuckle and turned back to the children. "How many of you live on cattle ranches?" he inquired. Several hands shot up.

"How many of you go riding in the hills with your daddies?" Other hands raised.

Josh leaned forward and said in his most mysterious voice, "Do you know that God is a cattle rancher?" He thrilled at the interest in the children's eyes. "God says in the Bible that he owns the cattle upon a thousand hills. I saw a lot of cattle yesterday but not that many!" He kept his attention on the children. "Even though God owns all those cattle, His Son, Jesus, is called the Good Shepherd. That's funny, isn't it?"

The children nodded, but Luther mercifully kept still. Josh went on. "A long time ago Jesus told a story that shows how much God loves everyone. We call it the story of the lost sheep." Josh glanced at the congregation. A small group sitting near the back wore broad smiles; Josh suspected they were the sheep owners. Others in the congregation scowled. Even Tim looked doubtful, but Ellie's blue eyes sparkled.

"A certain man had a hundred sheep. One day when he counted them, one was missing. The man left the other ninety-nine and went to find the sheep that had wandered away from the flock. The story says the shepherd was really happy when he found his sheep and brought it back where it belonged."

"I bet the sheep was happy, too," Caleb piped up.

Josh laughed and rejoiced when the congregation joined in. "I'm sure you're right, Caleb. You may all go back to your parents now." He stood, waited until they scrambled back to their places, then crossed to the pulpit and opened his Bible.

"Isaiah 53:6 says, 'All we like sheep have gone astray; we have turned every one to his own way; and the Lord hath laid on him the iniquity of us all.'" Josh closed his Bible and leaned forward. "You probably wonder why I chose to preach about sheep here in cattle country." He waited for a murmur to die. "I don't know much about cattle and sheep, but I know one important thing: You can herd cattle. Sometimes the ornery critters object and sometimes the herd stampedes, but cattle can still be driven."

Josh leaned forward, aware of quickening interest in the congregation. "Sheep can't be driven. They have to be led by someone who understands them and cares about them. Someone who is willing to give his life to save the flock." He paused. "The biblical account of the lost sheep doesn't list details, but the fact that the shepherd left the ninety and nine in the wilderness shows us the search couldn't have been easy.

"I've asked Miss Sterling to sing a song that tells what the search may have been like. In 1874 a man named Ira Sankey was on an evangelism tour in Scotland with Dwight Moody. Sankey tore a poem from a British newspaper, put it in his pocket, and forgot about it. At a service later that day, Moody asked Sankey for a closing song.

"It caught Ira by surprise, but the Holy Spirit reminded him of the poem. He took it out, said a prayer, and composed the tune as he sang. 'The Ninety and Nine' was Sankey's first attempt at writing a hymn tune." Josh nodded to Ellie. "Miss Sterling." He went back to his chair.

Ellie stepped to the front of the church. Abby played a few notes. Ellie began singing. The first clear note laid a hush over even the smallest child. Josh sat spellbound. Where had this rancher's daughter learned to sing like this? Ellie's voice surpassed the finest soloists who held highly paid positions at Bayview Christian. The words filled the sanctuary:

"There were ninety and nine that safely lay
In the shelter of the fold.
But one was out on the hills away,
Far off from the gates of gold.
Away on the mountains wild and bare.
Away from the tender Shepherd's care."

The song continued, painting unforgettable pictures of the obstacles the shepherd encountered in his quest to find the lost sheep. The congregation sat transfixed. When Ellie reached the final stanza, her voice swelled with joy:

"And the angels echoed around the throne,
'Rejoice, for the Lord brings back His own!
Rejoice, for the Lord brings back His own!'"

Ellie took her seat. Tears crowded behind Josh's eyelids. He rose and slowly walked to the pulpit. He struggled for words to match the triumphant ones lingering in the sunlit air. Finding none, Josh bowed his head and said, "Let us pray."

Chapter 9

When Joshua Stanhope called the children to the front of the church and courteously but firmly squashed Luther Talbot's attempt to interfere, Ellie Sterling wanted to stand up and cheer. Tim's wide grin showed he felt the same way.

The children crowded close to Josh. A sunbeam from the window behind the pulpit bathed the little group with golden light and glorified the young minister's face as he began the story of the lost sheep. Ellie clasped lace-mitted hands and glanced around her. Josh's rich, deep voice and simple re-telling of the timeless parable held the congregation spellbound. . .except for Amy Talbot. Face lifted toward Josh, her fingers toyed with the ruffles on her white dress. She coughed behind a dainty handkerchief, then dropped it and made a show of picking it up.

Ellie raged at the disrespectful, obvious attempt to attract the young minister's attention. Relief surged through her when Josh paid Amy no more heed than if she were a bug on the wall. He finished his story, sent the children back to their parents, and continued with the service.

Ellie drank in every word, finding new meaning in the familiar Bible story. Then Josh nodded to her. She slowly walked to the front of the church. *Lord, let me sing to Your glory.* Abby struck the opening chords. Ellie's earlier apprehension vanished. She opened her mouth and poured her heart into the song. Her heart thrilled at the look of understanding she saw in the faces turned toward her. Cattlemen and sheepmen alike knew every obstacle the Good Shepherd had encountered when He searched for His lost sheep. They, too, battled the elements of an often harsh land. Wild, bare mountains shaken by thunder. Steep and rocky trails and canyons. The desert. Flood-swollen rivers. Starless nights so black they hid dangers that threatened them. Thornbushes that tore into man and beast.

The expressions on the girls' and women's faces reflected their knowledge, as well. In spite of stern warnings, children sometimes wandered away from home. What agony mothers and sisters experienced until they heard the glad cry that showed a child—a lost lamb—had been found.

Never had Ellie felt the effects of a song so strongly. She closed her eyes and sang the final stanza with a power far beyond her own ability:

"There arose a glad cry to the gate of Heaven,
'Rejoice! I have found My sheep!'
And the angels echoed around the throne,
'Rejoice, for the Lord brings back His own!
Rejoice, for the Lord brings back His own!'"

The triumphant proclamation lingered in the sunlit air. Ellie returned to her seat, as exhausted as if she'd traveled every foot of the way with the Good Shepherd. Memory of the faces turned toward her and the glistening tear tracks on work-worn faces filled her with humility. Her heart swelled, and she silently thanked God.

Tim patted Ellie's hand, as if aware of her feelings.

Then Josh said, "Let us pray." Heads bowed. "Father, we thank Thee for this day and these, Thy beloved children. May the peace of God, which passeth all understanding, keep their hearts and minds through Christ Jesus. Amen." Josh smiled at the congregation. "Now if you'll give me time to get outside, I'd like to meet you all."

Luther Talbot pushed forward, protest written all over his disapproving face. "Our minister always greets people *inside* the church, not out," he announced.

Josh's easy laugh stretched Ellie's lips into a smile. She poked Tim when he showed evidence of wanting to let out a *yippee-ki-ay* after Josh replied, "God has given us such a beautiful day, I'm sure He won't mind if we step outside to enjoy it." He strode down the aisle, leaving Luther huffing behind him in hot pursuit, with Amy at their heels.

Before they reached the door, her clear treble floated back. "Oh Reverend, your sermon was *wonderful*! I don't know when I've been so touched." She giggled. "Please forgive me. Father said you don't like being called Reverend, but it doesn't seem fitting to call you Josh. How about Preacher Josh?"

Although Ellie couldn't see Amy's face, she could visualize the fluttering eyelashes and trademark innocence that were the finest weapons in the tiny blond's arsenal of charm. How would Josh respond? The first pang of jealousy Ellie had ever known attacked her. *Don't be foolish,* she told her wildly beating heart. *Josh is nothing to you.*

Is that so? a second voice whispered. *You've cared for him from the moment you met.*

Josh's amused voice broke into Ellie's turbulent thoughts and silenced the nagging voice. "I was called Pastor in San Francisco, but Preacher Josh will do. Now if you'll excuse me, we need to make way for others coming out."

"Bravo!" Tim whispered in Ellie's ear. "The Royal Canadian Mounties may always get their man, but I bet Amy Talbot won't. She seems to have met her match."

Ellie stifled a laugh. Yet as she and Tim followed the crowd surging outside to greet Josh, she wondered why Tim's comment should fill her with glee. Was it Christian to be glad Amy was getting the comeuppance she deserved? Besides, what was Joshua Stanhope to Ellie Sterling, or she to him?

She and Tim reached the doorway and stepped out into the sunshine. Sarah's laughing remark about the female population trying to attract Joshua Stanhope's attention had already come to pass. Girls and women in billowing summer dresses encircled him. High-pitched voices praised the sermon, the story, and Josh.

Don't set your cap for him, Ellie told herself. *Josh showed a clear preference for you at the fiesta, but look at him now.* Sarah's reminder that she had a running start didn't silence Ellie's doubts. She turned her attention to a group near her and concentrated on their comments.

"He's a likely young feller. Lookit the way he put ol' man Talbot in his place."

"Yeah, but he didn't preach much. Just told stories."

"That's the way I like it," someone approved. "Short 'n' sweet. Preachers that rattle on and on usually just keep repeatin' themselves."

"Wonder what the church board will do? Talbot looks mad enough to send Stanhope packin'." A laugh followed.

"I don't take much stock in what the Talbot girl says, but I kinda like the name Preacher Josh. It's friendly sounding."

"Pree-cisely," another drawled. "I figured he might be uppity, being from a big city and all. He ain't a bit like that." The speaker lowered his voice, and Ellie had to strain her ears to hear. "I hear tell his folks live in a swell mansion. Funny he'd leave all that an' some big church to come to Madera."

"Not funny at all," a crisp voice argued. "I wouldn't live in San Francisco if they gave me the place. Madera's good enough for me."

A murmur of agreement rose before the first speaker commented, "I shore vote for this new man. I aim to tell Talbot right now." He broke away and headed for Luther.

"Hey, wait for us!" A general exodus in Luther's direction followed. A moment later, Ellie saw the group of men surround the dour chairman. Her heart skipped a beat when they maneuvered him away from the crowd and under a large oak tree. Ellie couldn't hear what they said, but their jutting chins showed they'd met with strong opposition. What if Luther convinced them Josh wasn't worthy to be hired?

Ellie felt perspiration spring to her forehead. Dread tightened her fingers into fists. She clutched her arms around herself to suppress pain. The thought of never seeing Josh again was unbearable. How could he have staked a claim on her heart in such a short time? She held her breath and watched Matt, Seth, Red Fallon, and the four board members join the group under the tree. Now what?

It felt like an eternity to Ellie before Luther raised his hands with a disgusted look. He walked at a snail's pace toward Josh, dragging his feet all the way. "Reverend Stanhope, it has been decided to hire you, contingent upon—"

Loud cheers erupted, but Luther scowled. "As I was saying, the offer is contingent upon your performing acceptably for the next six months."

For the first time in their acquaintance, Ellie saw Josh's jaw tighten. His gray eyes darkened with anger, and his voice rang. "Mr. Talbot, I will be happy to serve Christ the Way, but I do not perform. Any minister who does isn't worth his calling."

Red Fallon stepped to Josh's side and glared at Luther. "We're hirin' a preacher, Talbot, not an actor. Put that in your pipe and smoke it!"

"Yippee-ki-ay!" Tim bounded over to Josh. "I'm gonna be the first one to shake our new preacher's hand."

The excitement on top of the reaction Ellie had experienced from singing proved too much for her. One hand over her rapidly beating heart, she slipped back into the empty church. She sank into a pew, trying to shut out the look Josh had given her just before she fled. And trying in vain to remember that anyone who walked so close to God could never be yoked with a girl who had never stopped hating her father.

Tim found her there a long time later. "C'mon, Ellie. Matt and Sarah invited Josh to the ranch for dinner. He's going with you in the buggy as soon as the rest of the folks here clear out." Tim sighed and rubbed his stomach. "Hope it's soon. Amy's hanging on till the last dog's hung, but I think Luther's about ready to drag her home."

It took a moment for his news to sink in. "Josh? Ride with me? What about you?"

"I already got a horse from the livery stable. Josh has to have a way to get back." Tim flashed a mischievous smile. "Now's your chance, sister dear. He's already interested."

Ellie didn't pretend to misunderstand. "Some chance." She couldn't keep bitterness from her voice. Bitterness and longing. "Can you imagine Gus Stoddard's daughter married to someone like Josh?"

Tim's smile disappeared. "You're Ellie Sterling now, not Ellie Stoddard." His loyalty brought tears. "What if Gus. . . ?"

Tim patted her hand. "Forget about him, Ellie. He was glad enough to get shut of us. Most likely, we'll never see him again. Peter or Ian either."

"Do you ever think about them?" Ellie turned her hand over and clung to Tim's. It suddenly seemed terribly important to hear his answer.

He shrugged. "Not much. They were mean. All three of them."

"Do you hate them?"

"Naw." Tim's brown eyes took on a poignant light. "I used to, but Seth says we gotta love God more than we hate people. We gotta forgive them, too, even when it ain't easy." His sigh sounded like it came up from the toes of his boots.

"If only I could find a way to be worthy of someone like Josh," Ellie whispered.

Tim cleared his throat and gave her fingers a squeeze. "You already are."

"Just ride close to the buggy," she pleaded.

"Sure. Can't let you and our new preacher go buggy riding without a chaperone."

Ellie smiled. Tim had returned to his usual impish self, but she'd caught a glimpse of the man he was well on his way to becoming.

To Ellie's dismay, Luther and Amy still had Josh buttonholed, even though the others had gone. Josh finally said to the Talbots, "If you'll excuse me, it's quite a ride out to the Diamond S, and they're waiting dinner for us. Miss Sterling, are you ready to go?" He nodded toward the buggy.

"You don't mean to say you and Ellie are riding ten miles unchaperoned!" Luther burst out. Disapproval oozed from every word, and Amy's smile changed to a pout.

Tim drew himself up into a picture of outrage. "Of course not. It wouldn't be proper." He pointed to a saddled horse. "I'll be riding alongside the buggy. We'd best be going. Solita doesn't like us to be late for meals."

"*Harrumph*. We will continue our conversation at another time, Reverend. Come, Amy." Luther strode off, but Amy sent a venomous glance toward Ellie before she tripped away and called, "Remember, Preacher Josh. You're to have dinner with us next Sunday."

Ellie could barely control herself at the look on Josh's face. It clearly said he did not enjoy the prospect of dinner at the Talbots.

He helped her into the buggy and asked, "Shall I drive?"

"Please." Self-conscious, she wondered what to say next. She needn't have worried. Josh began to ask about the country, the people, and Christ the Way Church. The trip to the Diamond S had never seemed shorter. By the time they arrived, Ellie knew Tim was right. Incredible as it seemed, "Preacher Josh" was definitely interested in her.

Chapter 10

Ellie had always scoffed at old wives' tales and oft-quoted sayings. When one came true, she chalked it up to coincidence. Yet a week after her discussion with Tim about their father and brothers, something happened that shook her skepticism. It also brought back memories she wanted to forget.

One evening, Seth came into the huge sitting room where the family had gathered after supper. A fire flamed in the huge fireplace and flickered on the colorful tapestries that brightened the walls. Seth walked over to Sarah and sat down beside her. His grim expression sent an alarm bell clanging in Ellie's mind.

"I'm glad you're all here." He slowly took a crumpled envelope from his pocket and pulled out a folded sheet of paper. "When Curly brought the mail home today, this letter was in it."

Ellie's body tensed. She shivered in spite of the warmth from the fire.

"It's from Gus," Seth said.

Tim sent a startled look at Ellie. "Talk of the devil and his horns appear," he mumbled, so low only she could hear him.

Ellie shushed him and turned her attention back to Seth. She'd seldom seen him as serious as when he told Sarah, "This concerns you as well as me."

She gasped, and her face paled. "What does Gus want?"

Seth's face turned thunder-cloud dark. "The usual. Money."

"So what's Gus whining about this time?" Matt barked.

Tim leaped up from the rug where he'd been sprawled at Ellie's feet. "The usual? This time? Has Gus asked for money before? How come I didn't know about it?"

"Settle down," Seth told him. "There was no need for you or Ellie to know. Matt and I took care of it."

Tim's eyes blazed. "You didn't send him money, did you?" he choked out.

"No. We won't this time either."

"Good." But Tim remained on his feet, fiery-eyed and rigid.

Heartache and shame that they were Gus Stoddard's children tightened Ellie's chest. Why must they face humiliation again, just when she was trying to follow Tim's lead and forgive her shiftless family?

Seth looked even more troubled. "Ellie, I'm sorry you and Tim have to hear

286

this, but you need to know what Gus has to say."

Ellie nodded, unable to get words out of her constricted throat.

Tim snorted. Tall and straight, he flung his head back and said, "I'd rather never hear what he has to say. Is he trying to get Ellie and me back?"

"He can't!" Sarah protested. "Matt made sure of that when we adopted you."

"Gus has ways," Tim reminded her. "Nothing could be worse than our being yanked back to St. Louis."

Amen to that, Ellie silently agreed. "Read the letter, please, Seth."

"All right." He unfolded the page and read:

"Dear Seth,

"I need yer help. Peter and Ian showed up and got in a fight on the docks. A feller died. The boys didn't kill him, but they got tossed in jail anyway. I would of sent a telegram but it takes every penny Agatha and me kin scrape together to get by. It don't seem right, us starvin when you and Sarah are livin in luxury.

"Wire five hundred dollars right away so we kin buy food and bail out yer brothers. You owe me, considering all I done fer you."

Seth threw the letter down. "Five hundred dollars? How dare that miserable excuse for a man come whining to Sarah and me after the way he treated us?"

Ellie cringed, but Tim ground his teeth, snatched up the letter, and read on:

"I can't stand knowin Peter and Ian might git hung. It's bad enough that I give up Timmy and Ellie when I wuzn't thinkin straight. Send the money to..."

Tim flung the letter toward the fire, but Ellie sprang from her chair and caught it.

"Why did you do that?" Tim hollered.

She shook her head. "I—I don't know. Something told me it should be saved." Tears dripped on the wrinkled page.

"Aw, Ellie, don't cry. I'm sorry I yelled at you." He looked so contrite that she mopped her eyes and hugged him, glad he didn't jerk away as he usually did when others were present.

Matt came across the room and held out his hand. "I'm glad Ellie saved it, Tim. Gus's story doesn't ring true. Seth and I will get to the bottom of this. We'll need the letter to investigate."

Ellie handed it to Matt, glad to be rid of the hateful thing. Barren of either *please* or *thank you*, it typified Gus's approach to life: wheedle, whine, and take, take, take. What would Matt discover when he investigated?

Early the next morning, Matt saddled up for the ride to Madera. Seth did the same. And Tim, who flatly refused to stay at the ranch. Matt would send a telegram to the lawyers who drew up the ironclad adoption papers on Ellie and Tim. "It won't take long for them to get the truth about the Stoddards," he said. "I expect an answer before nightfall."

Matt's prediction came true. Late that afternoon, the three horseback investigators returned. Tim leaped from the saddle and onto the veranda where the womenfolk sat waiting. Matt and Seth followed close behind. Tim's grin melted the cold, hard knot crowding Ellie's chest.

"Gus's story has more holes than a tin can used for target practice," he yelled.

"It sure does," Matt put in. "A dockhand who saw the fight cleared Peter and Ian."

The breath Ellie had been holding whooshed from her lungs. Her brothers weren't murderers. Thank God!

Matt continued. "The law released Peter and Ian. They left St. Louis before Gus wrote the letter!"

"That's not all," Tim announced with a look of disgust. "Gus and Agatha don't need food or anything else. Can you beat that? After all his bad luck at gambling, Gus made a killing on the *River Queen*. The lawyer said Agatha grabbed the money and invested it." A look of satisfaction crawled across Tim's excited face. "Serves Gus right."

Seth took up the story. "The lawyer also said that, according to gossip, Agatha only doles out a few dollars at a time to Gus. They have a cottage in a nicer part of town now. The old shack burned shortly after they left."

Good riddance, Ellie thought. She exchanged glances with Tim. His expression showed he shared her relief that the place where they'd endured so much heartache no longer existed.

"I learned a whole lot more from the lawyer." Matt laughed until tears came. "Agatha is the talk of St. Louis. Seems she's bound and determined to make Gus respectable. She descended on every gambling hall he frequented. She brandished an umbrella and threatened dire consequences to anyone who gave him credit. Agatha Stoddard is one determined woman!" Matt wiped his eyes, then sobered.

"I told the lawyer about the letter asking for money under false pretenses. He advised me to put it away for safekeeping. The lawyer is officially warning Gus that if he ever tries any more shenanigans, he'll be jailed for attempted extortion. I seriously doubt we'll be hearing from him again."

A collective sigh of relief went up from the group. Ellie felt a long-carried burden slip away. Was she finally unshackled from the past? A prayer rose from her grateful heart. *Lord, please help Pa. No sheep was ever more lost than he is.*

That night, Ellie lay in bed, watching the stars through her open window. Suddenly the significance of the prayer struck her. For the first time in years, she'd referred to her father as Pa, not Gus. Was it the first step toward forgiveness? She fell asleep pondering the day's events and thanking God for brighter tomorrows.

❧

Joshua Stanhope surveyed his new home and burst into laughter. "Lord, this parsonage could fit in the downstairs of the Nob Hill mansion with room to spare, but I love it. The church women sure made it shine." He breathed in the resinous smell of furniture polish and the woodsy odor of carpets beaten in the fresh, summer air. Gleaming windows offered an ever-changing parade of swaying tree branches and scolding squirrels. A well-trodden path led between the simple wooden dwelling place and the church.

Josh left his door open to the great outdoors as much as possible. It presented endless ideas for his sermons. He never tired of watching the squirrels and listening to the multitude of songbirds that filled his days with music. They lessened the heartache of the scene with his mother when he went to get his trappings for the move to Madera. Josh never dreamed he'd be hired after his first sermon so had arrived with only limited clothing and none of his personal treasures. Considering his mother's opposition to him leaving San Francisco, it hadn't seemed wise to ask for them to be sent.

The confrontation with her had been intense. So was Josh's parting with Edward. Only Charles Stanhope's firm handclasp and quiet "I'm proud of you for doing what you know you must" eased Josh's regret at causing his mother and brother pain.

He picked up a letter from the hand-hewn table. The words blurred, but he knew his mother's words by heart from many readings:

You will always be my son, Joshua, but I refuse to encourage you in your madness. I spoke to the board at Bayview Christian. They are giving you a six-month leave of absence so that you can come to your senses.

Charles says it isn't legal to withhold the income from your grandfather's trust fund, which I planned to do. However, I warn you: if you continue in your headstrong path, there will be consequences. I implore you to return to San Francisco where you belong. All will be forgiven and never mentioned again.

Your loving mother

Josh put the letter aside, but it had done its work well. For the dozenth time since it arrived, he asked himself, *Is it more than chance for Bayview Christian to approve a six-month leave of absence when my position here is "contingent upon performing acceptably for the next six months"? God, are You giving me a loophole in case things don't work out with Christ the Way after all?*

"No!" Josh slammed his fist on the wooden table so hard it made the bouquet of wildflowers one of the children had brought to his door jump. A sea of faces swam before him: Men, women, children. Old and young. Cattlemen and cowboys. Sheepherders. Townsfolk. Visitors who stayed in Madera before or after taking the scenic stagecoach trip to the Yosemite Valley. "I don't belong in San Francisco," he muttered. "I belong here among those who have welcomed me. And those who haven't. Namely, Luther Talbot."

"Did I hear my name?" a cold voice asked from the doorway.

Josh gritted his teeth and turned. The chairman of the board had a way of popping in like an out-of-control jack-in-the-box, especially on Saturdays. Josh knew from past experience the call would be one of three things: a critique of his latest sermon, a text for the next day, or a complaint about Josh's attempts to carry the gospel outside the church walls. Josh wouldn't stop. In the few short weeks he'd been in Madera, new faces had begun to appear in the congregation, thanks to his and Red Fallon's efforts.

Today's session was a repeat of many others. By the time Luther took his sanctimonious self away, Josh felt like he'd been thrown into a thornbush. Worse, trying to prepare the next day's sermon seemed impossible. How could he concentrate on God with Luther Talbot's presence lingering in the parsonage like a bad smell?

Longing to escape, Josh tramped to the livery stable and saddled Sultan. Matt had given him the black gelding shortly after Josh had returned from his trip to San Francisco.

"You need a good horse. Sultan's strong, smart, and gentle. Treat him well, and you'll have a friend for life," Matt had advised. "If you ever get caught out and don't know your way home, let Sultan have his head. He'll bring you back to the Diamond S."

Now Josh rubbed the gelding's soft nose and swung into the saddle. "You're everything Matt promised and more," he told the superb animal. Sultan stomped one foot and whinnied as if impatient to be off. Josh nudged him into a trot, then a ground-covering canter. Right now the more distance Josh put between himself and cantankerous Luther Talbot, the better.

Chapter 11

A shadow blocked the late August sunlight streaming through the parsonage doorway. Tim Sterling stepped inside. "Hey Josh, want to go cat hunting tomorrow?"

Josh stared at his grinning visitor. "Cat hunting! Who hunts cats? I thought they were welcome around here to keep the mouse population down."

Tim rolled his eyes and looked disgusted. "You sure are a city slicker! Not pussycats. Cougars. Mountain lions."

Josh eyed him suspiciously. "Is this another of your jokes?"

Tim shook his head. "Naw." His grin faded. "There've been a couple of cougar sightings. Yesterday, some of our hands combing the draws on the far north side of the range found a downed steer. We're going after the cat that killed it."

"What's a cougar doing on the Diamond S this time of year? I thought they stayed in the mountains until snow came."

Tim scowled. "This one didn't. Maybe he figured he'd get a head start on his buddies. Do you want to go on the hunt or not? Matt says you'll have to stay at the ranch tonight. We leave at daylight."

Josh hid his trepidation at the idea of chasing mountain lions. "Of course I want to go. I'll get Sultan and ride back to the ranch with you."

The next morning, a loud pounding roused Josh from deep sleep. He opened his eyes. How could the window of the parsonage have doubled in size overnight? Who had replaced his gingham curtains with rich, brightly colored draperies?

The pounding resumed, followed by an insistent call. "Get up and grab some grub, or we're leaving without you."

Josh laughed. No wonder he'd been disoriented. The guest room at the Diamond S had little in common with his humble parsonage bedroom. He sprang from bed, tingling with anticipation.

"Be with you in a minute, Tim." He poured water from a pitcher into its matching bowl and splashed his face. "No time to shave. Hope Ellie isn't up," he murmured, then laughed at himself. Living on a ranch meant Ellie had seen lots of unshaven men. He just didn't want to be one of them! His admiration for Ellie had grown by leaps and bounds ever since he'd met her at the fiesta. And each time the Sierra Songbird sang in church, Josh's hopes of some day winning her increased. "If I'm not a goner as Tim says, I'm pretty close to it," he admitted.

"You're slower than molasses in January," Tim accused when Josh followed him down the staircase to the hall and into the enormous kitchen. Josh cast a quick glance around. Good. No Ellie. Just Solita. She beamed and motioned Tim and Josh to the table. She set steaming fried eggs with chili sauce in front of them and a platter of warm tortillas.

"Huevos rancheros."

Josh dove into the egg mixture. "Solita, I don't know anyone in San Francisco who can make these like you do. Delicious."

"Gracias." Her white teeth gleamed in a broad smile. "They stick to the ribs, as Senor Tim says."

"They sure do," Tim said through a mouthful. He gulped down the rest and jumped to his feet when Matt, Seth, and Curly came in. Josh did the same.

The men stepped outside into gray dawn and headed for the corral. But Josh couldn't resist glancing back at the house. An upstairs curtain moved. A girl in a dressing gown appeared at the window, and a soft voice called, "Be careful."

"We will," Tim promised. He vaulted astride the powerful blue roan that stood saddled and waiting. Josh took Sultan's reins from the vaquero who held them and mounted. Matt, Seth, Curly, and several other cowboys swung into their saddles.

Josh chuckled, caught up in the contagion of Tim's excitement. How the Bayview Christian congregation would exclaim if they could see their former pastor now!

"What's funny?" Tim wanted to know. "Settle down, Blue," he ordered his horse.

"I was thinking about my church in San Francisco."

A wary expression crept into Tim's eyes. "You're not going back, are you?"

Josh lowered his voice. "Not unless Luther Talbot convinces folks to kick me out."

Tim shook his head. "He won't do that. Amy won't let him." He hesitated, then said with deadly intensity, "We're pards, right?"

"Of course."

Tim's jaw set. "I gotta warn you. There's talk around town. Amy's bragging she'll be Mrs. Joshua Stanhope before your six months are up." A grin chased away Tim's obvious concern. "Folks are saying she'd better get a move on."

Josh had never been more flabbergasted. "She. . .I. . .what makes her think I'm interested in her?"

"She's Amy. That's enough."

Josh's heart thundered. He bit his tongue to keep from blurting out that Amy would never be Mrs. Joshua Stanhope. The first moment he'd looked into Ellie Sterling's shy blue eyes, the title had been hers for the taking.

Tim waggled his eyebrows. "Don't forget. Cougars aren't the only cats around here." He bent low over Blue's neck and raced off, but soon returned. "Have you ever seen a mountain lion?"

Josh shoved aside the troublesome thought of Amy stalking him. "Hardly. They don't come to Nob Hill."

"I guess not." Tim pulled Blue closer to Sultan. "When Ellie and I first came out here, I was only eight years old and scared to death. Gus told us if we weren't good, the mountain lions would eat us."

"Who is Gus?"

Tim looked surprised. "Gus Stoddard. Ellie's and my pa. Didn't you know? I figured ol' man Talbot would've told you before now."

Josh shook his head. "I thought you were Sterlings."

Tim's eyes flashed. "We are. Gus sold us to Matt and Sarah a long time ago. Hey, don't tell Ellie I spilled the beans. She hates being reminded we used to be Stoddards." His face brightened. "We don't have to worry about it any longer. Matt got a lawyer to fix it so Gus can't bother us again without being in big trouble."

Good for Matt. From the sketchy information Tim had given, it appeared Gus Stoddard wasn't fit to wipe his children's feet.

Tim didn't seem to notice Josh's silence. He chattered on. "Guess what, Josh? The first mountain lion I saw looked like a sleepy, overgrown pussycat. Seth and I went camping in the mountains about four years ago. A dandy place. Good fishing holes. We were having a great time, but on the way back down the creek to our camp, we heard screaming. It sounded like a woman crying for help."

The look in Tim's eyes sent chills skittering up Josh's spine. "What did you do?"

"Seth said it had to be a mountain lion. They're cowards and don't usually attack folks unless they're cornered—or unless it's a mama cat with cubs. But I was glad Seth had his rifle." Tim grimaced. "Like a dummy, I'd left mine in camp.

"Anyway, Seth had already warned me never to run if I met a cougar and didn't have a gun. It's the worst thing you can do. You need to spread your arms out like an eagle's wings, make yourself look as big as you can, and yell like an Indian on the warpath. And pray hard!"

Josh gripped the reins tighter. "So what happened?"

"We came around a bend in the trail." Tim's eyes glazed over. "There he was, long and yellowish and not mean-looking at all. . .until he opened his mouth." Tim gulped. "That cougar had one sharp set of teeth." A red tide flowed into Tim's face. "I forgot everything Seth said and started to run. He shoved me so hard I hit the ground. He bellowed and threw his rifle to his shoulder, but the cougar leaped into the bushes just before Seth pulled the trigger. The shot missed him."

"Did you track him?"

"Naw. Seth said to let him go." Tim looked shamefaced. "I gotta admit I was glad. Hey, you look kinda pale."

"What do you expect?" Josh retorted. "After hearing your story, I'd just as soon keep my distance from any mountain lions."

"Do you want to go back to the ranch house? Or town?"

"Not on your life. If we see a cougar, you can do your eagle act and protect me."

Tim whooped, but Josh caught his look of relief when he set Blue to dancing across the range. Although Josh's heart persisted in turning somersaults, he realized he'd just passed an important test.

Dusk fell with no sign of mountain lions. The hunting party set up camp a short distance upwind of where the steer had been brought down. After supper, every trace of the day's camaraderie fled.

"I'm counting on the cougar returning to his kill," Matt said. "No sleep for us tonight. Good thing there will be a full moon. Check your rifles, and get in your places before it rises." He paused. "Be careful how and where you fire. We're out to get a cougar, not each other."

Josh's flesh crawled. Never in his wildest imaginings had he pictured himself lying on the ground, waiting for a mountain lion. His companions showed no signs of fear. Tracking cougars, working with ornery cattle, and hunting down rustlers were all part of their day's work. In place and invisible, they waited, with Tim motionless beside Josh. The night wore on. The moon climbed high into the sky. Josh's legs cramped from lying in one place. His nerves twanged. *Please be with us, God....*

A strong hand clamped on Josh's arm and cut off the rest of the prayer. "Don't move a muscle," Tim ordered, so low Josh had to lean close to hear. "He's coming."

Josh marveled at the young man's eyesight and hearing. He strained to see and hear. A rustle in the grass and the soft *pad-pad* of footsteps rewarded his diligence. A cougar, fully five feet long and gray in the moonlight, crept toward the kill.

A shot rang out from Josh's left. *Spang!* A horrid snarl followed. The cat exploded into the air and hit the ground running.

Tim leaped to his feet and raised his rifle. "Look out, Josh. He's winged and heading our way!" With no time to take aim, he pulled the trigger. The rifle misfired. It knocked Tim to the ground, flew through the air, and landed at Josh's feet.

The enraged cougar hurled toward them—snarling, spitting, and trapping them in a nightmare from which they might never awaken.

God, help me.

Josh grabbed the rifle by the barrel and bounded to his feet, vaguely aware of shouting and the sound of men running. The cougar sprang. Josh swung the rifle with strength multiplied by fear. *Crack!* The sturdy stock smashed against the animal's head. It split in two, but it had done its work well. The mountain lion fell to the ground with one claw scraping Tim's leg. The next moment, a hail of bullets ended the predator's life.

Josh shook like an aspen leaf in a high wind. "Are you all right?" he choked out.

"I reckon." Tim struggled to his feet. "Kinda dizzy though."

Josh looked down and gasped. Blood seeped through Tim's torn jeans. "You're hurt."

Tim's grin looked sickly in the moonlight, but he said, "Aw, it's just a scratch. Thanks to you."

"And to God." Matt forced Tim back to the ground, tore open his jeans and examined the wound. "You'll have a scar, but it looks worse than it really is." He snatched his bandana from his neck and bound Tim's leg before turning to Josh and gripping his hand until Josh winced. "It's a good thing you were here. None of us dared fire after the first shot, for fear of hitting one of you."

"Don't give me the credit," Josh protested. "I've never been so scared in my life! If God hadn't been with us. . ." The sentence died in his throat.

Matt's painful grip tightened. "Son, the real test of a man is in taking action when he's scared to death."

The words sank into Josh's heart to be mulled over at a later time. Right now, he was too close to the near-tragedy to concentrate on anything except thanking God for sparing his and Tim's lives.

Chapter 12

The staccato beat of horses' hooves the following day and Sarah's shout, "The men are home," sent Ellie flying through the ranch house doorway and toward the corral. Tim swayed in Blue's saddle, obviously in pain. Ellie saw her brother's torn, blood-stained jeans. Heart pounding, she rushed to him as Seth helped him down from the saddle.

Tim gave her a crooked smile and limped toward her. "Don't worry, Ellie. I'm fine 'cept for a love pat from a cougar who won't be killing any more stock."

"Thank God!" she burst out, throwing her arms around him.

"Yeah." Tim's smile faded, and he dropped one arm over her shoulders. "And Josh."

"Josh?" Ellie looked past Tim and met the steady gaze fixed on her.

"He saved my life."

Ellie sagged. "Saved your life!"

"Is there an echo around here?" Tim demanded. "If it hadn't been for Josh—"

"Time enough for that later," Matt snapped. "Seth, go to Madera and fetch Doc Brown."

"Not on your life!" Tim yanked free from Ellie, stumbled up the stairs onto the veranda, and dropped into a chair. "I don't need a sawbones for this little scratch. Matt already half killed me by drowning my leg with whiskey. Made me smell like a saloon." He beamed at Solita, who had stepped onto the veranda. "Solita's a good enough nurse for me. She'll fix me up."

"Sí, Senor. I will bring bandages and salve." The diminutive housekeeper's eyes twinkled. "But no more whiskey."

Tim grunted. "Good. If I hadn't had witnesses, you'da thought I'd been on a spree."

Ellie's eyes filled. How typical of her brother to make light of being hurt! She clamped her lips and held back a cry of dismay when the bandage came off and exposed the wound. There was no sign of infection, but the jagged gash ran from thigh to knee: far more than a scratch.

Solita carefully examined Tim's injury. "There is no need for stitches." She cleansed the wound, plastered salve on its length, and wound it with soft linen cloths. She also ordered Tim to bed for the rest of the day.

To Ellie's surprise, her brother yawned and mumbled, "Don't mind if I do. But first, I gotta tell Ellie what Josh did." He related the moonlight incident in a few short sentences that lost none of the drama, then yawned again and allowed Matt to carry him to bed.

Ellie slipped away. She must find Josh before he left the ranch and headed back to town. She couldn't let him get away without thanking him for saving Tim. Her heartbeat tripled. The music that had begun in her soul the day of the fiesta swelled into a song of praise. She loved Joshua Stanhope. Could she face him without betraying her feelings? She knew he admired her, but was her love returned? At times, she thought so. So often when they were together, Josh's steady gaze wrapped around her like a fleecy quilt. His smile settled over her like a rainbow after a storm.

Ellie raised her chin and told her traitorous heart to be still. She hurried outside. Josh stood beside Sultan, ready to mount. Thankful that everyone else had vanished, she ran toward him. "Please wait."

Josh turned.

Ellie reached him. She clasped her hands together and willed them not to tremble. "Josh, if it hadn't been for you, I might have lost Tim." A lump came to her throat. "How can I ever thank you?"

A beautiful light came into Josh's eyes. It softened the gray to the color of a misty dawn. He took Ellie's hands in his. "By marrying me."

Her mouth dropped. Surely she hadn't heard him right. "By. . .by. . . ," she stammered.

"Is there an echo around here?" Josh's teasing departed. "I know it's too soon. This is also not the time or place." He took in a deep breath and slowly released it. "I want you to know I've fallen in love with you, Ellie Sterling. You don't need to say anything now. Just keep this in mind: God willing, someday you'll be my beloved wife."

Josh released Ellie's hands, leaped into the saddle, and sent Sultan into a dead run. When they reached the bend in the road to Madera, he reined in, turned, and waved his sombrero. Then with a *yippee-ki-ay* worthy of Tim's best, he rode out of sight.

Ellie fled. Not to her room, where someone might discover her and want to know why she was so distraught, but to her promontory refuge. Her tumultuous heart kept time with the cadence of Calico's hooves. Josh loved her. He wanted her for his wife!

The words continued to beat in her brain as she reached the boulder on top of the promontory. Unable to contain her joy one moment longer, Ellie sat down, cupped her hands, and shouted into the valley, "Josh loves me!"

Loves me. . .loves me echoed back to her.

Ellie pressed her hands over her hot cheeks, still unable to believe it. How could a man as important as Joshua Stanhope love her? Yet he'd said, "I've fallen in love with you, Ellie Sterling."

Ellie's joy evaporated. "How will he feel when I tell him I was Ellie Stoddard for eleven years?" she asked Calico. "It looks like Gus is out of our lives, but Josh needs to know our background. Even if it doesn't make a difference to him, what about his family? What if the Lord calls Josh back to San Francisco? Would I ever fit in?"

Calico nosed her and stamped a foot as if in sympathy.

Ellie went on. "No one knows how I long to be someone, especially now. I need to be worthy of Josh's love. I'm past eighteen but all I've ever done is help around the ranch and sing in church. Tim and I have been dependent ever since we came here. It's time for me to do more." She stared down at the peaceful valley. "All Tim wants now is to ride and rope, but he may change his mind. Matt and Seth will pay for college if that's what Tim wants, but I wish I could earn money to help. I just don't know how."

The mare tossed her head and whinnied.

"I know, girl. It's time to go." Ellie mounted. "God, I'd really appreciate it if You'd. . ." her voice trailed off. She couldn't express what she wanted God to do, only that she needed Him to do something—anything—to satisfy her yearnings.

When Ellie left the promontory, she had no solution to her knotty problems. A conversation with Tim later that evening, however, brought comfort. Tim had slept most of the day and was as observant as usual. At Solita's decree, Ellie brought a supper tray to his room.

Tim wolfed down every morsel, then fixed a stern gaze on her. "You may as well spill whatever's bothering you."

"Josh asked me to marry him." Appalled at blurting out what she'd vowed to keep secret, Ellie covered her face with her hands.

Tim's fork crashed to his plate. "Great!" He frowned. "So, what's your problem? I told you Josh was a goner."

"He's in love with Ellie *Sterling*," she choked out.

Tim groaned. "Don't tell me you're still letting Gus spoil your life." He fell silent for a time, then added with obvious reluctance, "Besides, Josh knows Gus was our pa."

Ellie stiffened. "I suppose Luther or Amy told him."

"Naw. I did." Tim squirmed. "Don't look like that. It just came out. We were talking about cougars. I said Gus used to tell us the mountain lions would eat us if we weren't good. Josh looked disgusted and asked who Gus was. I told him, and we started talking about cougars again. Uh"—he squirmed again—"I said for him not to let on he knew 'cause you don't like being reminded about Gus."

Ellie realized her happiness depended on Tim's answer to a single question. "How did Josh take hearing we were adopted?"

Tim guffawed. "He musta taken it all right or he wouldn't have asked you to marry him." He sobered. "Josh is the best thing that ever happened to you besides our coming out here. Get it through your head that you're good enough for him or anyone."

For the second time that day, Ellie fled, hugging her brother's revelation to her heart alongside Josh's proposal. Yet the thought of not "being someone" remained.

Josh rode away from the Diamond S filled with disgust—not for telling Ellie he loved her, but for stupidly blurting it out next to a horse corral! No woman wanted to receive a proposal under such circumstances.

"It wasn't all my fault," Josh confided to Sultan after they rounded the bend in the road and slowed to a comfortable pace. "When Ellie looked up with those crystal-blue eyes and asked how she could ever thank me, it just popped out. Know what, old boy? I'm glad she knows, even if I picked a bad time and place. Wonder how long I should wait before asking her to answer?"

The question brought him out of the clouds and back to earth. "I can't even consider it until after my six months here are up and I know where I'll be." Josh shook his head. "Luther and his hangers-on are against me because I won't confine my ministry to the members. According to Tim, Amy is all that's standing in the way of my being fired. What will she think when she finds out I'm in love with Ellie?"

Sultan snorted.

Josh's spirits rose. "My sentiments exactly!" He began to whistle and rode the rest of the way to the parsonage, watching rose-tinted clouds in the west, his mind filled with rosy dreams of a future with Ellianna Sterling.

Chapter 13

The early September storm that slam-banged in from the Pacific Ocean paled in comparison with the fury in Charles Stanhope's face. He waved the special delivery letter that had just been delivered to him in the library. Edward had never seen his father so angry. Or heard him roar like the flames up the fireplace chimney.

"Letitia Stanhope, how dare you hire a private investigator to spy on our son?"

A wave of red mounted to her carefully styled blond hair. "You needn't shout. I did it for Joshua's sake."

Josh? Edward sagged with relief.

His mother held out her hand. "The letter's for me, is it not? Why did you open it?"

"I've been expecting to hear from our shipping office in San Diego. Thank God I opened the letter and found out what you are up to."

Curiosity overcame caution. "What does the letter say?" Edward asked.

His father cast him a quelling look but began reading:

"Except for a few malcontents at Christ the Way, Joshua has been well received. He's called 'Preacher Josh,' and people of all ages sing his praises, notably the young women who flock around him. Even in the short time he's been here, church attendance has grown substantially—especially among the ranch hands. It doesn't set well with the church chairman, but Joshua insists he must seek out those who are lost."

Edward wanted to applaud. So, good old Josh was carrying out his mission. Yet a pang went through him. He missed his twin.

His mother obviously cared little for the lost. "Just what I thought," she snapped. "A bunch of designing females making fools of themselves chasing Joshua. As if he'd ever look at anyone in that cow town."

"Don't gloat too soon." Charles gave her a stern look and resumed reading:

"According to gossip, those who plot to become Mrs. Joshua Stanhope may as well give up. The only girl your son has paid any attention to is a rancher's daughter. She sings in church and is called the Sierra Songbird. I have to admit, she has a nice voice."

Mother gave an inelegant snort. "What does an investigator know? She probably sings like a crow. Is that all?"

"Yes. Pay the investigator and dismiss him. I will have no more spying on my son. I trust him, even if you don't." He threw the letter into the fire and stalked out.

"He's my son, too," Mother flung after him. "Edward, what are we going to do?"

"Go to Madera."

A look of horror crossed her face. "You must be mad!"

Edward sat bolt upright. The idea grew like dandelions in spring. "Why not? We can find out for ourselves what's going on, meet this Sierra Songbird and"—his imagination took flight—"if she has any kind of voice, we'll bring her back with us, give her the finest training possible, and make her the rage of San Francisco. It will get her away from Josh."

Letitia wrung her hands. "You *are* mad. As mad as your brother."

"Not at all." Edward fitted his fingers together and played his trump card. "When Josh left Bayview Christian, you lost the prestige of being the mother of 'our fair city's most up-and-coming minister,' as the *San Francisco Chronicle* called Josh." A gleam in his mother's eyes showed he'd reached her. She dearly loved the limelight. "There's one chance in a million that the ugly Madera duckling could turn out to be a swan As her patron and discoverer, your social status would skyrocket."

The opposition in Mother's face gave way to consideration. "Your father won't hear of it." Her regretful voice told Edward he'd won.

He stood and stretched. "He'd do anything to help make peace between you and Josh. What's more effective than our visiting Madera and offering the local songbird a chance to soar?" Edward shrugged. "Who knows? It might even cause Josh to reconsider where he's supposed to be. Bayview Christian's still holding his place open, aren't they?"

"Yes." A conspiratorial look passed between mother and son.

Three days later Letitia and Edward ferried to Oakland and boarded the eastbound train.

❧

Josh thrust aside the sermon he'd been working on and headed for the Diamond S. "The only honorable thing to do is confess to Matt," he told Sultan. The black gelding pricked his ears into the listening attitude Josh knew so well. "How could I take advantage of Ellie when she was distraught over Tim?"

He repeated the question in Matt's office a short time later. Matt sat behind his desk with Josh standing across from him, feeling like a prisoner before a judge. "Ellie asked me what she could do to thank me for saving Tim." Sweat crawled up Josh's back. "I blurted out 'by marrying me.'"

Matt's voice cut like a skinning knife. "Did you mean it?"

Josh clenched his fists. "I never meant anything more."

Matt crossed his arms and tilted his desk chair back until it groaned. "So what's the problem?"

Josh swallowed, wishing he was anywhere else. "I should have told you how I felt and asked permission to keep company with Ellie before speaking out like that."

"Did you tell Ellie you love her and ask her how she feels?"

Josh felt himself turn pale. "You sure aren't making this easy. Not that I deserve anything else."

"What do you expect?" The chair crashed down on all fours. "A man comes to me, says he told my only daughter she could marry him because he happened to be in the right place at the right time, and—"

The words stung. Josh stepped forward and glared down at Matt. "It's not like that, Matt. I didn't ask anything from Ellie except for her to keep in mind that someday, God willing, she'll be my beloved wife." He met his friend's stern blue gaze squarely. "We've known each other a little less than three months. I'm twenty-seven. She's eighteen. I wouldn't expect her to love me now, although sometimes. . . " His voice lay down and died.

Mischief replaced the sternness in Matt's eyes. He got up from behind the desk, wearing a Cheshire-cat grin. One strong hand shot out and gripped Josh's. "Put her there, Preacher Josh. You may have my daughter's hand in marriage if you can win her. In the meantime, see that Tim 'keeps company' with you two unless you're in a crowd." His mirth changed to sadness. "Ellie was the target of vicious gossip as a child. It left scars. There's at least one two-legged cat in the vicinity who will scratch and squall if she thinks you're serious about Ellie."

"I know." Josh heaved a great sigh. "Tim already warned me that Amy Talbot has been making her intentions known all over town."

"It figures." Matt gave Josh a lopsided grin. "One thing. How will that San Francisco family of yours feel about Ellie?"

Josh's joy evaporated, but he wouldn't duck Matt's question. "My father will have reservations only until he meets her, Mother will huff and puff and try to blow my house down but will have to give in. My twin brother, Edward, will—"

"Twin brother! There are two of you?"

The look on Matt's face proved too much for Josh. He bent double laughing. "That bad, huh?"

Matt dropped back into his chair and stared until Josh felt impaled by his keen gaze. "No. It's just that I've heard twins sometimes share the same feelings." Matt cleared his throat and looked uncomfortable. "If your brother is like you, what's to keep him from falling in love with Ellie when he meets her? I'd hate to see her in a tug-of-war between brothers. Bad business. All three of you would lose."

Matt's insight sent a chill through Josh. "We look alike, but it ends there. Edward and I chose different paths in life a long time ago. Besides, he's already engaged." *Right,* a little voice taunted. *Beryl Westfield is like a burned-out comet compared with Ellie, who brings the sunlight. How can Edward or any man help falling in love with her? You were down for the count the first time you met her.*

"Well?"

Josh gathered his wits and replied, "Edward may have his faults, but I'm sure he has enough honor to never come between me and the woman I love."

Are you sure? the little voice persisted. *Absolutely sure?* Josh wanted to drown out the voice with a resounding yes, but doubts born of past experience rose. If push came to shove, would Edward let anything stand between him and something he'd set his mind on possessing? Time after time, the role of brother's keeper had lain heavy on Josh's shoulders. He'd given up much for Edward. If he fell in love with Ellie, as Josh knew could happen, must the older brother stand aside in order to keep Ellie from becoming a wishbone?

Matt leaned forward. "You can take my advice or not, Josh. But if I were you, I'd get a ring on Ellie's finger before that brother of yours ever meets her."

Josh's mouth dried. "A wedding ring?" His heart leaped at the thought.

Matt rolled his eyes. "No, you dolt. A brand. A sparkler. An engagement ring. Something to tell the world she belongs to you."

"You're all right with that?" Josh marveled.

Matt cocked one eyebrow and drawled, "Well now, Preacher, it really isn't up to me. One thing more. How are you going to support my daughter if Luther Talbot convinces folks you need to mosey on three months from now? I doubt you've saved much on the salary you get here."

Josh wanted to laugh. "I have income from a trust fund my grandfather left and saved quite a bit from Bayview Christian. The trust fund principal comes to me when I'm thirty, unless Mother finds a way to stop it. She didn't want me to leave San Francisco. By the way, this is privileged information."

"Of course." Matt's eyes twinkled. He stood, signaling the interview had ended. "You're a good rider. If Talbot succeeds in getting you kicked out, which I'm pretty sure he won't, I can always use another good hand."

"Thanks. I'll keep it in mind. Now I'd best be getting back to town before Luther sends a pack of hounds after me."

"He's about ready to," Matt warned. "His big gripe continues to be that you spend way too much time outside the church and parsonage."

"How do you feel about it?" Josh asked.

"You have to do both. Tend the flock and go after the strays."

Josh told Matt good-bye and headed back to Madera, pondering over the remarkable session and thinking of the rancher's final words. So much to do. If only there were more hours in a day! "There aren't," Josh told Sultan. "Hmmm. Wonder what's next?"

He didn't have long to wait. The eastbound train was grinding to a stop when Josh reached Madera. He tethered Sultan to the hitching rail in front of Moore's General Store and idly watched passengers descend to the dusty street. A heavily veiled woman paused on the platform at the top of the steps, with the porter attempting to assist her. A haughty voice commanded, "My good man, I can walk. Will you please let go of my elbow?"

Blood rushed to Josh's head and roared in his ears. The voice could only belong to one person. "Mother?" he croaked.

Letitia stepped down, followed by her grinning younger son. "Really, Joshua, must you gape?" She cast a disparaging glance up and down Main Street. "That's what comes of living in a place like this. Now, will you kindly take me somewhere so I can recover from our dreadful journey?"

She looked at the well-filled horse trough nearby and sniffed. "I presume there are accommodations with modern conveniences. Or is this where people here bathe?"

Chapter 14

"Mother!" Josh grabbed the woman's arm. He helped her from the street to the sidewalk that ran in front of the store, wishing the wooden planks beneath his feet would open and swallow him. He sent Edward a silent cry for help, but his twin had obviously been rendered speechless by their mother's rude remark. *Why are they here?* Josh wondered. *How can Mother, with all her social graces, be so insufferable? What is she trying to do, make me a laughingstock and undermine my work in Madera so I'll have to go home? The sooner I can get her out of here, the better.*

Before Josh could steer Letitia away, an elderly man hobbled his way through the crowd that always gathered to meet the trains. His cracked voice grated on Josh's ears. "Jumpin' jackrabbits, are there two preachers here or am I seein' double?" He shook his head as if to clear it. "Can't be. I ain't had a drink for nigh onto ten years."

This cannot be happening, Josh thought in despair. *It's like something out of a bad dream.* "You're all right," Josh said aloud. "Mother, Edward, this is my friend Dan Doyle."

Dan dipped his head to Josh's mother. "Pleased to meetcha, ma'am. You got a mighty fine son here. T'other one looks toler'ble, too." He cackled and held out a gnarled hand.

Mother ignored it, but Edward quickly reached out. "Thank you, Mr. Doyle."

Dan swelled with pride. Josh bit back a guffaw. *Bless Edward.* The old man probably hadn't been called *Mister* for years, if ever.

Edward turned to his brother. "About accommodations. . ."

Josh led his mother away before she could blurt out another derogatory remark. "It's just a short way to the Yosemite Hotel. You'll be comfortable there. By the way, where's Father?"

Mother made a sour face. "Traveling to San Diego on business." She fell mercifully silent, but Josh inwardly cringed. Her expression showed total contempt for Madera. On the other hand, Edward looked amused, even interested.

"It's rather picturesque, isn't it?" he exclaimed while they walked down Main Street. When they reached the Yosemite Hotel he stopped short and gazed at the imposing brick building. "Nothing wrong with that, Mother."

"It isn't too bad," she conceded.

Josh squelched the desire to tell her that years earlier before the original structure burned, Mace's Hotel had been a tiny wooden shanty that served as a saloon as well as a lodging place.

She stopped short and stared up the street. "Who is *that*?" She pointed to a bearded man leading a spirited horse. Dressed in a fine suit and tie, the man carried a gold-handled cane. A top hat completed the picture of elegance.

Josh battled the desire to repay his mother for humiliating him—and lost. "The captain."

She looked blank.

"Captain Russell Perry Mace. He's a hero. He hunted buffalo with Kit Carson, was wounded in the Mexican-American War, and spent years searching for gold before helping to establish Madera. He also served in the California State Legislature."

"Dear me, why would such a fine gentleman live in this godforsaken place?"

"The captain owns the Yosemite Hotel," Josh quietly said. "And God hasn't forsaken Madera, Mother. He sent me here." The instant the words left his mouth, he regretted them. Who was he to contradict his mother? Fortunately, her attention was so fixed on the captain that she either didn't hear or chose to ignore her son.

Edward snickered. "You'll have something to boast about to your friends, Mother. Meeting a hero and all that."

The captain reached them before she could reply. "Well, well, who do we have here?" He looked from Josh to Edward. "Twins, is it?" He didn't wait for a reply but turned to Letitia. "You, madam, must be their proud mother." He beamed at Letitia, who looked completely bowled over.

"Yes. I'm Mrs. Stanhope and this is Edward."

"Good. Good." The captain rubbed his hands. "Preacher Josh's coming to Madera is the best thing that's happened around here for a long time. I take it you and Edward will be staying at my hotel, Mrs. Stanhope? I'll be honored if you'll join me for supper. You, too, Preacher. Six thirty?"

Josh hoped his mother wouldn't blurt out that they usually dined much later. He sighed with relief when she merely said, "We'll be happy to join you, Captain Mace. Six thirty is fine."

"Good," he trumpeted. "Come in, and make yourselves at home." He led the way into the richly furnished foyer with its impressive staircase leading to the upstairs sleeping chambers. Mother's eyes widened, and her mouth fell open. Clearly, she hadn't expected this.

"Joshua, do you have rooms here?"

"No. I live in the parsonage next to the church." He glanced down at his dusty clothes. "I'll stable Sultan, get cleaned up, and meet you here." He beat a hasty retreat, his heart lighter than it had been since his family arrived.

Thanks to the opportune appearance of the colorful Captain Mace, maybe things would be all right.

Just before the outer door of the hotel swung shut, he heard his mother ask, "Do we dress for din—supper?"

"Some do. Some don't," the captain replied. "Wear what you like."

Josh chuckled to himself and hurried back to care for Sultan. How would Mother react to eating in the same room with sheepmen and cowboys, travelers, shopkeepers, and their wives? He shrugged. He could do nothing about it, except leave it to the Lord. But again Josh wondered, *Why are Mother and Edward here?*

He continued to wonder during the superlative dinner in the well-appointed dining room. Gaslight flickered on crystal and china. It gleamed on silver cutlery and tablecloths as starched and spotless as the pinafore-style aprons the waitresses wore. Josh rejoiced in the young women's usual efficient service. His mother could have no complaint about it, even though she looked askance at their fellow diners.

The captain took center stage. Josh had heard some of his stories before but enjoyed the talkative hotel proprietor's confession that gold mining wasn't all it was cracked up to be. "One day, I washed thirty-four buckets of dirt in the forenoon and made sixty-two and one-half cents. In the afternoon, I bought a sack of flour, a half pound of pork, and a dollar's worth of soap. It cost eight dollars."

Mother eyed him suspiciously, but Edward's eyes sparkled. Unless Josh was badly mistaken, his brother was having the time of his life.

When the last bite of the Lady Baltimore cake had vanished, the captain shoved his chair back from the table. "I imagine I'll see you in church tomorrow, especially Pastor Josh." He laughed heartily.

Josh held his breath, but Edward nodded. So did Mother.

"Good. Thank you for having supper with me." The captain pulled out Mother's chair. When she rose, he nodded and strolled out of the dining room.

Josh felt at a loss as to what to do next. "Would you like to see my parsonage?" he finally asked.

"Not tonight. I'm going to my room." His mother swept out, long skirts trailing behind her.

Thud. Josh's hopes fell to his toes. He turned to face Edward. "Is she ever going to forgive me?"

An unreadable expression came into his twin's eyes, an expression that left Josh uneasy without knowing why. "She's here, isn't she?"

Yet a question hammered in Josh's brain: *True—but what does it mean?*

≈

After a sleepless night spent reviewing the sermon he'd planned, Josh gave it up at dawn. "Sorry, Lord. With Mother and Edward in the congregation,

I simply can't preach about the Lost Son." He buried his head in his hands. "What shall I do?"

Silence followed. Peace came, first as a trickle, then like a river. It brought the feeling all would be well. Josh grabbed writing tools and began making notes.

A few hours later, he stepped behind the pulpit of Christ the Way, opened his Bible, and announced, "Our text today is from John 14." Pages rustled as the congregation found the place. Josh's heart thundered when he said, "Jesus told His disciples in verse 1, 'Let not your heart be troubled: ye believe in God, believe also in me.' In verse 27, He said, 'Peace I leave with you, my peace I give unto you: not as the world giveth, give I unto you. Let not your heart be troubled, neither let it be afraid.'"

He paused and closed the Bible. "Instead of preaching a regular sermon this morning, I'm going to tell you the story of a remarkable man." He heard a snort from behind him. *Please, God, don't let Luther Talbot make a scene.* Josh straightened. He wouldn't give the chairman a chance.

"Horatio Spafford and his wife lived in Chicago. They had four daughters, who ranged from eighteen months in age to twelve years. In the winter of 1873, the family joyously looked forward to a trip to Europe. The time for the trip grew close, but business difficulties forced Spafford to remain at home. Unwilling to deprive his family of the trip, he kissed them good-bye, bade them Godspeed, and promised to join them as soon as possible.

"Anna Spafford and the girls boarded a French steamer and began their journey. Tragedy struck off the coast of Newfoundland. The ship collided with an English sailing vessel, which ripped a huge hole in the *Ville de Havre*'s hull. It plunged to the bottom of the ocean within twenty minutes.

"Just before the ship sank, Anna gathered her girls and prayed. The icy North Atlantic swept over them. It took the three oldest girls, then snatched the baby from her mother's arms. Alone and near death, Anna was rescued by those in a lifeboat. Ten anxious days passed before the survivors landed in Wales. Anna wired her husband:

SAVED ALONE.

"Heartbroken, Horatio boarded the next available ship to England and was reunited with Anna. They returned to Chicago."

Josh paused and looked from face to face. "How many times does our faith weaken when we face adversity? Who among us could face such a loss and remain steadfast? My mother and brother are here today. I don't know what I'd do if I ever lost either of them or my father. Yet the Spaffords trusted God and kept the faith. Horatio later returned to where the *Ville de Havre* went down. A hymn came out of his pain."

Not a sound could be heard in the entire church. Josh saw tears trembling on his mother's eyelashes. Edward sat as if turned to stone. *Thank You, Lord.*

Josh looked at Ellie. Her glowing eyes reflected her love for the God who had delivered her and Tim from a life of sadness. "I've asked Miss Sterling to sing 'It Is Well with My Soul,' the song wrenched from Horatio Spafford's heart by tragedy."

Ellie slowly stepped forward. Abby struck a single note on the organ and stopped playing. Ellie clasped her hands against her pale yellow gown and began to sing:

"When peace, like a river, attendeth my way,
When sorrows like sea billows roll;
Whatever my lot, Thou has taught me to say,
It is well, it is well with my soul."

The glorious voice soared with triumph, needing no accompaniment:

"It is well. . .with my soul. . .
It is well, it is well with my soul."

Josh looked at Edward. Clearly astonished, his brother straightened in his seat and fixed his gaze on Ellie. So did Mother. The song continued. Josh saw his brother whisper to their mother. A satisfied smile appeared, but she never took her attention from Ellie.

"It is well. . .with my soul. . .
It is well, it is well with my soul."

Ellie had never sung so magnificently. Josh had never loved her more. Why then, did foreboding fill him? Another quick glance at his mother increased his apprehension. Whenever she looked like a pussycat who'd plundered the cream pitcher, it meant trouble. The unpleasant suspicion that his mother and Edward were neck-deep in some nefarious scheme perched on Josh's shoulder and clawed into him.

If not, why were they here?

Chapter 15

Josh barely got the final *amen* out before his mother and Edward left their seats and rushed up the aisle to Ellie. Letitia laid her gloved hand on the girl's arm and beamed. Josh hadn't seen her so fluttery since the mayor of San Francisco presented her with what Edward called a "do-gooder" award for work with various city charities.

"My *dear*," she gushed, "what a *mar*velous voice! And that song. . ." She dabbed at her eyes with her handkerchief and turned to Matt and his family. "You must be the Sterlings. Surely you are proud of this young lady." Her treble voice rang through the church.

Tim gawked. Ellie blinked. Sarah's eyes twinkled. The corners of Matt's mouth twitched as he said, "And you must be Mrs. Stanhope and Edward." He held out his hand. "I'm glad you came."

Josh wished he could say the same. It might be unjust, but he couldn't rid himself of the feeling mischief was brewing.

"Mr. and Mrs. Sterling, will you and your family be our guests for lunch at the Yosemite Hotel?" Edward laughed and corrected himself. "Dinner, that is."

"Thank you," Matthew said. "Sarah, Tim, Ellie, and I will be happy to accept. Our younger children can go home with my sister and her husband."

Edward gave them his most charming smile. "I'm sure Josh will be joining us."

You can bet on it, brother. I'm not letting you and Mother out of my sight until you're back on the train to San Francisco. Josh left the platform and came to the group. "Of course. Let's step outside. Folks will want to meet you." He maneuvered them down the aisle and into the yard. His heart warmed to the way the congregation flocked around his family. But when Amy Talbot, wearing a fluffy lilac gown and a here-I-go-a-hunting look approached Edward, Josh wanted to howl with mirth.

Wide-eyed and innocent, she peered up into Edward's face, then clapped her small hands. "I declare, you really are alike as two peas in a pod." Amy giggled. "What a blessing to have two such handsome men in church today!" She batted her eyelashes. "You know, Mr. Stanhope, we're all simply crazy about your brother. If you plan to stay for a few days, Father and I would love to entertain you. I'm Amy Talbot, and my father is chairman of the church board."

If looks could kill, Josh judged, *Amy would be dead at Mother's small feet.* She started to reply, but was drowned out by Tim's hoarse laugh. Josh saw Ellie elbow him, and Tim changed it to a fit of coughing; Josh's sentiments exactly.

Edward, suave as usual, shook his head. "I'm afraid we'll have to turn down your invitation, Miss Talbot. We'll be returning to San Francisco as soon as we finish our business here."

Business? What business? Josh's premonition of storm clouds lurking just beyond the closest hill increased with Edward's almost imperceptible nod to his mother.

The crowd began to disperse. Amy and her father, who had unbent long enough to be introduced to the Stanhopes, lingered, obviously in hopes of being included in the dinner invitation. They didn't leave until Tim broadly hinted, "If we don't mosey along to the hotel, we may not be able to all sit together."

Luther cast him a withering look. "Come, Amy." He started off. Amy flounced after him, but turned and called back, "Don't forget! If you decide to stay longer, my invitation still holds," then tripped after her rigid father.

"Whew! Is this what preachers have to put up with?" Edward asked. "Glad I didn't become one. What do you think, Miss Sterling? Is everyone here really crazy about my brother?" He offered his arm.

Ellie sent Josh a pleading glance before placing her fingertips on Edward's arm. "Not everyone. But Tim is right. We'd best be on our way."

"Mother?" Josh held out his arm, seething inside. What audacity! He lowered his voice. "Why are you and Edward here?"

Her cat-in-the-cream expression returned. "For your own good, Joshua." She refused to elaborate on the walk to the hotel.

Dinner seemed endless in spite of the banter that flowed around Josh. Ellie and Sarah said little; Tim, nothing at all. Edward and Mother dominated the conversation, extolling the wonders of San Francisco but always coming back to Ellie's singing. One by one, the other diners left. When only the Sterlings and Stanhopes remained, Mother turned to Matt and delivered a verbal blow. "Edward and I had a reason for coming to Madera other than seeing Joshua." She tapped her fingers on the table. "We want permission to kidnap your daughter."

Josh's first thought left him shaking. *Matt was right. I should have gotten a ring on Ellie's finger before she met Edward.* The next moment, the full impact of the plot struck him. It took all of Josh's control to keep from raging at his mother. He set his teeth in his lower lip and tasted blood, the only way to hold back words that once spoken, would haunt him forever.

Sarah gasped. Ellie sat as if frozen. Tim uttered a smothered protest, flung his napkin to the table, and leaped to his feet.

Matt straightened in his chair. His eyes turned midnight blue. "I beg your pardon?" Icicles dripped from his voice.

Edward stepped into the breach. "I'm sorry Mother was so blunt." He sounded sincere, but from long experience, Josh knew better.

"We don't really want to kidnap her." Edward leaned forward, and his eyes gleamed. "We want to take Miss Sterling to San Francisco and give her the finest musical training available. Josh told us how well the Sierra Songbird sings. Hearing her this morning in church confirms his opinion. Think of the good your daughter can do. We have the ability to help her become the toast of San Francisco and make a fortune. This is also a once-in-a-lifetime opportunity to touch lives with her God-given talent—"

"She's already doing that!" Tim interrupted, hands clenched in a fighting stance. "You think folks here come to church just to hear Preacher Josh?" His voice rose. "They don't. They also come to hear Ellie sing. You may be our preacher's mother and brother, but you've got some nerve showing up and trying to take Ellie away from us!"

"Sit down, Tim," Matt ordered. His eyes flashed fire. "I should apologize for my son, but I won't. He said exactly what I'm thinking. Unless I'm sadly mistaken, Josh feels the same way."

All eyes turned toward Josh. He started to speak, then caught sight of Ellie's face. She hadn't moved since Mother had fired the opening salvo in what surely would be a relentless war to get her own way...and the Sierra Songbird. A quick look at Mother's tightly buttoned mouth showed how long and hard that battle would be.

Josh jerked his attention back to Ellie. Every trace of color had left her cheeks. Her lips trembled. Her eyes looked enormous. He started to agree with Tim and Matt, but something in Ellie's face stopped him: a wistful expression that showed Edward's plea had kindled a spark. *Tread lightly.*

The unspoken admonition curbed Josh's tongue. "Ellie?"

Obviously distraught, she stood so abruptly that her chair crashed to the floor, then ran out of the dining room.

Josh rounded on Edward. "How could you?"

He raised one eyebrow. "This doesn't concern you, Josh. It's between Miss Sterling and her parents."

"And her brother," Tim reminded.

"Of course." Edward rose and helped their mother to her feet. "Why don't we go to our rooms and give you a chance to find the lady involved and think it over?"

"If we think it over until Judgment Day, you still can't have Ellie," Tim growled. "I gotta go find her." He raced out.

Mother, who had remained silent during the encounter, smiled and patted Sarah's hand. "I'm sorry, dear, it's just that we have your daughter's welfare at heart. Her chances here are quite limited. You mustn't be selfish and hold her back."

Josh had never in his life come so close to disliking his mother. Couldn't she see what she'd done? She and Edward had shot the day to smithereens. Not trusting himself to speak, he went to find the girl he loved.

❧

When Ellie left the dining room, she fled to the place in Madera that offered refuge: Christ the Way Church. Knowing she'd be pursued, she ducked behind buildings and through the alley instead of staying on Main Street, where she could be spotted. Yet once she reached the church, she reconsidered. It was the first place they'd look for her. She needed time alone to grasp everything that had happened.

A large oak tree a little distance away offered sanctuary. Ellie sped toward it and sank to the ground beneath its sheltering branches. The day's events whirled through her mind, starting when Tim had helped her down from the buggy in front of the church. . . .

"Hurry or we'll be late." Ellie's heart sang as usual, knowing she'd soon see Josh. She and Tim went inside and found their places. A slight stir at the back of the church caused heads to swivel. Ellie blinked. Why was Josh sitting down beside a middle-aged blond woman wearing the most stylish hat that had been seen in Madera in years? He should be up front sitting beside frowning Luther Talbot, who insisted on occupying a seat on the platform during each service.

Tim poked Ellie. "Who's the fancy dame? Where'd Josh get the duded-up suit?"

Ellie shook her head and turned toward the front of the church.

"It ain't Josh after all," Tim reported, head still craned toward the back row. "He's just now coming through the door. The other guy's gotta be Josh's twin. Betcha the woman's their mother."

Ellie gulped. Had Josh mentioned her to his family? Had they come to look her over? She pushed the thought aside and concentrated on the service. When Josh finished the story of Horatio Spafford and beckoned to her, she stepped forward. She forgot about Josh's family until she sang the last line of her song, "It is well, it is well with my soul." She breathed a silent prayer of thanks and discovered a pair of gray eyes identical to the young minister's steadily regarding her. No, not identical. The newcomer's gaze held impudence. Josh's did not.

Ellie returned to her seat like one in a trance. She suffered Mrs. Stanhope's and Amy's gushing, Edward's invitation, and the walk to the Yosemite Hotel with the wrong brother. Charming he might be, but he wasn't Josh. Ellie wished with all her heart that he would trade places with Edward. And when Mrs. Stanhope said, "We want permission to kidnap your daughter," Ellie wondered if the woman was quite mad.

Now she buried her face in her hands. Snatches from the glowing picture

Edward had painted sank into her soul. *"Finest musical training available. . .the good your daughter can do. . .the ability to help her become the toast of San Francisco. . . make a fortune. . .once-in-a-lifetime opportunity. . .touch lives with her God-given talent."*

Ellie slipped to her knees. "Please help me, God. I can't leave Josh! He loves me and wants me for his wife. That's what I want, too." Yet her traitorous heart clamored to be heard. With a cry of despair, Ellie confessed, "Lord, I've asked You for years to help me be someone. No one but You knows how much I want to be worthy of Josh. Could this be Your answer? The Diamond S has been like the end of the rainbow, but do You have greater treasure waiting for me in San Francisco?"

Her heart beat faster. "What if everything Edward describes comes true? I could serve You and save money to provide for Tim instead of being beholden to Matt and Seth. I could also become someone Josh would be proud of no matter where You lead him. Besides, it's not like it would be forever."

Ellie raised her head. She looked at the church. She thought of her family and life on the ranch. Sobs wracked her slender body. How could she bear to give up all she knew and loved? Yet she'd asked for an opportunity to be someone. What if God was calling her to the city the way He'd called Josh to Madera? How could she accept? How could she refuse?

Chapter 16

Josh gritted his teeth and marched through the front door of the Yosemite Hotel. If he stayed in the dining room one minute more, he would erupt like a volcano and say words that could never be recalled. How dare Mother patronize Sarah and accuse her of selfishly holding Ellie back? Church members and nonmembers alike heaped praise on Sarah. They obviously considered her one of the finest women in the valley, and according to Red Fallon, Sarah was a true angel of forgiveness. As for Edward, Josh's anger burned hotter with every step.

He caught sight of Tim loping down Main Street ahead of him. "Wait up," Josh called. Tim glanced back, paused, and waited. A white line around the boy's tightly closed mouth and the lightning that flickered in his eyes warned of an impending storm. It broke when Josh reached him.

"Your brother's not much like you, is he?" Tim burst out. "You'd never come up with a fool idea like taking Ellie to San Francisco."

"No." A world of regret poured into Josh's reply and a look of understanding passed between them. "Not that she isn't talented enough. She is. Edward's right about that, but high society is no place for Ellie. She's far too unsophisticated for the circles in which Mother and Edward travel."

Fear darkened Tim's eyes until they looked almost black. "Yeah, but Ellie may not think so." He kicked at the road, and swirls of yellow dust rose. "Did you see her face when your brother was spouting about this being her big opportunity? And then she ran out! I wanted to hit your brother for making her look like that."

"So did I," Josh confessed. "I wish he and Mother had never come to Madera."

"Same here. I'm afraid Ellie may fall for all that stuff. Come on. We gotta find her." Tim cocked his head to one side. "She probably went back to the church." He started on, easily keeping pace with Josh's long strides. "Hey, I guess being a preacher doesn't stop you from getting mad, does it?"

"No." Josh produced a feeble grin. "It just keeps me from hitting folks!"

Tim grunted but fell silent. Josh suspected that for once he didn't have a reply.

When they reached Christ the Way, Josh warned, "We need to go in quietly. If Ellie's praying, we don't want to bother her." He opened the door, and they stepped inside. Only silence from the empty room greeted them.

Tim looked wise. "When things bother Ellie, she likes to go off by herself. She probably figured the church is the first place we'd look for her. We'll find her outside somewhere."

It didn't take long to discover Ellie's refuge. Josh spotted her beneath the huge oak tree, a yellow-clad figure drooping in a way that tore at his heart. Unwilling to interrupt her solitude, he put his finger to his lips and motioned Tim back. They retreated to the church steps and waited without speaking. Josh could sense waves of pain and helplessness coming from the boy beside him. Tim stood on the brink of manhood, ready to leave his little-brother role and become Ellie's protector.

Josh longed to offer words of comfort, but they stuck in his throat. Edward and Mother had stirred Ellie's interest, or she wouldn't have run away to be alone. What would it mean to his future with the girl he loved? Could she withstand the persuasiveness of Letitia and Edward Stanhope, the lure of adulation?

Josh tried to brush aside his anxiety, but it stuck to him like a hungry mosquito. So did doubts about Edward. Josh had seen the astonished delight in his brother's face when Ellie sang. Edward knew and loved good music. He could have been an accomplished pianist if he'd cared enough to practice instead of chasing after other interests. Would loyalty to his twin overcome the impact of Ellie's freshness and innocence while Edward helped her climb to the pinnacle of success? Josh closed his eyes and silently prayed, *Not my will but Thine be done.*

At last Ellie rose and came toward them. Her tear-stained face bore mute witness to her inner turmoil. Love for Josh shone clear and true in her beautiful eyes, but she had obviously been deeply affected by his family's proposition.

❧

Letitia and Edward Stanhope extended their stay at the Yosemite Hotel. They suffered the twenty-mile round-trip to the ranch and back to plead with the Sterlings to allow Ellie to accompany them back to the city. They again pointed out the advantages Ellie would have. She felt like a wishbone, torn between clinging to the security of the life she knew and loved and the life the Stanhopes offered—most of all, the chance to be someone and make a difference in the lives of others. Prayer brought little peace. She wavered between saying no outright and agreeing to go for a short time.

The turmoil created by the Stanhopes' persistence didn't end with Ellie. Or with Tim or Josh, drawn together by common concern. It profoundly affected the Diamond S family and friends. Matt, Sarah, and Seth adamantly opposed Ellie's going to San Francisco. To Ellie's amazement, Seth's wife, Dori, firmly disagreed.

"Remember when I just had to go to school in Boston?" she asked Matt early one evening in the sitting room before the fire when the discussion raged hot and heavy. Ellie sat in a shadowy corner at one side, listening without speaking.

Her brother made a face. "Do I ever! Do you remember how you hated it?"

Dori tossed her dark curls. "Do I ever!" she mimicked, bright blue eyes shining. "Even though it became a disaster, I'm glad I went."

"Why?" Tim demanded from his spot on the floor in front of the fire.

Dori sobered. "I had to go away in order to appreciate what I have here." She smiled at Seth. "I have a feeling Ellie will do the same."

He shook his head and looked troubled. "After the freedom of living on the ranch, I'm afraid she will be like a wild bird in a cage."

It felt strange being discussed as if she were not present, yet Ellie remained silent and allowed the talk to flow around her.

Solita spoke for the first time since the conversation began. For once, her timeworn brown hands lay idle in her lap. "If our Sierra Songbird goes to the city and Dios does not wish her to remain, no bars will hold her." She turned to Ellie, and her black eyes softened. "Senorita, what does your heart say?"

The moment of truth Ellie had dreaded ever since the Stanhopes dangled the promise of fame and fortune before her lay heavy in the quiet room. Only the crackle of the fire and the happy laughter of children at play outside the front door broke the silence.

Ellie clenched her hands until the nails bit into her palms. Tears sneaked past her eyelids. She knew they left glistening tracks on their journey down her cheeks. Her voice came out barely above a whisper. "I've prayed and prayed about it. I don't want to leave you and the ranch, but I feel like I must go." It was out, the words she'd known must be said but that would change her life, perhaps forever.

Tim, who had been unusually quiet during the exchange, leaped to his feet and glared at her. "For crying out loud, are you crazy? What about Josh? The minute you leave, Amy will be—"

"Tim!" Matt interrupted. "That's enough. We appreciate how you feel, but this has to be Ellie's decision: no one else's."

Tim gave him a rebellious look and stalked out. Ellie put her hands over her burning face, glad for her dimly lit corner. But Tim's question refused to be ignored. What about Josh? Just this afternoon Matt had called Ellie aside and repeated the interview in which Josh confessed his feelings and received permission to keep company with her.

"He's only been here a short time, but I believe Josh loves you the way I love Sarah," Matt had said. "He's a fine man, Ellie. You'll never do better."

Now, still ecstatic over Matt's affirmation, Ellie's decision to leave Madera faltered once more. How could she go hundreds of miles away into a new and perhaps frightening world when the love she wanted more than life itself remained in Madera? The next moment she steadied her churning mind. Surely Josh's love—and hers—could endure a short separation. Besides, as Solita said, if God didn't want Ellie to stay in San Francisco she could come home as Dori had.

The thought comforted her. *I truly believe You want me to go, Lord,* she prayed that night while lying in bed and looking out the window at the winking stars. *It's my chance to become worthy of Josh. And to rid myself forever of the stigma of being Gus Stoddard's daughter.* She fell asleep, dreaming of cattle and cable cars, cowboys and creek beds, and the clang of the city the Stanhopes had described.

The dream changed to an all-too-familiar nightmare, but one Ellie hadn't had for years. The sounds of San Francisco and the San Joaquin Valley changed to childish voices, taunting and cruel: *"You ain't nothing, Ellianna Stoddard. Neither's your Pa. Trash, that's what you are—and you ain't never gonna be nothin' else."*

The cry of a coyote awakened Ellie, mocking as the voices in her dream. Instead of the sickening feeling that had always followed the dream, however, determination flooded through her. "You're wrong about me," she fiercely whispered to the haunting voices. "With God's help, I'll show you, San Francisco—and the world."

Her mind raced. Her purpose grew. "I'm going to work hard and become everything Edward and Mrs. Stanhope promised: rich, famous, and a blessing to others. I had enough trouble as a child to be called Job's granddaughter. This is my chance to have people look up to me, not down on me. I will learn to be a wife of whom Josh can be proud."

When Ellie again fell asleep, no dreams troubled her. She awoke resolved to carry out the vow she had made in the night hours—and sent word to the Stanhopes she was willing to leave Madera.

Two days later Ellie shook the dust of her past off her new, stylish boots and left for San Francisco with Mrs. Stanhope and Edward.

Ellie bade Josh a heart-wrenching good-bye. When he clasped her hands as if he'd never let her go, Ellie wanted to fling herself into his arms, regardless of the crowd at the station. Only the desire to become worthy of the unguarded love shining in Josh's eyes kept Ellie true to her course. The last thing she saw when the train wheels began their *clackety-clack* to carry her away was Josh waving from the steps of Christ the Way Church. Tim stood beside him, somber faced and with arms crossed.

Ellie's vision blurred. For one wild moment, she longed to cry out, "Stop the train!" Instead, she raised her chin, set her face toward the west, and didn't look back.

Chapter 17

Ellie glanced around the passenger coach. She stifled a giggle, but her eyes stung. How different this was from the common car in which she and Tim had huddled on their trip from St. Louis to California! She closed her eyes and pictured two frightened children facing an unknown future. There had been no gingerbread trimmings, no polished brass lamps hanging from the ceiling. Certainly no stained-glass transoms to reflect rainbow colors across the rich, plush seats.

She thought of the dining car with its spotless white tablecloths and well-trained attendants. She and Tim had been too timid to even sneak a peek into the dining car when they came to Madera. Ellie forced the comparisons out of her mind. *That was then. This is now.*

"Well, we're on our way," Edward said.

His laugh and resemblance to Josh sent a twinge through Ellie. *Oh dear! Only a few miles lie between the speeding train and home, and I'm already missing Josh. This will never do.* She dismissed the thought and put on a bright smile. "Yes."

Mrs. Stanhope settled herself more firmly in her seat. "We need to talk about you, Ellie." She raised one eyebrow. "The first thing we'll do when we get home is take you to a good hairdresser and modiste." She gave Ellie's well-cut traveling gown a nod of approval. "Your clothing is fine for Madera, but San Francisco fashion demands—"

"Hang San Francisco fashion!" Edward cut in. "You're not going to turn the Sierra Songbird into a bird of paradise."

Ellie gaped, unable to believe her own ears, but Edward wasn't through.

"Look at Ellie, Mother. See how her hair curls under at the nape of her neck? And the way her soft bangs curve across her forehead? It makes her look like a page from the days of knights and ladies." His eyes sparkled. "When she sings, she must wear simple, tunic-style dresses that highlight her uniqueness."

Mrs. Stanhope bridled, and her mouth set in a stubborn line. "As if you know about fashion and the proper dress for ladies!"

"I know what will set the Sierra Songbird apart." Edward stroked his chin with long elegant fingers. "Yellow. Lots of yellow, like sunlight and the meadowlark's breast. Surely your fancy dressmaker can create a costume such as I've described.

"We're also not going to let some music professor turn Ellie into an opera singer. Her charm is in who she is. A few lessons in proper breathing will be all she needs." A gleam brightened his eyes. "Ellie, do you play guitar? Do you know some old ballads?"

Ellie blinked. *What on earth. . . ?* "One of our Mexican workers taught me to play the guitar, and I know dozens of ballads. I've even written a few."

Edward crossed his arms and donned a satisfied smile. "Good! I'll usually accompany you on the piano, but a guitar will be perfect for some of your songs."

Mrs. Stanhope clapped her gloved hands. For the first time, Ellie saw the older woman show genuine excitement and delight. "You're getting back to your music, Edward? I am so happy."

Ellie caught a glimpse beneath Mrs. Stanhope's outward surface. A true mother's heart beat in her tightly corseted body, at least as far as Edward was concerned. The recognition went a long way toward helping Ellie warm up to her patroness.

She sighed, wishing Mrs. Stanhope could accept Josh for who he was. Her wish gave birth to a question: What if God was leading her to San Francisco for a greater purpose than fame and fortune? A purpose even more important than ministering to others with her voice? The prayer of the thirteenth-century monk, Saint Francis of Assisi, came to mind. Ellie had written a simple guitar accompaniment and often sang the timeless words:

> *Lord, make me an instrument of Thy peace;*
> *where there is hatred, let me sow love;*
> *where there is injury, pardon;*
> *where there is doubt, faith;*
> *where there is despair, hope;*
> *where there is darkness, light;*
> *and where there is sadness, joy.*

Ellie's heart filled to overflowing. *I still want to be someone, Lord,* she prayed, *but the greatest gift I could ever bring to Joshua would be reconciliation with his family. Help me sow seeds that You may cause to grow.*

Mrs. Stanhope's voice grated into Ellie's prayer. "One thing. Don't worry about expenses. As your sponsor, I am happy to take care of your needs."

Ellie raised her chin, feeling a red tide sweep into her face. "Thank you, Mrs. Stanhope, but that won't be necessary. Matt and Seth gave me ample funds to carry me until I can begin to earn my own way."

"That will be sooner than you think," Edward promised. "We'll start by having you sing at Bayview Christian."

Josh's church. Ellie's mouth went dry. How could she sing to a congregation she suspected was waiting for their former preacher to come to his senses and return?

"Trust Me."

The words that had brought her through good times and bad stilled Ellie's trembling hands. God knew what He was doing. All she had to do was cling to His promise to never leave or forsake her. Ellie jerked her attention back to what Edward was saying.

"After that, we'll let it be known you're available for home musicales and soirees."

Dazzled by the glittering future he painted, Ellie felt her enthusiasm rise to match Edward's. Not to be outdone, his mother broke into the plans.

"I have a splendid idea!" Her face glowed. "Ellie, when you feel ready, we'll have you do a benefit concert for the Occidental Mission Home for Girls." Sadness replaced her joy. "It's too bad there has to be such a place, but thank God for Margaret Culbertson. She rescues young Chinese girls from slavery or worse."

Mrs. Stanhope set her lips in a grim line. "Desperate parents in Canton, China, sell their daughters for less than forty dollars each. Countless other girls, some only six or seven, are kidnapped and hidden aboard ships. Once they reach America, they are smuggled into San Francisco and other ports."

"How can they get past immigration?" Ellie protested. A lump came to her throat, thinking of those unfortunate girls. What she had suffered at Gus's hands was nothing compared with the girls' plight.

Edward gave a scornful laugh. "Immigration officials can be bribed. The Chinese slave traders pretend to be the girls' relatives. They carry false papers that let them smuggle the girls into Chinatown, which is only a few blocks from Nob Hill, where we live. The girls are abused and forced to work such long hours many of them don't last long. They're called the 'Children of Darkness,' and live without hope."

He clenched his fists. "I'd like to get my hands on some of those yellow slavers! They're the scourge of San Francisco. They bribe police officers to cover up for them. Many lawyers work pro bono on the girls' behalf, but it's often impossible to obtain justice. San Francisco is a beautiful city. Many good people live in Chinatown, but it also holds opium dens, and the yellow slave trade is an indelible stain."

Ellie shuddered. What kind of place was this?

Mrs. Stanhope took up the story. "They hate Margaret Culbertson. She established the Mission Home on the very edge of Chinatown in 1874 and began raids into its dark heart. She's saved many girls from bondage. Margaret cares for their spiritual as well as their physical needs. She's one of the most courageous women I've ever met. I wish I could be more like her."

Edward patted his mother's plump hand. "You do a great deal. It takes money to keep the Occidental Mission Home going. You're tops at shaming some of our miserly leading citizens into making donations."

Her eyes twinkled. "Only because they get their names listed in the paper."

Ellie fell silent. She had never met anyone like this society matron. Mrs. Stanhope's warmhearted concern for the Chinese girls appeared at odds with her obvious desire for recognition. Perhaps she believed she'd been divinely appointed to carry out on earth the plans God made in heaven.

Edward, identical to Joshua in looks, also seemed a mass of contradictions. His bringing his mother to Madera to find a singer didn't make sense to Ellie. She pondered it while the train continued its headlong rush toward the City by the Bay. But when they left the train and boarded the ferry at Oakland, everything except her surroundings fled from Ellie's mind.

Fog hung low over San Francisco Bay, so thick she could barely see the opposite shore. Whitecaps kicked against the ferry. Ellie's nostrils twitched from the unfamiliar smell of salt. "It's not much like the Mississippi River," she mumbled, then put one hand over her mouth, thankful that the chill breeze whipped away her words. Nobody in San Francisco knew her as anyone other than Ellie Sterling. She needed to guard her tongue and keep it that way.

A mournful whistle blew. Edward helped the women off the ferry. Ellie gaped at the crowded dock and streets. Pushcarts jostled carriages. Peddlers offered their wares, screaming at the top of their lungs. Ellie shrank against Mrs. Stanhope while Edward secured a rig and said, "Nob Hill, driver." They climbed inside. The sound of horses' hooves clattering over the cobbled streets made Ellie homesick for Calico. Oh, to be back riding the range instead of in the midst of such confusion!

There was so much to see that Ellie soon forgot everything but San Francisco. The streets went up and up until it seemed they would reach the sky. A cable car clanged its way down a steep hill.

"I'll take you on the cable car someday," Edward promised.

Excitement filled Ellie. "Thank you."

They reached the top of the hill and climbed another. At last the coach stopped in front of a large, imposing house. Ellie smothered a nervous giggle. The dark brick Stanhope mansion, with its turrets, lace-curtained bay windows, fancy iron scrollwork, and balconies resembled a haughty, aging queen squatting on a throne, looking down on everyone else. Could a simple rancher's daughter ever feel at home here?

The ornate front door opened. Ellie expected a uniformed butler, but a smiling, gray-haired replica of Edward and Josh came down the steps, hands outstretched. "Welcome to our home, Miss Sterling. I'm glad you're here."

Ellie looked into Charles Stanhope's steady eyes and shyly put her hand in his. The cold knot that had parked where her heart should be ever since they boarded the ferry left. No matter what lay ahead, she'd found a friend... perhaps even an ally, if needed.

Chapter 18

From the time Ellie met Beryl Westfield, Edward's dark-haired fiancée seized every opportunity to belittle Ellie when they were alone. Yet in public, she fairly oozed sweetness and light toward "our Sierra Songbird."

"Don't pay any attention to Beryl," Edward advised Ellie one day after walking in while Beryl was making a snide comment.

Beryl glared at him and rushed out, but Edward only laughed.

"Her nose is out of joint because she pursued Josh before we got engaged. She couldn't get him. Beryl is thirty-two, five years older than we are; almost old enough to be your mother. Besides, she's also upset because I've mended my lazy ways in favor of promoting you and practicing."

Edward frowned. "Josh tries to like Beryl for my sake, but it's rough going." He clasped his hands behind his head. "Sometimes I don't like her either."

Ellie gasped. "You're going to marry someone you don't like?"

Edward had the grace to look ashamed. "I need a wife." A glint came into his gray eyes. "Too bad I didn't see you before my brother did!"

"Please don't talk like that, Edward." Ellie took a deep breath. "You mustn't marry anyone you don't love with all your heart."

"Is that the way you feel about Josh?"

Ellie sensed that a great deal hung on her answer. She could not give an evasive reply. "Yes, Edward, but it's between us and God, not you. And especially not Beryl. Now if you'll excuse me, I need to practice."

"Wait, Ellie." Edward caught at her sleeve. "Don't hold it against me for asking. Comparing a girl like you with Beryl Westfield makes a man wonder."

His comment troubled Ellie, but anxiety over her first public appearance in San Francisco left little time to worry about Edward.

At last the big day came. Ellie's knees shook as she left the Stanhope pew and started to the front of Bayview Christian Church. The distance up the richly carpeted aisle loomed longer than the miles that stretched between Madera and the Diamond S. She felt sweat trickle inside her gloved hands and smoothed down her pale yellow sleeves. Would her wobbly knees be able to carry her up the richly carpeted aisle? Would a single note come out of her parched throat? Why had she agreed to make her San Francisco debut in Joshua's church? Far better to have first sung at a home musicale.

"Trust Me."

The unspoken reminder blunted the edge of Ellie's fear. Her throat cleared. She walked to her place beside the organ, turned, and faced the congregation. " 'It Is Well with My Soul' is my favorite hymn. Before I sing, I want you to know how the song came to be written." She paused. For a moment the richly colored stained-glass windows changed to clear glass in her mind. Sunlight streamed through them into Christ the Way Church and bathed Joshua Stanhope in its golden rays.

The image faded, but it had strengthened Ellie. She clasped her hands and said, "Horatio Spafford was a remarkable man. He, his wife, and four young daughters lived in Chicago. . . ." Ellie saw quickening interest replace the expressions of boredom and curiosity on the faces turned toward her. When she finished the story, she nodded to the organist. He struck a single note, and Ellie's bell-like tones rang throughout the cathedral.

"When peace, like a river, attendeth my way. . ." Her voice soared with triumph, just as it had when she sang in Christ the Way. "It is well. . .with my soul. . . . It is well, it is well with my soul."

With my soul echoed back from the vaulted ceiling. Ellie looked at the Stanhope pew. Mr. Stanhope wore a look of peace that thrilled her heart. If no one else had been touched, he had. Tears coursed down Mrs. Stanhope's cheeks. Had she also been inspired by the song? Ellie's gaze turned to Edward. She saw approval in his eyes and a softening in his face. It made Edward look more like his twin than ever.

The fourth occupant of the pew looked neither exalted nor touched by the story and song. Beryl Westfield, gowned in the latest fashion, raised one haughty eyebrow and pursed her lips when Ellie walked back to the pew. Ellie's joy at the congregation's obvious approval dwindled. The enmity in the older woman's face made her shudder. She hadn't faced such dislike since the days of being taunted for being Gus's daughter. She hated the feelings Beryl stirred up. Everyone else she'd met in San Francisco had been kind. Must there always be a serpent to spoil the Garden of Eden?

Busy trying to overcome her resentment, Ellie barely heard the choir's final presentation and the benediction. She returned to reality when the Reverend Michael Yates, Josh's red-haired substitute, reached her. "Smashing, Miss Sterling. Absolutely smashing." Admiration shone in his hazel eyes. "What a team we make—you with your singing; I with my preaching!"

Edward made a choking sound. Ellie wanted to poke him. No matter how pompous Michael sounded, as a minister he deserved respect. Not wanting to encourage him, she said, "I'm glad you liked my song." Michael Yates had made his lofty ambitions clear at their first meeting. He'd also done everything but add how proud he'd be to have the Sierra Songbird help him climb the ladder to success.

Even if there were no Joshua, I couldn't care for this man, Ellie thought. *He appears far more interested in how rapidly he can rise than in being God's servant and leading souls to Christ.* How different Michael Yates was from Josh, who had walked away from the position Michael obviously coveted.

❧

Josh crumpled the third version of a letter to Ellie and tossed it toward the big woodstove in the parsonage. He missed his target, just as he missed Ellie. She'd only been gone a few weeks, but it seemed like forever. Josh pulled the single letter she'd written to him from the pocket above his heart, smoothed out the creases, and spread the pages on his table. Worn from many readings, they threatened to fall apart. He read the words he had already memorized:

Dear Josh,

I hardly know where to start. San Francisco is beautiful, ugly, inviting, and terrifying. I am in awe of its magnificent structures but appalled at the stories I hear about the yellow slave trade. I sometimes want to flee, but the continuing belief that God has put me here for a reason prevents my turning tail and running.

Almost everyone has been incredibly kind. Your father is everything I wish mine had been. Your mother treats me like an honored guest and delights in advising me about proper dress. To my surprise, she approves of everything I brought from home. However, she has insisted on having some gowns made for more formal occasions and when I perform.

Edward is really a dear, not at all what I expected when I first met him. He's so much like you that when I'm with him, I sometimes forget he isn't you!

Josh raised his head and gazed out the window. September had waved farewell and ushered in October. Tree branches swayed in the gentle breeze. Busy squirrels searched for winter store. Peace lay over the smiling land but failed to touch Josh.

"The last thing I need is for Ellie to start thinking Edward's just like me," he muttered, cringing at the thought. "Such an idea could lead to heartbreak. If ever two persons were unequally yoked, they are Ellie and my brother."

She could be the making of Edward, a little voice mocked. *Beryl Westfield is a self-confessed infidel. Ellie is the finest example of Christian womanhood. Beryl attracts with her sophistication. Ellie appeals because of her lack of sophistication.*

Josh grunted. "Lord, if I gave up Ellie, which I'm not going to do, there's no guarantee Edward would change permanently, even if he won her."

The little voice remained mercifully silent, so Josh returned to the letter:

I never dreamed how different San Francisco could be from the Diamond S. Edward has taken me to ride the cable cars and to Golden Gate Park, always suitably chaperoned of course. We ride there, but it's nothing like being on Calico. I long to be on her back and riding with the wind in my face.

The Pacific Ocean took my breath away. So did walking along the Embarcadero with its salty, fishy smell. Two of my favorite places are the Conservatory in Golden Gate Park and the Palace Hotel. Edward says I may someday be able to sing there, but not until I'm better known. I couldn't believe it when the carriage we were in drove right into the Grand Court. Forgive me for gushing about things you know so well. They're all new and strange to me.

Ellie went on to describe her first solo at Bayview Christian and added:

When I sang "It Is Well with My Soul," I didn't expect the congregation here to react the same as those at Christ the Way. But they did. Your mother and Edward say it must become my signature song. No matter where or what else I sing, I'm to save the story and song for the end of the program. Your father agrees. He says nothing else can reach people like the song. I'm glad. Each time I sing it, I think of you telling the story of it being ripped from the depths of a hurting heart. It makes me homesick, but it also makes me proud to pass the story on. My prayer is that it may touch lives the way it touched mine.

By the way, Reverend Michael Yates approves of me. He says we make a great team because of my singing and his preaching. The first time he said it, I wanted to laugh. Edward nearly disgraced himself by choking. You should have seen the look Beryl gave him.

Josh slammed his fist on the table. "This is the last straw. I not only have to worry about Edward, but this Yates clown is obviously on Ellie's trail, too. So he thinks they make a great team. Not if I have anything to say about it. Yates has another think coming." Josh returned to the letter once more:

I miss everyone and long for the time when God leads me back to Madera.

Ellie

Josh left the pages on the table and sought the silence of his church. He knelt before the altar and bowed his head. *Lord, bring Ellie home to me,* his heart cried. *I need her so much.* Fear of losing her and the weight of recent events fell heavily on Josh's bent shoulders. Slowly but surely, Luther Talbot and his cohorts were making inroads on Josh's acceptance.

"Lord, my hopes for happiness here seem short lived," he prayed. "All I want is to find and serve those who need You. Now I'm facing a mountain of resistance. Luther, the board, and many of the congregation frown on my desire to spend time outside the church walls. They continually remind me I was hired to minister to the flock already securely in the fold, not go chasing after wild sheepherders and cowhands."

Josh stopped his prayer long enough to mutter, "I can't believe Luther's latest complaint." He mimicked the board chairman's accusing voice. "'You've been here since June, Reverend. What good has come of all your gallivanting around? Only one of those lost sheep you've been so eager to bring to the Lord has come to the altar.'"

Josh chuckled. "I bit my tongue to keep from telling Luther that one soul saved in the time I've been here isn't so bad. Noah preached for 120 years and only succeeded in saving eight people from the flood, including himself."

Laughter gave way to depression and doubt. "Was I wrong in thinking Madera is where You want me to serve? And that Ellie is the woman You've chosen to be my wife—even though Edward can make her San Francisco's Sierra Songbird?"

Hours later Josh returned to his home with his concerns unresolved. "Well Lord," he prayed as he lay in bed watching the brilliant stars filling the sky outside his open window, "Your answers are *yes*, *no*, and *wait*. This time it must be *wait*."

An owl hooted from the spreading oak tree. A coyote yapped for its mate in the distance. Its mournful wail sounded as lonely as Josh felt. Yet the crooning of the crisp, early October night wind soothed the troubled young preacher, and at last he slept.

Chapter 19

Ellie sat by the window of her bedroom in the Stanhope mansion. If only the sun would break through the heavy gray fog blanket that obscured the usually magnificent view! Thankful that for once she had a few minutes to herself, she breathed a sigh of relief. Ever since she'd arrived in the city, life had galloped at a pace that sometimes left her disoriented. After her first solo at Bayview Christian, she'd been deluged with invitations to sing, thanks to an enterprising reporter who'd been in church that Sunday. He'd helped launch her whirlwind rise to fame with a glowing review of her solo in the *San Francisco Chronicle*. Then he periodically added tidbits guaranteed to pique the interest of persons looking for something new and worthwhile.

A demanding knock sounded on Ellie's door. Before she could respond, it slammed open. Beryl Westfield, face contorted with fury, rushed in. "You innocent-faced minx! Have you seen this?"

The discordant voice jerked Ellie from her solitude. She peered at Beryl. Impeccably dressed as usual, the hatred in Beryl's black eyes made Ellie cringe. Beryl flung a copy of the *Chronicle* at her and demanded, "Read that!"

Ellie caught the paper before it struck her in the face. She glanced down. Her image stared back at her from beside the bold headline: Sierra Songbird Soars.

"What's wrong?" Ellie faltered. "It's just an article."

"Just an article?" Beryl raved, hands clenched into fists. She took a menacing step toward Ellie. "Read the whole thing!"

Ellie blinked. Had Beryl gone crazy, to come tearing in, raging like this? "Read it!"

Ellie shrank from the older woman, who stood watching her like an avenging angel. No, more like someone under Satan's control. Beryl evidently wouldn't leave until she got what she'd come for. Ellie read the headline again, then the article:

Sierra Songbird Soars

San Franciscans are taking note of a newcomer to our fair city. Miss Ellianna Sterling first captivated the congregation (and this reporter) at

328

Bayview Christian Church with her remarkable voice. Miss Sterling is the protégée of Mrs. Charles Stanhope, well-known benefactress and champion of the downtrodden.

Sought after for soirees and musicales by San Francisco's finest, the Sierra Songbird, as she is known, is winning both high praise and our hearts. Her modest dress, simple ballads—including some she has written—and her hymns have shaken San Francisco. Sterling's simplicity and lack of vanity impress even the most jaded music lovers. She prefaces the heartfelt rendition of her signature song, "It Is Well with My Soul," with the story of how it came to be written. Few of us remain dry-eyed when confronted by the author's unwavering faith.

Neither can we resist the expression on the songbird's face when she sings, "Even so, it is well with my soul.'" It bears mute but compelling testimony: Whatever others choose to believe, it truly is well with Ellianna Sterling's soul.

The Sierra Songbird is often accompanied by Edward Stanhope, whose proficiency at the piano has until now been unsuspected. The dark-haired man and the yellow-gowned singer make a striking couple. One cannot help wondering if there would be wedding bells as well as church bells in their future were it not for Edward's engagement to Miss Beryl Westfield.

Tickets are now being offered at premium prices for a concert benefiting Mrs. Stanhope's favorite charity, The Occidental Mission Home for Girls. It is one event this reporter plans to cover, and not just to get a story.

Ellie let the paper slip through her fingers to the rich Oriental rug. She had run the gamut of emotions while reading it. Joy. Excitement. Gratitude for the reporter's kind words about her singing. The thrill of knowing God was using her to touch lives. But the comment about a wedding and church bells destroyed Ellie's pleasure and filled her with disgust. She jumped from her chair and faced Beryl.

"Why did the reporter have to spoil all the nice things he said by hinting at a romance between Edward and me?" she cried. "It isn't true, Miss Westfield. Edward is my friend, nothing more."

Beryl's eyes narrowed into cat's eyes. "If that's true, then why has he been making me a laughingstock by escorting you all over the city?"

"We always have a chaperone," Ellie told her. "Maria or one of the other maids accompanies us."

Beryl brushed her comment aside. "Even if I believed you, which I don't, it doesn't matter. My friends mock me because Edward is never available when I want him." She drew herself up to her full height and glowered down at Ellie. "Edward has also begun to hint that perhaps we aren't suited for one another. I pleased him well enough until you came." Venom dripped from every word.

Snippets of a conversation from weeks earlier popped into Ellie's mind:

"Sometimes I don't like her myself."
"You're going to marry someone you don't like?"
"I need a wife."
"You mustn't marry anyone you don't love with all your heart."
"Comparing a girl like you with Beryl Westfield makes a man wonder."

"Well?" Beryl's harsh voice sent the memory flying, but not before Ellie's heart leaped. She'd come to like Edward—first because he reminded her of Josh, then for his dedication to helping her succeed. If he was having second thoughts about joining his life with Beryl, it was all to the good.

Ellie carefully hid her elation at the thought. "I have told you the truth, Miss Westfield. I have nothing more to say. Now will you please leave my room?"

Beryl's face went chalk white. She raised one hand as if to strike. Then she said, "Watch your step. To quote that Bible you so piously hide behind while trying to worm your way in where you don't belong, 'Pride goeth before a fall.'"

"It's actually 'Pride goeth before destruction, and an haughty spirit before a fall,'" Ellie told her.

The unwelcome guest gave Ellie another scorching look and marched out. Shaken, Ellie sank back into her chair. "Lord, what am I doing here?"

"Trust Me."

Ellie buried her face in her hands and cried out, "I do trust You, but it's hard! I haven't done anything to deserve such treatment."

"Neither did My Son."

The silent reminder poured healing into Ellie's hurting heart. She continued to sit by the window and look out into the gray day, taking stock of her present life. At times, her St. Louis childhood seemed distant and unreal. Even her years on the Diamond S were gradually losing their luster when compared with the glory of rising from obscurity to being sought after. Only her love for her family and Joshua remained constant.

"I'll enjoy it while it lasts," she vowed. "Someday Joshua and I will be reunited. In the meantime, I'm saving money in case Tim needs it. Also, when the time comes, I won't have to go to Joshua like a penniless beggar girl."

Joy welled into Ellie's throat and rippled out. "I'm also helping Josh, even though he doesn't know it. Lord, thank You for making Mr. Stanhope so understanding. When I told him I wanted to send my tithe to Christ the Way Church anonymously he arranged it. I'm sure he never said a word to Mrs. Stanhope or Edward or they would have asked why I'd do such a thing."

The solemn chime of a clock put an end to Ellie's rejoicing. She'd be late for her music lesson if she didn't hurry. She washed her hands and face, tidied her shining hair, and ran downstairs, carrying her hooded cloak. To her dismay, Beryl stood with Edward in the great hall. Her rigid stance showed she still burned with anger.

Edward looked up. "Beryl reminded me of an important engagement this afternoon, Ellie. She's helping Mother with the arrangements for the benefit concert, and of course they need my expert advice. We'll drop you off on the way, but I don't know how long it will take. I've told our carriage driver to pick you up after your lesson. Sorry."

"There's no need to be sorry." Ellie slipped into her cloak and followed them out to the carriage. She climbed in, being careful to leave the place beside Edward for Beryl. When they reached her music teacher's studio, she stepped down and said, "Be careful. It looks like the fog is getting worse."

"We will. I'll see you at home later," Edward called as they trotted away.

Ellie hurried inside, glad to get out of the penetrating moisture that threatened to soak through her heavy cloak. She greeted her teacher and the lesson began. Partway through, however, a message came. Her instructor read it and blanched.

"I have to leave, Miss Sterling. A dear friend has taken ill and needs me."

"It's all right," Ellie assured him. "I can wait here. The Stanhope carriage will come for me at the regular time."

He looked dubious but apologized again and left.

Ellie busied herself with straightening piles of music that lay askew, but soon tired of the task. Why stay in this empty studio when it was less than a mile from home? She had time to walk and be there long before the driver left to pick her up.

Once outside, she hesitated. "Don't be foolish," she told herself. "You can't get lost between here and Nob Hill." Ellie pulled the hood of her cloak over her hair, clutched its voluminous folds around her body against the encroaching cold, and confidently started up the street.

All too soon, the fog thickened. It changed to a drizzle. Its eerie *drip-drip* added to the chilling atmosphere. Ellie increased her pace, anxious to get out of the murk that swallowed up the street signs. A few blocks farther on, she murmured, "Better to wait in the studio than in this pea soup." She shivered with cold and turned to retrace her steps. Her foot slipped on a pebble. Ellie tried to regain her balance, but fell, hitting her head on the cobblestone street.

Dizzy and disoriented, Ellie staggered to her feet and rubbed her throbbing head. She tried to remember whether she should be walking up the hill or down. Did it really matter? If she kept walking, she'd get somewhere. Yet each uncertain step brought new fear. Where *was* she?

She rounded a corner. Dim lights flickered through the fog curtain. Thank goodness! Light meant help lay just ahead. Ellie broke into a run. More lights appeared, still faint, but enough to show alleys on both sides of the street. Stairs led to second and third stories. Dark, shadowy forms huddled in gaping doorways. Muffled voices speaking a language Ellie didn't understand floated through the fog.

She stopped short and peered through the gloom at a brightly colored banner with strange black symbols. Her heart hammered with fear. Confused by the fog, she had stumbled into Chinatown—the last place she should be alone with night coming on.

Yellow slave traders. The scourge of San Francisco. Opium dens. Children of Darkness. Many good people in Chinatown, but a stain on the city.

Ellie's stomach lurched. She turned to flee, but a heavy hand caught her by the shoulder. A disembodied voice gloated, "I've got you now. 'Tis about time."

Ellie tried to wrench free. She could not. She tried to scream. Only a squeak came out of her constricted throat, so muffled by the fog no one except her captor would ever hear her. *Dear God, why didn't I stay at the studio where I belonged?*

Chapter 20

The grip on Ellie's shoulder tightened. The fog-hoarsened voice ordered, "Don't try to fly, little birdie. You and your kind are for belongin' in the paddy wagon, not on the streets."

Your kind? Paddy wagon? What did he mean? Ellie twisted around and peered into her captor's face. She sagged with relief. Enough light shone on brass buttons marching down the burly figure's chest to identify him. A policeman. The biggest, most forbidding policeman she'd ever seen. Surely he'd get her out of her predicament and back to the Stanhopes!

A none-too-gentle shake brought doubt hard on the heels of Ellie's relief. "Is it the cat's got your tongue?"

Ellie's mind churned. Icy fear licked at her veins. Her body shook. What if this policeman with the iron grip was a devil in disguise? One of the police officers the Chinese smugglers bribed to wink at their dark deeds? Terror turned Ellie legs to overcooked spaghetti. Only the firm hold on her shoulder kept her from tumbling to the wet cobblestone street.

The policeman leaned down until his broad, scowling face was level with Ellie's. He gave a muffled exclamation and released her, but caught her with both hands when she stumbled and nearly fell. "Miss Sterling? Faith and mercy, why are you for bein' in such a place?"

The rich Irish voice dispelled fear, but Ellie tried twice before she could give a disjointed explanation. "The fog. I lost my way. Thank God you're here!"

"I'll also be for thankin' God. Beggin' your pardon, but with the hood over your head and you bein' out on such a night I mistook you for. . .uh—" He broke off.

Ellie wrinkled her forehead. "How did you recognize me?"

The policeman's brogue deepened. "Thanks to the *Chronicle*, everyone's for knowin' the Sierra Songbird. Come along, colleen. You're safe with Clancy. I'll for shure be havin' you home shortly."

Ellie had to run to keep up with her rescuer's long strides that gobbled up the distance between Chinatown and Nob Hill. When Clancy delivered her to the Stanhope mansion, she impulsively said, "I didn't know there were Irish guardian angels, but you were mine tonight."

Clancy's laugh rang out, warming Ellie in spite of the chill night. "I've niver been called an angel before, but I'm glad 'twas me who found you." He scowled and became the grim policeman who had frightened her. "Don't you be for runnin' around alone at night, *mavourneen.* There are spalpeens in this city who would delight in clipping our songbird's wings, cagin' her, and holdin' her for ransom."

Ellie shuddered at his warning. "I promise." She held out her hand, and Clancy engulfed it in his. "Will you come in?" she invited when the door swung open and Edward stepped out. She could see Mr. and Mrs. Stanhope standing in the hall behind him.

Clancy shook his head. "I'm on duty." He raised his voice and called, "She's for bein' safe," then respectfully touched his hat and vanished into the fog.

"Ellie? Where have you been? Why was that policeman with you?" Edward took her arm and led her into the hall. The heavy door closed behind them. Light from the chandelier in the great hall streamed down, a welcome contrast to the dark, miserable night lurking outside the mansion. It showed the worry lines etched in the three faces turned toward her.

Suddenly aware of her disheveled appearance, Ellie sensed her nerves starting to unravel. If she related the Chinatown incident now she'd be forced to run the gauntlet of horrified questions and relive her terror. She couldn't handle it. Ellie bit her lips to hide their trembling. "My instructor had to leave early. I started to walk home but lost my way. A policeman found me and brought me home. Please excuse me. I need a hot bath and dry clothes." She slid out of her sodden cloak and handed it to Maria, who had come into the hall with a concerned look on her pretty face.

"Go draw a bath for Miss Ellie," Mrs. Stanhope told the maid.

"Sí." Maria disappeared with the cloak. By the time Ellie slowly trudged upstairs, the Mexican girl had already poured a generous amount of fragrant bath salts in the claw-footed tub and stood waiting to take away Ellie's wet clothing when she shed it.

"Gracias," Ellie told her.

Maria's eyes sparkled with fun. "Senorita, you look more like a robin with its feathers ruffled from a windstorm than our songbird!"

"I feel that way, too." Ellie yawned.

"Do not fall asleep in the bath," Maria warned. "Senora Stanhope says dinner will not be served until you come. Senor Marvin Stanhope is to be a guest."

She whisked away, leaving Ellie to luxuriate in the scented water.

Ellie felt tempted to ask for dinner in her room but reconsidered. Ever since arriving in San Francisco, she'd been eager to meet Charles's brother— who defied Stanhope expectations by serving down-and-outs at his Rescue Mission.

Ellie finished her bath and towel-dried her hair until it curled under against the nape of her neck. She slipped into the pale blue dimity dress Maria had laid out for her and fastened the ribbons on her flat slippers. Her heart quickened to double time. What would the man Joshua admired so deeply think of her? Had Josh mentioned her to his uncle? If so, would the street missionary find her worthy of his beloved nephew?

One look into Marvin Stanhope's keen gray eyes set Ellie's doubts at rest. He bore a strong resemblance to the other Stanhope men. Ellie immediately felt at home with him and delighted when placed beside him at the glittering dining room table. He plied her with questions about Joshua.

Ellie clasped her hands and spoke more freely than she had felt comfortable doing except to Josh's father. She tingled with excitement. "He is wonderful," she said, aware of Marvin's keen interest and the way Mrs. Stanhope and Edward leaned forward to hear. "If it hadn't been for Joshua, a mountain lion would have killed my brother, Tim."

Mrs. Stanhope's silver fork crashed to her fine china plate. Her face paled, and she stared at Ellie. "A mountain lion! Why haven't you told me about that?"

Ellie wished she had bitten her tongue instead of blurting out the news in an attempt to show how splendid Joshua was. "I—I'm sorry. I knew it would worry you."

Mrs. Stanhope's voice rose a full octave. "What happened?"

"A rifle shot wounded the lion. It came toward Tim and Joshua. Tim's rifle misfired and knocked the lion down. The rifle landed at Josh's feet. He grabbed it and knocked the beast senseless. The other men came and killed it."

Mrs. Stanhope raised a handkerchief to her lips with trembling hands. "I knew no good would come of my son going to Madera." She whirled toward her brother-in-law. "This wouldn't have happened if you hadn't lured Joshua to your mission when he was only a boy."

"Settle down, Mother. Uncle Marvin didn't send Josh to Madera. God did." Edward spoke gently, and his father nodded in agreement.

Edward's unexpected defense of his brother caught Ellie by surprise. She wouldn't have expected him to admit that God was responsible for Joshua's choice. Was the prodigal twin softening toward spiritual things? *Please, Lord, let it be so. I can hardly wait to write and tell Josh what Edward said.*

Some of the color returned to Mrs. Stanhope's face. She beckoned to Maria, who gaped in the background. "You may serve dessert now."

When the maid left the room, Ellie said, "You can all be proud of Joshua. He's doing a great deal of good under difficult circumstances."

Mrs. Stanhope bridled. "Why should my son be experiencing difficult circumstances after all he gave up here?"

For the second time, Ellie regretted speaking before weighing her words as she'd been doing since coming to San Francisco. Her heart sank. "Some of the board members disagree with his methods."

Edward chortled. "That's nothing new. I remember hearing of trouble in the ranks of Bayview Christian a time or two over Josh's. . .uh. . .sometimes unorthodox means of getting his message across." Not giving his mother a chance to answer, he immediately turned back to his uncle. "How are things at the mission?"

Ellie gave a secret sigh of relief and drank in every word of their guest's reply. But when he turned to her and said, "Miss Sterling, would you consider coming to the Rescue Mission and singing?" the hush that fell over the diners left her paralyzed. Edward's mouth fell open. His father's eyes twinkled. And Mrs. Stanhope looked as if she'd been turned to stone. Why didn't someone say something to break the shocked silence?

Ellie thought of her Chinatown ordeal. The Rescue Mission was located in one of the worst parts of San Francisco. Panic sent perspiration crawling down Ellie's body. How could she deliberately go to a place so filled with danger and sin? Something terrible might happen to her.

"Trust Me."

Ellie swallowed hard and took a deep, unsteady breath. When she released it and spoke, her words came out in a whisper. "I will go."

"No!" Edward leaped to his feet, overturning his chair. It crashed to the costly carpet with a muffled thud. Fury mottled his face. "Are you insane? I won't hear of it. It isn't safe." He glared at his uncle. "How dare you make such a suggestion? Unspeakable things happen down there."

His uncle softly replied, "Psalm 118 says, 'The Lord is on my side; I will not fear: what can man do unto me?' Ellie will be perfectly safe. You can deliver her in a closed carriage with a bodyguard if you wish. Once inside the mission, every man there will fight to defend her should the need arise, which it won't." The zeal in the man's eyes made him look more like Joshua than ever. "Edward, Letitia, think. Who needs the Sierra Songbird more? Those who already know the way, the truth, and the life? Or the lost sheep?"

A glorious light crept into Charles Stanhope's face. "I will personally take Ellie to the mission." He raised a commanding hand when his wife started to protest. "The subject is closed. Marvin is right. Ellie can do more good with her songs and stories down there than we may ever know." He smiled at Maria, who had brought a silver tray holding frozen pudding to the table. "I suggest we finish our dinner and prevail on our songbird to favor us with a number."

To Ellie's surprise, Mrs. Stanhope and Edward subsided, but the storm clouds hanging heavy in their faces showed they didn't consider the matter settled. Ellie did. She had given her word.

Weary beyond belief from the day's events, Ellie found herself wound tightly after their guest left. Her brain raced like a caged squirrel. *Beryl. The* Chronicle *article. Chinatown. Marvin Stanhope's plea.* Knowing she would not sleep until she rid herself of the memories, Ellie snatched writing materials and wrote a letter to Tim, a letter in which she poured out all her wrought-up feelings.

At last she slept. The next morning, the hastily written missive began its journey to the Diamond S.

Chapter 21

A few days later, Edward stalked into the breakfast room where Ellie was having a solitary meal. He flung a copy of the *San Francisco Chronicle* on the table in front of Ellie. "Read this," he thundered. "How did that meddlesome reporter get wind of it?"

Ellie glanced down:

Sierra Songbird to Perform at Rescue Mission

The latest news about Ellianna Sterling, who has captured the hearts of San Franciscans with her incredible voice and sweet personality, is indeed shocking. Miss Sterling plans to visit one of the meanest streets in our city and sing at the Rescue Mission. The mission, which offers 'soup, soap, and salvation,' is operated by Marvin Stanhope, long considered eccentric for turning his back on society in favor of a life of service.

An unnamed source confirms that what began as a rumor is now fact. When asked why she would even consider such an outrageous venture the Sierra Songbird replied, "Jesus went to the lost sheep. Should I do less?"

This reporter is torn between applauding the young lady's courage and dashing to her rescue like a knight in the days of old.

"How can the reporter know this?" Ellie cried. "Who is his unnamed source?" She fixed an accusing stare on Edward. "The only person I told how I felt was you!"

The anger in Edward's face changed to chagrin. He clutched his head in both hands. "I was so upset about your going to the mission that I blurted it out to Beryl. Ellie, I am so sorry."

Appetite gone, Ellie pushed back from the table and slumped in her chair. "This must be her revenge for the speculation about us."

Edward dropped into a chair next to her. "It's more than speculation, Ellie. I've broken with Beryl for good. She blames you." A corner of his mouth lifted in a lopsided smile. "It really is your fault, you know. No man in his right mind would marry a woman like Beryl when there are girls like you in the world."

"Stop." She raised her hands in mute appeal. "You know how I feel about Joshua."

338

"Don't worry about it." Edward cocked one eyebrow and became his usual fun-loving self. "If good ol' Josh were anyone but my twin, I'd fall in love with you. He is, and I won't." A scowl replaced Edward's teasing expression. He folded his arms across his chest and added, "I can't say the same for the present pastor of Bayview Christian. Watch your step, Miss Sterling, or you'll be Mrs. Michael Yates in spite of yourself. He's determined to get to the top. What better way to achieve success than with the Sierra Songbird as his wife?"

Ellie didn't say so, but Edward's evaluation matched her opinion of Michael. He never lost an opportunity to praise her and send languishing looks her way. Suddenly lighthearted by Edward's promise not to fall in love with her, she brushed aside the thought of Michael, clasped her hands, and gave a mock sigh. "Oh, to be loved for myself alone, not just to help fulfill someone's ambitions."

Edward twirled an imaginary mustache in the best stage villain tradition. "Beware, my pretty. Greed and ambition lurk in the hearts of men."

Ellie laughed at his nonsense. "Are we practicing this morning as usual?"

Edward abandoned his dastardly role. "Of course. You want to sing your best for the derelicts as well as for society—unless I can talk you out of going to the mission."

"You can't."

"I know. You, young lady, are a very determined person."

A few hours later, Ellie had need of every ounce of determination she could muster. Maria appeared at her open door. Her dark eyes sparkled. "You have a visitor. Senor Yates is waiting in the library. Senora Stanhope says you are to come at once."

"Bother!" Ellie laid down her Bible. "Just when I thought I'd have time to study."

The Mexican girl came closer. "You read about *Jesús*, sí?"

"Sí." Ellie smiled at her. "Jesus is my best friend."

Maria touched the silver cross she wore. "I love Jesús, too. But I think Senor Yates wants to be more than a best friend." She clapped one hand over her mouth and left before Ellie could reply.

Unnerved by Maria's comment, Ellie reluctantly went down the curving stairway. Singing at Bayview Christian meant working closely with the Reverend Michael Yates. She'd known for some time he saw her as a means to an end, and it troubled her. If he'd come to declare his intentions to marry her, how could she turn him down without incurring his wrath? She entered the room lined with rare editions and fine paintings and chose a chair rather than the settee in order to distance herself from her uninvited guest.

After inquiring after Ellie's health as if she were an invalid, the young minister said, "Miss Ellie, I've come to lay my heart at your feet and beg for your hand in marriage. I need a wife." He gave her an ardent look. "In all my many travels I've found no one so eminently suitable as you."

Ellie covered a giggle with a cough. The first part of his proposal sounded like it had been lifted from an advice to the lovelorn article in the *Chronicle*. Ellie had started to read THREE EASY WAYS TO ASK A LADY TO MARRY YOU, but had been interrupted after the first suggestion: *"Be bold."*

I wonder what the other two ideas were. Ellie stifled another giggle. *Michael must not have read them either. Telling me he's found no one else suitable surely couldn't be part of the article.*

Michael paced the room, and his smooth voice painted their future in eloquent, glowing terms. Face aflame with zeal and self-importance, he ended by saying, "Think of it, Miss Ellie. There's no limit to what we can do together. We'll lead multitudes to Christ. First we conquer San Francisco, then the nation. I'll go down in history as one of the greatest preachers of all times." He placed one hand over his heart. "And you will be my inspiration."

Although disgusted by his conceit, the prospect of the glorious future he promised sliced through Ellie's common sense. What an opportunity to show those persecutors who had made her feel like Job's granddaughter!

As if sensing her response, Michael knelt at Ellie's side and captured her hands. His hazel eyes gleamed. "I'm determined to marry you. Help me fulfill my dreams."

Ellie came to earth with a dull thud. His dreams? What about hers? Even if she loved Michael, which she didn't, as his wife she'd never be more than a small star hitched to a flaming comet. "I don't love you."

He squeezed her hands. "You will." Confidence rang in every word.

It sounded to Ellie like a veiled threat. She remembered Edward's warning: *"Watch your step. . .or you'll be Mrs. Michael Yates in spite of yourself."* How could she convince him otherwise?

Tell him who your real father is, a little voice replied. *If Michael knew your background, he'd thank his lucky stars for saving him. Of course, telling him would also bring your house built on sand crashing down around you and end your career.*

Never! She snatched her hands free and exclaimed, "Michael, I love another man."

He leaped up and glared down at her, face redder than his hair. "Stanhope, I presume. Why have you been leading me on and making me think—"

Ellie shot out of her chair and planted her hands on her hips. She wanted to scream but kept her voice low. "Reverend Yates, I've never led you on. You're the one who has obviously planned a future and worked me in like the missing piece of a puzzle. I don't fit into your life. I never will."

A vein throbbed in Michael's throat. He gave an unpleasant laugh. "Edward Stanhope has nothing to offer you but a tarnished reputation. When you come to your senses you'll be knocking on my door, begging me to marry you. Just don't count on my still being available." He stomped out, leaving Ellie cold and shaken.

"Edward?" she whispered. "Reverend Yates thinks I'm in love with Edward." Unwilling to meet anyone until she could control herself, Ellie took refuge in her room. She couldn't set Michael straight without betraying Joshua. Edward knew she loved his twin. His parents did not. Ellie shivered. Would Michael add to the speculation already running rampant about her and Edward? What if it reached Joshua? The idea appalled her.

Ellie clenched and unclenched her hands in an effort to relax. "As long as Reverend Yates believes I may come running to him, he will hold his tongue," she told herself. "I should be safe from unfounded rumors—at least for now—because of his pride."

Tired of the whole mess, Ellie flung herself on her bed. Why must life be so complicated? If again given the choice between the Diamond S and San Francisco, which road would she take? There, she'd been Ellie Sterling, adopted daughter of Matt and Sarah. Here, the city lay at her slippered feet.

Honesty compelled her to confess, "Lord, I don't know. I miss Josh and Tim and home, but. . ."

Ellie fell into a troubled sleep with her questions unanswered. Hours later, she awakened from a jumbled dream crying out, "What would San Francisco say if they knew me as Ellie Stoddard, not Ellie Sterling?"

Late one afternoon, drumming hoofbeats jerked Josh from the sermon he'd been preparing. A clear voice shouted, "Whoa, Blue!"

Josh sprang out of his chair and into the yard.

Tim Sterling shot out of the saddle, eyes blazing. "Ellie's gotta come home. She's being ruined and coulda got herself killed." He coughed and slapped dust from his pants. "Gimme some water. I'm dry as a bone."

Dread filled Josh's soul. "Come in before someone hears you." Once inside, he brought a tall glass of water and motioned for Tim to sit down. "What's this all about?"

Tim drained the glass and dropped into a chair, breathing hard. He tossed Josh a wrinkled letter. "See for yourself."

Josh unfolded the pages and silently began reading:

Dear Tim,

I hardly know where to begin. San Francisco is both breathtaking and terrible. Thanks to the Stanhopes and a reporter who heard me sing, I've been praised until I'm in danger of being spoiled. Sometimes I wonder why I'm here, but most of the time I'm too busy to think clearly. Besides, I know God wants me here.

I don't like being talked about, but I'm learning to accept it. Being the target of gossip isn't new to me, and it's the price required for rising to the top, as I'm determined to do.

Josh stopped reading. Disappointment swept through him. "I hate hearing Ellie talk like that. It sounds as if she's already starting to change."

"Yeah." Tim slumped in his chair and stuck his lower lip out. "I'd like to yank her back here where she belongs."

"So would I." Josh returned to the letter:

My life is mountaintops and valleys. Edward has been wonderful, but his fiancée doesn't like me. She's the only one who makes me feel like an intruder. Definitely a valley experience!

I had an adventure late this afternoon. I decided to walk from the music studio to the Stanhopes. I got turned around in the fog and ended up in Chinatown.

"Chinatown!" Josh felt himself pale. The writing blurred. The letter fell to his lap.

Tim hurtled from his chair and paced the floor. "If a policeman hadn't found her, who knows what would've happened? That's not all," he raved. "She's gonna go sing at your uncle's Rescue Mission. Red Fallon told me what it's like down there." Worry lines added years to his face. "I don't care if your dad and brother are going with her. Why don't you tell Ellie to get back here where she belongs?"

Josh spread his hands helplessly. "I can't do that, Tim. No one can but God."

Tim turned his back on Josh and said in a muffled voice, "I know, but He'd better hurry up before something awful happens to her."

Josh got up and gave Tim's shoulder a comforting pat. "God knows best, even when we don't understand. I get the feeling Ellie thinks San Francisco is the pot of gold at the end of the rainbow."

"More like fool's gold." Tim whirled toward Josh. "Why don't you go find out what's happening? Don't tell Ellie you're coming. Just show up." He didn't wait for a reply, but glanced out the door. "It's getting late. I gotta go. Don't forget what I said."

Josh watched his young friend vault to Blue's saddle and ride off in the threatening dusk. Forget? As if he could. Tim's startling suggestion and the news about Ellie had triggered temptation. Why not chuck his job, go to San Francisco, and fight the brother Ellie found "wonderful" for her love?

"Sorry, Lord," he mumbled. But when morning followed a sleepless night, Josh had reached a decision. His trial period would be over in a few weeks. He'd give Luther Talbot and his whiners an ultimatum: Either Preacher Josh would be free to minister outside the building as well as inside, or they could get themselves another man. And the day his six months ended, Josh would catch the first train west and leave his future in God's hands.

Chapter 22

A glorious rainbow hung over San Francisco on the morning of the day Ellie was to sing at Marvin Stanhope's mission. Ellie drank in the sight from her bedroom window. She needed to talk with Mrs. Stanhope, but couldn't tear herself away until the last shimmering remnant disappeared.

Ellie found Mrs. Stanhope reading in the library. The girl had long since discovered the way to her sponsor's heart was to ask for advice, so she went right to the point. "I know you don't approve of my going to the Rescue Mission, but I need your help."

Mrs. Stanhope sighed. "I don't approve, but Charles assures me you won't be in any danger. I must admit that good has come from the *Chronicle* article about your singing there. Tickets for our Occidental Mission Home for Girls benefit concert are sold out. There's also a long waiting list." Her blue eyes gleamed with excitement.

Ellie remembered her experience in Chinatown and shuddered. "I'd sing my heart out to help Margaret Culbertson's work."

"Good for you!" The approval in the older woman's voice thrilled Ellie. In the weeks she'd been in San Francisco, her patroness had gone from pride in her protégée to obvious fondness. After the first concert, she'd made Ellie feel like a daughter of the house. Ellie felt red flags fly in her hot cheeks. God willing, perhaps one day Mrs. Stanhope would be willing to accept her as Josh's wife.

"What is it you need?" Mrs. Stanhope inquired.

Ellie put aside her daydreams. "I need advice on how to dress tonight. Should I wear a simple calico? I don't want to be so dressed up the men will be uncomfortable."

Mrs. Stanhope fitted her well-manicured fingers together. "Let me think." She wrinkled her forehead. "You're right in not wanting to cause embarrassment. It isn't the socially acceptable thing to do."

Ellie suppressed a grin. Leave it to Mrs. Stanhope to think of that.

"On the other hand, I'm sure the. . .uh. . .residents at the mission have seen your picture in the *Chronicle*. If you dress too plainly, the men may think you feel they aren't worthy of fine clothes."

"I hadn't thought of that." Ellie looked at her sponsor with respect. It seemed out of character, yet why should it? Autocratic and determined to have her own way, Mrs. Stanhope had a warm heart, as evidenced by her concern for the young Chinese girls in the city.

"Let's go look over your wardrobe."

"All right." Ellie trotted up the stairs after Mrs. Stanhope.

One by one, Ellie's lovely gowns were inspected. "Wear this new white muslin," Mrs. Stanhope advised. "It's pretty but simple. Wear a yellow sash, and I'll order a corsage of yellow roses."

A rush of admiration for her contradictory benefactress filled Ellie. "I don't suppose you would want to come with us," she blurted out.

"I? Go to the Rescue Mission? I wouldn't be caught—" She broke off.

Ellie saw an unexpected struggle between dismissing the idea and breaking through layers of conventionality. It encouraged her to say, "Perhaps you'd find out why Joshua's life changed after going there."

Mrs. Stanhope sniffed. "I hardly think that would happen."

"Please?" Ellie felt as if she were fighting for her future. "Just this once? I'd really like you to be there for me." *And for Josh,* she silently added.

"My goodness, but you're persistent." A long-suffering look etched itself into Mrs. Stanhope's face. "If it means that much to you, I suppose I should go, although it's against my better judgment." She bustled out. Ellie wanted to cheer.

❧

Ellie would never forget the expression on Marvin Stanhope's face as his sister-in-law swept into the Rescue Mission. It matched her husband's and son's disbelief when she had blandly announced she planned to accompany them to hear Ellie sing. But after the first shocked moment, Marvin rose to the occasion.

"Thank you for coming." He led his guests to chairs at the front of a shabby room that smelled of cleanliness and boiling coffee. To Ellie's relief, both the room and its occupants had obviously been subject to strong soap and water. Mrs. Stanhope didn't turn a hair, even when a motley collection of unfortunates filed in and filled the chairs. Others stood at the back. It seemed as if every derelict for miles around, as well as the *Chronicle* reporter who sang Ellie's praises, had come to hear the Sierra Songbird.

Edward sat down at the old but surprisingly well-tuned piano. Ellie had carefully selected a program designed to appeal to this particular audience. "Please sing along if you know the words," she invited. At first no one except Edward and the newspaper reporter responded. Then grumbling bass and cracked baritone voices joined in on "Aura Lee," "Sweet Genevieve," "Beautiful Dreamer," "Silver Threads among the Gold," and a dozen others.

Ellie's heart swelled. Long ago in this very room, Red Fallon had met the Master because of a young man who fearlessly braved a dark alley and rescued him. Her pride in Joshua multiplied a hundredfold.

She gradually shifted from ballads to hymns. At last, Ellie picked up her guitar and signaled to Edward, who joined his parents. After singing "Amazing Grace," she struck the first notes of "It Is Well with My Soul." A quick glance into the sin-hardened faces with seeking eyes stilled her fingers. These men knew far too much of tragedy. They didn't need a song with a history of death and loss.

Ellie's heart pounded. "I'd like to end with 'The Ninety and Nine,' one of my favorite hymns." She played a single note, laid her guitar aside, and began to sing:

"There were ninety and nine that safely lay
In the shelter of the fold.
But one was out on the hills away,
Far off from the gates of gold.
Away on the mountains wild and bare.
Away from the tender Shepherd's care."

Feeling she was battling despair and hopelessness, Ellie continued her song. She saw expressions change. Dead-looking eyes sparked to life. The reporter leaned forward as if to make sure he didn't miss a note. Mrs. Stanhope brushed away tears. Her husband radiated satisfaction. Edward looked more serious than Ellie had ever seen him.

She triumphantly sang the final words:

"And the angels echoed around the throne,
'Rejoice, for the Lord brings back His own!
Rejoice, for the Lord brings back His own!'"

A great stillness fell over the room. The bubble of a huge coffeepot on a nearby stove sounded loud in Ellie's ears. Then a storm of applause reached the rafters. Ellie's tears flowed, and she stumbled to a seat.

Marvin Stanhope walked to the front. His face glowed with love. "There is greater rejoicing in heaven over one lost sheep who is returned to the fold than for all those who never go astray. Please bow your heads."

A ripple of movement crept through the audience.

Ellie could scarcely contain her feelings when Marvin said, "Tonight the Good Shepherd is seeking those who are lost. He is not out on some wild, bare mountain or in a deep valley, but here with us. Lord, if there's one in this place who is willing to follow You, let that person come forward."

After what felt like an eternity, a wizened old man shuffled to the front. "Pray for me," he said.

Ellie heard little of the prayer that followed. Her heart thudded against the walls of her chest until it seemed it would burst. Had God led her to San Francisco, not for fame and fortune, but to teach her what Joshua had learned long ago? Service to God through serving His children was what really mattered.

≈

A few days later, Josh sat at his table, reading the excited letter from Ellie for the fifth time. It had taken that many readings to fully grasp her news. What magic had Ellie used to persuade Mother to go with her to the Rescue Mission, a place she'd sneered at for years? His heart leaped. Could it be the first step in reconciliation?

"Yoo-hoo! Preacher Josh, are you home?" a girlish voice called, interrupting Josh's fervent prayer of thanks.

Josh gritted his teeth. He'd always heard trouble came in threes. Trouble came in twos in Madera: Luther and Amy Talbot. He stepped outside. There was no way under heaven he'd allow Amy inside the parsonage unless others were present. What did she want now? She'd plagued him with invitations until his excuses had worn threadbare.

Amy flitted toward him, a vision in pale pink from parasol to slippers. Lovely, except for her cold, china-blue eyes. "May we go inside? It's warm for October."

"We'll go to the church."

She pouted. "Abby Fallon's practicing on the organ. I want to talk to you alone."

Josh inwardly shuddered. "I hardly think your father would approve of that."

Amy fluttered her eyelashes and looked sly. "He doesn't have to know."

"You think anyone in Madera can do anything without being found out? Besides, I'm on trial here." He regretted the words the second they popped out.

Amy raised a delicate eyebrow. "Father won't dismiss you unless I say so."

Josh didn't trust himself to answer. He led Amy into the church, ushered her into a pew at the back, and sat down beside her. "Keep practicing," he called to Abby. "You won't bother us."

"She bothers me," Amy grumbled, then looked down at her gloved hands. "She can't hear us, can she?"

A warning bell rang in Josh's brain. "No."

Amy's eyes gleamed. "I want to ask you a question. If a girl—a young woman—wants a certain man, is it unmaidenly for her to ask him to marry her?"

Josh gaped like a fish out of water.

"Well?"

Josh found his voice and got to his feet at the same time. He purposely raised his voice, loud enough for Abby to hear. "Miss Talbot, I hope you are jesting. It would not only be unmaidenly, but improper for a young woman to ask a man to marry her."

It didn't seem to faze the bold girl. "Even when marrying her means saving the man she wants from being fired?"

Josh could barely conceal his dislike. "Absolutely. Now if you'll excuse me, I need to speak with Abby." He stepped back into the aisle, but her shrill voice followed him.

"You'll rue this day!" She elbowed her way past him and ran out of the church, banging the door behind her.

Josh walked to the front of the church and stared at Abby.

"What's Amy up to now?" she asked.

"That spoiled young lady thinks she can have everything she wants, including me."

Abby's giggle brought a reluctant grin. "I probably shouldn't have told you," Josh apologized.

Abby sobered, and a worried look came into her dark eyes. "I'm glad you did. Knowing Amy, you may need a witness." She rested her hands on the keyboard. "Don't forget that a woman scorned, especially one like Amy, is big trouble."

"Let's forget her and talk about the hymns for Sunday," Josh suggested. "A much more pleasant subject."

Abby nodded, but before they finished deciding on what songs best fit Josh's subject, the door slammed open. Luther Talbot stormed in with Amy right behind him.

"Reverend Stanhope, what's this I hear about you insulting my daughter?" he bellowed. "She came home in tears and refused to repeat whatever it is you said to her. You may do things differently in San Francisco, but we don't stand for such here."

Josh felt anger begin at his toes and crawl its way up. "Keep your voice down. This is the house of God." He ignored Luther's gasp and fixed his gaze on Amy's smirking face. "Tell your father the truth, or I shall."

Amy's eyes widened, and she put on an aggrieved air. "Why, Preacher Josh, whatever do you mean?"

Sickened by her pretense, Josh turned to Luther. "Mr. Talbot, is your daughter in the habit of asking men to marry her?"

Luther's jaw dropped. "What are you talking about?"

Josh didn't give an inch. "I'd hoped never to repeat our little conversation, but since Amy chooses to play innocent, you need to know what happened. I did not insult her. I did tell her it's unmaidenly and improper for a young woman to ask a man to marry her—and only after she asked. Mrs. Fallon heard what I said."

Luther grabbed his daughter by the shoulders and shook her. "Is that true?"

"I was only teasing the preacher," she whimpered. "He took it all wrong."

Josh's temper boiled over. "Was it also teasing when you asked if it would still be inappropriate if marrying her meant saving the man she wanted from being fired?"

Amy burst into sobs, freed herself, and stumbled out the open door.

Josh watched Luther's prominent Adam's apple go up and down before the gaunt man said, "I may have been a bit hasty." He turned on his heel and marched out, his spine stiffer than a hickory walking stick.

Abby's laughter released some of Josh's fury. She rocked back and forth on the organ bench, then wiped away tears. Mirth, however, soon gave way to concern. "This isn't going to endear you to either Luther or Amy."

Josh stared at her. "It also won't improve my chances of staying on at Christ the Way." He walked out and headed for the livery stable. The best medicine for getting the Talbots and their doings out of his system was a long, hard gallop on Sultan.

Chapter 23

Joshua Stanhope stared at the red-circled date on his calendar. Tomorrow, November 30, ended his six-month trial period at Christ the Way. And tomorrow he'd board the train to San Francisco.

Would he be back? The grim-faced church board had silently listened when Josh laid down his conditions for further service: freedom to serve outside the church as well as inside. But Luther Talbot's noncommittal "We'll let you know" indicated that unless God intervened, Josh would be out of a job.

A pang shot through him. "Lord, I've come to love the church and most of the people. Glad I'm getting away though. I can hardly wait to see my family and Ellie."

Fear nibbled at his anticipation. What would he find? The girl he loved or a changed young woman?

Josh brushed the disloyal thought aside but fought depression all the way to San Francisco. Mother had been friendly when she and Edward came to kidnap Ellie, but how did she feel now that she'd gotten what she wanted?

When the carriage reached the mansion on Nob Hill at dusk, Josh paid the driver and strode up the walk and onto the porch. He thought of the lost son who came home to his father's house from a far country, sick and uncertain of his welcome. Although Josh's circumstances differed, new understanding of the young man's feelings filled him. *Why didn't I tell my family I was coming? Father would have rushed out to greet me, just like the lost son's father,* he reflected. Josh raised and dropped the heavy knocker. The door opened.

"Senor Joshua," Maria gasped. "You are home?"

"Yes, Maria." He stepped into the brightly lit hall. "Where is the family?"

"In the drawing room." She scuttled ahead of him, talking all the way. "I do not think they are expecting you. Senorita Ellie would have told me."

Josh thanked her and pushed open the heavy drawing room doors. Heart beating like a bass drum, he stepped inside, leaving the doors open. "Howdy, folks." *What a dunce. I haven't been home in months, and I say howdy?*

Three shocked faces turned toward him. Mother's hand flew to her throat. Edward and Father leaped up and met him halfway across the room. Father gripped Josh's hand. "Welcome home, Son."

Edward pounded on his shoulder. "Great to see you, old man. Why didn't you tell us you were coming?"

"I wanted to surprise you."

Mother's chin wobbled. "You certainly have, Joshua. I—we've missed you."

Relief threatened to buckle Josh's knees. He hurried across the costly rug and knelt beside her chair. "I've missed you too, Mother. All of you." He looked around the lavishly furnished room. "Where's Ellie—Miss Sterling?"

A rustle behind him whipped Josh around. A soft voice said, "I'm here."

Josh stared. The white-robed girl in the doorway looked like she'd stepped out of a painting. "Ellie?"

"Don't you know me?" She glided to him and held out her hand.

Josh folded it in his. "I'm not sure," he told her. "You look different—"

"Of course she looks different," his mother interrupted. "Surely you didn't expect her to look the same as when she lived on a ranch. Not that there's anything wrong with ranches," she hastily added. Her unaccustomed tact surprised Josh. Evidently Ellie wasn't the only person who had changed.

"I'm glad you've come," Ellie said.

The feel of her soft hand in his and the expression in her eyes made Josh feel better.

In the days that followed, however, he realized how much Ellie had changed. Not only in dress, but in the confident way she carried herself. . .and how she fit into city life. Josh searched in vain for the Ellie he'd fallen in love with: the girl in the yellow calico gown that made her look like a western meadowlark. Did she still exist? Or was San Francisco changing the Sierra Songbird into a society peacock?

Early one chilly morning, Josh climbed high atop a hill overlooking the Pacific Ocean. "Lord, it seems everyone at Bayview Christian expects me to come back, except Reverend Michael Yates. I no longer belong in San Francisco. I can't stay, even if it means losing Ellie—and it may. She seems so thrilled with her success here."

Josh stared unseeingly at the rolling waves breaking against the shore far below. "I feel like a man without a country. I want to go back to Madera, but surely I'd have heard if they plan to keep me." He groaned. "If they don't, how can I ask Ellie to give up all this for a preacher without a church?"

Hours later, the cold drove Josh back to the mansion on Nob Hill. Strange. After only six months, he felt more at home in the Madera parsonage than in the home where he'd been born. He raised his head and clenched his jaw, determined to corral Ellie.

So far, trying to get her alone had been futile. His opportunity came that afternoon. Edward was out and about; Father at his shipping office. After lunch, Mother retired to her room for a nap. Josh told Ellie, "We need to talk."

Her eyes darkened. "I know." She led him to the library and motioned him to a chair, as if she were the daughter of the house and he a mere guest. "How's everyone on the Diamond S?"

"Fine, but I don't want to talk about them. When are you coming back to Madera where you belong?" Josh saw her stiffen at his blunt question.

"I belong here." Ellie leaned forward. "I'm doing a great deal of good with my singing. Everyone says so."

"More than in Madera? Is singing to throngs of people more important than seeing lives changed at the hand-hewn altar in Christ the Way?"

Every trace of color fled from her face. She stared at if seeing Josh for the first time.

"Tim thinks you're settling for fool's gold instead of real gold. Has all this glitter spoiled you?" He waved at the luxury surrounding them.

The harsh words hung in the air. Ellie's eyes looked enormous. "Do you think so?"

"I don't know. I—"

A tap on the door cut into Josh's reply. He got to his feet. "Yes?"

Maria entered, holding a letter. "For you, Senor. It came this morning, but you were not here." She handed it to Josh and scurried out.

Josh glanced at the envelope. His world turned black.

Ellie slipped from her chair and came to his side. "Is it from the church board?"

"No. From Tim." He tossed her the unopened message. "He's probably blasting Luther and his buddies for getting rid of me. Here, you read it." He watched Ellie slit the envelope and unfold the single page. Tears sparkled on her lashes. She glanced down and began to laugh. "If this isn't just like Tim! No greeting, just this:

"Luther called a secret meeting of those who don't want you here. Red got wind of it. He rounded up members and a bunch of cowhands and sheepherders who like you.

"They busted into the meeting. Red up and told the board Jesus came to save folks with the gumption to admit they're sinners. He said God's love ain't s'posed to be kept locked up inside the church. You shoulda heard folks cheer!

"It shook the board up (specially when Red hinted a new board could get picked). Anyhow, they voted to let you run things your way. Hurry home before they change their minds."

Josh gave a great shout. "Well, God bless Red Fallon!" He gently grasped Ellie's shoulders. "Now that I have a job again, will you marry me, Ellie? Right away?"

Ellie clasped her hands around his arm and gazed into his face. She looked stricken. "I want to marry you, but until God lets me know my work here is done, I can't."

Josh stared down into her troubled face. The sincerity in her voice could not be ignored. "I can't argue with what you feel God is telling you to do, Ellie. Just make sure you're hearing Him right." Josh bent and kissed her upturned lips, then released her and left the room.

❧

Ellie watched Josh go. She longed to rush after him and erase the bitter disappointment in his eyes. She could not, so she flew to her room for refuge. Her respite, however, was short lived. Just before dinner, Maria appeared.

"The senor from the newspaper is waiting to see you."

Ellie rebelled. "Tell him I can't see him."

Maria shook her head. "He said it is *muy* important."

"All right." Ellie smoothed her hair and went back to the library.

The reporter's sober countenance frightened her. "Miss Sterling, the *Chronicle* received an anonymous message today. I regret bringing it to you, but others may have also received it." He handed her a sheet of paper.

Bold black words stared up at her: "*Ask the Sierra Songbird about her real father and jailbird brothers.*" The page slipped to the floor. Ellie wanted to flee. Just when she thought herself over the past, a dozen malicious words had brought it all back.

"What do you want me to do with this?" the reporter asked.

An old saying came to mind. *Tell the truth and shame the devil.* "You need to hear and write the truth." Ellie saw admiration sneak into his watching eyes. "Come back this evening after I have time to talk with the Stanhopes."

He nodded and left. Ellie sank to the settee. "Lord, I dread telling them, especially Mrs. Stanhope. Well, whatever happens, I'll be free from the fear of discovery. I just hope it doesn't cause more trouble for Joshua." She went to her room and donned her prettiest dress. Somewhat calmed by the knowledge that God was still in control, she went down to dinner. When the meal ended, she quietly said, "I have something to tell you. May we go into the library, please?"

Mrs. Stanhope looked startled. "Of course." She rose and led the way. With a silent prayer for help, Ellie waited until everyone was seated in the restful room.

"The *Chronicle* received an anonymous message today," she began. "It said to ask me about my real father and brothers." She fixed her gaze on Mrs. Stanhope and told the story of Ellie Stoddard who became Ellie Sterling. She spared none of the details, even though they seemed more sordid than ever when related in this luxurious setting. Ellie watched Mrs. Stanhope's face grow mottled with rage, change to disbelief, soften with compassion, and grow tight-lipped, but the older woman didn't interrupt.

Ellie ended with, "I'm sorry for the embarrassment this will cause you, but I intend to give the reporter the full story. He's coming back tonight." Her self-control broke. Tears dripped. "I wish I'd told you everything before I agreed to come here."

Mrs. Stanhope turned to Joshua and glared. "Did you know about Ellie's past?"

A steely look came into his gray eyes. "Yes, but not how bad it really was."

"And you didn't see fit to tell me."

Ellie cringed. Would this cause another rift between mother and son?

Josh's lips curved into a smile of incredible sweetness. "Stoddard or Sterling, Ellie is the most wonderful girl in the world."

"Amen," Edward put in.

"Do be quiet, Edward. This doesn't concern you."

To Ellie's dismay, he began to laugh. "Wake up, Mother. The truth is written all over Josh's face. Ellie's going to be my sister, and I couldn't be happier!"

Mrs. Stanhope pinned Ellie with a stare. "Do you love my son? Has he told your father—Mr. Sterling—that he wants to marry you?"

"Y—yes, but I haven't said I'd—"

Mrs. Stanhope went into her take-charge mode. "Then I suggest you do so at once. No one will dare cast aspersions on a future Stanhope." She stood and started toward the door. "Charles, tell the reporter to drop a hint about Joshua and Ellie in his story." To Ellie's utter amazement Mrs. Stanhope's eyes twinkled. Genuine affection lurked in their depths. "This has been a most surprising evening, but I always wanted a daughter. With a little more training, you'll do nicely, my dear."

She swept out, leaving Edward cackling like a laying hen and Ellie in a state of shock.

Mr. Stanhope quietly said, "I couldn't be more pleased, Joshua. Edward, stop laughing and come with me. Your brother and Ellie need to be alone."

The door closed behind them. Through blinding tears, Ellie saw Joshua coming toward her. The next moment she was safe in his arms.

❧

The next issue of the *Chronicle* carried a story that Ellie considered a masterpiece:

SCURRILOUS ATTEMPT TO CLIP
SIERRA SONGBIRD'S WINGS FAILS

A vicious effort to discredit Miss Ellianna Sterling has come to naught. An anonymous message, "Ask the Sierra Songbird about her real father and jailbird brothers," aroused the ire of this justice-loving reporter. In an exclusive interview, Miss Sterling frankly stated she was born in St. Louis, Missouri, as Ellianna Stoddard and was raised in poverty. At age eleven, she and her younger brother came to live with their stepbrother and stepsister in Madera.

Matthew Sterling—owner of the largest cattle ranch in the San Joaquin

Valley and married to Miss Sterling's stepsister—legally adopted Ellianna and Timothy.

While it's true that Miss Sterling's older brothers were jailed, they were soon cleared and released from the trumped-up charge.

Cowards who refuse to sign messages need not send them to the Chronicle*—especially to this reporter. Nay, go ahead and send them. They make a perfect lining for the bottom of birdcages.*

On a happier note, tittle-tattle has it that wedding bells may someday ring for Joshua Stanhope and the Sierra Songbird. When asked about the rumor, the elder Stanhopes and their son Edward simply smiled and looked pleased.

Chapter 24

San Francisco took up arms in Ellie's defense after the scorching *Chronicle* article appeared. Letters to the editor poured in. Then the enterprising reporter tracked down the envelope that brought the anonymous letter.

It was postmarked Madera.

"Amy Talbot probably wrote it," Josh said. "The *Fresno Expositor* and the *Madera Tribune* both ran the article and mentioned the postmark. Eventually the culprit will be exposed, punishment enough."

Ellie agreed. She knew only too well how it felt to be the subject of gossip.

The next day, she hid tears and told Josh good-bye. "Your visit was too short."

"I need to get back to Christ the Way." Josh brushed away the lone tear Ellie couldn't hold back. "It's only a few weeks until Christmas." He kissed her ring finger. "I'll have something special for you when you come home."

"All I want is you."

Josh's eyes twinkled. "You already have that!" A quick kiss, and he was gone.

The following morning, Ellie sat by her window and stared out into rain mixed with sleet. Tree branches bent and shivered in the wind. Ellie already missed Josh. Homesickness for the Diamond S and the promontory where she'd spent so many happy hours overwhelmed her. She longed for rolling rangeland and canyons instead of tall buildings and cobblestone streets. For clear, crisp mornings untouched by fog.

Ellie wrapped herself into a colorful shawl Solita had made. The red, white, and emerald green reminded Ellie of Christmas. She closed her eyes and thought of last year's program at Christ the Way. Everyone had brought gifts to the altar. Not gold, frankincense, or myrrh, but food, clothing, treasured toys, and money—some from those who had little to spare—for a family who had lost their home and possessions to fire.

Ellie hadn't written even one song since she'd come to San Francisco. Now words tumbled into her mind. She snatched writing materials and let them pour out:

Tell me, kind shepherds, when you came to the manger,
What gifts did you bring to the new little stranger

Who quietly lay asleep on the hay?
We had no fine gifts on that glorious night
When the fields were ablaze with a heavenly light.
So our voices we raised in worship and praise.
Tell me, oh Wise Men who came from afar,
What did you bring when you followed the Star,
And found Him that day in the house where He lay?
Gold, frankincense, myrrh
From far distant lands.
We bowed down in wonder and kissed His small hands.
Tell me, good people, what gifts do you bring,
To the Savior who loves us; the King of all kings?
Will you open your hearts and invite Him to stay—
Or, like the innkeeper, turn Him away?
Or, like the innkeeper, turn Him away?

The perfect title came to mind: "Ballad for a King." Ellie bowed her head. "Lord, You've given me the gift of song. I'm trying to use it for You, but I want to do something more to honor Your Son. I just don't know what."

"Forgive."

The word pierced Ellie's soul. She let tears flow while she took a fresh sheet of paper and wrote: *I forgive you, Pa. Ellie.* She placed it in an envelope that she sealed and addressed. Then she tucked her poem inside her dress to nestle above her heart and ran downstairs.

Warmed by the poem's presence, Ellie buried her letter among the others to be posted. Her heart pumped with joy. "Lord, I haven't felt this clean since I was baptized in the stream on the Diamond S. Pa probably won't reply, but I'm free." She danced upstairs and into her room.

Mrs. Stanhope sat by the window. Her hands nervously pleated and smoothed a fold of her costly skirt. "Ellie, I have to tell you something."

Dread shot through Ellie. "Is Josh hurt?"

"No, it's something else. Would it break your heart to spend Christmas here?"

Ellie's knees gave way. She dropped to the bed. "Why?"

"Governor Markham has asked for a private musicale at our home. It's your chance of a lifetime." Mrs. Stanhope sighed. "Unfortunately, the governor and his wife are only free on Christmas Eve."

Ellie's dreams for the holidays fled. How could she say no when Mrs. Stanhope had done so much for her? Ellie had grown to love Joshua's mother since being welcomed to the family. She'd also seen the older woman slowly become a more understanding person.

"You don't have to stay." Josh's mother rose and patted Ellie's hand. "Pray about it and do what you feel is right. We won't hold it against you if you go home as planned." She frowned. "I've known Henry Markham for years and have already told him you might not be available. He should have picked a better time." She marched out.

Ellie stared after her. The unexpected advice to pray and willingness to leave the decision in Ellie's hands were more effective than pleading or reminders of duty. "Lord, how will everyone at home feel, especially Joshua?" Her throat constricted. "Besides, if I stay here, I'll be so disappointed I won't be able to sing."

She stood and started for the door, intending to tell Mrs. Stanhope she couldn't give up her plans. Yet a feeling that more than Governor Markham's whim hung on her decision stopped her. The tumult in her soul gradually stilled. She bowed her head and whispered through her unhappiness, "I'll stay."

"Perhaps you can go home for New Year's," Mr. Stanhope said when Ellie announced her decision, but Edward shook his head.

"Sorry, Ellie." He looked genuinely regretful. "The only time we could reserve the Palace Hotel is on New Year's Day. I know you sing for more than money, but this performance will bring in an incredible sum. It will also be your largest audience."

Ellie could barely hide her distress. She couldn't afford to turn down such an opportunity. She'd had to dip into her slow-growing savings too many times. She also thought about the spectators. The rich as well as those at the Rescue Mission needed to hear the gospel. Perhaps one among them would be touched by her singing. "All right, but after that, I need to go home."

"Speaking of going, we need to go practice," Edward said. "How about right now?"

"Of course."

The afternoon sped by. Mrs. Stanhope's news and Ellie's turmoil had driven away all thought of her poem until she went up to change for dinner. She removed her dress and shook it. No page fell to the rug. Ellie searched her room and retraced her steps from earlier that day without success. "A servant must have found and disposed of it," she decided. "It's foolish to inquire about a scribbled piece of paper. I can write it again." The hustle and bustle of the upcoming holidays, however, pushed it from her mind. So much to do. So many places to go.

By Christmas Eve, all Ellie wanted was to lie on her bed, look out into the star-filled sky, and think of the Christmas Star that shone close to two thousand years earlier. Instead, she donned a new yellow silk gown and filled the drawing room with music. Governor Markham, his wife, and the other guests called her back for encore after encore.

Free at last, Ellie stole away from the adoring crowd and escaped to her bedroom. The contrast between the merriment and the first Christmas saddened her. "Father, does anyone here except me think of the humble stable where Your Son was born?" She pressed her face to the window, glad for its cool touch. "Joshua is right. I've been dazzled by the glitter. Jesus said, 'Where your treasure is, there will your heart be also.' Well, my heart and treasure are in Madera. Lord, how long must I stay here?" Discouraged and lonely, she cried herself to sleep.

꙰

New Year's came and went. Ellie surpassed herself at the Palace Hotel concert, but once the excitement of performing in such a splendid place died, she grew restless. God showed no sign of delivering her. "I'll stay because I feel it's Your will," she prayed, "but it would be easier if I knew why." Heart heavy with unshed tears, even the familiar admonition, *"Trust Me,"* failed to bring comfort.

A few days later, Mrs. Stanhope summoned Ellie to the library. Ellie had never seen her in such a state. "Ellie, we have wronged you."

"It's my fault." Edward held out a printed piece of sheet music that read: *"Ballad for a King," by Ellianna Sterling. Music by Ludwig Karl and Edward Stanhope.*

Ellie blinked. "What—how. . . ?"

Edward paced the floor. "I found your poem on the staircase and showed it to a composer friend. Ludwig said it had worth. We set it to music."

Ellie clapped her hands. "That's wonderful!" She turned her attention to Letitia. "But why did you say you've wronged me?"

Tears spilled down the older woman's face. She shook her head and didn't reply.

Edward stopped pacing. "Mother was thrilled when I told her. She wanted to rush to you with the news. So did I—until I realized what it meant. Ludwig predicts it will bring you large royalties and open the door for you to write other songs."

Ellie felt she stood at the edge of a mystery. "I still don't understand."

"You've been good for all of us, especially me." Edward's eyes glistened. "Ludwig wants me to continue as his collaborator."

"What exciting news," Ellie cried, but Edward shuffled his feet and looked uncomfortable.

"It's only part of the story. This is the only printed copy of your song. I made Ludwig promise to keep it secret for a time. I also selfishly convinced Mother that we needed to keep you here as long as we could—even though Josh had slipped and mentioned your dream of helping your brother. Don't you see, Ellie? This opens the way for you to go home. You can write anywhere."

Ellie's brain whirled. "Why are you telling me this now?"

He looked ashamed. "You'll have to sign a contract for the song to be published. Anyway, Mother insisted you be told. She will tell you why."

Mrs. Stanhope dabbed at her eyes and sent Ellie a pleading look. "I wanted to believe Edward was right. I hoped your being here might bring Joshua home, even though deep in my heart I knew it wouldn't happen. Remember the night at the Rescue Mission when you sang 'The Ninety and Nine'?"

Ellie thought of Josh's mother brushing away tears. "Yes."

Mrs. Stanhope sniffled. "I can't explain it, but the story of Jesus leaving the flock and going to help the lost sheep reminded me of Joshua when he said he was going to Madera."

Ellie couldn't have been more shocked if the roof had opened and a meteorite had hurled into the quiet library. Her heart hammered with understanding. God had led her to San Francisco for unknown reasons, but none as important as this.

Mrs. Stanhope continued. "After Edward showed me 'Ballad for a King,' I made a copy of it. I didn't tell him, but I read it again and again, especially the last stanza:

"Tell me, good people, what gifts do you bring,
To the Savior who loves us; the King of all kings?
Will you open your hearts and invite Him to stay—
Or, like the innkeeper, turn Him away?
Or, like the innkeeper, turn Him away?"

"I've always tried to do right and help others, but I've realized I'm just like the innkeeper." Letitia raised her tear-stained face. "No more. This morning, I gave Jesus a gilt-edged invitation to live in my heart."

Ellie felt torn between the desire to weep for joy and shout with laughter. How like Mrs. Stanhope to surrender her life to the Lord in such a manner! Ellie sprang from her chair, ran across the room, and knelt at the woman's side. "I am so happy!" She clasped Letitia's hands in her own. "This is the greatest gift you could give to God, me, and"—her lips trembled—"to Joshua."

"He already knows. I sent a telegram an hour ago." Mrs. Stanhope turned to Edward with a look of undeniable longing. "Now if only—"

Edward raised his hands in mock protest. "Don't preach, Mother. One minister in the family is plenty." But Ellie noticed an unaccustomed softness in his attitude. Her heart throbbed. Perhaps someday Edward would—

"*Trust Me.*"

The words rang in Ellie's heart. *Lord, my work here is finished. Although I've often been rebellious, I can say like the Apostle Paul, I have fought a good fight, finished my course, and kept the faith. Now I'm free to fly home to Madera—and Joshua.*

Valentine's Day 1893

Sunlight poured through the windows of Christ the Way Church. It bathed the couple standing before the altar in radiance rivaled by Preacher Josh's face when he glanced down at Ellie. Her spirit rushed out to him. What had she ever done to deserve such happiness?

"With this ring I thee wed."

Joshua's vow touched Ellie's soul. She looked into his shining gray eyes, then at the ring he placed on her waiting finger. Her heart soared. It had been a long, hard flight before the Sierra Songbird found priceless treasure: a golden circle without beginning or end. . .just like her heavenly Father's love.